THE RISE AND FALL
OF THE WONDER GIRLS

Sarah May is an intimate observer of society (AKA curtain-twitcher of the highest order). She is the author of five previous novels: *The Rise and Fall of a Domestic Diva*, *The Rise and Fall of the Queen of Suburbia*, *The Nudist Colony*, which was shortlisted for the Guardian First Book Award; *Spanish City* and *The Internationals* which was longlisted for the Orange Prize. She lives in London with her theatre director husband and their two children.

Praise for Sarah May's novels:

'This is writing at the level of myth: fully formed, recognisable, unique' *Guardian*

'May's shrewd sideways glance makes this a novel moving and menacing by turns. Her ensemble – aerobics-obsessed Linda, rebellious Dominique, the creepy Niemans – are often gruesome, but all too convincing' *Observer*

'The narrative is beautifully observed, with the subtle touch of a writer who makes every action and mannerism feel plausible. Sarah May has a rare talent for melding the farcical with the tragic, and has produced a novel which – but for an ending worthy of Tom Sharpe – is a scathingly successful piece of social commentary' *Daily Mail*

'Sarah May has brought the obsessions, ambitions and class paranoia of Thatcher's Britain beautifully back to life. It's a visceral read, but this is one book you'll be happy to read in a r̶   *Daily Express*

'An ol   *Sun*

By the same author

The Rise and Fall of a Domestic Diva

The Rise and Fall of the Queen of Suburbia

The Nudist Colony

Spanish City

The Internationals

SARAH MAY

The Rise and Fall of the Wonder Girls

HARPER

Harper
An imprint of HarperCollins*Publishers*
77–85 Fulham Palace Road,
Hammersmith, London W6 8JB

www.harpercollins.co.uk

A paperback original 2009
1

ISBN-13 978-0-00-732210-7

Set in Meridien by Palimpsest Book Production Ltd,
Grangemouth, Stirlingshire

Printed and bound in Great Britain by
Clays Ltd, St Ives plc

Mixed Sources
Product group from well-managed
forests and other controlled sources
www.fsc.org Cert no. SW-COC-1806
© 1996 Forest Stewardship Council

FSC is a non-profit international organisation established
to promote the responsible management of the world's forests.
Products carrying the FSC label are independently certified
to assure consumers that they come from forests that are managed
to meet the social, economic and ecological needs
of present and future generations.

Find out more about HarperCollins and the environment at
www.harpercollins.co.uk/green

For Gabriel

This book has been a long time coming . . . my heart-felt thanks, in particular, go to Clare Alexander for her indomitable energy and enthusiasm; Clare Hey for her acute editorial observations and for nurturing the book in the beginning; and to Katie Espiner for her unflinching sense of vision.

Contents

*four virgins go
fruit picking*

– summer –

1

Summer was shimmering and at its height as Tom
Henderson drove his piebald red Volkswagen out of
town with three seventeen-year-old virgins in the back.
It was Ruth who – sitting in the middle between Vicky
and Saskia – suggested fruit picking.

Tom said he'd drive them.

He had just about enough petrol to get there and back.

The windows were down and there was a Led
Zeppelin CD playing that jumped when they went over
potholes or when they braked suddenly like Tom was
braking now, at a set of red lights. As soon as the car
stopped, the 32°C with humidity that had been forecast regained its full weight.

'Jump them,' Vicky Henderson ordered her brother.
'It's, like, B-Movie empty – there's nobody around.'

'The lights are red.' Tom exhaled, uninterested.

'This is fucking unbearable.' Vicky groaned and
turned irritably to Saskia, slumped against the opposite door, her face obscured by her hair, which had settled
there when the car stopped. 'Why are you wearing
jeans? Aren't you like melting?'

Saskia, high, was staring through the open doors of the Baptist Church they'd drawn level with – at an outsize flower display looming white in the shade of the vestibule. She looked down slowly at her denim-clad legs and shrugged.

'Yeah –'

The lights changed at last. They left the Baptist Church behind and a hot breeze started blowing through the car again.

There were a lot of churches in Burwood. In fact, they still *built* churches in Burwood. The newest was completed only six months ago – at around the same time as the North Heath housing estate, whose population it had been built to serve. There was a pub next to the church, clad in the same bright sandstone, serving western-style BBQ ribs to the hungry faithful.

'And you're tanned,' Vicky carried on. She hadn't finished with Saskia. 'If I had your legs I wouldn't be putting them in jeans.'

Saskia sighed and continued to stare out the open window, her hair blowing around her face. She was thinking about the south of France where she'd spent most of July; thinking in particular about her father lying drunk and untidy on a poolside sun lounger while she tried to drag a yellow and white striped umbrella over to him so he wouldn't get burnt. That's how she spent most of her time: stopping her father getting burnt – one way or another. At least in France she'd had Ruth for company when Richard Greaves lost consciousness, which he did most afternoons.

She turned her head to look at Ruth, who was sitting beside her, and her eyes caught Tom's in the rear view mirror. Last summer Saskia had been in love with Tom. She kept a darkly detailed diary noting his every movement, gesture and look, and stole things from his bedroom that she never gave back – a ball of elastic bands, a pair of worn sports socks, a Smurf pencil sharpener, a Radio Mercury sticker, and a library copy of a D.H. Lawrence book he'd spilt aftershave over.

This summer she didn't love him any more.

Catching her eye now, in the rear-view mirror, Tom felt bad about the hours his university girlfriend Ali and he spent talking and laughing about Saskia's 'hinge-less passion' – a phrase coined by Ali – and the way he'd just handed Saskia up to Ali, who could be cruel.

'How's Ali?' Saskia said suddenly.

'She's in India,' Vicky put in. 'Her parents think Tom and her are too close.'

'And what does Tom think?' Ruth asked suddenly – loudly, out of shyness.

'Tom doesn't think.'

'Shut up, Vick –'

Ruth kept her eyes on Tom – taking in his thighs, throat and wrists – and wondered what it would be like to sleep with him as the red Volkswagen left behind the retail parks where the good people of Burwood bought pet food and hot tubs, hitting a leggy stretch of road lined by garages, off licences, discount bedding stores, pubs that welcomed families and sold salad in kegs, Indian restaurants – one called Curry Nights had been made infamous a couple of years ago when an Alsatian carcass was found in one of their bins.

'I went to school there,' Ruth said, as they passed the primary school where she'd had her hand driven onto a rusty nail by another girl and had to go to hospital to get a tetanus jab.

Nobody said anything.

It was too hot to worry about somebody else's memories.

They passed the St Catherine's Hospice and the flat above it rumoured to house Burwood's only prostitute. Local press refused to comment on the prostitute or the Alsatian carcass in the bins at Curry Nights, and it was the *News of the World*, in the end, that covered both stories. Burwood also appeared – that same week – in the *Financial Times*, featuring as one of the ten towns in the UK where men lived longest.

Burwood ranked number four.

Burwood was a good place to live.

From the air, the town looked like an untidy circle surrounded by a band of green separating it from London to the north and Brighton to the south. In other words, it had a lot more going for it than most places viewed via satellite.

Burwood long pre-dated its Domesday Book entry, and was now flourishing and thriving its way into the twenty-first century with an all-pervasive aura of stability and permanence that breathed promise to the world-weary. So saying, Burwood had its fair share of anarchists – the most notable being a poet who, two hundred years ago, published political tracts and distributed them from a hot-air balloon, unsettling everyone before eloping with an underage girl called Harriet. In cases such as this, however, it was town council policy to disinherit – no matter how famous their anarchic sons and daughters later became.

The Hendersons, hugely influenced by the *Financial Times* article – and the fact that the town's historic centre already felt familiar, having been used by the BBC on a regular basis to film Jane Austen adaptations – were by no means the first immigrés, and wouldn't be the last.

Burwood ended now abruptly on its eastern side, which was also its most picturesque. They'd driven through all the rings of the town's life from its pre-medieval centre to the helplessly conservative, sprawling suburban villas built with optimism after the Second World War, and with disproportionately small windows behind which a whole generation came to terms with the horrors of war and the legacy of those horrors . . . perennial-filled borders, trimmed lawns and terrifying stretches of leisure time spent struggling to define the word 'peace'. They'd passed through the industrial estates and were, finally, beyond the reaches of the executive satellite estates – by products of the post-1986 housing boom. Burwood's last house was an old brick cottage shared by two octogenarian brothers who had been Conscientious Objectors in the last world war.

The red Volkswagen turned off the main road into open country, following a lane that sank beneath banks of hedge and forest where there was sudden shade and the sound of water before rising again in order to cross fading green and yellow fields. The forest was beech and ash and had once stretched from coast to coast, covering the land Burwood now stood on. Deepest darkest forest had been replaced by deepest darkest suburbia, where modern man and woman sought refuge, as their forest-dwelling ancestors had sought it in the forest. Like them, they mistook the shade-dappled depths for a place of innocence where a simple life could be led.

'I hope they have raspberries,' Ruth said, to nobody in particular. 'I told mum I'd get raspberries.'

Vicky stared at her. She couldn't imagine what it would be like to have a conversation about anything

– let alone raspberries – with her mother, Sylvia Henderson.

'Isn't Grace working at Martha's Farm?' Saskia said after a while, trying to pin her hair back with her arm.

Ruth watched Tom suck in his left cheek and move his hands on the steering wheel.

'I thought she already had a job?' Vicky said, irritated that she didn't already know this.

'Yeah, but this is like a holiday job.' Saskia let go of her hair again.

'Why didn't she say?'

'Probably thought you already knew.'

'Well, I didn't.' Vicky turned to Ruth. 'Did you know?'

Ruth shrugged. 'I kind of lose count of the number of jobs Grace does.'

'Yeah, well, some people's parents can't actually afford to send their children to university so they have to pay for it themselves,' Tom said from the front.

Ruth, upset, looked away.

'There are loads of grants and stuff for people like Grace,' Vicky said, defensive. Upsetting Ruth was her territory.

'People like Grace?' Tom cut in, angry.

Ignoring this, Vicky carried on, 'In fact, she'll probably be better off by the time she finishes – not like the rest of us, up to our eyes in student-loan debt. Cambridge are offering her a scholarship anyway, so what's the big deal.'

Saskia said slowly, 'I thought she was going for that NASA one at Yale?'

Vicky, no longer interested, didn't respond.

Grace was one of their group, and Vicky was tyrannical about having up-to-date information on all members. She considered the group – *her* group – a profound social achievement given that she'd only started at Burwood Girls' in Year 11. First she successfully penetrated an already-established group, then she amputated the excess, re-forming a splinter cell comprising core members only: Grace Cummings, Saskia Greaves and Ruth Dent. She put her rapid rise down to not only getting them into Tom's university parties but even some London ones as well. Who else on all Satan's earth could have got them into Lilly Allen's brother's eighteenth for fuck's sake?

They turned right off the lane into Martha's Fruit Farm and tried looking for a space in the field full of cars. In the end they parked at the top near a ridge of trees where there was a sandpit.

Ruth, worried, said, 'D'you think they'll have raspberries?'

'Will you shut up about raspberries.' Vicky pulled her skirt off the back of her legs, which were covered in an imprint of the car's upholstery.

'I only mentioned them once.'

'You mentioned them like about a hundred times,' Vicky said, moving off between the rows of parked cars, the air heavy with the scent of fruit on the turn.

They straggled slowly down the field whose early summer ruts had now been baked hard by the sun. By the time they got to the weighing-in hut at the bottom, all three girls had linked arms, their heads resting on each other's shoulders.

2

Tom stayed in the car with the door open and lit another joint, sucking on it slowly while watching a black Labrador play in the sandpit just beyond the bonnet of the car. Through the windscreen he could see Burwood in the distance, but there was no resonance for him in the view. The Hendersons moved down from London two years ago and he'd only lived there a couple of months before leaving for university. He'd felt more at home in Bolivia than he ever had in Burwood.

An elderly couple – fruit picking veterans – returned to their car, a purple Nissan parked next to Tom's. Their determined faces were sweating under matching white sun hats with 'Crete' embroidered above the visors, and as they lined up their baskets of fruit on the roof of the car, he saw that they were still wearing the surgical gloves they'd bought with them to pick fruit in, now stained purple.

He finished the joint then got out of the car and, without bothering to lock it, followed the others down the field.

There was a crowd of people round the weighing-in shed and a woman inside was barking at them to get into a queue, but people were too hot and laden with fruit to comply.

As the crowd shuffled forward, broke up then re-formed, Tom caught sight, briefly, of his old black and silver racing bike leaning against the side of the shed; the one he told his mum he'd sold to Grace last summer – only he never sold it to her, he gave it to her.

He remembered clearly riding it round to Grace's house and Grace answering the door in a dressing gown, holding one of her sister Dixie's dolls. Up until then he'd never realised Burwood even had a council estate. He'd rung the doorbell and while he waited, staring at a patch of wall next to the drainpipe where a lump of pebble-dash had fallen off, he'd decided that he was going to give Grace the bike.

Grace, in her dressing gown, stared at him.

He prompted her. 'The bike?'

She carried on staring at him before switching her gaze to the bike. 'The bike – shit. Sorry. Just a minute.' She disappeared back indoors.

Too late, Tom realised that she was getting the forty pounds they'd talked about on the phone the day before.

'Wait –' he called out, wanting to follow her, but just then there was the slap of wet feet on pavement and Grace's nine-year-old sister, Dixie, appeared round the side of the house leaving a trail of wet footprints behind her. She stood on the corner in a pink polka dot bikini with bows at the side, water glistening on her legs, watching him through a pair of goggles and wearing a smile that was missing two bottom teeth.

They took to each other immediately.

11

'Who are you?'

'I'm Tom.' He held out his hand and Dixie shook it wetly in hers.

'Yeah, but who *are* you?'

'A friend of your sister's.'

'Like a boyfriend?'

'No, just a friend.'

Dixie contemplated him. 'I never saw you before.' She paused. 'I'm having a sleepover tonight.'

Before Tom had time to respond to this, Grace reappeared at the front door and Dixie ran off up the side passage and into the back garden again.

'Forty pounds, right?' Grace handed him an envelope.

'Leave it,' Tom said, embarrassed.

'You said forty pounds – on the phone.'

'Yeah, but –'

'What?'

Grace looked angry.

'It doesn't matter – about the money. I mean, just take the bike. I changed my mind about the money.'

'What made you change your mind?'

'I don't know.'

'You said forty pounds. On the phone.'

'Yeah, but –'

This had gone on and the sun had moved round the side of the house until it was filling the front garden.

Now Tom saw her, standing over by the ice cream van with her back to him. While he was watching, she stood up straight, laughing. She looked like she was having a good day. He should go before she saw him.

'Hey, Tom.' She'd seen him – was smiling straight at him.

'Hey.'

She came across the grass in her flip-flops and a bottle-green T-shirt that said 'Martha's Crew'. Grace didn't look like she belonged to anyone's crew – let alone Martha's. Tom watched the boy in the ice cream van watching Grace.

'What brings you out here?'

He hadn't seen her for a year, and this wasn't the kind of thing – a year ago – she would have said.

'I'm my sister's chauffeur.'

'She's here?'

'Somewhere.'

'Anyone else?'

'Saskia – Ruth.'

'I didn't know they were back from France.'

Tom didn't say anything.

She squinted across at the fields laid out below the weighing-in hut, trying to pick out her friends.

He saw that her fingertips were stained purple.

'You're not picking anything?' she said.

'No –'

For some reason this made her smile.

'How's the bike doing?' he asked

'The bike's doing fine. Only one puncture so far.'

'You should change the tyres to Kevlar – they won't ever puncture.'

'Okay –'

Was she laughing at him?

'They sound expensive though – and I still owe you for the bike.'

'Fuck that,' he said, genuinely angry.

She was about to say something when a voice started yelling, 'Grace – Grace,' from inside the hut.

'Shit – I better get back.' She disappeared into the

13

crowd round the weighing-in hut and didn't look back.

Tom and the boy in the ice cream van were left staring at each other. The afternoon felt suddenly pointless – as though it had been going on for too long.

3

Vicky followed Ruth to the far end of the raspberry field, whose boundary was marked by a narrow strip of woodland unable to cast any shade because the sun was too high in the sky and falling on it at the wrong angle. The earth was hard and tufted and, with a serious headache beginning due to the day's dope diet, Vicky kept losing her footing. She picked the biggest raspberry she could find, put it in her mouth then spat it out again.

Ruth stopped picking. 'You okay?'

'Tastes funny.' Vicky wiped her mouth. 'Do they taste funny to you?'

Ruth took one of the raspberries out of her punnet. 'Tastes fine. Maybe you just got a bad one.'

They carried on picking, the heat close around them.

'Where did Sas go?'

'Redcurrants.'

Vicky, bored, had stopped picking and was now just trailing after Ruth. 'Redcurrants?'

'Said she'd never picked redcurrants before.'

'What d'you do with redcurrants?'

Ruth continued to make her way up the row, too intent on picking to respond to this.

Behind her, Vicky said, 'Matt was meant to phone at twelve today. He's been on holiday and he said he'd phone when his plane landed, but he never did. No message – nothing. I'm meant to be going to a party with him this weekend.'

She looked up instinctively as a plane went over-head, nosing down towards Gatwick. 'I can't believe you and Sas didn't meet anybody in France – like, anybody at all.'

Ruth had stopped picking and was staring at something in the distance, her shoulders so taut with concentration that Vicky had one of her brief, habitual anxiety attacks that their GP at Park Surgery refused to prescribe her Diazepam for.

It was the plane – the plane that flew over just then; it had crashed. She just knew it. Any minute now there'd be smoke and debris and the field would be full of soft, torn, bloodied body parts. Any minute now the silence would end and she'd see freshly twisted wreckage and freshly dead people. What if Matt's flight had been delayed? What if Matt was on that plane?

The two blues she took out of her pocket now and put into her mouth had, until recently, belonged to her mother, Sylvia, whose anxiety attacks their GP at Park Surgery had been happy to prescribe Diazepam for.

She'd been taking Sylvia's prescription Diazepam since she was fifteen – when the burglary nightmares first started. It was the same every night – she'd wake up around two, convinced she heard someone crossing the gravel drive, walking up the side of the house and letting themselves in through the patio doors. She'd lie in bed flushed with fear and barely breathing, listening to the intruder's footsteps on the stairs, and waiting for her bedroom door handle to start turning. That's when she'd take the Valium, put on her i-pod, and curl up under the duvet – whatever the weather.

'What is it?' she tried not to scream.

Ruth, distracted, said, 'Does that look like Mr Sutton to you?'

'Mr Sutton?' Vicky's eyes grazed the fields spread out around them, still looking for smoke, still sniffing the air for blood.

'Over there.' Ruth pointed.

Vicky felt herself start to calm down. The sky was clear – no smoke. The plane that had gone overhead had landed safely.

'I'm sure that's him.'

Vicky looked. Ruth was right. In the next field was their Art teacher, Mr Sutton – whose home address they'd taken from confidential staff files so they could send an anonymous Valentine's card.

Mr Sutton was the youngest male member of staff at Burwood Girls', and taught art under an overwhelming barrage of oestrogen that manifested itself in the various totemic gifts he was recipient of – from an envelope full of pubic hair to a photograph of a pair of bare breasts.

'What's he doing here?'

'Picking fruit – like everybody else.'

'Shit – look at me.'

'He's two fields away, Vick.'

'Yeah, but *we* can see *him*. So are we going over – saying hello?'

Ruth was blushing. Confident – and often caustically funny – with family and close friends, she was pathologically shy with most other people.

'Come on – you know you've got a thing about him.'

'I know, but –'

'And we haven't seen him for ages.'

Ruth shrugged and turned away. 'Wait – he's with someone.'

'Who?'

'He's talking to someone.'

As Vicky continued to stare, the gradient of the field, which sloped gently downwards, seemed suddenly much steeper. The next minute she grabbed hold instinctively of one of the raspberry canes as the entire field lurched out from under her feet.

She'd never had such an intense or sudden attack of vertigo before.

'Vick?' Ruth said, turning to her, worried. 'What happened? You looked like you were about to black out.'

'Vertigo – I just took some Valium.'

'What colour?'

'Blue.'

'How many?'

'Two – like, 20mg or something. Don't look at me like that.' Vicky broke off. 'It's Saskia!'

'What?'

'The person Mr Sutton's talking to – it's Saskia.'

4

Still high, Saskia drifted down between the rows of netted redcurrant bushes able to feel every crevice and ridge beneath the thin soles of the sandals she'd bought at a market in the south of France. Mel and Tony were pre-divorce friends of her father's. Richard Greaves had known Mel since university and the Greaves stayed in their villa at St Julien most Julys. During the first week, before Ruth arrived, Mel drove Saskia to the local market – a girls only trip – and for a whole two hours she'd tried to be Saskia's mother, then she got bored with the idea and moved onto something else. Before she got bored she bought Saskia the sandals she was now wearing – had worn all summer, in fact – and a bracelet made of bottle tops that African immigrants were selling on blankets, which Ruth had admired when they picked her up from the airport in Montpellier. Saskia had been so pleased to see her she'd almost given it to her before changing her mind and deciding to keep it.

A plane passed overhead. She watched its shadow move solidly over the ground and redcurrant bushes, her eyes following it as it ran over the rows – until she saw Mr Sutton. *Was* that Mr Sutton from school – picking redcurrants just like her, approximately five rows away? She wasn't convinced it was. Saskia believed in UFOs; she believed in ghosts, parallel universes and monsters like the Yeti that evolution had stranded, and sometimes she got confused and saw things out of the corner of her eye that never quite materialised when she really concentrated.

No – Mr Sutton was definitely there. He was waving at her.

Saskia didn't wave back, she just carried on staring.

He hesitated then made his way over to her row.

'Hey,' he said, pleased to see her. Saskia was one of a handful of pupils going on to study art at degree level, and he kept this coterie of girls close.

Saskia finally emerged from what her grandmother used to refer to as one of her 'brown studies' – lapses of attention that had induced her mother to have her tested for epilepsy as a child – and smiled back at Mr Sutton.

He was wearing shorts and a yellow polo shirt. The effect was stodgy and preppy and just not him at all. Her dad wore polo shirts; they'd been bought for him by his ex-wife, who was also Saskia's mother, because he never knew what to wear when he wasn't wearing a suit. Now her mother was dressing a different man, and although her dad made an effort – post-divorce – not to wear the polo shirts, he also made the mistake of not throwing them away. He came across them when he was looking for something to decorate in and after that they once more became fixtures in his casual wardrobe even though they were covered in paint stains and smelt of white spirit.

For this reason, although she didn't know it, Saskia had always associated polo shirts with helplessness, and seeing Mr Sutton wearing a yellow one confused her because he'd never struck her as helpless before. It was like somebody had got to him before he could get to himself, and it made her feel sorry for him.

He must have read something of what she was thinking in her eyes then because he paused, suddenly awkward. 'What are you picking?'

'Redcurrants.'

He held up his punnet. 'Me too.'

She nodded, gesturing to the redcurrant field they were standing in the middle of. 'Yeah –'

'I can't believe I just said that.'

She nodded again. 'Yeah –'

He laughed. 'So – how's it going?'

'Fine. How's your summer been?'

He had no idea how his summer had been. 'I went to South Africa.'

She didn't ask him who he went with – if anybody. 'How was it?'

'I can't remember.'

Saskia laughed.

He twisted his neck like it might be stiff. 'What about you? What have you been up to all summer?'

'I went to the south of France with my dad.'

'Get any painting done?'

She shook her head. 'I had some ideas – made a few sketches.'

'I'd like to see them.'

She nodded, aware that she had no intention of showing him the sketches she made after seeing Tony and Mel in the kitchen that night when she'd got up for some water. 'We were staying with some friends of dad's,' she blurted out, trying to distract herself from the memory of Mel bent over the marble kitchen surface, her breasts pushed into a pile, her hands gripping the edge of it, and Tony behind her. It had looked fierce and ugly with about as much choreography involved as taking a crap, and now she was scared of the whole thing. 'They had a pool and stuff.'

'Sounds great.'

'Yeah – the first couple of weeks were, then my dad and his friend Tony sort of remembered that they never really got on and that my dad's always fancied his wife.' Saskia heard herself saying it and couldn't believe she was saying it, but couldn't stop herself. 'And Tony, who's been holed up in paradise for about two years too long, was like drunk the whole time and then dad got drunk and then they started rowing.' She paused for breath, horrified. She hadn't told anybody this – not even Ruth, who'd actually been there – so why was she telling Mr Sutton in the middle of a field of redcurrants?

He was staring at her, about to say something when suddenly there was a woman standing next to him wearing black wraparound sunglasses that made her look like a beetle. She'd appeared from nowhere, had her hand on his arm, and was smiling at them both.

Behind the glasses, Saskia recognised Ms Webster who'd taught her Physics in Year 9. For a moment she wondered what on earth Ms Webster – who also coached the Burwood Girls' Netball A Team – was doing at Martha's Farm as well. Then she realised: Ms Webster was here because Mr Sutton was here; Ms Webster was here *with* Mr Sutton.

He'd been to South Africa with Ms Webster. They'd lain on the beach together, swam in the sea together, and had sex in a hotel – and other places – together. Now the yellow polo shirt – Ms Webster was wearing the same one – made sense.

'Typical,' Ms Webster said loudly, triumphantly, holding a basket full of redcurrants up in the air.

Saskia stared at her, her mouth hanging open awkwardly.

'So much for his contribution to jam making.'

Saskia didn't know what to say – she'd never had a jam-making conversation before.

'I just saw Grace as well,' Ms Webster carried on.

'Grace works here,' Saskia said without thinking. It sounded mean – when all she'd meant to do was say something because she couldn't carry on standing there with her mouth hanging silently open, feeling like she'd just got drunk in high heels.

'Well – we'd better be going,' Ms Webster said, her hand still on Mr Sutton's arm, turning him round, steering him away. 'Enjoy the rest of your holiday.'

'I will.' Saskia was jabbing the front of her sandal repetitively against a ridge of earth and now the crust cracked and crumbled.

Mr Sutton turned back towards her. 'I'm in and out of school the next couple of weeks – if you've got anything you're working on or want to show me before the beginning of term.'

'Thanks –'

Another tug on the arm and he was led away again, only to break free a second time.

'Oh – and I hope that's not permanent.'

Saskia stared at him. She had no idea what he was talking about.

'Your neck. The scorpion.'

Her hand went to her neck. 'No, it's – no.'

He smiled, paused, then turned and walked away with Ms Webster.

Saskia kept her hand on her neck, covering the

temporary tattoo that had come free with one of her music magazines. Her eyes followed Mr Sutton and Ms Webster in their matching polo shirts and South African sun tans all the way to the weighing-in hut.

They were arguing.

By the time Vicky and Ruth reached Saskia, standing inert still in the field of redcurrants, the black Peugeot convertible belonging to Ms Webster had left Martha's Farm in a loose trail of dust. Neither the driver, Ms Webster, or the passenger, Mr Sutton, looked like they were going home to make jam.

'Did you speak to him?' Vicky asked, breathless still from the Valium-induced attack of vertigo.

Saskia nodded vacantly.

'And?'

'What?'

'What did he say?' Vicky was beginning to lose patience.

Saskia was about to mention his reference to her tattoo when she decided not to. 'I don't know.'

'Sas –' Vicky insisted.

'He went to South Africa – on holiday.'

'South Africa?'

Saskia sighed, her hands dropping to her sides. 'With Ms Webster.'

'Webster?' Vicky screamed, the screams echoing across the fields. 'No – fucking – way. Are you sure?'

'She was standing right here in front of me, Vick. They were wearing matching clothes.'

'Like – how matching?'

'Yellow polo shirts, shorts and Birkenstocks.'

'That is so depressing. How come we didn't know anything about this? How did she get to him?'

'End of last term,' Ruth said.

Vicky turned on her. 'Why didn't you say?'

'I don't know that – I'm just guessing. Staff drinks and stuff.'

'Staff drinks and stuff? They went to South Africa together, Ruth – they're practically married.' She paused. 'Webster. Why didn't I see this coming?'

'Webster's okay,' Ruth ventured then paused. 'Isn't she?'

'Webster's not okay, Ruth. She's like the wrong side of healthy, like too healthy, like under all that lycra she wears she's got no genitals or something.'

Nobody said anything.

Saskia's hand remained over the temporary scorpion tattoo as they trailed slowly over to the weighing-in hut, expecting to find Grace there – only to be told by the boy in the ice cream van that she'd already gone.

'She had to leave early – something about a puncture. I offered to take her home in the van, but –' His eyes moved curiously over all three of them as Vicky emptied her raspberries into Ruth's already full container and stepped away from the hut, crushing the ones that fell beneath her sandals. She stood, bored and dizzy, aware of the ice cream boy's eyes on her, but too overwhelmed by the thought of Mr Sutton and Ms Webster to react.

The ice cream boy stared at the red spots in the dust and tried hard to think of something to say. He was still trying as the girls walked back up the field towards Tom's car.

'Webster's totally wrong for Sutton,' Vicky started up again then broke off, staring into Saskia's punnet. 'Why *did* you pick redcurrants?'

Saskia stared at the redcurrants, trying to remember.

'I wanted to paint them. Remember that triptych I did of the rotting quince?'

'No.'

'I was thinking about doing another one with red-currants.'

'Morbid.'

'It's only fruit.'

They got to the top of the field where Tom was sitting in the sandpit, banging on an old plastic cup with a lolly stick and making a child with blond curls laugh.

'Looks like I've got to go, little man,' he said when the girls arrived. 'See you around.'

Vicky glanced at the toddler without interest as Tom handed him the plastic cup and stick and watched him try to reproduce the sound he'd been making.

'Did you manage to meet up with Grace?' Tom asked as they got back in the car.

'No – she already left – had a puncture or something. We'll probably catch up with her on the road. Can we get some windows down?'

5

They caught up with Grace about a mile down the lane where it left the fields and sank into forest.

Tom slowed the car when he saw her up ahead on the opposite side of the lane, pushing her bike.

'Isn't that *your* bike?' Vicky said, staring.

'I sold it.' Tom threw the rest of the joint he was smoking out the window.

'When?'

'Last summer.'

'To Grace?'

'You know I did.'

They pulled up alongside her.

Vicky leant out the back of the car and gave a slow, exaggerated wave.

'You should have said,' Tom called out.

'About what?' Grace called back.

'Needing a lift.'

'I don't need a lift.' She smiled at him.

Saskia and Vicky were leaning out the car, waving.

'You've got a puncture.'

'I know, but I didn't want to leave the bike.'

'Come on, get in,' Tom said, 'I'll put the bike on the roof rack.'

Without waiting for a response, he drove past her and carried on for a couple of hundred yards, until he got to a passing place where he pulled in, got out the car and jogged back to where Grace was.

'There's some rope –' he called back to Vicky, who was hanging out the window still, watching him '– in the boot.'

She pulled her arms and head back into the car and let her head flop against the back seat.

'Are you getting the rope out the boot?' Ruth asked.

'No – I'm too depressed about Sutton and Webster.'

'I'll get it.' Ruth got out of the car, stretching herself. She poked at the junk in the boot, looking for the rope.

Through the open hatchback, she saw Vicky climb between the two front seats and get into the driver's. The next minute, Vicky started the car up and put it into gear. It jolted forward then stalled, the boot flapping.

Tom broke into a run back towards the car as the engine started up again and a basketball rolled out of the back onto the lane.

Saskia got quickly out of the car and joined Ruth as the engine started to grate.

'Vicky!' Tom yelled, sprinting now, his footsteps loud on the tarmac. 'You're flooding the engine.'

Grace was wheeling her bike towards Saskia, Ruth and the car when there was a series of sharp splintering cracks in the woods to their left and two deer broke suddenly out of the dense line of trees, passing so close their flanks grazed Saskia and Ruth before they swerved, hooves slipping on the hot road surface, stopping Tom in his tracks, vaulting the basketball then disappearing into the woods on their right.

They were gone, leaving behind them an unsettling silence that hadn't been there before.

Tom, shaking, hadn't moved. 'Shit –'

'I never saw deer so close before,' Ruth said, breathless. 'I mean, I felt them – they actually touched me.'

Grace dropped her bike on the side of the road and went up to Tom. 'You okay? Something must have scared them – in the woods.'

Vicky got out the car and walked towards them. 'What was that?'

'Deer,' Grace said.

'They passed so close, they actually touched me,' Ruth said again.

Ignoring Ruth, Vicky said to Tom, 'I think you're out of petrol.'

'Out of petrol? You just flooded the fucking engine.' He was angry with himself for being so shaken by the deer.

'I didn't flood the engine – you're out of fucking petrol.' Vicky turned and started to walk off up the lane.

'Where are you going?' Tom called out after her.

'Home.'

'How?'

'The bus – there's a stop at the top of the lane on the main road.'

'So you're just going to leave my car in the middle of the fucking road?'

'It's your fucking car.' Vicky carried on walking.

Tom didn't say anything. He picked up the basketball and started to bounce it rhythmically on the road.

Ruth, Saskia and Grace hesitated, uncertain how the argument between brother and sister had started or how it had got to this point. Vicky had already disappeared round the bend and out of sight.

After a while, Ruth shut the boot. 'You want help pushing it or something?'

'No point – we won't get it started in second without a hill. I'll come back later with dad and pick up some petrol on the way.'

Just then the ice cream van from Martha's Farm came up behind them, sounding its horn. The boy inside leant out of the window. 'What happened?'

'The engine's flooded or something,' Saskia said, diplomatic.

Tom carried on bouncing the ball.

The boy in the ice cream van turned to Grace. 'They caught up with you then.'

'Yeah.'

'D'you want a lift?'

'My bike.'

'We'll get that in the back no trouble.'

Grace hesitated and glanced at Tom, who kept his eyes on the ball and didn't look up.

'I've got room for one more,' the boy said, pleased.

'I don't mind getting the bus,' Ruth put in.

Saskia drifted slowly towards the ice cream van. 'You sure?'

Ruth nodded as Grace turned back to Tom. 'How are you getting home?' she asked over the soft rhythmic beat of the ball on the road.

'We'll get the bus – it's fine,' Ruth said again, trying not to look at Tom, who didn't comment on this.

Saskia got up into the front of the van, excited. 'Can we put the music on?'

The boy didn't respond – he was too busy watching Grace standing beside the van with her bike.

Tom stopped bouncing the basketball.

'I think I'll walk back.' He paused, looking at Grace. 'You feel like walking with me?'

She didn't say anything; within seconds was standing beside him.

'What about your bike?' the boy said, quietly devastated, and trying not to sound frantic.

Tom turned to Grace. 'We can lock it to the roof rack and I'll take it home with me when I come back for the car later. You've got a lock for it?'

Ruth's momentary decisiveness was gone, and its departure left her looking stranded.

'Ruth,' Saskia called out from the ice cream van, and the next minute, Ruth was climbing up beside her as Tom started to bounce the basketball again.

The van pulled away, the boy glancing in the rear view mirror at Grace.

Grace and Tom stood in the road and watched the van disappear, a canned version of *Au Clair de la Lune* starting up the moment it was out of sight.

At the sound of the music, they smiled suddenly at each other.

Feeling immediately lighter, Tom kicked the ball hard, into the forest.

'Why did you do that?'

He shrugged, still smiling, then lifted her bike onto the roof of the car. Grace chained it to the roof rack.

After checking the doors to make sure they were locked, he jumped down into the ditch the deer had vaulted earlier.

'You coming?' He watched her, waiting for her to change her mind.

31

'Which way are you going?'

'Shortcut.'

She jumped down into the ditch beside him. 'I'm wearing flip-flops.'

'You're not in a hurry for anything?'

She shook her head.

'So we'll go slow.'

She hesitated then followed him into the woods.

suburban satire

– autumn –

6

Bill Henderson woke at 5:15 just like he did every morning, including weekends, only at the weekend he didn't have to get up. Today wasn't a weekend, and the world was even more silent than usual due to the heavy fog October had pushed over Burwood during the night. Bill didn't know about the fog yet, but the silence was so intense he woke with the sound of a low pitched hum in his ears that he thought was the under-floor heating they'd had installed downstairs until he remembered that the central heating wasn't programmed to come on until seven because Vicky said the sound of it woke her up. It was the same sort of humming he heard Scuba diving that summer because of water pressure.

Still puzzled, he executed the neat sideways roll he'd perfected over the years, which enabled him to vacate the marital bed in the early hours without waking Sylvia. Landing softly on the carpet in a stress position, he moved silently out the room. He then crept downstairs to the loo where he peed in the dark because switching the light on triggered the extractor fan.

They'd been in the house over two years, but in the dark mornings, half awake, the layout sometimes caught him out. He aimed his pee as best he could in the glow from the sitting room sidelights that were on timer switches and programmed to come on at five in the morning. Not flushing the chain was also part of the morning's silent routine, one that contributed to the sometimes overwhelming feeling in Bill that he had in fact died without realising it, and was haunting rather than living in his home.

He padded through to the kitchen, put the cooker hood light on and poured himself a glass of milk, which he drank standing in front of the fridge where there was a diary kept up with magnets that had survival maxims for life as a woman written over them – that Sylvia, drunk, read out to him like he hadn't heard them a million times already.

He checked the diary every morning, with a fledgling curiosity at this early hour for the insight it gave him into the lives lived by his wife and daughter during the week. There in front of him was a list of cryptic biro scrawls that held the key to everything happening in this house he'd paid for and that he felt like no more than a squatter in. It occurred to him that all he would ever need to surmise about these two people – one to whom he was bound because of a religious ceremony, and the other through genes – was contained here in this diary.

Today's list was long:

5km / hair @12 / POKER / flowers – Panino's / Tel. Tom re. nxt w/e – Ali coming?

Then, in caps, with an asterisk either side:

Then, in lower case and without asterisk:

rem. Bill

It was strange seeing his own name written in the diary.
Puzzled, but not particularly concerned, he put his empty
glass down on the surface and stared around the kitchen.
He was forgetting something. He'd stood in this exact spot
the night before and Sylvia had asked him to do something first thing in the morning when he got up;
something important, and now he couldn't remember.

He went through to the sitting room, still trying to
recall what it was, and attempted to operate the pulleys
that opened the curtains – curtains that had cost them
more than a month's mortgage payment.

They swung heavily apart, not responding to his touch
as they did Sylvia's, and there he was all over again in
the pyjama bottoms and T-shirt he wore to bed. The
T-shirt infuriated Sylvia, who couldn't understand why
he refused to wear both parts of the two-part sets she
bought him. Even when he explained that he didn't
like to end his day in the same way he began it by doing
up a row of buttons. She still didn't understand.

He enjoyed observing himself hovering above the
lawn's dark outline while simultaneously suspended in
a fragile replica of the sitting room.

This morning he looked like he was standing in a
cloud and it took him a while to realise that nothing
untoward had happened to the outside world; it was
only fog.

He waved at himself and smiled, then, suddenly embarrassed, went back upstairs to the spare bedroom where

he kept his minimal wardrobe of mostly suits, clothes to play golf in and a couple of outfits he wore when they went out socially as a family. These were the outfits he stood in while listening to people whose names he forgot as soon as they told him, talking about operations they'd had or cars they drove. Sylvia's people.

He dressed without looking at himself in the mirror, shaved in the downstairs bathroom where he kept his shaving soap and cologne, then left the house, tiptoeing across the gravel that marked the threshold between him and the dawning day.

Two Fridays a month he went up to London to do a day's auditing at Pinnacle Insurance's Head Office.

Today was one of those Fridays.

7

Sylvia Henderson was between diets, and sleeping badly. She woke about thirty minutes after Bill Henderson left for work, and couldn't see anything when she opened her eyes because of the black-out blinds she'd bought to ease her irregular but persistent bouts of insomnia. She knew, instinctively, that Bill wasn't there. The smell of him in the bed was always stronger once he'd left it. After unconsciously processing this fact about Bill – that he'd left for work – she stopped thinking about him.

They'd been married too many years for her to think about him when he wasn't physically present.

In fact, even when he was it was sometimes difficult.

Tomorrow night, Sylvia was having a poker party.

Nobody in Burwood had ever had a poker party before.

If only Bill would stop creeping and shuffling about, and start acting like the sort of man who was married to the sort of woman who held poker parties for forty people.

The Hendersons had been to hell and back, which *wasn't* to say they'd been to the Congo, but *was* to say that Bill Henderson had lost his job – unexpectedly – and had a breakdown. Leaving Sylvia to conceal this fact from just about everybody they knew (including themselves) while simultaneously attempting to sell the 1.2 million London home in order to get rid of the 600k mortgage, pay Vicky and Tom's final terms' school fees (£8,500), and put together the Henderson re-location package.

She'd been looking for somewhere they could shine – after The Crash, the Hendersons needed to shine – and chosen Burwood after seeing an article in the *Financial Times* ranking it as fourth highest in the country for male life expectancy, and eighth lowest for teenage pregnancy. These figures spoke affluence, and with the proceeds from the sale of their London Life, the Hendersons bought number two Park Avenue – the largest house on the street – and set about making arrangements for their own Second Coming.

The house had been undervalued for a quick sale – messy divorce, the estate agent who showed her round explained, with as much polite regret as he could muster.

Bill got the job she persuaded him to apply for at Pinnacle Insurance after pumping him with Prozac until he was well over the limit, and in spite of the fact that he was holding out for a job teaching maths at a school in Malawi, which she knew he wouldn't get because she'd shredded his completed application after promising to send it recorded delivery.

Sylvia's rise to top of the pile here on Park Avenue had been – much like her daughter Vicky's at Burwood Girls' – astronomical. Most of their neighbours had been easily won over by her Phoney Femme Fatale persona

– everybody, that is, apart from the doctor's wife at number five, who had an unsettling sense of humour, and the two retired diplomats who lived with their Down's Syndrome daughter at number seventeen.

Both the doctor's wife, however, and the two diplomats, had accepted invitations to her poker party.

Sylvia was going to win.

8

While Sylvia lay in bed not thinking about Bill, Bill moved slowly through the fog on Hurst Road in the same direction and with the same frantic plod as the other commuters – towards the station that connected them with the country's capital: London.

The behaviour of the human traffic on the pavement was the same as the traffic on the roads, despite the fact that they didn't have a vehicle. Bill had been classifying them over a long series of Fridays. There were the tailgaters who stayed on your heel and refused to pass even when you slowed down virtually to a stop; the centre crawlers who seemed to take up the entire pavement and refused to move over; the obsessive overtakers who insisted on accelerating past you only to immediately slow down so that you were forced to overtake in turn only to find them once more accelerating on your right in a repetitive pattern that could cover the entire Hurst Road stretch to the station itself.

He never spoke to his fellow commuters – nothing more than shifting shapes in this morning's fog – and yet over the past two years their faces had become more familiar to Bill than his own family's: to the extent of noting absences on the platform, and wondering why. He'd filled in the hundreds of hours spent toeing the line along the front of Platform 2 while waiting for delayed trains spuriously christening his fellow commuters. There were Zombie Extra, Sid Steroid, The Obliterator, Super Slut, Hobo Becoming, War Criminal, and Dartford Tunnel (so-called for obvious reasons involving over-use by members of the opposite sex), who would have got the title of Super Slut if Super Slut hadn't already been taken. For some reason they rarely showed together for the 6:08 train. Something that had initially led Bill to the conclusion that Dartford Tunnel was Super Slut on a bad day, which she in fact wasn't.

Super Slut always got a seat on the train, and Sid Steroid always stood as close to her as he could; close enough to share both his inherent and artificial body odours. If Bill ever stopped to think about it – which he didn't – he'd realise that he spent a disproportionate quota of the day's emotions on these commuter fictions: from wondering whether the festive season would bring about some sort of consummation for Sid Steroid and Super Slut to wondering how it was that Zombie Extra and The Obliterator always managed to get through the train doors first even when they'd been standing at the back of a platform cluster.

He'd served up a few of his better stories to Sylvia – such as the time Zombie Extra took a seat vacated by a generous gentleman for Super Slut and how it had come to blows between Zombie Extra and Sid Steroid – but Sylvia wasn't interested. Sylvia was only interested in the names of people at Pinnacle Insurance who held more senior positions than him.

In fact, she hadn't only been uninterested in his Zombie Extra versus Sid Steroid story, she'd looked worried and initiated one of her off-the-wall discussions on how St John's Wort was a genuinely effective herbal alternative to Prozac for the treatment of depression, and how it had changed Barbara Phelps's husband's life.

When he'd asked who the fuck Barbara Phelps was (let alone Mr Phelps who had a Life), she'd looked at him and said, 'Precisely.'

He continued to stalk through the fog towards the station.

Sylvia had revisited the St John's Wort conversation again last night and this had somehow run into a criticism of his lack of initiative when it came to Tom and spending time with Tom. Despite speaking to Tom on the phone and seeing him when he came home to visit and get his laundry done, Bill hadn't yet chartered a yacht for the weekend and learnt to sail it across the Channel like Mr Phelps, who had a Life, had with his son – cross-Channel sailing being, apparently, the Litmus test for those who were, and those who weren't paternally engaged. So their relationship was completely dysfunctional.

He was still thinking about last night as he reached the traffic lights just outside the station and drew level with Zombie Extra. Poised on the edge of the kerb and ready with the rest of them to make a road-dash across now heavy traffic, he remembered what it was Sylvia asked him to do last night.

'I forgot to empty the dishwasher.'

It wasn't until Zombie Extra turned to stare at him that he realised he'd said it out loud.

9

In the darkness, Sylvia's ears clearly picked out a tapping, scuffling sound and for a moment she thought it was Bill – maybe he hadn't left for work yet after all. She lay still and concentrated. There it was again. It wasn't Bill.

She'd been hearing it for about a week now and told herself they probably had mice. Whatever it was, it sounded like there was more than one of them, which meant they were breeding.

Not wanting to spend any more time alone in the dark, she hit the light switch she'd had installed – one on her side of the bed, one on Bill's – and the bedroom was instantly illuminated with just the right wattage: low because her eyes had become increasingly light-sensitive recently. Rachel Dent, the Hendersons' neighbour to the right and Sylvia's best friend of two years, said it was a side-effect from the Botox, but Dr Forbes said this was unlikely, and Rachel was only saying that because she had a needle phobia and couldn't do Botox herself. Sylvia had a top-up done earlier in the week ready for tomorrow night's poker party, and was eager to see if the Botox magic she'd got so addicted to had taken place – it usually took about three days for her face to process the age-defying contents of the injection.

The small, busy sounds stopped and she got quickly out of bed in the camisole and French knickers she still had the body to carry off.

Putting on the kimono Tom brought back for her from China, she went into the en-suite to check on her face. It really was unbelievable. She pushed up her sleep-ridden brown curls (L'Oréal colours 232, 141 and 303) pulled out some grey strays – and could have passed for Debra Winger in *An Officer and a Gentleman*, on only £300 a shot. Given that Botox Heaven was so accessible, she couldn't understand why there weren't queues round the block for it. The number of her friends who hadn't tried it yet – and who were in her opinion wilfully sabotaging their few remaining prospects – amazed her. Surely electing not to do Botox was as close to self-harm as a woman her age could come without actually drawing blood.

She smiled.

Her face, above her top lip, remained expressionless but she felt that this lack of expression gave her poise and a definitive sort of elegance; the sort the late Princess Diana used to have.

Sighing, she yelled, 'Vicky!' through her daughter's bedroom door before going downstairs and into the kitchen. There was Bill's milk glass by the sink, which meant he'd forgotten to empty the dishwasher again. She was half tempted to leave it until the evening, but that would only irritate her all day. Like that time he kept forgetting to empty the bin and she'd hauled it out into the middle of the kitchen floor, where it had stood, overflowing, and all he'd done was walk round it day after day – not getting the point.

'Vicky!' she yelled again, up through the ceiling this time, as she got the pan out the cupboard and started to make porridge.

Porridge was good for her. It had been good for Kate Winslet. The nutritionist had told her that. Sylvia had gone through a bad patch two years ago, just before they moved, skipping breakfast and living off crackers, bananas and emetics. The morning bowl of porridge had done just what the nutritionist promised: re-instated regular bowel movements and aided weight loss. The resulting weight loss far exceeded her expectations when she realised it wasn't just her own jeans she could now fit into, but her seventeen year old daughter's as well. She made a point of trying on Vicky's jeans – her weight barometer – once a week.

She went to the foot of the stairs. 'VICKY!'

There was the sound of a toilet flushing and water running.

She went back into the kitchen and laid out two bowls on the black marble surface she still wasn't convinced went with the granite floors.

Vicky rounded the corner, bleary and grey.

Sylvia, concentrating, filled the two bowls with porridge before looking up. 'What happened?' she said, taking in her daughter.

Vicky hauled herself onto the bar stool and stared at the steaming bowl of porridge. 'When?'

'I don't know when, but you look like shit.'

'Thanks.'

'Are you feeling okay?'

'No.'

'Ill?'

'Don't think so.' Vicky stuck her spoon into the

47

porridge then let it drop against the side of the bowl. 'I can't eat this.'

'It's what the nutritionist prescribed – plus it's freezing out there.'

'You've been out already?'

Ignoring this, Sylvia said, 'So you need something hot inside you.'

'I can't.'

'You'll be hungry mid-morning, and end up buying a muffin.'

'And?'

'And –' Sylvia faltered. 'That's no way to eat.'

'That wasn't what you were going to say.'

'What was I going to say?' Sylvia pulled herself up onto the other stool.

'I don't know – something about muffins and getting fat.' Vicky paused. 'You think I'm getting fat?'

'I think you should eat your porridge – you need to eat properly . . . out all the time . . . takeaway pizza.' She paused. 'There's no balance.'

'Are we still talking about food here?'

'What else would we be talking about?' Sylvia started to eat. 'It just occurred to me . . .'

'What?'

'That your jeans haven't been through the wash much recently.'

'So?'

'So?'

'So, I don't like wearing jeans all the time and anyway we're not even allowed to wear them to school.'

Sylvia nodded slowly. 'Well, we all need to be careful.'

'I don't believe this. You've started already and it isn't even eight o'clock.'

'You're the one who won't eat their porridge,' Sylvia observed.

'I was diagnosed bulimic less than two years ago and you're telling me I'm fat? I mean, I'm like no therapist or anything, but I'd say that's dangerously counter productive.'

'Is that a threat?' Sylvia asked. 'As I recall, you had symptoms of mild bulimia – that's not the same as being diagnosed bulimic. It was to do with the depression and the binge eating and you're over that now.'

'Yeah – over that; all done and dusted with that one.'

'Are you trying to initiate a conversation about depression, Vicky? Is this a cry for help?'

'A cry for help? If I'd gone down that road I'd have fucking lost my voice by now.'

'Are you trying to tell me you're depressed again?'

'I love the way you stress the "again"; like, here we go *again*, here's Vicky getting all boring and time-consuming *again*.'

'So are you?'

'What? Still boring?'

'Depressed –'

'Noooo!' Vicky shouted.

Sylvia waited. 'Your porridge is getting cold.'

She watched as her daughter picked up the spoon and shoved in mouthful after mouthful, until the bowl was empty. 'You want to watch you don't get indigestion.'

Vicky stared at her, her mouth full.

'I just need to know you're on top of things. This is an important year for you. I know you're hearing it from your teachers, but you need to hear it from me as well – and dad.'

'Dad doesn't even know what year it is – and you

never made O Levels let alone A Levels. So what are you talking about?'

Sylvia resisted the instinctive urge to take a swipe at her daughter's face – primarily out of respect for the fact that Vicky had actually made the effort to put make-up on this morning. She used to hit Vicky a lot as a child and was of the opinion that a 'tap' never hurt anyone. Vicky had – possibly – been tapped more than Tom, but then Vicky had been a difficult child, even as a toddler. 'Curdled,' her mother used to call it. Some children just came out like that – curdled. So, ignoring the reference to her lack of higher education, Sylvia said, 'I just want you to know that your dad and me are behind you at this point, which means you're free to focus on the opportunities ahead.'

'Oh my God, you're talking in platitudes. Did you take an evening class or something and not tell us?'

Sylvia drew herself slowly off the bar stool and Vicky instinctively flinched as she took a step towards her.

'Why are you so angry?'

'Because I'm sick of you talking to me like I've screwed up already when I haven't even taken my mocks yet.' Vicky stopped. 'This is about me not getting Head Girl, isn't it? You think me not getting Head Girl was because I'm not on top of things.'

'I didn't say that.'

'God, it must have been awful for you having to break the news to all your friends – about me not getting Head Girl. How humiliating for you.'

'So I thought you'd get it – what's wrong with that?'

'I keep telling you but you won't listen – there's no way anybody other than Grace was going to be Head Girl this year.'

'So it was a foregone conclusion?'

'Pretty much.'

'But I thought you said people voted?'

'People did –'

'You're making it sound like the whole thing was rigged,' Sylvia said, interested.

Vicky, who'd been staring strangely at her, got down from the stool, went over to the dishwasher, opened it – saw it was full – then shut it again.

She turned round, arms folded. 'Have you had something corrective done?'

Sylvia, startled, said, 'What?'

'Your face – it looks like somebody just ironed it.'

'A good night's sleep.'

'Ruth reckons you've had corrective surgery.'

'When did she say that?'

Vicky shrugged. 'I don't know. Some time. I asked Tom and he said "no", but now I'm not sure. There's definitely something different going on with your face.'

Sylvia touched her face with her fingertips then held protectively onto her throat under her daughter's gaze.

'Have you been getting Botox?'

Before Sylvia had time to defend herself, Vicky's face contracted suddenly.

'What is it?'

'Sick – I'm going to be sick.'

She ran past the breakfast bar and upstairs.

Sylvia waited.

The sound of retching – distant – came from upstairs.

She went to the foot of the stairs. 'Vicky? Are you okay?'

No response.

'There's air freshener up there – not the one with the orange lid that smells like old men – I'm writing to Airwick about that one. There's a can with a blue lid – Topaz Haze or something? – use that.'

Still no response.

'And you might want to have a shower while you're up there. Your hair looks like it could do with a wash. I know you already did your make-up, but –' She paused; her throat felt hoarse. The sound of banging came from upstairs. 'Vicky?'

She needed a boyfriend, Sylvia thought; that was the problem. She walked slowly back into the kitchen, opened the dishwasher and shut it again.

Rachel must have mentioned the Botox to Ruth – why else would Vicky have come up with that crap about her having corrective surgery? Well, who needs any sort of Heaven at seventeen – least of all one where they inject you with Botox?

10

Vicky went next door to number four where the Dents lived – in a house half the size of number two, built in the fifties on a plot where stables for number two used to stand. She walked to school most mornings with Ruth – partly out of convenience but primarily because out of all her group, it was Ruth she liked best. Ruth had been the first friend she made in Burwood as an unwilling urban transplant who spent most of her time shut in her room dazed with loneliness and the amount of time she spent on Facebook.

The friendship had been engineered, in the beginning, by their mothers – Sylvia, in order to offload, and Rachel out of generosity – and in many respects it mirrored the burgeoning friendship between Sylvia and Rachel themselves, who became inseparable when Rachel started to emulate Sylvia. After bringing the Hendersons back from the brink, meeting somebody who wanted to *be* her was the best thing that could have happened to Sylvia.

It was the same for her daughter, Vicky.

Despite inauspicious beginnings – Vicky initially

mistook Ruth's choking shyness for aloofness – Ruth was soon buying Vicky wholesale.

Vicky had been to a pathologically competitive girls' school in London that regularly provided the worlds of business, banking and government with leaders. It was intimated to the girls that reproduction was for the weak and stupid and that using your womb as nature intended was a less suitable fall-back position in life than having a breakdown and doing VSOS in Central Africa. Vicky had been on track for 12 GCSEs – including Ancient Greek and Chinese – and total mental and emotional collapse.

Ruth's early feelings for Vicky, clouded as Vicky was in the aura of the city she'd been forced to leave behind, were ones of reverence, and Ruth's reverence healed Vicky in a way nothing else could have done. The more Ruth wanted to be Vicky, the more Vicky loved her. Ruth understood that, for Vicky, living in Burwood was like living with a permanently infected wound. Despite having spent the past nine years of her life happy in this small commuter town nestled in the valley of affluence between the North and South Downs, she now learnt to actively despise it – and the people in it – for Vicky's sake.

Just as when Vicky fell in love with Mr Sutton, Ruth was expected to do the same in order to keep her company.

While Vicky was often cruel to Ruth – nobody else was allowed to be.

During the cruel phases, Ruth maintained a sobbing silence and simply waited for Vicky to come back round.

Saskia was nowhere near as devoted as Ruth, but she was swayed by the Aura of London surrounding Vicky. A complicated home life and an inherent and distracting talent for painting prevented Saskia from becoming worshipful, but Vicky liked her because she was beautiful.

She liked Grace the least.

Grace had so many part-time jobs – including raising a younger sister their mother was never home to raise herself – that she was rarely able to commit to the social life of the group, and this bored Vicky. Any latent chance of real intimacy had now been buried under Grace's appointment as Head Girl.

This morning the Dent family – apart from Ruth – were already out on the drive.

Nathan Dent, Ruth's stepfather, was trying to get something off his shoe and Rachel Dent was trying to get into the car because she was volunteering at the hospital that morning. The Audi estate was emitting the mellow, warning ping it had been programmed to make when the driver's door was left open too long.

'My shoe,' Nathan said over the voice of the Sat Nav, Giselle, who was trying to initiate conversation.

He stared down at the toe of his right shoe. What he had taken for a mark was in fact a cut in the leather. Between yesterday evening and this morning, something had either wilfully or unwittingly lacerated the leather across the toe of his shoe. The shoe was now irrevocably damaged . . . flawed . . . imperfect. Imperfection brought on nausea and panic, which led to bouts of unaccountable rage – like the one he experienced briefly now, standing on his drive on a Friday morning.

'It's ruined.'

Rachel looked down at the shoe he'd pushed through the gravel and fog towards her for inspection.

'Where?'

'There. Completely ruined.'

'Is not so bad. Can't you get repair?' She'd dropped her pronouns and forgotten her tenses like she used to do when she first learnt English; something she only ever did when she got anxious.

'*It* is not so bad. Can't you get *it* repair-*ed*. Look, I know you don't care.' He paused, but Rachel didn't respond to this. 'But the shoe's beyond repair and – for me anyway – that's frustrating. I walk home in a perfect pair of shoes and by the next morning – mysteriously – they're completely ruined.' He paused again. 'And that's frustrating.'

Rachel continued to remain silent. She wasn't being obtuse, she just had no idea what she was meant to say – how to respond without aggravating him further, which she was bound to do. With an effort, she leant suddenly forward, aiming clumsily for his cheek, and missing as Nathan turned to meet her kiss. Her lips bounced uncomfortably off the side edge of his chin and she mumbled 'sorry' – aware that it was last night she was apologising for . . . for having fallen asleep when he wanted to make love to her.

Nathan calmed down as soon as her misjudged lips touched his face. The shoe was forgotten. 'Okay, well – I'd better be off,' he said, sounding almost cheerful now, and even managing a small smile.

Rachel watched him walk down the drive in his beige CIA Mac, nodding at Vicky Henderson who was backed up against the red brick wall that separated number two Park Avenue from number four. He got to the gate post, which was fast becoming obscured in bamboo, stepped in a puddle, cursed, shook his foot, then crossed the road, narrowly avoiding the bus going into town that nobody ever used because everybody in Burwood owned a car. Even the elderly shunned using their bus passes in favour of battery operated mobility aids.

By the time Nathan got to the junction with Hurst Road, he was wearing the tight smile he wore most of the time for his dealings with the world: a quietly over-bearing, sarcastic smile that the majority of people were unwilling to probe behind.

Nathan Dent was the product of an over-hygienic childhood; the recipient of a slow, trickling paternal and maternal love, so you couldn't blame him really – for his smile. You couldn't blame him for the other legacies either – the propensity to dress like he sold audiovisual equipment in Currys, and the habit of scrubbing at his hands and nails with a toothbrush when they got dirty. His childhood had left him with a bitter taste in his mouth and a capacity for measuring himself out – both professionally and personally – in careful, dispassionate doses. Marrying Rachel, in fact, was the most ambitious thing he had ever done in his life. It was also, importantly, the only time he'd ever not been in control of himself. He turned down Hurst Road and across the park to the offices of Pinnacle Insurance where he sat in a booth and protected the world against itself.

'You okay?' Vicky asked Rachel, embarrassed. She had to say something – she'd been standing there the whole time and was still backed up against the wall, shoulder to shoulder with brick and bamboo.

Rachel smiled at her – confused by the question. 'You?'

Vicky nodded.

'You don't look it.'

'A bit fluey – that's all.'

'What's your temperature?'

57

'My temperature?'

'You look like you've got a temperature – you didn't take a reading?'

Vicky shook her head – did the Hendersons even have a thermometer? – too close to tears to speak. Ruth's mum always had this effect on her. She remembered the time she'd been upset and Rachel had hugged her and kissed the top of her head. She couldn't remember what it was she'd been upset about, but she remembered Rachel's warmth.

It was strange – number two Park Avenue was full of family photographs . . . hanging on walls, sitting in frames, secreted in albums, and yet Vicky had virtually no memory of ever having been held or embraced by Sylvia. At number four Park Avenue, there were no photographs and yet Rachel was forever hugging Ruth – it was one of the things that struck Vicky most when she first got to know the Dents. Mother and daughter did other things as well as hugging: swapped books, had manicures, make-overs . . . even spent entire days in spas together . . . things that baffled Vicky, who spent most of the time drowning under matricidal urges.

Ruth appeared then at the front door.

'You want me to lock this?' she called out to Rachel.

'Go ahead.'

'What was all that about?'

'When?'

'Out here – just now. I heard dad shouting.'

Rachel shrugged and opened the driver's door.

'You girls sure you don't want lift to school? I'm going straight past there.'

'We're fine,' Ruth said.

'Last chance?'

'We're fine, mum.'

58

'Okay –' Shaking her head, she took out the sunglasses she wore whatever the weather from the glove compartment. Then, putting the car into gear, accelerated hard so that pebbles from the drive sprayed up against the body of the car and caused scratches that would at some future date be detected by Nathan, who would expect a full explanation including the use of pronouns as well as the definite and indefinite article.

11

Left on the drive, Vicky and Ruth checked to see what the other one was wearing. The style the sixth form at Burwood Girls' went for was nineteen-twenties shot through with eighties Gothic – retro silk dresses in pastel shades over black tights with pumps gone to seed and lots of costume jewellery: Goth flappers.

They were both appropriately dressed.

'We're going round the long way,' Vicky announced.

'But, Vick, we're already running late.'

'I want to check in on Sutton.'

'Sutton?' Vicky rounded on her. 'Oh, Sutton – yeah, okay.'

'Are you feeling alright?'

Ruth nodded, preoccupied, and they started to walk.

The long way took them on the route past Mr Sutton's new house on Dardanelle Drive and sometimes they got a sighting of him leaving for work on his bike. At the beginning of the Michaelmas term he and Ms Webster had moved in together and Vicky had to get the new address out of the files in Mrs Harris's PA's office.

'Your dad's a total fuck up,' Vicky said as the Audi disappeared out of sight into the fog, Rachel waving enthusiastically. 'And your mum's so nice, I mean – how did it happen?'

Ruth shrugged. 'Nathan's okay. I know how he comes across, but –'

'What?'

'He's always been pretty good to us.'

'Shit, listen to yourself, Ruth. Save me the passion.'

'Passion's what he's up against, Vick. She fell in love with my dad during a war – they used to make love while the Serbs up in the mountains above the house were firing down on them. That's what Nathan's up against.'

Vicky stared at her. 'She told you that?'

'I was conceived under gunfire.'

'You talk about that stuff?'

'I'm her daughter – who else would she talk to about it?'

Vicky, walking beside her, couldn't even begin to contemplate initiating a conversation with Sylvia about her conception. Would Sylvia even remember?

Fifteen minutes later, they were crouching behind the line of conifers that ran alongside Mr Sutton and Ms Webster's front lawn.

'Webster's car's still there,' Ruth noted, whispering.

Just then the front door opened and Julia Webster herself appeared, yelling something over her shoulder back into the house. She was wearing a North Face jacket and a lot of fleece on her outer extremities.

'My God – have you seen the fog?' she called out.

'She looks like she's going on a field trip,' Vicky observed.

Ruth let out a muffled snort.

Julia remained poised in the porch. 'I'm going,' she said into the fog.

After a while Mr Sutton appeared, barefoot, a tea towel in his hands.

Ruth and Vicky gripped each other's arms.

'Why does he have to look so fuckable?' Vicky hissed, taking in the jeans and T-shirt he was wearing.

Ruth murmured faithfully, in agreement – her mind elsewhere – and they continued to watch through a natural peephole where some of the hedge had died.

Julia tilted her face up and as Mr Sutton leant dutifully to kiss her, she grabbed deftly hold of his chin and kept their faces together.

'Grotesque,' Vicky mumbled. 'Like – genuinely grotesque.'

Julia checked his face briefly as they pulled apart, unsure how to read what she saw there – despite the fact that he was wearing a smile – and went over to the sports car, opening the door.

'Don't forget – IKEA tonight,' she said lightly.

'Shit.'

'You forgot.'

He nodded and pulled his shoulders up to his ears before letting them drop again. 'Do we have to?'

Through the peephole in the hedge, Vicky and Ruth were still holding onto each other.

'It's bookshelves for you we're going for. I just thought you might want your art books out of those boxes they've been in all summer.'

'Okay –' he responded, flatly.

'You don't sound like it's okay.'

'I don't?'

'No, you don't.'

Ruth and Vicky worked hard at stifling the excited

laughter that was threatening to erupt from behind the line of conifers.

Julia stared at him. 'We'll talk about it later.' She hesitated, forcing a smile. 'You're sure you don't want a lift?'

'No – I'll cycle.'

'Well, don't forget your lights. You'll need them in this fog.'

'I won't.'

Julia hesitated again then got in. She gave a light wave before putting the car into gear and reversing off the drive.

Mr Sutton continued to stand in the porch, slowly drying his hands on the tea towel he was holding as the car's engine revved without resonance, pumping out carbon monoxide fumes that hung in the fog and had nowhere to go.

Vicky felt suddenly nauseous.

Eventually the car moved off and Mr Sutton waved vaguely as it disappeared into the fog. After a while, he went back inside.

As the door shut, Vicky clutched at Ruth's arm.

'They're not going to last,' Ruth said, jubilant.

Vicky shook her head, rapidly.

'Vick? What is it?'

'I think I'm going to be sick.'

'You can't,' Ruth said as the colour left Vicky's face and she started retching uncontrollably over the hedge, shaking with the force of it.

'Vick?' Ruth, worried, pulled back as much of Vicky's hair as she could while Vicky held onto the street sign for Ypres Drive, panting and waiting for the shaking to subside. This part of Burwood had been developed in the sixties and seventies, built on land once farmed by tenant farmers who lost their lives in the First World War. Without the men to labour on it, the land became untenable. By the time there was the labour force the world had changed and the men had changed with it.

'Tissue,' she said, through her nose, trying not to swallow in case it triggered another gag reflex.

'It's got Olbas oil on it,' Ruth said, trying to shake the pencil shavings off. 'Mum got a box of them when I had flu that time.'

'I don't care what it's got on it, I'm puking my guts up here, Ruth.'

Vicky blew her nose, wiped her mouth then spat into the tissue before pushing it into the hedge.

'D'you think you should go in today?'

'I'm fine. Apart from the fact that my mouth tastes disgusting.' She took a bottle of water from her bag, swilling a couple of mouthfuls and spitting them into the hedge as well.

'You just puked in a hedge, Vick.'

'I'm fine.'

'You're taking too much Valium.'

They started to move away then stopped suddenly as the front door opened and Mr Sutton appeared, carrying his bicycle over the threshold.

Ducking again, they watched him try to put on his helmet, struggling with the catch until, frustrated, he finally managed to get it done up. Then he switched on his lights and cycled off into the fog, the red light on the rear of the bicycle blinking at them.

'They're never going to last,' Ruth said again as the red light disappeared.

Vicky didn't say anything. She took a couple more

sips of water and held onto her stomach. Her throat hurt and she could taste nothing but vomit.

They started walking in the direction of school again – Ruth waiting for Vicky to comment on the row they'd just witnessed.

'What if I'm pregnant?'

Ruth stopped. 'Pregnant?'

'The puke – that's the second time this morning – and I'm late.'

'How late?'

'About four days.'

'Is that normal?'

'No.'

Vicky carried on walking and Ruth had to break into a run to catch up. 'Wait – Vick!' She was about to grab hold of Vicky's arm when her phone started to ring.

'Are you getting that?'

'Like – no. I mean –'

'What?'

'Could you be – pregnant?'

The phone stopped ringing.

Vicky nodded.

Ruth rounded on her. 'You and Matt? You never said anything.'

'You know – when I went up to town for that party in Pentonville with those weird Welsh guys.'

Ruth took this in. 'So – have you said anything to Matt?'

'What – about being four days late? I'm not filling his head with all this shit just because I'm late.'

'You're the one who said you thought you were pregnant.' Ruth paused. 'You did take precautions, right?'

'Like, no – of course.'

'So how could you be pregnant?'

'It's only like ninety-eight percent protection. Maybe I'm the two percent that got away.'

'Ninety-eight percent?'

'You never read the back of the packet?' Vicky broke off. 'We talked about babies and stuff – that weekend.'

'You only just started sleeping with him.'

Vicky shrugged.

They passed the school coaches that brought girls from outlying villages, parked on Richmond Road, and the pavements became suddenly dense with girls from the lower and middle schools, in uniform.

They turned in at the school gates, making their way in the same direction as the rest of the morning traffic between borders full of pruned rosebushes towards the main building. The younger girls walked in clusters, fast, socks falling down, bags slipping off shoulders and hair coming loose from clips and bands they were only just learning how to put in themselves.

A teacher, semi concealed by the wall of uniformed bodies, called out, 'Come along, girls.'

'You should take a test, Vick.'

'I'll give it a few more days.'

'There's a chemist up on Grace's estate – it's where everyone goes.'

'Who's everyone?'

'Come on – you know what I mean,' Ruth lowered her voice to a whisper. 'That's where Tina Branston went.'

'So that's like – what – one other person?'

Ruth didn't say anything.

'Move along girls,' the same teacher called out again.

Vicky had a sudden memory of walking through reception at the end of the summer term and seeing Tina

Branston there, so heavily pregnant she could barely walk. Flanked by a teacher, she was en route to the isolation room opposite the Head's office where she sat all her GCSE exams so as not to be a distraction – or pollutant – to the other girls. Vicky remembered catching Tina's eye – and being the first to look away.

'You make it sound like people are heading in their droves up to the chemist on Meadowfield Estate when you're talking about one other person. Tina fucking Branston.'

'Sorry,' Ruth mumbled. 'Anyway this is totally different to Tina Branston. I mean, as of January you'll be able to vote, have a credit card, get married – you're practically adult. Tina was like only sixteen or something. Plus she didn't even know who the father was. Plus you don't even know if you're pregnant.'

'Tina Branston had a boy,' Vicky said. 'She posted a picture of him on her Facebook.'

'How come Tina's got computer access? I thought she was meant to be like completely poverty-stricken?'

'You can pick up a computer for like a couple of hundred quid, Ruth, or maybe she stole it – I don't know, but the point is she posted it there for everyone to see and it was like, fuck you all, I did it, I'm happy. Now what are you going to do about it?'

'Yeah –' Ruth said, unconvinced.

'And people said some real shit about her.'

'Vick – we said some real shit about her. In fact, we said some real shit *to* her.'

'Don't you sometimes wonder?' Vicky carried on, no longer interested in Tina Branston.

'About what?'

'About the point of all this?'

Ruth took in the parked bicycles in the shed and

lines of girls moving towards the group of Victorian buildings whose roofs were barely visible in the fog. This was how things were and they didn't bother Ruth, but she kept this to herself.

'Matt was talking about dropping out,' Vicky carried on. 'He says the course is shit and that all the lecturers are on ego trips and can't be bothered to teach under-graduates. As a student you're just revenue to the university and loan bait to the banks. He was talking about this commune his friend lives on down in Sussex – they make cheese and stuff and sell it. He was talking about going to live down there for a while; getting his head straight.' Vicky paused. 'He was talking about me maybe going with him.'

'Vicky, you can't –'

'Why not?'

'Girls!'

It was Ms Hadley – popularly referred to as Bride of Quasimodo – a disabled teacher who'd been hired, impressively, well before the era of equal opportun-ities. She taught English, had goggle eyes and crutches, the rubber stoppers on the bottom of them sounding strange as she made her way through the fog towards them. In Year 7, Ruth had locked her in the book cupboard and hidden her crutches. She'd scared herself – it stood out as the singular large-scale act of cruelty in her life so far, and she still didn't know what came over her that day.

'Are you seriously thinking about not going to university?' Ruth whispered.

'I'm seriously thinking about not even finishing my A Levels.'

'Vick –'

'I just want to be with Matt.'

'But what would you do on this commune?'

'I don't know – make cheese?'

'How come he even knows about it?'

'I told you – he's got a friend there – Ingrid.'

Ms Hadley was standing in front of them, legs splayed awkwardly beneath the long skirts she always wore. 'Bell's rung,' she said, her voice sounding automated through lack of intimate conversation with anyone.

Vicky stared at the silver and turquoise necklace she was wearing, and wondered how cripples could be bothered to adorn themselves – especially female ones. What was the point?

Ruth flicked her eyes over Ms Hadley's deformed chin, at the point where it sank into her neck, then looked away.

Thousands of girls had passed through Ms Hadley's withered hands over the years, but she never forgot a face and she'd certainly never forget Ruth's because it was Ruth who locked her in the cupboard that day. She'd cried, as silently as she could, behind the locked door and that was something she hadn't done on school premises either before or since, in all her long career. So, no, she'd never forget Ruth.

Ruth smiled awkwardly.

Ms Hadley didn't return Ruth's smile; she just carried on staring.

She carried on staring as the girls shuffled past her, legs and sticks splayed over so much of the pavement they had to pick their way through the pruned rose bushes in the borders.

'Freak,' Vicky whispered, when they were still within earshot.

'Vick –' Ruth warned her.

'So, what? You know what she keeps in the back of her car? A snow shovel – all year round.' She paused. 'Hadley's probably on the FBI's most wanted list.'

'For what?'

'Killing sexually attractive young girls.'

They went into the main building by the entrance to the side of the Upper Hall and the first person they saw was Mr Sutton standing at the foot of the stairs.

'Hey, you two,' he said brightly, under the impression that this was their first meeting of the day.

Vicky hated it when he said this, lumping her and Ruth together as though they were children.

'Catch up later.' He grabbed hold of the banister, setting off at a run up the flight of stairs to the top where the art department was.

Vicky turned on Ruth. 'Why did you do that?'

'What?'

'You waved.'

'So?'

Vicky did an impression. 'It was idiotic.'

'So? Where are you going?'

'I need to find a water fountain – I can still taste vomit in my mouth. I'm sorry,' she said, grabbing hold suddenly of Ruth's hand and squeezing it.

'It's okay.'

'Will you come with me – to get the test?'

'Course. Have you told the others?'

'Not yet. Listen – I'll see you at break.'

Ruth nodded. 'It'll be okay. You know that, don't you? I mean – even if you are – it's only a fucking baby. It's not like the end of the world or anything.'

Vicky smiled and gave Ruth's hand a final squeeze then pushed forcefully through the set of double doors and disappeared down the corridor.

Ruth hesitated at the foot of the stairs then got her phone out her bag. One missed call. She checked the number and smiled – a new sort of smile she'd been wearing for about two months now, one that Nathan had noted across the dining table, and that unsettled him.

12

Saskia Greaves swung her legs out of bed and made her way over to the window where she opened the curtains – still just about hanging from the few remaining plastic hooks attached to the rail. Her bedroom window usually commanded a view over the strip of wasteland that was their back garden, the neighbour's garden to the right – containing a miniature Swiss chalet housing two blood-hounds – and beyond this the Unigate milk float depot.

This morning the drone of the milk floats sounded distant and all she could see of them through the bank of fog was their headlights. There was another light hovering at eye level – one of the floodlights that went on at around 4:00 a.m. and was usually attached to an arching branch of steel – now suspended in fog.

She stood motionless, her mind moving rapidly.

Turning away from the window, she put the toadstool night light on that she'd had since childhood and picked up her mobile. She went back over to the window.

We need 2 talk. Tonite. S

Once the text had been sent, she remained by the window, tapping the mobile gently against her teeth.

At last, sighing, she moved over to the pile of clothes heaped against the chest of drawers. There was no wardrobe in the room. The chest of drawers were here when they moved in, only the bottoms had since fallen out of the drawers so she'd just started leaving the clothes in a pile by the side instead. This meant it was sometimes difficult to separate the washed from the unwashed clothes and after a while they all got the same smell – damp wallpaper, rotting carpet and other things the survey had failed to shed light on and that Richard Greaves hadn't really been in a fit state to take on board at the time of purchase.

She found a couple of tops in monochrome shades and then put on the skirt she'd taken off the night before and thrown on the floor by the side of her bed, the legs of which had broken on one side so that it was propped up with National Geographics and manuals for computer software that no longer existed.

Then she went downstairs where there were no curtains at any of the windows – apart from a blind in the kitchen – so the morning's low calibre lighting had already made its way in.

Picking up a slice of pizza from the box on the coffee table – last night's? The night before that? – she wandered through to the kitchen, opened the fridge door, stared inside, shut it again then took a couple of bites from the slice of pizza and started to make coffee.

She checked her dad's timetable, blue-tacked to the wall, and saw that he had morning classes starting at nine.

'Dad!' she yelled from the foot of the stairs, her mouth full of pizza. 'You've got a nine a.m. start. Dad!'

She took a cup of coffee upstairs and went into the only other bedroom in the house, pulling the duvet back enough to reveal the small head and sleep-ruffled grey curls of Richard Greaves. Then she went over to the fitted wardrobe and selected one of the dark heavy suits – first checking for cigarette burns and other stains – and hung it on the sliding door, the one that was still in its runners, where he'd see it when he woke up. The other door was propped against the wall with a serious dent in it, Richard having recently crashed into it when drunk.

His suit collection pre-dated their post-divorce move to the two-bedroom terrace overlooking the Unigate milk float depot. It was the legacy of his producer at Sky TV days, and most of the collection still fitted him despite the weight he'd put on. The suits had lost a lot of their original impact because they no longer had any expectations of the man wearing them – but the cut couldn't be denied.

Saskia had stored them in a box when he got fired and the box had been put in the van along with every-thing else when they left their old house on the north side of Burwood. They'd stayed in the box while he took a year off on his redundancy money and tried to write a book, and they'd come back out of the box a year ago when he'd taken the job as a Media Studies teacher at Burwood Technical College.

'Dad – time to get up – come on.' She stood at the foot of the bed and waited as the duvet shifted and Richard rolled onto his back.

She went over to the curtains and opened them. 'There's a thick fog out there today – look.'

But Richard didn't look; he was too busy watching her – and had stopped being interested in fog a long time ago.

'You okay?' he said after a while.

Saskia smiled at him, but didn't say anything.

'What's that you're eating?'

'Pizza.'

He sighed. 'You out tonight?'

'Maybe. What about you?'

Richard nodded slowly. 'There'll probably be drinks after work.'

'Who with?'

'People.'

They stared at each other.

'Well,' Saskia said at last. 'Just let me know.'

Richard sighed again.

'Come on, you've got to get up – you've got a nine a.m. class.'

'Not today.'

'Yes – today; it's the module on sitcoms and you've got notes for it already – those ones we worked on this time last year; I put the green folder by your bag next to the door. Come on –' She lifted the duvet and tickled his feet.

'Okay – I'm up.'

She leant over and gave him a kiss on the forehead before disappearing into the bathroom and putting on her make-up. After this she picked up another cardigan from the pile in the corner of her room, and a scarf that she wrapped round her neck at least four times before poking her head round his bedroom door once more and yelling, 'UP!'

'I'm up,' he mumbled, sitting swaying on the side of the bed.

'See you later.'

'Yeah. Love you.'

'Love you too.'

She went back downstairs, unlocked the front door and stepped out into the fog.

13

Sitting on the edge of the bed, Richard Greaves listened to his daughter leave the house, and waited. Sometimes she forgot stuff she had to come back for, but not this morning.

He exhaled loudly, unaware he'd even been holding his breath, and collapsed backwards onto the bed. This morning he was feeling the *most* unhappy he had felt since he'd first started waking up in the morning feeling unhappy, which was about five years ago. Something terrible had happened in his life; more terrible than discovering the love letters written by a man called Peter Jenkins to his then wife, Caro; more terrible than being laid off from Sky TV and having to pay most of his not generous redundancy package to Caro and her new partner, Peter Jenkins; more terrible than living in a two up two down overlooking the Unigate Dairy depot. What made it worse was that he couldn't talk to anybody about it; not even his sister – the only member of his family he was still on speaking terms with – and definitely not Saskia.

He lay there staring up at the ceiling, which had

been hastily wallpapered in order to hold it together – by the son of the woman who died here – before they put it on the market. The upstairs bedrooms had also been washed in a single coat of magnolia that the wallpaper underneath – a ghostly pattern of miniature posies – could still be seen through. The imprints of the elderly woman's furniture could be traced as well, in the pile of the carpet from the decades it had stood there.

The lamp hanging from the ceiling was a deep, helpless burgundy, and had tassels. There were brown stains on the inside of the shade where water had, at some point in time, dripped through the ceiling. Sometimes he was so hung over when he woke in the morning that he thought he heard the lamp muttering at him in a language he couldn't understand – a dead language like Aramaic. His sister phoned him while that was happening once and told him he sounded like crap and he'd asked her how a person who was getting taunted by a lampshade – in Aramaic – was meant to sound, and then she'd hung up.

This morning it wasn't taunting him – in Aramaic or anything else.

Sighing, he rolled over and felt under the bed for the bag of cocaine he kept taped to the frame.

His dealer lived on a farm about three miles out of Burwood. He bred spaniels for gun dogs and Richard came across him because he had a lap top that was playing up – this was when he was writing his novel – and the spaniel breeder did a sideline in computer repairs. Richard left the farm with a fully functioning lap top and 4g of pure Bolivian – yet another of the breeder's sidelines, it transpired.

Hauling himself once more into an upright position,

he shook out a line onto the small metal tray with a picture of the Natural History Museum on it that he kept by the side of the bed specifically for this purpose.

He did the line, closed his eyes, and waited.

When he opened them again, the surfaces in the room had become sharper and brighter. By the time he got dressed in the suit Saskia had hung out for him, the interior of the house was virtually dazzling.

Downstairs, he felt that the kitchen could almost pass as the sort of kitchen other – ordinary – people had.

He poured himself a glass of milk and stood drinking it, staring at the two photographs Blu Tacked to the fridge door – the only two photographs in the entire house, in fact. One was of him and Saskia scuba diving in France, and the other was of him standing at the bottom of a trench in the Somme where a relative of his had died during the First World War.

You could tell a lot about a middle-class family from examining their fridge. A well-stocked interior indicated physical health, and a well-stocked exterior (fridge magnets) indicated an attempt, at least, in projecting emotional health. The Greaveses' fridge was both empty, and unadorned – apart from the two photographs.

Richard picked up his bag and the green folder containing Saskia's notes for that morning's class on sitcoms and, feeling fretful – the only discernible trace of his earlier despair – but remarkably buoyant, pulled the front door loudly shut.

That was all he had to do.

As long as he left for work in the morning, kept the front garden clear of litter, and put the right recycling in the right bin, he was left alone.

The world didn't care that a coke-addicted divorcee lived at number twenty-four Carlton Avenue with a daughter he was incapable of looking after – or that he'd slept with a minor in one of the upstairs bedrooms.

Richard took the same amount of cocaine most mornings to help him out of bed, out of the house and into the dark green Skoda that had been designed with Saabs in mind. He used to make people laugh – his ex-wife, Caro, included – at his Skoda jokes, but that was when he drove a Saab. Now, as a Skoda driver, he wasn't entirely sure of his footing when it came to telling Skoda jokes, and didn't know any jokes about Saabs.

The fog was beginning to lift and the early morning world of Burwood shone through the diminishing grey as he drove the Skoda out of town towards the new bypass and Technical College.

Once there he made his way to the far end of the car park and parked beneath a bank of Scotch pines where traces of fog still hung. This was where he always parked because nobody else ever did.

He shunted his seat back, picked up the bag of cocaine he kept on the floor under the driver's seat, and did another line from the Skoda's dashboard. After this he got his phone out his bag and dialled the number he'd been thinking about dialling all morning. She didn't pick up. He thought about leaving a message, but in the end decided not to.

Still clutching the phone, he got out the car and headed towards the glass and steel college building. It wasn't until he got half way across the car park that he realised how cold his legs were.

Feeling suddenly sick with fear, he checked to see that he'd remembered to put on the suit trousers – he'd once got as far as the bypass before realising that he was only half dressed. Yes, he was wearing trousers; it was his socks that he'd forgotten to put on.

Reassured, he passed through the automatic doors into reception where he saw Polly – who taught textiles and made her own clothes – standing waiting for him.

'Richard,' she said, coming towards him in one of her own designs, her voice long and mellow from decades of breathing exercises. 'I was hoping to catch you –' She paused, hauling her hair slowly back over her shoulders and laying a hand on his arm. 'Everything okay?'

He'd once made the mistake of crying in front of her when he gave her a lift home, and now she thought she had Fast Track Access to him.

He stared at her hand, but it didn't leave his arm.

'I really need you to confirm re. the Transcendental Yoga Retreat.'

Lost, he probed his mind for references to a Transcendental Yoga Retreat. Was this something they'd actually discussed? Her tone seemed to suggest so – at a worryingly concrete level. Her tone seemed to suggest that she was going to carry on probing his Chakra points until he caved in – and said 'yes'.

While waiting for a response, her hands started brushing at the shoulders of his jacket, dusted with fallout from his nostrils after the line he did on the Skoda's dashboard.

Could he tell Polly about his problem?

'Look at all this dandruff. You're stressed,' she said. 'I've got some wonderful oil for scalp conditions.'

Their eyes met.

'I just don't know if it's my thing – a Transcendental Yoga Retreat.'

'Did you go to the site?'

He shook his head.

'Go to the site – have a look at it – then make your mind up.' Her hand was still on his arm.

'The thing is – I've got quite a lot of complicated personal stuff going on at the moment.'

Polly nodded, interested.

Richard looked around him.

The college building was optimistically open-planned so ironically reception – the main thoroughfare into the college and usually crowded – was often the best place to have a private conversation.

'I've been involved with someone.' He broke off when he saw the look on her face. 'Not seriously,' he said quickly. 'I mean – for me.'

'I didn't realise,' Polly mumbled, upset.

'I should never have started it.'

'So – you're breaking it off?'

'Trying to.'

'Why trying to?'

'She's not getting the point.'

All this was good – what Polly wanted to hear – and she would have been reassured by it, exuberantly so, if it hadn't been for the fact that Richard's facial expressions were changing by the second and there were beads of sweat along his upper lip.

'She doesn't understand the . . . impossibility . . . I mean, it's my fault for starting it in the first place, but the . . . impossibility . . . of it carrying on.'

'So talk to her . . . tell her.'

Richard let out a strange, high-pitched giggle.

'I keep trying to, but she's obsessed. It's her age –'

'Her age?'

Richard nodded. 'I mean, she's quite young.'

'How young?'

'Young.'

82

'How young?'

He scrunched up his face. 'Seventeen.'

'Seventeen!'

A group of students turned round and stared at them then swung away again, laughing.

'For fuck's sake, Richard.'

He winced. 'I know.'

'No, you don't know.' Polly paused. 'She's not a student here, is she? Please God, don't tell me she's a student here.'

He shook his head. 'Look, I really need to talk –'

'I'm no professional.'

'I just need to talk – to somebody. Later? After school?'

The bell sounded and she started to move off through reception.

'Please –' he called after her.

She turned and looked at him before disappearing through the double doors leading to Art & Textiles.

He shuffled over to the reception desk, feeling cold inside, and slid his elbows across the glass surface. 'I don't suppose –'

The receptionist turned, in her headset, to look at him.

'I don't suppose you keep spare pairs of socks behind there, do you?'

She carried on looking at him, sighed, and turned back to her magazine and the article on celebrity house foreclosures she'd been reading.

14

On the Meadowfield Estate – Burwood's only council housing – Grace Cummings was tying a French plait in her ten year old sister Dixie's hair while Dixie, who was going through a major *Sound of Music* phase, tried to pick out the tune for 'Edelweiss' on a mouth organ she got in a Christmas cracker the year before.

Their mother – Nicole Cummings – had been working at Fleurs, the florist, for a year now. She used to have a job cleaning until Grace bullied her into applying for the one at Fleurs when it was advertised in *The County Times*. Despite the early start – which left Grace in charge of getting Dixie to school – working with flowers had changed Nicole in a way nothing or nobody else ever had. For the first time in her life, she had a career rather than a job, was sitting exams to get accredited and even – poised on patchy lino inhaling the green perfume of cut flowers on the threshold between life and death – nurturing a silent ambition to run a florist's of her own one day.

When Grace had finished, Dixie shook her head

smiling and ran a hand over her hair. 'Emma's going to be so jealous.'

'Here, put this on,' Grace said, handing her a duffel coat that used to belong to her.

'Not that one – it's scratchy.'

'It's the only one you've got and it's cold so put it on.'

Dixie conceded. 'D'you want to be a hairdresser when you grow up?'

'Not really,' Grace said, distracted.

'So what d'you want to be?'

'I want to go up in space.'

'People still need their hair cut in space.'

They were running about five minutes late.

'Who's picking me up from tap tonight?'

'Me.'

'Can I wear my tap shoes to school?'

'Where are your school shoes?'

'I left them in the back of the car.'

'You're sure?'

Dixie nodded.

'What about your trainers?'

'Can't find them.'

Before the job at Fleurs, Nicole had been seriously thinking about re-locating to Perranporth in Cornwall – to a council flat overlooking the beach and some municipal palms.

She didn't sleep well, and didn't read the *Financial Times*, so didn't know about the reassuring statistics concerning crime, teenage pregnancy and male mortality – or that Burwood was a good place to live. Only last week she dreamt she woke at two a.m. – to the sound of the neighbour they backed onto beating his disabled wife with a shovel, out in the garden. When she looked out the bedroom window, however, there

85

was nobody there – no grunting, enraged shovel-wielding husband, and no terrified, disabled wife scrunched up on the lawn in threadbare moonlight. Unfortunately there was nobody lying beside Nicole in bed, and when she got up there was no article attached by magnets to her fridge door that she could read in order to dispel her fears. So the dream stayed with her, made worse by the fact that she was sure she'd heard an ambulance in a nearby street just before dawn, and hadn't seen the disabled woman since.

Eventually they left the house, Grace pushing her bike and the metal plates on the bottom of Dixie's tap shoes ringing out on the pavement, the echoes muffled by fog.

They cut down an alley where Grace remembered being pushed into a pile of nettles when she was about Dixie's age. The attack was still vivid in her mind because she hadn't seen it coming, and couldn't understand it. Like the time that girl in the red anorak had put a stone inside a snowball and knocked out part of her tooth so that now she had a different coloured bit in one of her front teeth.

'Emma says she can do the splits but I haven't ever seen her do it and every time I ask her to show me she comes up with some excuse so now I don't know whether to believe her or not.' Dixie paused, waiting for Grace to comment, but Grace – who'd been even more distracted than usual this morning – didn't have anything to say. 'She says she can sit on her hair as well but I've actually seen her do that. So –' Dixie swung her head, pleased at the slapping sound the French plait made against the back of her coat.

'I hope Ms Jenkins isn't sick today. She was sick last week and we had Ms Clarke whose hair's pulled back so tight you can see all the veins on her forehead. She makes us put our heads on the table with our thumbs up and keeps on shouting "Silence" even when nobody's talking. How can you talk less than silence? She made Emma and me sit apart and I had to share with Mandy who smells like going to the toilet and has to go to the hospital to have her bath 'cause her mum's in a wheel-chair. That's what Emma says.'

'When am I going to meet Emma?' Grace said at last, making an effort.

'Emma's mum says she's not allowed to come to our house so I've got to stop asking her. It's because of the dogs near us – the ones that don't wear leads that might have rabies.'

'She said that to you?'

Dixie nodded. 'Maybe her mum'll let her come now you're Head Girl.'

Grace ran her hand protectively over Dixie's hair.

'Ms Jenkins said microwave food isn't good for you – is that true?'

'Probably.' Grace felt exhausted and the day hadn't even begun.

They were almost at the school crossing where she'd recently agreed to leave Dixie and let her go through the school gates on her own.

'I told Ms Jenkins you were Head Girl, but she already knew. She said one day they were going to have to put a blue plaque up on the school to say you'd been a pupil there.'

Grace smiled.

'What's a blue plaque?' Dixie asked.

'It's like a sign – they put them on buildings when a famous person's lived or worked there.'

Dixie stopped. 'Are you going to be famous?'

'Who knows?'

Grace watched her younger sister cross the road with the Lollipop Lady, who gave her some sweets. When Dixie got to the other side she waved the sweets triumphantly in the air.

She gave a final wave before disappearing through the gates into the crowd of children and parents.

Grace could still hear the tap shoes. She waited until she couldn't hear them any more before getting on her bike, preoccupied, thinking about what Ms Jenkins had said about the blue plaque, and feeling suddenly tearful.

As she stopped at the next set of lights, she heard somebody call out her name. 'Grace! Grace!' It was her Physics teacher and Form Tutor, Ms Webster, in the car that had pulled up beside her.

'I didn't see you at netball practice yesterday,' Ms Webster shouted through the open window.

Grace played Wing Defence on the B team. She should have been on the A Team, but her commitments at home prevented her from going on any of the tours.

'Sorry about that,' she shouted back.

Ms Webster nodded, looking at her. 'Anything wrong?'

Grace shook her head, her mind still on blue plaques.

The lights changed to green and she waved, moving instinctively forwards.

A few seconds later, Ms Webster overtook, calling out, 'I'll see you at school.' She wiped at her face where something wet had fallen then accelerated past Grace, who kept her head down because she'd started – inexplicably – to cry.

15

Down in the basement gym at number two Park Avenue, Sylvia Henderson was listening to *The World's Greatest Arias* and focussing on the weights because she'd noticed movement in her underarms recently – a lack of solidity that bothered her. She was used to working out with Rachel – who was still trying to get pregnant at the age of forty-four – in between Rachel's miscarriages.

As she gasped and a whole host of sopranos sang, her eyes flickered over the garden, on eye level and bleak at this time of year in its early winter wash of browns. The garden was one of the few things in her Brave New Suburban World that frightened Sylvia. Even more so when she'd realised that in Burwood you weren't only expected to spend time *in* your garden but *with* your garden.

At the Park Avenue Residents Association Summer Barbecue there was a large-scale trade in cuttings, which had alarmed Sylvia into drinking herself way above her limit and spending far too much time with a man with halitosis who kept chewing at his nails.

Despite having walls still papered in Laura Ashley and floors carpeted in dog hairs, Dr Fulton's wife, Jill, had a social standing on the Avenue it was difficult to de-stabilise due to her horticultural reputation.

Sylvia enjoyed eating in the garden; she enjoyed getting Tom to light the fire pit when he was home – Bill was too depressed to be trusted with this task – and enjoyed sunbathing on her Plantation recliner. She didn't enjoy anything that required her to kneel or wear old clothing, and anyway – lost interest once the summer was over.

She'd gone to a nursery just outside Burwood that was often on TV and spent vast amounts of money on plants guaranteed to give architectural effect, but still couldn't make the garden come together. It overwhelmed her – and it knew it.

She could feel it now, in its winter nudity, taunting her – and wished the fog hadn't lifted.

Shifting her eyes away from the garden, she continued pulling weights until the phone started to ring.

She answered it, panting.

'Mum? Are you okay?'

'Tom –'

'You sound weird.'

'I'm down in the gym.'

'Is now a good time to talk?'

'About what?'

'The weekend.'

Tom sounded tense; stressed. His usual lightness – that herself and others found so endearing – wasn't there.

'Listen, mum – I don't think I'm going to make it.'

'Tom –'

'I know.'

'My poker party.'

'I know –'

'I've told everyone you're coming.' She indulged rapidly in the image of Tom in his Dinner Jacket moving through her guests. 'What am I going to say to people? My God –'

In her distress, she'd inadvertently turned back to face the garden and was now staring at the randomly planted oleanders, olives, Dicksonia antarctica and eucalyptus trees looking like a band of horticultural misfits that had broken rank for the final time, never to re-group again under her command. She knew she'd seen *Day of the Triffids* alone, at an impressionable age, and she knew trees couldn't walk but she was now convinced they were moving towards the house. She could feel them peering in at her. Soon they'd be tapping on the glass, their branches fiddling with the catch until they managed to slide through the windows.

'We've barely seen you since the summer –' She kept her eyes on the trees.

'I know.'

'And I haven't seen Ali for I don't know how long.'

Silence.

Sylvia started to panic.

Turning her back on the garden, she headed for the stairs leading up from the basement and started to climb through the house, enraged. 'Is Ali okay?'

'She's fine.' Tom paused. 'Actually, we've decided to take a bit of a break.' Another pause. 'Mum?'

'From what?' She tried not to yell down the phone.

'Well – each other.'

'Is this Ali or you speaking?'

'It's mutual.'

'Why the hell didn't you say something to me sooner?' she finally exploded.

'Because I knew this is how you'd react.'

'And how am I meant to react? You work together, Tom – you and Ali just work.'

'Actually, mum, we've kind of realised we don't.'

'This is the first blip that's all; this is something you need to overcome – not walk away from.'

'It's not a blip – and we've talked about it, and we're not sad.'

'But I've bought Ali's Christmas present – I bought her parents' Christmas present. There are pictures of Ali on this year's Christmas card.'

Sylvia had reached the upstairs bathroom, and was now looking in the cabinet for her Valium. Where the fuck had all the 2mg whites gone?

'Is something wrong? Tom?'

In the silence that followed, she tried to make as little noise as possible while searching the cabinet for the pot of 2mg whites.

'Like what?'

She couldn't believe the only pills she had left were the 10mg blue ones.

'I don't know, like . . . have you been unfaithful?'

'No! Mum–'

With the phone hooked under her chin, she managed to shake a couple into her hand. 'Because stuff like that – painful as it is – should never get in the way of a relationship as strong and special as yours and Ali's.' She put the pills in her mouth and took a couple of sips of water straight from the tap while holding the phone away from her so that it was facing out the window.

'I'm speaking from experience, Tom. So when it comes to you and Ali –'

'Mum, wait!'

'What?'

'Are you talking about dad? God –' Tom exhaled loudly, without waiting for an answer.

'That was years ago – I thought you knew. Look, my point is we've been through it – and we're still here.' Sylvia hesitated, eyeballing herself in the mirror. 'Don't get upset about it now.'

'I'm not upset, I'm –' Tom, suddenly nauseous, sought for the right word. 'Disorientated. Profoundly disorientated. Shit, mum – did I know her?'

'Isabella? No. She was a summer intern, she wouldn't have come to the house.'

'Isabella –'

'You didn't know her, Tom,' Sylvia said, getting pissed off with the conversation. 'It was the summer before you started at Bessemer. Look, it doesn't matter,' Sylvia was trying not to sound irate. 'I want to talk about you and Ali.'

'Actually, mum, I'm kind of devastated right now –'

'So it's Ali who was unfaithful?' Sylvia shouted – disbelief taking hold of her.

'No – I'm talking about dad and this Isabella person, I mean –'

'Fuck Isabella, Tom, I was using her as an example.'

'An example? Mum, I'm trying to deal with the fact that when I was growing up, dad had an affair.'

'For two weeks – with a summer intern. Get over it, Tom – I had to.'

What on earth had made her tell Tom about Isabella? She hadn't thought about Isabella for years. Tom had Bill's predilection to become fixated with things that didn't concern him. An early symptom of hereditary depression? Now she was getting morbid.

Up until Isabella, she thought women only collapsed on celluloid, she didn't realise they collapsed on real carpets in real houses in front of real husbands – who smelt unfamiliar. Bill had been her life. After Isabella she'd literally swallowed herself whole, and vowed never to be that vulnerable again. She realised that she could either spend the rest of her life constantly afraid that Bill would leave her – a time-consuming and all pervasive fear – or she could train herself to fall out of love with him.

She looked around her.

Where was she?

The bedroom.

What was she doing in the bedroom?

What had she been doing before the bedroom?

She'd been in the bathroom – talking to Tom and taking Valium.

'But, mum –'

'Don't get morbid about it.'

'I'm not.'

'Stay focussed.'

'On what?'

'You and Ali,' Sylvia yelled.

'There's no stuff like that between Ali and me, and even if there was – we don't have over a decade's worth of marriage and two children behind us.'

Ignoring this, Sylvia said, 'So, what stuff is there?' There was hesitation – slight, but detectable nonetheless – and she noted it. 'You're not depressed, are you?'

'No, I'm not depressed. I just broke up with my girlfriend.'

'A minute ago you were talking about trial separation.'

'I just said that, so as –'

94

'What?'

'To go easy on you.'

The panic was coming back, she could feel it – in spite of the 20mg of Diazepam now going to work on her system. He couldn't expect her to give up on the idea of Ali just like that. If she'd sat down and written a list of everything she wanted in a girlfriend for Tom – she'd have written Ali. One day Tom and Ali were going to have a beautiful wedding – she had a file on the computer with a codename where she kept all her downloads from wedding research conducted on the internet – and after that they were going to have beautiful babies.

Before she could stop herself, she let out a quick, gasping sob.

'Mum, come on –'

'I'm sorry – it was just all going so well.'

'Well, it's hardly like the four horsemen are tap dancing on the roof of the house, is it?'

'First there was that business with Vicky not getting Head Girl – now you and Ali. On top of everything else.'

'Like what?'

'Like dad's job; like the relocation; like dad's depression.'

'Dad's not depressed.'

'You don't live here any more Tom, you don't know.'

'Isn't that just stress?'

Sylvia sighed. She loved talking about Bill's depression and it made a change, talking about it with their son, but she didn't really have time. She had a hair appointment with Barry at Kutz (it looked even worse in neon) in less than forty-five minutes. 'Shit.'

'You okay?'

'Late for something. Listen, I just don't want Ali and you making any rash decisions.'

'Mum, I told you –'

'You told me you were having problems,' Sylvia cut in. 'You just need to give each other some space – not ultimatums.'

She smiled confidently at herself in the cabinet mirror, despite the fact that the sun was shining outside now and casting long winter shadows across the bathroom walls, making the room feel as though it was tilting from side to side. She held onto the sink, still smiling, mouthing the word 'ultimatums'.

'Why don't you come down this weekend anyway – on your own. We can talk some more.'

'I can't.'

'If your account needs topping up –'

'Mum – please.'

Tom sounded tired. Depressed? If that was Bill's legacy to Tom, she'd kill him.

'Come down for Sunday lunch then.'

'Okay. Okay –'

'I'll transfer the money for the train fare.'

'I don't need money.'

'Boys your age always need money, Tom.'

'Mum – wait. What happened? To Isabella?'

'You're breaking up – see you Sunday.' Sylvia ended the call so quickly she dropped the phone in the sink and had to retrieve it before heading into the bedroom to change. She thought about the charm she'd bought for Ali's Christmas present – the Tiffany pagoda – and wondered whether she shouldn't just post it to her anonymously. Ali would think it was from Tom, and Tom wouldn't say anything because he'd be too embarrassed. Quite frankly, if Tom wasn't going to put the effort in, she was because there was no way The Hendersons were losing Ali.

Humming along to *The World's Greatest Arias* still playing down in the basement, she was about to leave the house when the phone she was carrying started ringing in her hand.

'Mum – listen.'

It was Tom – he'd changed his mind – Ali and he were coming to the poker party tomorrow night after all.

'About dad –'

Sylvia stopped. 'Tom, I've got to go.'

'It feels weird – me knowing about Isabella and him, and him not knowing I know.'

'Why weird?'

'Can I talk to him about it?'

'Not at the moment – no.'

'I know – now's not a good time – this whole working at Pinnacle Insurance thing's really taking its toll, isn't it?'

'He said that to you?'

'He was devastated when he didn't get that promotion they'd been prepping him for at the old place for like the past decade. Like – devastated.'

'He said that to you?' Sylvia said again.

'Then they brought in that guy like about my age and he was meant to be managing dad but he knew shit and dad like lost it with him.'

Sylvia had no idea what Tom was talking about, but the worrying thing was, it all sounded true.

'When did he tell you all this?'

'We do talk, mum.'

Well this was the first Sylvia had heard of it and why choose now to spring this latent father/son relationship on her? Two years ago Tom wouldn't have been able to identify Bill after a road accident where his head had remained intact. In terms of intimate parenting, Sylvia had always been under the impression that she had exclusive rights on Tom, and exclusivity meant a lot to her.

'Well don't get sucked in, that's all I'm saying.'

'Sucked in to what?'

She opened the front door and stood in the tiled porch, staring at the morning world. The fog had gone, and now thick white sunlight cut through the cold air, which smelt faintly of petrol. She checked to see that none of the trees from the back garden had crept up the side passage to lie in wait for her on the drive – no, the coast was clear. Nothing out there but a laurel that needed pruning (so Jill advised her), and a pampas grass that had suffered from suicidal levels of low self-esteem for the past two decades – almost as long as she and Bill had been married, in fact – and was now enjoying a comeback.

'Depressed people can be devious, Tom – and they're adept at creating a chain of need.' Sylvia paused as a roaring sound started up over the wall at the Dents' property. 'You've got your whole life ahead of you,' she said over the noise, before trailing off, uncertain. Was she even talking about Bill any more? Or Tom for that matter?

'Mum – dad's NOT depressed,' Tom said, sounding genuinely angry. 'He's fucking broken.'

The line went dead.

She tried not to think about this – about any of this. She never had liked broken things – even as a child. That's why she walked out on her mother at fifteen.

She crossed the drive towards the Hendersons' new Lexus 4×4 and checked over the wall to see what was going on at the Dents. This suburban affliction had been acquired within days of moving in. In London – even in the part they'd been living in – you didn't look over walls because somebody was invariably getting mugged, raped or stabbed in their own front garden, and it was better not to know. If you knew you had to do something about it, and when the police got involved those things dragged on. If you didn't look, you didn't know, and life carried on.

Over the wall at number four, Rachel Dent was wearing a safety helmet and ear muffs while operating a petrol-powered leaf vacuum.

She saw Sylvia, waved, and turned the machine off. 'You're going out?'

Sylvia nodded. 'I've got about a million things to do before tomorrow.'

Rachel slid off the ear muffs. 'What's that?'

'I said – I've got about a million things to do before tomorrow.'

'Oh.'

Rachel hadn't picked up on the 'tomorrow' reference. Had she actually forgotten the poker party?

'I was going to finish up here and come over.'

'Everything okay?' Sylvia asked, turning away and opening the car using the remote.

Rachel was staring bleakly at her, the visor on the helmet now pushed up.

'I was meant to be working at the hospital this morning, but they already had my shift covered. I got the wrong day or something.'

Sylvia had no interest in Rachel's voluntary work at the hospital – why work for free doing something you could get paid to do – and blamed Jill Fulton, the doctor's wife, for putting Rachel up to it in the first place.

'I was really looking forward to doing something that

would take my mind off the stomach cramps I've had since this morning.'

'Something you ate?'

Rachel continued to stare bleakly at her. 'Something I ate? No – I think it's my period coming.' She started to cry.

Sylvia was shocked – plus she wanted to look at her watch, but was aware that looking at your watch was on the list of things not to do when your neighbour was sobbing in front of you.

And Rachel *was* sobbing now – so violently, in fact, that the helmet's visor had slipped back over her eyes.

'But it hasn't actually started, has it?'

Rachel shook her head, the suction pipe from the leaf vacuum scraping against the wall. 'What if it does?'

'Well it means the IVF failed, I guess.' This came across as more flippant than intended – even to Sylvia – who was trying hard not to lose patience. Her appointment with Barry was a reality; tomorrow night's poker party was a reality – Rachel's period was still only conceptual. 'This is only your fourth course – it's going to take time.'

'I don't have time – I'm forty-four years old.'

Rachel being forty-four was precisely Sylvia's point. Why on earth would a woman of forty-four want to have another child? Rachel had been through it once already; she knew the full extent of the horror. Why re-live it?

Rachel was forever counteracting any of Sylvia's talk on liposuction with the stock phrase, 'You just need to tone what you've got.' She'd like to see Rachel stand by her mantra when her shoes were getting caught up in her stomach every time she tried to take a step forward.

100

'I think about how it was with Ruth. When I got pregnant with her, I was living on a kitchen floor in darkness. The shutters were down the whole time because they were firing on us. Then they started using mortar shells from up on the mountain and the house was shaking so much we were like fleas on a dog's back on that kitchen floor.' She paused, caught up, her eyes no longer blinking. Then, appealing suddenly to Sylvia, who had just managed to take a look at her watch, she said, 'How come I lose a baby between this house and Sainsbury's when I managed to keep one inside me during a war?'

Sylvia should have been sitting in a swivel chair in Kutz with Barry's hands on her shoulders talking about layers and lights – five minutes ago – and she wasn't even in the car yet. She didn't have the reserves right then to go over Rachel's miscarriage again so gave a slow, blank smile and waited for the moment to pass. In the silence that followed, Rachel's tears turned to sniffs as she wiped repetitively at her face.

'I had cramps with Vicky. All the pre-period syndromes, and I just thought oh, well, it isn't going to happen this time. Only they never came to anything and before I knew it, I was pregnant with Vicky.'

Rachel's eyes were turned full on her – behind the visor. 'Really?'

Sylvia nodded. She'd never seen a face so full of hope before and the effect was disorientating.

It wasn't until she'd started to speak that she was even aware of this memory.

'That was with Vicky?'

'With Vicky.'

Rachel reached over the wall with her free hand and gave Sylvia's arm a squeeze. 'Thank you,' she said. Then again, 'Thank you.'

Sylvia smiled, unexpectedly released from the moment.

Rachel made no attempt to go back to her leaf vacuuming so in the end Sylvia left her standing by the wall and got into the car with a sense of relief.

She put the car into gear and pulled off the drive, waving at Rachel – who didn't wave back; didn't even look up in fact as the car drove past her.

Sylvia was so busy staring at Rachel that she didn't see Jill Fulton cycling past the entrance to their drive, waving enthusiastically. She stopped just in time as Jill – poor Jill, who cycled everywhere but never seemed to lose any weight – swerved to avoid the Lexus's bumper, which was on shoulder level.

Sylvia followed her slowly to the end of the road, fascinated as always by the absence of woman in the woman. There was Ruth trying to come to terms with the fact that another five grand's worth of IVF was just about to bleed its way out of her womb – and she'd still gone to the effort of making herself up; even after deciding to spend the morning in a protective helmet with visor.

Jill was married to a man who made national news last year by operating on himself while under local anaesthetic, and she couldn't even be bothered to dye her greys.

Sylvia had put 'smart dress' on the poker party invites, but what did 'smart dress' mean to somebody who hosted the Residents Association Summer Barbecue in shorts and a Batman T-shirt; who mended their own guttering and shared Christmas Day with needle exchange patients?

Sighing, she headed into town and was soon sitting in Kutz with Barry's stroppy hands on her shoulders. He only cheered up when she asked after his boyfriend

– who'd just bought him some Prada shoes on e-bay for a civil ceremony they were going to that weekend.

He had the print-out in his trouser pocket to show her and because she was so late and Barry had still agreed to keep the appointment she had to sit there and listen to the minutiae of the bidding history, like the most stress anybody in the world had ever suffered was having to live through the last two minutes of a bid on a pair of Prada shoes that were probably fake anyway.

Sylvia wanted to scream at him, 'Try life as a heterosexual for a change,' but in Kutz, she was outnumbered.

She came close to pointing out that if he'd chosen a boyfriend on a better salary than Mark, who drove trains, he'd be able to afford real Prada new, but in the end she kept quiet because Barry had scissors in his hand and tomorrow night she was hosting Burwood's first ever poker party.

16

By the time Vicky, Ruth, Saskia and Grace made their way through the school gates, it was already getting dark. The late afternoon was full of the head and tail lights of semi-stationary traffic, exhaust fumes and the sounds of children no longer confined by routine.

'So – are we going back to yours?' Vicky said.

Saskia shrugged. 'Can do.'

'Is your dad going to be there?' Ruth asked.

'Shouldn't be – he was going out for drinks after work today.'

'Who with?'

Saskia looked at her. 'Why would I care? Why would you care?'

Grace dug her hands in her pockets and pulled her scarf up over her mouth, breathing deeply into the acrylic stripes. 'Listen – I'll see you all later. I've got to get Dixie from her dance class.'

She started to cross the road.

'Wait – are you coming to B-52s tonight?' Vicky called out after her.

'Can't,' Grace called back, 'I've got a late shift at Sainsbury's.'

The others carried on walking through the mass of bottle-green uniforms making their way up the road.

'Have you told Grace?' Saskia asked.

Vicky shook her head.

Nobody was surprised – nobody told Grace anything any more. Partly, it was to do with her being Head Girl, and the inevitable distance this put between her and her peers – even peers she'd known since the age of eleven. But there was something else – less transient – that only Ruth knew about, and would have mentioned, only Grace herself hadn't yet, and so she didn't feel she could. Ruth had gone swimming one Sunday – she swam at least three times a week – and, crossing the park afterwards, saw Grace and Dixie on the roundabout with Tom Henderson.

After a while, Saskia said, 'Vicky – d'you think you are?'

'Could be.'

'What'll you do?'

'Depends.'

'On what?'

Vicky hesitated. 'I don't know.'

'You wouldn't keep it, would you?'

'Jane Linton had an abortion before the summer holidays,' Ruth put in. 'Her boyfriend was so supportive, like – really sweet about it – gave her the money and everything.'

Saskia stared at her then turned back to Vicky. 'You wouldn't keep it, would you?' she said again.

'I don't know.'

'You said you and Matt had already talked about kids and stuff,' Ruth reminded her.

'Yeah – he wants to do a better job than his parents did with him.'

'Yeah, but the point is, do you?' Saskia said.

Vicky shrugged.

'Tell her about the commune and the goats and how you're going to make cheese and stuff,' Ruth said, excited.

Vicky sighed, less convinced in front of Saskia. 'Matt's got this thing about moving to a commune, helping teach in the school there and maybe keeping some goats to make cheese.'

'So he's going to make goat's cheese and he wants you to make it with him?'

'We could all go,' Ruth put in.

Vicky didn't say anything.

'You should get the morning after pill – you don't need a prescription or anything, you can get it straight from the chemist.'

'Only this isn't the morning after,' Saskia pointed out.

'Well, Larissa was four days late last month and *she* got the morning after pill and as soon as she took it her period started.'

'Ruth – that doesn't make any sense.'

'What I'm saying is – with Larissa it was, like, psychological,' Ruth concluded.

They headed in silence through Burwood's town centre, passing Panino's, who were doing the catering for Sylvia's poker party. Arno – the proprietor – who was standing in the window and saw them pass, waved.

Three hours after waving to Vicky Henderson from behind his shop window Arno and his wife would have a row, and Arno would end up putting her hand in the sandwich toaster and switching it on. But – as the girls passed the coffee shop and Vicky returned Arno's wave – none of this had happened yet.

'Where are we going?' Vicky asked Saskia.

'We're getting the kit from Cramplins.'

'Can't we just go to Boots? You know – right now the anonymity of a franchise is looking really appealing.'

'Vick – school's just come out, the chances of seeing someone we know in Boots is, like, beyond high. Nobody goes to Cramplins – apart from people buying surgical shoes and incontinence pads.'

'I thought it shut down,' Ruth said.

'In the process of – which is even better.'

'Will Cramplins even sell pregnancy testing kits?'

Saskia pulled her down West Street – a legacy of Burwood's early days as a cattle market when drovers used to bring herds in from the west – stopping in front of an old-fashioned chemist. The original wooden shop front was still intact and the windows of frosted glass advertised the fact, in chipped gold leaf, that it was a dispensing chemist.

M. R. Cramplins had been on West Street when bona fide Victorians walked the streets of Burwood, and the current Cramplin was great-grandson of the original M. R. Cramplin.

A home-made sign was posted across the window with the words Closing Down Stock Clearance written on it in black felt tip.

'Here?' Vicky was unconvinced.

'It's closing down – they'll be gone this time next week so who cares?'

They didn't see the man with the camera standing behind them – Jamie the photographer from *The County Times* – whose flash went off as they stopped in front of the shop window.

'Hey, girls,' said Jamie, irritated, 'you want to move along a bit?'

They stared at him before shuffling towards the door, which had a circular sign hanging above it with an eye painted on it.

Vicky paused, and turned to Ruth and Saskia. 'You're all coming in, right?' she whispered, aware of the photographer.

'Course,' Ruth said, taking hold of Vicky's arm.

'I can't do it.'

'Vick – you've got to,' Saskia hissed.

Vicky turned to Ruth. 'What about that chemist up on Grace's estate you were telling me about? We could go there.'

Jamie took a picture of the girls as they went into the shop. Frank, who was doing the piece on Burwood's oldest shop closing down, had asked for straight pictures of the shop window, and Mr & Mrs Cramplin, but Jamie liked the idea of the three schoolgirls going in – Cramplins' last customers pay homage. Or something like that.

As they pushed open the door, the bell inside the shop clanged – then the girls disappeared.

Inside the shop it was empty – there wasn't even anybody behind the mahogany and glass counter.

Vicky's eyes worked rapidly over shelves full of Scholl podiatric products – insoles, corn plasters, shoes – stacked next to back supports and incontinence pads. This wasn't a shop for people who still had sex.

Then Saskia re-appeared beside her with a Predict box and Vicky was seriously considering shop-lifting when a man with over-groomed white hair, wearing a shirt and tie – the sole survivor of three generations of Cramplin chemists – appeared behind the counter.

He'd been upstairs – speaking to Frank Barlow, the journalist from *The County Times*.

Saskia pushed the Predict box into Vicky's stomach. 'Just do it,' she mumbled.

Vicky shuffled across the carpet and dropped the box onto the counter.

'Are you paying cash?' Mr Cramplin asked, without looking at the box.

'What's that?'

'Cash?'

'Cash. Yeah.' She slid the money over the counter.

The entire transaction was conducted without her once looking up, focussing instead on a flat-faced ring with a trident engraved on it that the chemist was wearing on his index finger.

The next minute Mrs Cramplin appeared from behind the curtain at the back of the shop in the blue suit and floral blouse she'd put on for the interview with Frank Barlow from *The County Times*.

Frank Barlow himself stood just behind her.

Vicky grabbed at the bag and, ignoring Mr Cramplin's, 'Your change!' ran for the door, followed by Ruth and Saskia.

They disappeared into the October afternoon, the bell ringing behind them.

17

Sighing, Mr Cramplin ran his hand over the counter.

'Last customers?' Frank asked.

Mr Cramplin looked at him then blinked and looked away. He didn't like Frank Barlow.

'What did she buy?'

'I'm sorry?'

'I might finish the piece with it.'

'With what?'

'Your last customer.'

'Oh.' Mr Cramplin nodded.

'So – what did she buy?' Frank asked again.

'Personal items.'

Mrs Cramplin let out a sound half way between a giggle and a grunt.

She'd spent thirty-five years in a marriage she'd never wanted to a man she thought she could change; a man who had taken away her old life without ever giving her a new one.

Despite this, up until now she'd always been loyal, but suddenly – with the shop half packed up – just didn't see the point any more.

'She was buying a pregnancy testing kit.'

Frank Barlow stared at her. 'What – the girl who just left?'

'And the other one.'

'Only one of them bought a kit,' Mr Cramplin corrected her. He never had been able to tolerate the way his wife stretched and twisted the facts; robbing them of their vital simplicity.

'Well the other one was in at the beginning of the week – the one standing near the door with the long hair.'

Frank Barlow was nodding to himself, digesting this. 'So you sold Predict kits – it was Predict, wasn't it? – to two of those girls?'

'That's it,' Mrs Cramplin said.

Mr Cramplin didn't say anything.

'It's because we're closing down – they think they can come in here and it won't matter.'

At last Mr Cramplin turned to Frank Barlow. 'You won't be writing that up in your piece, will you?'

'Course not,' Frank said, automatically.

There were a lot of things that twenty-eight years of life on earth hadn't given Frank Barlow, but one thing he had limitless reserves of was instinct, and he'd been following it blindly for as long as he could remember, which had left him very little time for self-diagnosis.

He'd been born and grown up in Burwood, and the town felt like a father who'd done his job without criticism, and without love, which had given Frank a certain shallowness – occasionally illuminated by a craving for violence. He'd had one of his violent moments this afternoon, listening to Mrs Cramplin unravel thirty-five years of marriage in a sing-song whine. It had been so intense, in fact, that he'd had to grip onto the sides of the chair he was sitting on in order to prevent himself from dropping to the floor by her feet and tidying up her ankles with a carving knife; trimming away all the mottled purple and grey flesh spilling over the rims of her shoes because it was setting his teeth on edge. The moment had passed.

He'd left Burwood – for a year – at the age of eighteen and tried to find another life for himself in London, but been unable to. So he'd returned home with the thought that if he couldn't escape, he'd at least leave his mark, and one day bring the town he hated to its knees. He let his mother sort up a job for him on *The County Times* and after three years got a promotion that enabled him to rent a flat in the new block overlooking Waitrose. Once he had his own place he started to seriously date the sort of seventeen-year-old girls who would never have dated Frank Barlow at seventeen, but who were happy to spend a year of their lives with him now he was in his twenties. He spent money on them, cooked for them in his flat, and put up with their banality in bed. Then they left – usually for university – and lost all interest in ever seeing Frank Barlow again. So the girls lasted a year each, and were renewed on an annual basis, and this was the rhythm of his personal life.

It was Frank who'd uncovered Burwood's only prostitute, living in the flat above the St Catherine's Hospice shop. He'd sold the story to the *News of the World* – through an internet company that brokered deals between the media and people with stories to tell – after the Editor at *The County Times* decided not to run it. His exposé on the paedophile photographer – Mike Wedmore, who'd had a family portrait studio on East Street for over thirty years – had gone to the *Sun*.

He'd spent the morning with the mother of a fourteen–year-old boy who had committed suicide because he was being bullied at school – Danehill, where Frank Barlow had also been a pupil, and also been bullied – and had taken a pencil with a rubber monster on the end from the boy's desk without knowing why. He could feel it now in his coat pocket as he walked with Jamie, the photographer, back to his car.

'So – you got the girls going into the chemist?' Frank said, turning to him.

'Yeah,' Jamie responded, pleased. 'I know that wasn't the brief, but I thought you'd want me to.'

He waited for Frank to comment on this, but Frank didn't.

They got into the car in silence.

18

'Stinks in here,' Vicky said when they got to number twenty-four Carlton Avenue.

'Yeah,' Saskia agreed, turning on the kitchen light.

Ruth disappeared into the lounge where she crashed onto a pink bean bag with unicorns on it next to the coffee table.

The bean bag and sofa were the only pieces of pre-divorce furniture in the house, and both were still covered in dog hairs belonging to Chet, the black Labrador the Greaves had when Saskia was growing up and whose tail she'd held on to while learning to walk.

Vicky appeared in the lounge doorway reading the instructions on the Predict box without really taking them in.

'Let me have a look.'

She passed the box to Ruth and slumped down on the sofa among the deceased Chet's hairs, staring up at the ceiling.

'That's the most depressing lampshade I've ever seen.'

Saskia came through from the kitchen as Ruth put the Predict box on the coffee table.

All three of them stared at it.

The room was dark because nobody had thought to switch any lights on, but there was enough of a glow coming from the kitchen to see by.

Vicky pulled hard on the ends of her scarf. 'Got anything to drink?'

'Jack Daniels – maybe. Vodka – maybe,' Saskia said. Nobody moved.

Vicky got a small Tupperware pot out of her bag, unwrapped the tinfoil package inside and put two pills in her mouth.

'You take those into school?' Saskia asked.

'The 2mg are white – they could be Ibuprofen.'

'You might be pregnant, Vick,' Saskia said.

'Yeah, but I don't know yet, do I? Anyway, it's not like I'm shooting up on heroin.'

'I read somewhere that a lot of heroin addicts have perfectly normal babies,' Ruth put in.

'Yeah,' Saskia agreed, 'if you can call a neo-nate addicted to heroin normal.'

Vicky hauled herself off the sofa and picked up the kit.

'You going up?' Saskia asked.

'Obviously.'

'You want me to come with you?'

Vicky shook her head and disappeared upstairs – the lampshade on the ceiling, vibrating.

Saskia and Ruth were wary of each other without her. Something had changed since the summer, and while Ruth knew what that was – Saskia didn't.

Saskia rolled herself a cigarette and pulled one of her legs up, pressing her chin into her knee until it hurt. She looked suddenly much older.

'What are you thinking about?' Ruth asked.

'Sex,' Saskia said, without looking at her, flicking ash from the cigarette in the direction of the coffee table.

'Sex is weird,' Ruth said, after a while. 'I mean – at first.'

'Yeah,' Saskia agreed. 'And sort of disgusting.'

Ruth nodded and they started to relax. 'Then it gets better.'

They looked at each other and were on the verge of speaking – simultaneously – when upstairs, the toilet flushed, and at the sound of the flush, Ruth automatically got up. 'I'm going upstairs to see how Vick's doing,' she said, suddenly awkward again.

Saskia followed her to the foot of the stairs – there wasn't room for both of them up there on the minuscule landing. She stood hugging herself, resting her head against a patch of wall spongy with damp.

'Vick?' Ruth called out. 'You okay?'

'No.'

'Can I come in?'

'No.'

'Vick – open the door.'

'Just give me a minute.'

Without thinking, Ruth drifted into the bedroom next to the bathroom, which belonged to Richard Greaves. It smelt of unwashed linen, stale alcohol, rotting carpet and bad dreams. The bed was unmade and there was a collection of glasses and cups on the night table. The floor was covered in discarded clothes, and a single shoe. The whole scene bothered her, but for some reason it was the single shoe in particular that brought her unexpectedly and for no reason almost to tears. She picked it up, scanning the room inadvertently for the other half of the pair, but there was no sign of it.

Then the bathroom door opened and Vicky was standing there.

'The test was positive,' she said blankly, staring at Ruth in the middle of the bedroom holding Richard Greaves's shoe – barely registering her.

'Vicky!' Saskia called out from the foot of the stairs.

Vicky left the bedroom, followed by Ruth – who put the shoe tidily under the bed – and as soon as Saskia saw Vicky's face, she said, 'You're pregnant.'

Vicky nodded then started crying and soon they were all crying without knowing why, and hugging each other – Vicky burying her face hard in Ruth's suede jacket – the one she'd bought on their last trip together to Camden Market.

19

Bill Henderson was drunk.

He got drunk alone – as he did most things these days – at a commuters' pub on a balcony overlooking the main concourse at Victoria Station.

He sat on an insubstantial metal chair that left ridges on the underside of his legs and drank three pints of some industrial brew that looked drinkable under the pub's neon blue signage. As he did this, the mellow computerised announcements informed him that first one then another Portsmouth Harbour train – the ones he needed for Burwood – were departing from Platform 19.

The concourse below was full of immobile clusters of commuters standing in front of the departure boards with their heads tilted back. From up on the balcony they looked like chickens in suits – especially when one of the clusters surged suddenly forward and through the barriers; a stampede only held up by inconsistencies such as people with children, suitcases, crutches or other physical disabilities. He'd once seen a mob making a final dash for the 18:24 push a woman with a buggy onto the tracks because they didn't want to wait for the 18:43.

He remained sitting on the balcony listening to announcements for trains going to places he'd never been to and couldn't foresee ever having a reason to go to, until he'd finished his third and final pint.

It was almost half seven by the time he finally got on a Burwood train, and he had to hold onto the railing as he went down the flight of steps leading from the balcony back down to the concourse.

The trains weren't so busy on a Friday night – he got a seat and fell asleep as soon as the train started to move. While he slept he had a dream, which was strange in itself, given that he'd stopped dreaming about a decade ago. Stranger still was the fact that it was about Sylvia, and in the dream Sylvia was naked. Conscious, he couldn't remember what his wife looked like naked, but in the dream her hair was down, she was sitting in front of an electric fire and she had poker cards in her hands.

He woke at a station called Horley and tried to remember whether Horley came before or after Burwood. Horley came before. The train had been held up for forty minutes there last week because someone had thrown themself out the window of one of the new part-ownership flats overlooking Platform 1, onto the lines.

As he came to blearily, in public, he became aware that the collar of his jacket was wet with drool, and his right cheek pockmarked with the indent from the seat's upholstery. The woman opposite – who'd been on the train since Victoria and since Victoria been reading a self-help manual on how to get rich through hypnosis – looked at him then looked away, definite disgust on her face.

In a panic, he checked to see that his eyes hadn't rolled out of their sockets in his sleep; that what was left of his hair was still on his head; that he hadn't inadvertently peed himself.

It was then that he realised he had an erection; obvious through his suit trousers.

He stared at the woman opposite then at his own reflection in the carriage window, helplessly pulling his jacket around him.

While Bill Henderson was getting drunk at Victoria Station, Sylvia Henderson was getting drunk over a recipe for chicken and coconut curry that she'd cut out of a magazine, put in a clear plastic wallet and then filed under 'c' in her recipe folder. This folder, which she'd been compiling since the children were small, gave her an inordinate amount of pleasure – more pleasure, in fact, than her matt black Le Cornue stove, which she'd been wanting half her life.

Once the curry was simmering she went through to the sitting room and put the garden lights on, startling a fox that was crossing the lawn. The fox stopped dead in its tracks, panting rapidly, then swung its head and stared at her – mouth open – before running in a long low slide behind the evergreen bush that the man at the garden centre promised her would have a hedonistic fragrance in May.

The garden floodlit – pinned down; mounted – was the only time she felt comfortable with it. Humming, she put on the Robbie Williams CD Tom bought her last summer after they'd been to see him in concert together at the O2, then went back through to the kitchen and mixed herself a vodka martini. Bill never worked late these days – he'd lost his drive because of the depression – and the earlier he came home, the more they drank. Their one bottle a night had accelerated to two, and the only way to curtail further acceleration was early evening cocktails.

Sylvia tried phoning Tom's girlfriend, Ali – who she'd been trying to contact all day – but Ali didn't pick up.

Irritable, she finished the vodka martini, swept the vegetable debris off the bench – missing the bin, which wasn't like her – and mixed herself another. She then made her way unsteadily towards the oversize American fridge and clung onto the handle, swaying as she stared into its brightly illuminated bowels looking for a bunch of coriander.

She found the coriander, swung back towards the bench and started to cut into it with a handbag-size knife that cost the better part of a hundred pounds – something to do with the number of times the steel in the blade had been folded.

Knives were the one piece of kitchen equipment she'd been able to get Bill interested in. While they were still in London – before he got made redundant and before he got depressed – he used to do amazing things to joints of meat in front of a pleasantly inebriated Sunday lunch audience.

She stopped chopping and stood with her abdomen pressed against the kitchen bench and the knife with the folded steel blade raised in her right hand. She looked poised enough to do one of two things expertly – cut open her stomach and pull her intestines out onto the chopping board in a deft, classic rendering of seppuku *or* cut the carrots into the two millimetre thick slices recommended in the recipe for chicken and coconut curry. In the event, she remained motionless, thinking about the past.

Sylvia often thought about the past; had in fact got to that point in her life when she spent more time thinking about the past than the future, under the illusion that the past was something she had control over. When she thought about the past she tended to restrict it to the recent past. She rarely plunged as deep as she had suddenly, inadvertently just done. To the time when she first met Bill – just after the dreary, frightening years of hostels and washing clothes in sinks.

It was Bill who taught her how to play poker – when they first met. This memory, uncalled for, had rushed through her while on the verge of bringing the knife down to make contact with carrots and chopping board. She remembered sitting on an orange and brown carpet in front of an electric heater and Bill talking her through the cards, but she'd been too busy looking at the way the light from the heated elements moved over his wrist and lower arm to really take in the cards. Later they took off their clothes and never finished the card game.

Despite the clearness of the memory, she began to doubt that first poker game had ever really taken place. Had Bill's hair ever been black and thick enough for her to grab handful after handful and for it to never run out? Had he really ever made her laugh – so much she'd bruise her rib cage from the inside? How improbable to think that a young girl who looked just like her and a young boy who looked just like Bill had ever played strip poker on a brown and orange carpet covering the floor of a bed-sit.

Then the front door opened and Bill walked into the kitchen, only for a moment it didn't look anything like him. Where were the long smooth arms, black hair and shining eyes? Had he dressed up as an old man to make her laugh? Shuffling across the kitchen floor in his old jacket and grey wig, mouthing something at her, he looked so ridiculous, she started to laugh.

The night was cold and dark and Burwood's rush-hour had been and gone hours ago. Exhausted, Bill hung about the deserted taxi rank, but no taxis showed so after five minutes he started to walk along the empty streets home, wondering if a curfew had been imposed on Burwood. A couple of times, unnerved by the silence, he turned round, half expecting to see a line of tanks rolling down the road behind him.

He put his key in the front door to number two Park Avenue fully intending to tell Sylvia about his erection, but the first thing he saw when he walked through to the kitchen was the debris from supper preparations on the floor by her feet, which wasn't like Sylvia, who hated the kitchen looking used. Then, as she turned round, he saw blood running down her wrist and disappearing down her sleeve. There was a smudge of it on the edge of the bench.

She wasn't smiling at him, but she was at least looking at him in a direct, focussed way – happier than he remembered her looking for a long time.

'You're bleeding,' he said, gripped by a sudden notion that she'd been standing at the kitchen bench, cutting her wrists.

She looked down and started to laugh.

He stood swaying, in the middle of the kitchen floor, wondering about the muscular tic that had started up in her left cheek.

20

'What is this?' Vicky said, pushing her spoon through the chicken curry.

Sylvia had somehow managed to get the food onto the table and candles lit without immolating herself. The achievement of sitting down to a family meal, as recommended by countless TV chefs and various politicians – with a teenage daughter who dreamt of matricide and who didn't have a boyfriend despite being a size eight, and a husband with depression – had exhausted her. When Tom was still at home they used to eat together most nights. Now the fractured Henderson family made a concerted effort to sit round the same table once a week because once a week was as much as any of them could stand. The original idea of an informal family supper had, over the course of the eighteen months since Tom left home, metamorphosed into something unnervingly ceremonial.

It reminded Bill of the Last Supper, but the participants at that only had to do it once.

'Chicken curry,' Sylvia said, in response to the question.

Vicky dropped her spoon. 'It's got coconut in it – I hate coconut.'

'Since when?'

'Since forever. It's like the one thing I don't eat and every time we have supper together you like obsessively make something with coconut in it.'

Sylvia swallowed loudly, and considered this – making a mental note to book a facial for Vicky because she had flaky patches on her forehead. 'What did I make last Friday?'

'Thai curry – with coconut milk.'

Bill remained silent.

'You're drunk,' Vicky added, staring at her.

Without a word, Sylvia picked up Vicky's plate, grazing the back of her hand across one of the candle flames, and walked with the jerky deliberation of somebody trying to appear sober into the kitchen. With the same deliberation, she held her burnt hand under the cold tap before tipping the contents of Vicky's plate into a sieve and rinsing the entire meal under warm water.

She walked back into the dining room. 'I took the coconut out,' she said, and started eating again.

After a while, a steady throbbing pain starting up in her left hand, she said, 'Tom's not coming to the party tomorrow – he phoned this morning.'

'How was he?' Bill asked.

Sylvia stared at him. 'He's not coming to the party,' she said again. 'Something to do with him and Ali.' She peered through the candle flames at Vicky. 'Did he say anything to you about Ali?'

Vicky shook her head. 'I haven't spoken to Tom for weeks.'

'Will you phone Ali for me?'

'Why?'

'To find out what's going on between them two.'

'I'm not phoning Ali.'

'She might pick up if you phone.'

'She might not want to speak to any of us. What d'you want me to say anyway? Ali – please don't split up with my brother. My mum doesn't want you to?' Vicky paused, staring at her plate. 'Creepy.'

'Nobody said anything about Tom and Ali splitting up,' Sylvia said loudly.

'For Christ's sake, mum, her parents took her to another continent this summer to get her away from Tom.'

Sylvia was stunned. 'Is that why they went to India?'

'They're just kids,' Bill put in, blandly.

'Who do they think they are?' A spasm shot uncontrollably up her left cheek.

'They'll work something out,' Bill mumbled.

Sylvia turned on him, outraged. 'Is that really how you think things happen – that they just work themselves out?'

'I didn't say that.'

'Things never just work themselves out. Look around you. Go on – just take a look around you,' she yelled, her hand pressed firmly over her left cheek. 'You think all of this just worked itself out?'

'Sylvia –'

'There was somebody behind the scenes, Bill, making it all happen. There's always somebody behind the scenes – only you've never been there, have you? You just shuffle from one set to the next and – eureka – it's all fully decorated, furniture in the right place, even people in the right place.'

'Mum – leave him alone.'

'Shuffle?' Bill said.

Sylvia turned back to him. 'What?'

'You said "shuffle".'

Sylvia shrugged.

'You think I shuffle?'

'I don't think, I know. You're a shuffler, Bill – always have been; always will.'

Vicky had her elbows on the table and her thumbs in her ears. When she was younger and they used to argue, Tom and her would slide slowly off their chairs and under the table then crawl, one behind the other, to the nearest exit. Sometimes she'd pause in the doorway and look back at the table and see her father give up and slump forwards as though somebody had just pulled out his spine. If it hadn't been for Tom, pulling her away, she would have gone running back into the room and thrown her arms around him.

She remembered one of her parents' worst rows – the one they had before leaving London when Bill picked up his plate of food and hurled it against the dining room wall. All four of them – Tom was still at home then – had sat in their seats and watched chicken risotto slide down the walls until Bill left the house and Tom disappeared upstairs. Sylvia, sobbing, put on a pair of Marigolds, ran a basin of hot water and started to scrub the chicken risotto from the Sanderson wallpaper, which wasn't washable. When Vicky got up and tried to leave the room as well, she said, 'Don't leave me.'

Only Vicky had. She left Sylvia kneeling on the floor in her Marigolds and went out into the night in search of Bill, who she was terrified would just carry on walking and never come back if she didn't find him.

She did find him – standing in front of an estate agent's window.

'There's a cat in there,' he'd said, unsurprised to see her.

Vicky had looked through the glass, beyond the pictures of houses sold and for sale and into the empty offices, but couldn't see a cat.

Sylvia was saying, 'I happen to like Ali. I happen to think Ali's good for Tom. I also happen to have spent most of last week – time I didn't really have given that this weekend we've got a poker party with more than forty people coming – designing the Christmas cards on which Ali appears, and now I've –'

Vicky pushed her chair back suddenly.

Bill, concerned, said, 'Vick? What is it?'

'You look like you're about to throw up,' Sylvia said, irritable, falling briefly sideways as her right elbow missed the edge of the table. Unsteadily, she poured herself another glass of wine, rivulets running smoothly down the crystal she'd bought herself as a moving in present when Bill failed to mark the occasion.

'It's the coconut,' Vicky said, her hand over her mouth.

'I washed it out.'

'I can still smell it.'

'Go and have a lie down, love,' Bill said.

Sylvia started to laugh the unsettling, guttural laugh of a woman taking a good look at a slice of her own life.

Bill and Vicky were staring at her.

'What is it?' Bill said.

'"Go and lie down, love,"' she repeated in flawless mimicry of Bill. 'I don't think you have ever . . .' she carried on, turning to him '. . . in all our married life together ever told me to go and lie down.' She dissolved into laughter again.

Bill didn't react to this. It wasn't something he'd ever thought about.

She turned back to Vicky. 'Don't worry – I'll sort the dishes – I mean, it's not like I stood and made supper as well. You must be *so* tired.'

Vicky ran from the room and Bill stood up to follow her as the fan in the downstairs toilet started up.

'I'm sure she'll be able to vomit unaided,' Sylvia mumbled.

'She's not well,' Bill insisted as the sound of Vicky retching became clearly audible above the sound of the fan and the silence in the dining room. Vicky re-appeared in the doorway.

'D'you feel better now?' Bill asked.

She nodded, dazed, and poured herself a glass of water.

'Are you going out tonight?' Sylvia asked, watching her.

Vicky shook her head. 'I was – but not now. I'm going upstairs – to clean my teeth.'

'She's not well,' Bill said again.

'It's Friday night,' Sylvia said, trying not to raise her voice.

'So? I've been puking my guts up – in case you hadn't noticed.'

'You're seventeen.'

'I'm going to bed.'

'If you never go out you'll never meet anyone.'

'I don't want to meet anyone. Plus, there's nowhere to go anyway in this shit hole.'

'I thought everybody went to that bar – B-52s?'

'Oh. Yeah. I forgot about B-52s. Forgot how much I enjoyed being touched up by twenty-somethings – or worse – who forgot to leave Burwood.'

Nonplussed by this – what else did Vicky think twenty-somethings wanted to do to teenage girls? – Sylvia said, 'I heard that some famous actors from that film they're shooting were there last week.'

'If you're so keen why don't you go yourself?'

'Vick –' Bill warned her.

'Wait. I did see John Hurt.'

'John Hurt?' Sylvia was excited.

'Yeah, it was disgusting. We were dancing and stuff and he came up to Ruth.'

'Ruth?' Sylvia put in, offended.

'He's like eighty or something and he was trying to get her to go back to his room at The King's Head. Like, how disgusting is that?'

'Ruth,' Sylvia said again.

Why had the octogenarian actor approached Ruth when Vicky was so much thinner?

Vicky surveyed the table – and her parents. 'I'm done here.'

'Vick – you've hardly touched your food – you've got to eat.'

'She does eat,' Sylvia snapped, unsure how much more of Bill's concern for his daughter she could stand. If Tom was here, he would have known how to bring an end to this, but Tom wasn't here and she was too drunk to do anything other than stumble through an ill-constructed counter-attack, which had more to do with Bill's concern for Vicky than anything Vicky was saying or doing. Sylvia was getting distracted now as well – the bulb in one of the sidelights had just blown, and she added it to the mental list she was assembling of things to do before tomorrow night's poker party.

'You're not yourself,' Bill said. Then, as he saw tears start up in his daughter's eyes, 'Vick – what is it?'

She shook her head.

Sylvia wasn't sure how she'd managed to slide so far down in her seat, but her chin was swinging dangerously near to the remains of her chicken curry. Hauling herself upright, and oblivious to the exchange going on between Bill and Vicky, she said, 'She has to be eating somewhere – she can't even fit into her jeans any more.'

Vicky turned on her. 'Will you stop going on about my fucking jeans – I can't fit into my jeans because I'M PREGNANT.'

In the silence that followed, Bill held Vicky's gaze.

Part of Sylvia's mind simply stopped. The other part came to rest once more on the sidelight whose bulb had just blown. No need to panic – it was a standard Phillips forty-watt pearl. They sold those everywhere. No need to panic.

Vicky carried on crying.

In the past few seconds Bill's cheeks had sunk in on themselves – to such an extent that the lower half of his face looked hollow. 'How?' he croaked at last, clearing his throat and repeating himself. 'How?'

'How d'you think?' Vicky said through tears.

'Who?' Sylvia asked, turning her mind reluctantly away from the forty-watt pearl light bulb.

'No-one.'

'Well, it wasn't an immaculate conception.'

'Have you thought about –?' Bill paused. 'You know –'

Vicky nodded, sobbing. 'I don't think I can.'

Bill digested this. 'You don't have to make any definite decisions – not right now – but it's something we should talk about.'

Vicky, still sobbing, nodded again.

Sylvia, who had her elbows propped on the table

and her head in her hands, said, 'You do know whose it is, don't you?'

'Of course,' Vicky responded, angry for the first time.

She was holding on tightly to the back of the chair, aching for someone to hold her, hug her – even if it was her mother.

'And you've told him?' Bill carried on.

'I can't get through. He's not picking up.'

'Does he have a name?'

'I'm not saying.'

Sylvia cut in with, 'And this – nameless person – he's, what? Your boyfriend?'

'It's not like that.'

'Like what? You're pregnant, for Christ's sake. Why didn't you say anything?'

'About what?'

'Having a boyfriend.'

'He's not my boyfriend.'

'Do we know him?'

Vicky shrugged. 'What does it matter?'

'What does it matter?' Sylvia let out a muffled snort.

Bill continued to watch his daughter. 'And how d'you think he'll feel about – this?'

'How the hell should I know?' Vicky paused. 'We did already talk about kids, though.'

'You talked about kids?' Bill exploded. 'Vicky – you're seventeen!'

Sylvia started, as it occurred to her for the first time that Vicky had in all likelihood fallen in with some Charles Manson-like character. The whole thing sounded vague – sectish.

'Seventeen – yeah – I'm at my childbearing prime.'

This confirmed Sylvia's acolyte-of-Charles Manson suspicion.

'Is that what this . . .' Bill struggled '. . . wanker said to you?'

'He's not a wanker, and it's a biological fact.'

Bill and Vicky stared at each other – they hardly ever argued.

'So what I'm meant to wait till I'm like forty or something by which time I'll be infertile and need IVF?'

'You don't have to wait till you're forty, but you could at least wait till you've been to university and lived a little.'

'I don't want to go to university. I don't want to rack up over thirty grand's worth of debt that it'll take me the first decade of my working life to pay off – if I even get to have a working life by the time the economy's through with us.'

'So when exactly did this revelation about Higher Education occur to you?' Sylvia said.

Vicky shrugged again.

Both her parents were staring at her now.

'What?' she screamed at them. 'Got any better ideas?'

'About a million,' Bill said sadly.

'Yeah, well you might want to try some of them yourself 'cause I'd rather do anything – anything – than get to the age of fifty and end up like you.'

'I'm not fifty,' Sylvia said.

Vicky turned on her. 'I mean – like, how many milligrams of Valium d'you swallow every morning so that you can do even one day of your life?'

Bill checked his wife. 'You're taking Valium?'

'On prescription. It's in the bathroom cabinet, Bill, right next to your razors. What – you never even noticed?'

Vicky was slowly backing away from the table towards the door.

'You don't even like each other,' she shouted when she got there.

Sylvia stood up, preoccupied. 'Have you told anybody else?'

'Does it matter? It's going to start to get pretty bloody obvious soon.'

'You're not having the baby, Vicky, you know that don't you?' Sylvia said, quietly.

Bill tried to reach out for his wife's arm, but the only part of her he could reach was her left hip and there wasn't anything there for him to hold on to. 'Sylvia –'

She shook him off.

'It's my choice,' Vicky said.

'You just fucked up your last choice.'

'I HATE YOU.'

'I'M DEVASTATED.'

Vicky went running from the room and upstairs, slamming her bedroom door shut.

Sylvia and Bill looked at each other as Sylvia sat back down at the table, with its strewn remains of the once-a-week family supper.

She exhaled slowly and stared through the dining room window – a small bay with window seat put in by the previous owners – at the garden.

The trees had been listening, she could tell. They'd crept closer to the house and although they'd been quick to shuffle back into place just before she'd looked up at them, she could tell.

'Look at them,' she said out loud.

Bill finally roused himself. 'What?'

'Out there – in the garden. The trees.'

Sighing, he got to his feet and went over to the window.

'They're watching us.'

134

His eyes scanned the floodlit garden he had very little feeling for. 'Watching us?'

Sylvia nodded. 'They're watching. And waiting.'

Bill looked at her. 'Sylvia – they're trees.'

She nodded as if he was getting the point. 'And they're waiting,' she said again.

'For what?'

A muscular spasm rippled quickly through her left cheek. She felt it.

Bill saw it.

'I don't know, but they're waiting. Do I *look* fifty to you?' Sylvia said after a while, turning to face him. 'When I told Ruth I was forty-eight she nearly died, literally died of shock,' she carried on, unconsciously working her hand under her chin and over her throat, checking for sagginess. 'Just didn't believe it –'

Bill cut her short with, 'Sylvia!'

'What?'

'Vicky's pregnant –'

Sylvia nodded slowly, her hand still on her throat. 'That's not the point.'

'What's not the point?'

'Vicky being pregnant. The point is – who else knows?' She paused, thoughtful. 'D'you think she does it on purpose?'

'Does what?' Bill said, impatient.

'Making an announcement like that the night before my poker party – when she knows how much work I've put in. It's taken me over two months to co-ordinate this. The poker@home people, the caterers, the flowers . . . tomorrow night there are going to be over forty people here in this room, Bill.'

'Fuck the poker party.'

'It's our last chance,' she yelled.

'At what?'

'Us –'

Bill didn't say anything.

'Two years ago,' Sylvia carried on, quietly now, 'we nearly went under. We did nearly go under, Bill. You've got no idea what it was like for me.'

She could feel herself straining towards him, but Bill kept his distance. He was no longer even watching her, but observing her instead.

'There were moments when there was so much darkness; so much darkness,' she said again, 'and nothing made sense.'

Bill turned away from her, towards the windows, and after a while there was a light smile on his face.

This was because he'd seen one of the foxes he'd been watching for months now, in the garden.

Sylvia didn't know this, but the smile gave her hope – until Bill said, 'Why did we move here?'

'We got tired,' she explained, 'tired of the noise – the helicopters at night – the gunshots – the two burglaries – Tom getting mugged. We needed some space.'

'I wanted to go to Africa.'

'I know you did, and we talked about that, but –'

'The Gambia's meant to be beautiful.'

'Tom was about to do A Levels, Vicky GCSEs. It never would have worked. It was a beautiful idea, Bill – and I listened to you, I did listen, but it would have taken a lot of energy we didn't have to make it work. If we'd been twenty-eight still, maybe, but we're not twenty-eight any more.'

'Were we ever? Right now I feel about a hundred.'

'We made the right decision. It was a risk – moving here – but it was the only way we could give ourselves a last chance.'

'Last chance – is that how you see moving to Burwood? More like a fucking death wish.'

'I don't accept that, Bill. I've put so much in – so much, and we're almost there.'

'Where?'

'On top of things again.'

'Vicky just told us she's pregnant.'

Ignoring this, Sylvia said, 'And it's a long time since we've been on top of things, and I want to share that with people. Tomorrow night's poker party –'

'Our daughter's pregnant,' Bill yelled.

'I know,' Sylvia yelled back. 'I was here.'

'Well start acting like you were.'

Sylvia flinched, memories crowding in: of the chicken risotto running down the walls of their old London home and Bill walking out on her.

'Where did we go wrong?' Bill said suddenly, helplessly.

'We didn't.'

'We must have gone wrong somewhere. How did it happen – and who is this prick she's talking about?'

'I've got no idea. Vicky and me . . . we don't talk.'

'None of us talk.'

'That's not fair, Bill – we talk.'

'When we're drunk – and we're always drunk, have you noticed that?'

He turned away from her to look out the window again, but the fox had gone.

Every muscle in Sylvia's body was clenched, and she kept checking, irate, on the trees in the garden – convinced she could hear them shaking with laughter.

'We're going to get through this, Bill,' she said, 'this is just something else we need to get through, and we will get through it.'

'We didn't put enough in.'

'To what?'

'Vicky!'

'Vicky's a black hole, Bill. Nothing you put in has any effect.'

'So maybe we should have tried putting something rather than nothing in.'

'Maybe you should have thought about that when you were working twenty-five hours out of every twenty-four, and still found the time for that woman – Isabella.'

Bill stared at her. That word was taboo – they'd agreed never to say that word again; never even to think that word again.

'You want to know something about Isabella? Something I never told you at the time?'

'No.'

'Isabella was you, Sylvia. She was you.'

'What – only ten years younger, a foot taller, blonde hair, and with an Italian accent?'

'I wanted to be with you – I just wanted to be with who you used to be before –'

'What?'

'You stopped caring about us.'

There was a moment's silence, and during that silence Sylvia lost all control – her mouth opened and fell away from her, and she couldn't breathe. Then it passed.

'That's nice, Bill. So you were getting free therapy and sex all rolled into one? Sounds like you were onto a good thing.'

Bill started to leave the room. 'I can't take much more of this.'

'Where are you going?'

'Upstairs. To see our seventeen-year-old daughter who's pregnant.'

'There's no way she's having that baby,' Sylvia called out after him. 'You can tell her that – from me. We haven't been through what we've been through for this to happen. Not now. She's having an abortion – even if I have to do it myself. There's no way I'm becoming a grandmother.'

21

Next door, at number four Park Avenue, Nathan Dent was chewing slowly, silently, on the stew Rachel made that afternoon, his eyes on his step-daughter, Ruth, who seemed unusually pre-occupied, which wasn't like her. Most of the time she was shy and watchful, and in this respect she was much more like him, which was strange given that she was Rachel's from her first marriage and he'd only inherited her. Ruth came as part of the package that was marrying Rachel.

He first met her when she was eight – and Rachel and he had known each other for six months – in the National Gallery, by a painting of a rhinoceros.

Nathan had never been in the National Gallery before – something that had shocked Rachel – and never been out with women who made arrangements to meet in galleries. He usually dated women with thin, hectic laughs, who liked to get drunk quickly, have loud thumping sex, and make plans for the weekend.

Rachel was a war widow with a child – who he met at an event hosted by Pinnacle Insurance to mark the underwriting of a syndicated loan to a Turkish bank.

She was wearing black and white and walking round the room with a bottle of champagne in her hand and a plate of crab crostini in the other.

On the other employees of Frobisher Catering, Ltd the thin bow-tie looked demeaning, but not on Rachel, who managed to wear it with a sense of irony that went with her hair and eyes.

He noticed that men's eyes picked her out – watched her approach and followed her retreat – his own included. When she paused in front of them with the champagne and crab crostini, the men found themselves passing comments that were sent lightly and intelligently back – with an ambiguous smile. Nathan's feet continued to tread the granite floor of the atrium at Pinnacle Insurance's London offices; he laughed, shook hands with people he knew and people he didn't, and felt vaguely reassured by the insecure echoes rising up into the atrium – as his life changed.

When he left, he did something he would never have done if he hadn't been drunk and Rachel hadn't been who she was. He took off his name badge, wrote his number on the back of it then slipped it back into the plastic holder with the telephone number facing out – and handed her the badge as he left.

She phoned the next day, and six months after that he met her daughter – Ruth – in front of a painting of a rhinoceros in the National Gallery.

He knew, with a lover's instinct, that if it didn't work between Ruth and him, it would never work between Rachel and him – and so he was terrified. He didn't like children. He never got on with them when he himself was a child, and this hadn't changed.

He'd heard about the war and the conception of Ruth under shellfire. He'd heard about the death of Marin,

Rachel's first husband. He'd learnt that it was possible to be jealous of the dead as well as the living. How could he hope to compete with this uniformed stallion who kept going for hours on end to the rhythm of exploding mortar shells?

Ruth and Rachel got to the painting of the rhinoceros first that day.

He came upon them with a gallery plan grasped sweatily in his left hand.

Ruth was standing completely still in front of the painting.

Rachel's head was moving round, in search of him.

They were holding hands.

Seeing them like this, he realised that he'd already met the child in the relationship, and that was Rachel.

Rachel continued to look for him in the air-conditioned crowd as Ruth turned instinctively round and stared straight at him. She smiled – he smiled back, and even waved. It was going to be alright.

He'd sensed nothing but warmth and curiosity from Ruth – even relief. There was no trace of anything anxious let alone malignant. Ruth realised at that first meeting that Nathan didn't want anything from Rachel, he simply wanted to be with her, and bear the weight of her.

Here was somebody who was going to help her with Rachel, and she responded by taking him to see her favourite pictures. Nathan, who was thirty-five at the time, didn't have any favourite paintings so was happy to be led, still clutching his floor plan, by Ruth. The understanding and complicity that had started that afternoon had stayed between them throughout the years that followed.

He fell in love with the daughter in the same way he had with the mother – quickly and intensely. The deep, unashamed sensuality that connected Rachel and him was replaced by an intellectual bond between him and Ruth that he remained deeply perceptive of and attached to – even during the difficult teenage years when Rachel and he finally decided to try for children of their own.

Which was how he'd noticed, with an ever increasing despair, the growing distance not just between Ruth and him, but Ruth and her own life. Especially since the summer.

There had been distances before: puberty, obviously, then the relocation to Burwood, made possible by the death of his parents and sale of his childhood home – a terrace in a Croydon suburb. Then there was the first miscarriage – the screams and confusion it had taken Ruth months to get over; the second miscarriage and the arguments between Rachel and him, growing in length and cruelty. Their cruelty was making them selfish; forgetful.

He had to make an effort – somehow – to close this distance. He couldn't bear the thought of Ruth leaving home, which she'd be doing in only a year's time – with this void between them still.

'Is there chilli in this?' Ruth asked suddenly, looking at Rachel.

Nathan remained silent, carefully finishing his mouthful.

Rachel, who was miles away – who knew where – looked up at her daughter then Nathan then, briefly, the room surrounding them, confused. 'What's that?'

'I said,' Ruth laboured the words, irritable, 'are there any chillis in this?'

'Ruth –' Nathan checked her. This rudeness and need to be argumentative were new.

Rachel stared down at the stew. 'Just one – I think.'

'You said you wouldn't put chillis in any more.'

'Did I?' Rachel smiled vaguely at her, then sat back in her chair, her left hand – Nathan noted – held protectively against her stomach.

Then Ruth's mobile started to ring.

'No phones at the table,' Nathan said, aware that he wouldn't have said that six months ago.

Ruth stood up, holding the phone.

'Is okay,' Rachel put in, tired.

'No *it* is not okay.' Here was the cruelty. He could feel it coming.

'I'll phone back – just give me a minute. Don't go anywhere.' Ruth rang off and sat back down at the table, on edge.

'No phones at the table.'

'I heard,' she said, staring at him before turning to Rachel. 'Is it okay if I go out tonight?'

Rachel nodded. 'I thought you were going swimming.'

'I am – I'm talking about afterwards.'

'Out where?' Nathan asked.

'B-52s.'

'What's B-52s?'

'I've been going there for like over a year now – why the sudden interest?' Ruth responded, sullen.

'It's not interest,' Nathan said, a sudden, sharp smile on his face, aware that Rachel was watching him. 'It's a formality we have to go through that's all. You want to go out and I need to know where you're going.'

'All the kids go there,' Rachel put in, unsure whether this was Nathan's clunking attempt at humour or whether he was just being cruel.

'I'm aware of that,' Nathan said, 'it's just – if she ever doesn't come home and we have to call the police and they have to launch a search, it would be less embarrassing if we knew where it was she hadn't come home from.'

'That's a terrible thing to say,' Rachel said slowly, staring at him.

Ruth stood up again. 'I'm going out.'

'You're not finished,' Nathan called out after her. Then, to Rachel, 'She's not finished.'

Rachel was still staring at him, wide-eyed, as if seeing something she hadn't seen before.

'That's a terrible thing to say,' she repeated.

Nathan agreed – was himself stunned at what he'd just said. What had happened to them? They had no more regard for each other than colleagues forced to sit round a boardroom table together – which was where he might as well be, he conceded, for all the love and security he felt.

In the silence that followed, they heard Ruth's heavy footsteps coming back downstairs, followed by the front door slamming shut.

'She's gone,' Nathan said.

For a moment, Rachel looked startled – before sinking back into herself. 'She's nearly eighteen.'

'She didn't even say goodbye. We don't know who she's gone with – or when she'll be back.'

'No –' Rachel yawned.

'For God's sake, Rachel,' he yelled, aware without even being conscious of it that his left hand was throwing the fork he'd been holding across the room towards nothing in particular. It rebounded off the wall and fell onto the carpet where it left an unpleasant brown stain.

'I've got pains in my stomach,' she said, once the fork had landed. 'They started this morning. It's my period coming.'

145

'You don't know that.'

'It's my period, Nathan,' she said, her eyes wide, leaning back in her chair with her hands pressed into her abdomen.

'But it hasn't actually started yet, has it?'

She shook her head.

They looked at each other then looked away – at the remains of stew on the three plates, the vase of yellow roses pushed down to the far end of the table, and Ruth's chair – recently vacated and twisted away from the table at an angle still. Nathan looked down at his own hands, gripping the edge of the polished dining table. It was a poised, quiet, unendurable moment.

Two miles away, Ruth was diving into deep water at Burwood Leisure Centre. Even before breaking the surface, she felt happily detached from number four Park Avenue. After swimming eight hundred metres, she got smoothly out of the pool, enjoying the attention of the two life guards – one of them sucking absent-mindedly on the whistle in his mouth.

A couple of months ago, she would have buckled under their gaze, but now she walked slowly along the edge of the pool towards the changing rooms, smiling to herself.

Fifteen minutes later and smelling strongly of chlorine, she got into a green Skoda that pulled up next to the pavement where she was standing in the leisure centre car park.

Saskia's father, Richard Greaves, was behind the wheel.

22

Vicky sat at her desk with the Girls World Father Christmas bought for her when she was nine – all the way from the North Pole. Girls World was the older sister she never had and she used to spend hours making up the plastic face and combing the blonde nylon hair. It had received a lot of the child Vicky's love. Then puberty struck and she went through an aggressive stage of defacing Girls World with biros, felt tip pens and scissors. Hair had been hacked off in clumps and lips coloured black. After the torture years, Girls World was relegated to decorative kitsch, and now served as a book end.

Tonight she'd taken it off her shelves and sat at her desk scrubbing at the pubescent defacements. There was nothing she could do about the holes she'd driven through the ears with a screw driver so she hung a pair of earrings in those. Then, with her make-up bag in front of her, she set to work on the moulded plastic face, and this was how Bill found her when he padded softly into the bedroom a few minutes later.

'Vick? How you feeling?' She didn't respond. 'Still sick?'

'No – that's gone.'

He noted the Girls World on the desk and saw that she'd been crying.

'I just wanted to say –' He stopped in the middle of the room, stranded and helpless. 'Whatever you decide we're here for you. You know that don't you?'

Ignoring this, Vicky said, 'Which colour d'you think? For the lips?'

'You have got options.'

'Yeah, plenty. I was thinking of going for marshmallow pink.'

'Vick – you don't have to keep this baby. We don't expect you to.'

She swung round to look at him then back to the Girls World. 'Did *she* send you up here to say that?'

He shook his head, sadly, and remained in the middle of the room, trying to remember the last time he'd actually been in his daughter's bedroom – if at all, in fact.

'She hates me.'

'She doesn't hate you,' Bill said automatically. He might even have meant it – been able to provide evidence, if pushed. 'Did you manage to get through – to this bloke?'

'Bloke?' Vicky thought about this then shook her head. 'Everything's shit at the moment,' she mumbled, concentrating on the lipstick. 'Everything's just totally shit.'

Inclined to agree with her, Bill moved over to the window and stared out at the back garden. Then he saw it – picking its way steadily but hesitantly across the floodlit garden – and felt suddenly uplifted.

'What is it?' Vicky said, seeing Bill jerk upright.

'The fox.'

He turned to her and his face had been transformed to such an extent that she felt instinctively drawn to the window as well.

'Look – he's stopped.'

Just then the fox flicked its face up at the window, one leg curled up under its chest, its mouth open.

'Did you see that?' Bill said.

The fox blinked then moved out beyond the reach of the floodlights into the borderland between number two and number four Park Avenue.

'He's early tonight – doesn't usually come till around two in the morning; maybe three.'

'You're up then?'

'Can't always sleep,' he said without looking at her.

For some reason they'd started whispering when the fox first appeared and were still whispering now even though it had gone.

'You're not happy, are you?' Vicky said after a while.

He put his arm round her and she leant her head on his shoulder as the lights in the garden went out so that they were left looking at the reflection of themselves beyond the window, out there in the night.

'We'll get this sorted – it'll be okay,' he said, unsure whether it was even Vicky he was talking to any more.

23

As Paul Sutton turned into the drive of number forty-four Dardanelle Drive, Julia came into view – crossing the lawn in an apron and Marigolds. She had a bucket in her hands and stopped when she saw him.

'There was puke,' she said.

'Puke?' He got off his bicycle.

'In the hedge. I came out with the rubbish and smelt it.' She paused under the streetlight that shone into the garden. 'Someone puked in our hedge.'

Paul, unsure how he was meant to react to this and unable to fathom her upset, said, 'Kids – drunk.'

'It's disgusting,' she said, following him, distracted, into the garage.

'What's that?' he said, sniffing at something hot and sweet in the kitchen.

'I got us a Chinese on the way home – want to watch it in front of the football?'

He put his bicycle lights down on the surface. 'I'm not in tonight – I'm meeting up with Craig – at the pub – remember?'

'Tonight?'

150

'Yeah – tonight. We talked about this.'

'But it's Friday night.'

'I know, but tonight's the only night Craig could make.'

Julia paused, unconvinced. She would have remembered if Paul said he was going out with Craig.

'You said it was okay – we didn't have anything planned.'

'I just got a Chinese – for two – and the football's on.' Julia paused again, thinking. 'Why didn't you say anything earlier?'

'Because it was all arranged.'

'But this morning I was talking about maybe going to IKEA tonight – to get the bookshelves – and you didn't say anything about meeting up with Craig then.'

Paul shrugged, picked up the front bike light he'd just put down on the surface and clicked it on. 'Maybe I just forgot. I don't know –'

They both stood staring at the bike light, until Paul switched it off and they were forced to observe each other, uncomfortable.

'Well, why don't we have the Chinese then I can come out with you. Phone Craig – tell him you're running late.'

'I could –'

'But?'

He stared at her. She was still wearing the Marigolds and they made her look distraught.

'There was something he wanted to talk to me about. Something – Look –' Paul broke off.

Julia felt afraid. There was something wrong – Paul's posture, the way he was fiddling with the light and staring fixedly at it so that he wouldn't have to look at her. Only minutes ago, she'd wanted to engage him

151

and get him to talk. Now she was terrified of him saying a single word more.

'It's fine,' she said, louder than intended, and affecting a smile. 'Let's just eat this then you can go. It's in the oven, ready.'

She put the foil cartons on the tray in silence and as Paul followed her into the lounge he thought about the fact that while Julia was often irritating, it was difficult to be angry with her because she was never unreasonable. This was one of the problems with Julia. Or rather, one of his problems.

It was the same with the trip to South Africa that summer.

It was Julia who came up with the idea and Julia who arranged the whole thing, which somehow gave him licence to be irritable with her when they arrived even though South Africa had only been a suggestion of hers and there was nothing stopping him disagreeing and coming up with an alternative.

Which was how he came to find himself, at sunset on a Friday in August, on the top of Table Mountain with Julia beside him.

At some point a German had proposed to his girlfriend and everybody cheered, and he'd seen the look on Julia's face.

'Did you think about the bookshelves?' she said, sucking some chow mein off her chopsticks, her eyes on the screen. 'We could go to IKEA tomorrow.'

Paul watched Rooney bypass centre-field, while in his mind he ran through what it would be like getting into Julia's Peugeot tomorrow and driving up through Purley to Croydon – possibly one of the most depressing drives in the developed world.

'Paul?'

'What's that?'

'The bookshelves – IKEA – tomorrow.'

'Oh. Yeah –'

'So – you're okay with that?'

'Yeah.'

'You don't sound okay.'

'I don't?'

'No, you don't.'

It occurred to Paul that they'd already had this conversation. They had – on the drive this morning. They'd got to this point and Julia had backed off.

'So – what do I sound like?'

'Like you'd rather saw your own foot off and eat it.'

He stared flatly at her, surprised. Were they actually going to have a row?

'It's okay,' she carried on, smiling suddenly, 'we don't have to go to IKEA – there are other places to get bookshelves.'

They weren't going to have a row.

'D'you think we could put the bookshelves on hold?' he said after a while.

'We've been putting them on hold since the summer.'

'It's just I've got stuff I want to work on this weekend.' He paused. 'An application.'

He still had his eyes on the pitch on TV, but he could feel Julia watching him now.

'Application as in "job application"?'

He nodded, chewing rapidly on some sweet and sour pork.

'You never said anything.' She shook her head. 'So – what is this job?'

'Head of Education and Projects Manager at The Salt Mills.'

'The Salt Mills?'

153

'It's a gallery.'

'So it's not a teaching post.'

He looked at her then looked away. 'I'm no teacher, Julia. I don't want to teach – this isn't what I want to do.'

'This –'

Their shoulders were almost touching and yet Julia looked shrunken – miles away.

'Why didn't you say?'

When he didn't answer, she said, 'And where is this gallery? I mean – will you have to commute or what?'

'Bradford.'

She jerked herself upright and the plate of chow mein slid off her lap, the sofa, and onto the floor. 'Bradford? Paul –'

Paul's eyes followed its downward course. 'What?'

'What?' she barked back at him. 'What will you do if you get it? And when exactly were you going to say anything to me about any of this?'

'Jesus Christ, Julia, I haven't even applied for it yet.'

'But if you get it –'

'If I get it –'

'We'll have to re-locate.'

He didn't say anything for a while and then when he did he was aware that he sounded more aggressive than he'd meant to. 'So we have to give a month's notice on this place.'

'This place?'

'What's the big deal?'

'My job's here – in Burwood. I'm happy here. I'm happy here in Burwood.' She bent over and attempted to scrape the chow mein off the carpet, but gave up. 'Sorry for being so fucking boring.'

'Julia –'

'Sorry for loving my life. Here. With you.'

She curled up in the corner of the sofa and started to cry.

'Julia,' he said again, inexplicably relieved by the tears – it was the first time Julia had cried in front of him. 'I'm twenty-six years old.'

'So am I,' she sobbed.

'I just want –'

'What?'

'To live –'

'THANK YOU,' she bellowed through tears and mucus; a gasping disbelief still, behind the tears, that they were even having this conversation.

She looked around her, protectively, at the house they'd rented, unfurnished, and tentatively chosen furniture for. She was happy here; hadn't thought – until it happened – that it was possible for a person to be so happy.

'And what about me?'

He faltered, unnerved now. 'Well – you could come. If I got the job.'

'To Bradford? I don't want to go to Bradford.'

'Julia – I need to get out.'

'Of what?'

'This whole fucking place,' he said expansively. 'You can't take a leak up a back alley here without getting tazered.'

'So you want to relocate to somewhere where you can piss in the street?'

'Nothing might come of it.'

'We've said too much for nothing to come of it.'

He got to his feet.

'Where are you going?'

'Out – to see Craig. I said I'd meet him at nine.'

He left her on the sofa, in front of the TV, and went to get his coat.

She heard him in the hallway and didn't move. She heard the door to the garage slamming shut behind him and still didn't move. He was taking his bike. It wasn't until she heard the garage door opening that she got up off the sofa and went to the front door as Paul emerged, wheeling his bike out into the night.

She stood with her arms by her side and her head tilted against the doorframe. Her shadow was falling – long – across the front garden.

'I love you,' she said, stifled, trying not to yell.

He thought about this then got on his bike.

She must have started crying again without realising it because her face felt suddenly wet.

'You need lights.'

'I'm fine.'

'You need lights, Paul,' she called out after him as he cycled past her car and turned onto the road.

She stepped out of the front porch and crossed the lawn to the pavement.

He was at the T-junction and turned onto the main road without looking back.

Her feet were wet and there was grass stuck to the soles of them. What was it that had happened here tonight? Where had it come from?

She went back indoors, trailing blades of grass, and stood in front of the TV and remains of Mr Li's, not seeing any of it.

Then she picked up the phone and slowly dialled Craig's number.

'Craig? Yeah, it's me, Julia. Listen – I'm trying to get hold of Paul, is he meeting up with you later? Oh. Right. Okay –'

She rang off.

24

Paul cycled across Burwood through deserted streets. There was nobody about apart from the odd gaggle of teenagers grouped under a lamppost, trying to reconcile themselves – after hours spent in front of games consoles having their sensory and intellectual perceptions honed to a GTA-style street life – to the empty streets of Burwood. Where the only criminal offence they were likely to bear witness to was mobility aids exceeding their 8mph limit. These had become a genuine hazard – a toddler nearly got run over at the multi-storey car park in a mobility aid stand off. There was a perceptively laconic piece about it in *The County Times* – by Frank Barlow.

As he cycled past one group a girl's voice called out, 'Mr Sutton!'

There was a chain reaction of laughter after this, but he didn't look back.

The moon was almost full. He checked it every night – a leftover habit from his rural childhood. He didn't think about Julia.

He rode downhill, standing upright on his pedals,

swerving to avoid a fox that ran, low, across his path. He wasn't going to the pub, and he wasn't meeting Craig.

On Carlton Avenue, the pavements had been dutifully lined with wheelie bins ready for tomorrow's collection. The green and brown bins stood in virtually unbroken lines – the only gap in the formation was outside number twelve, where he got off his bike.

He knocked on the door of number twenty-four and waited. The battery on the bell had burnt out months ago and you could tell, from the outside, that the inhabitants of number twenty-four weren't the sort of people who put new batteries for doorbells on their shopping list; weren't the sort of people who wrote shopping lists.

He knocked on the door again, louder this time, putting his arm up to the glass and pressing his head against it.

Then it opened and he saw Saskia Greaves standing in the dark kitchen. It was dark in the house behind her as well and even from the doorway he could smell the stale, tragic smell that always hung inside number twenty-four Carlton Avenue. The smell he was convinced he became impregnated with after being there; that he was forever waiting for Julia to pick up on, but that she never did.

He waited on the threshold, unsure. 'I'm sorry – I couldn't get away any sooner. Sorry –' he said again then paused. 'We had a row.'

'I fell asleep,' Saskia said after a while.

She didn't ask the sort of questions an older person would ask. She didn't ask what the row had been about – whether he'd said anything to Julia about them. She just stood there, considering him, in the clothes she'd worn to school that day – the clothes he'd taught her in, period five.

'Can I come in?'

She nodded, her hand going out for the radiator, which was always cold.

He shut the door quietly behind him and they stood in the dark kitchen, watching each other.

'Your dad?'

'Out – obviously,' she responded, irritable.

He kept his coat on, and could feel his right trouser leg was rolled into his sock still to protect it from the bike chain. It made him feel suddenly ridiculous.

Saskia's hair was untidy; there was some sort of food stain down the front of her top, and her eyes looked bright in the darkness.

'It was about Bradford – the row.'

'Bradford?'

He nodded. There it was again – the lack of questions. 'It's a town, in Yorkshire. There's a job I saw. I love you,' he finished, aware that he sounded frantic.

'I'm pregnant,' she said, gently pushing herself away and pulling herself back towards the radiator, her hair swinging lightly. 'That's why I needed to see you.'

'I love you,' he said again.

She slammed herself suddenly back against the radiator. 'God –'

'Sas –'

She pulled her hair back from her face and bit on her lip, not looking at him.

'What d'you want to do?'

'I don't know. I don't know anything about what's going on here. D'you have to pay for an abortion or can you get one on the NHS?'

'Is that what you want to do?'

160

'If you have to pay, you'll give me the money, won't you?'

He could have hit her then.

'I'm seventeen, Paul,' she screamed at him – as though he wasn't getting the point. 'I don't want a baby. You don't want a baby.'

'I don't know,' he said lightly, smiling. He tried to take hold of her, pull her towards him, but she jerked away, wanting distance between them – distrustful of his close proximity now she knew the price of intimacy.

'Come on, Paul,' she said, sounding briefly much older than him.

'I'm not going anywhere – you know that, don't you?'

Then she did start crying. 'Why's this happening to me?'

'To us. We can sort it out.'

'Is that what you want?'

'I want you to be okay. I want us to be okay.'

'Us? Okay? You're my fucking teacher – how can any of this be okay?'

'The teacher stuff's incidental. I've always said that.'

'The teacher stuff?' She'd moved away from the wall and radiator and started pacing within the metre square of kitchen floor, waving her arms wide when she spoke, pulling her hair back behind her ears when it fell over her face and stuck to her lips. 'It's tabloid stuff.'

She had beautiful hands. A painter's hands.

'I'm going for this job up in Bradford. If I get it – will you come with me?'

'What about art school?'

'Take a gap year and have the baby – our baby.'

'In Bradford?'

'I just need to get out of teaching, Sas – get a year under my belt doing something else. There's no way we could stay in Burwood anyway – if you had the baby.'

'If I had the baby.'

'If you had the baby – you could reapply to art school in a year's time.'

'Only I was thinking of art school in London.'

She'd stopped pacing and was standing still looking at him, pulling on the sleeves of her cardigan until they were covering her hands.

'You want me to have the baby, don't you?'

'I want us to be together.'

'What about Ms Webster – Julia,' she corrected herself.

'There's no "about Julia".'

'You're practically married.'

'How come?'

'You live in the same house.'

'Sas – I could pack my stuff tonight. In fact, most of it's still in boxes 'cause I never unpacked it.'

She carried on staring at him for a second longer before disappearing down the dark hallway towards the lounge where she slumped on the sofa, switched on the sidelight, and rolled herself a cigarette.

'You can't smoke that,' he said from the doorway.

She was curled up in the corner of the sofa, her free arm wrapped around her.

He sat down next to her and she carried on smoking.

He pulled her feet out from under her and put them onto his lap, but she pulled them back.

'None of this was meant to happen,' she said after a while, sounding sad – heavy.

'But it did.' He leant over and took the cigarette out of her mouth, pressing the stub into the surface of the coffee table – already covered in ash-coloured polka dots. 'And I'm not sad.'

'Hey –'

'I'm not sad at all. In fact, –' He started to kiss her. 'I've never been happier.'

'You're fucking nuts. Are you even meant to do this when you're pregnant?'

'It's fine.'

'Paul!'

'What?'

She pushed him away, but he stayed poised against the palms of her hands.

'I don't even know how many months you're pregnant for. I mean, before the baby comes.'

'Nine.'

'I thought it was eighteen.'

'That's elephants.'

She started to laugh, her arms collapsing slowly.

'We're fucked – you know that, don't you?'

Paul didn't say anything.

'If I keep this . . . this . . . thing,' she carried on, 'who do I say the father is? I can't say it's yours, can I.' She broke off as a rattling sound started up against the patio doors. 'What's that?'

'Rain.'

25

Five miles away, in a Forestry Commission car park that got overcrowded in the summer months with people who did the woodland trail circuit past ponds their prehistoric ancestors used to extract iron ore from, Richard Greaves sat with his hands clutching the green Skoda's steering wheel even though the car was parked and the engine off. He wasn't thinking about his ancestors – or even his direct descendants.

Ruth Dent was in the passenger seat, sobbing quietly with her mouth open and her hands held tightly together, clutched in her lap. Her swimming kit was on the floor by her feet and her hair was still wet, drying slowly into curls.

The rain must have stopped – it was no longer banging on the roof of the car.

'It should never have happened,' Richard said, staring through the windscreen at the dark mass of trees surrounding them. His nostrils were full of the smell of chlorine, and he had a sudden memory – unbidden – of Saskia at a swimming gala when she was about eight. She'd been entered for the twenty-five metre front crawl, but been too terrified to dive in at the deep end when the starter pistol cracked, and so was left alone toeing the water, crying.

The sight of her standing there in her swimming costume and cap had broken him, but Caro – furious at her daughter's cowardice and failure – hadn't let him go over.

A car passed on the road behind, its headlights sweeping briefly – unintentionally – through the interior of the Skoda, picking out Richard's signet ring and a Christmas bauble Saskia had hung from the rear view mirror last year.

'I thought you wanted it to,' Ruth said, through tears.

'You should have a boyfriend – your own age.'

'What – who'd rather play Halo 3?'

Richard looked at her sideways. 'I don't know what happened this summer.' He sighed. 'What I was thinking – what I was feeling then, was wrong. Those feelings came from a fucked-up place, Ruth. If my wife had never left me, none of this would have happened.'

'But she did leave, and it did happen. All of it.'

'It happened once – that's all,' he reminded her.

'Well, once is enough, isn't it?' She put her elbow on the arm-rest and turned to look at him. 'What I want to know is – what changed that day I cycled over to see Sas and she was out and we went upstairs and you broke my locket? I mean – I'd been over at yours like about a hundred times before – we'd been in France together – and nothing. Why that day?'

'I don't know. It was hot. I was exhausted. You were beautiful.'

She smiled at him, eager, running her hand down his leg.

He picked the hand off and laid it gently in her lap.

'And it should never have happened, and I'm deeply – deeply sorry it did.'

She put her left hand in her mouth and bit nervously on the nails. 'I'm not.'

'You're the sweetest thing, Ruth.'

She gave a short, bitter laugh. 'But?'

'It's too fucked up to be love.'

'Love is fucked up.'

'True,' he conceded. 'But not like this. I want you to be happy.'

'That's love.'

'That's parenting.'

'That really is fucked up.'

'Yeah – maybe you're right.' Richard ran his hands up and down the steering wheel as Ruth started chewing on her nails again.

He stared through the windscreen at the outline of forest, moving in the wind. The movement gave the trees a strange intent and he felt suddenly unwanted by them. He and Ruth shouldn't be here.

'It has to stop,' he said quietly, his eyes still on the trees. 'That's why I phoned you. You have to stop calling me – sending me stuff. It has to stop,' he said again.

'Are you still in love with your wife?'

'No.'

'Are you in love with anybody?'

'I love Saskia.'

'That makes me jealous.'

'She's my daughter. Parents love their children. They're not "in love" with them – it's different.'

'I'm still jealous.'

'You're beautiful,' he said, turning back to her, running his knuckles down her cheek.

'Not beautiful enough.'

'And I'm finding this incredibly hard, but none of this should have happened, Ruth – none of it.'

'I don't know whether we're breaking up or whether you're asking for forgiveness. When you phoned this morning – said you wanted to see me – I thought –' She broke off. 'Why are you doing this? You don't even sound like you.'

He smiled sadly. That late August afternoon, he'd inadvertently given Ruth all the parts of himself he liked the least, and these were the parts Ruth fell in love with – or thought she did, and maybe at seventeen it amounted to the same thing, he couldn't remember. Either way – and despite the wrong he'd done – afterwards, he was suddenly free of those parts of himself. Those parts Caro had never come to terms with; the parts she judged him for and in the end lost interest in trying to change, putting her energies instead into leaving him. He didn't blame her. But Ruth – at only seventeen – had swallowed them whole and now they'd disappeared without a trace.

When he turned away this time, she felt him leave her.

His face had changed.

'You can't leave me,' she blurted out, unable now to conceal her panic. 'You've changed me too much. I'm different.'

Richard didn't respond.

For the first time since divorcing Saskia's mother – Caro – he felt divorced, and it was because he'd managed to bring an end to the temptations of Ruth. He'd been travelling downwards ever since Caro left him, and always wondered what lay at the bottom of the pit. Now he knew: Ruth was at the bottom of the pit, and he was down there with her. Richard Greaves, fifty-one-year-old divorcee, was fucking a seventeen-year-old girl. That was the bottom of the pit, and now – finally – he was ready to get out.

The first thing he was going to do when he crawled out was take the cocaine from under his bed and throw it away because he wasn't going to die in Burwood.

He was going to hire decorators and builders – sort out the house.

He was going to buy patio furniture at out of town stores on Sundays.

He was going to start running again.

He was going to get Saskia and him new bikes and they were going to do circuits at the country park on Saturdays and watch the Canada geese return to the pond from Alaska.

He was going to start dating the hippy at work – Freya – and maybe even go on that Transcendental Yoga thing with her.

It was going to be okay. Normality, which he'd spent much of his life to date sneering at, struck him now as one of humanity's profoundest achievements.

He was not going to live the life of an ageing predator.

He was going to live the life of a man whose first marriage hadn't worked out – whose does, even when they actually stay married? – with a wonderful daughter, who was leaving home this summer to go to the Slade.

That was her dream.

Saskia had dreams – among the empty pizza boxes and furniture that belonged to other people.

He had a sudden memory of them arriving at a holiday cottage they used to rent in Cornwall every August and the way Saskia had opened the car door before it had even stopped and run towards the cottage where every year, for a week, they were all together;

all happy. She'd run with her hair swinging across her back, her face – skewed round briefly towards them – stretched wide with excitement.

It was unbearable.

He wanted to run after her, and scoop her up to the sky, limbs flying as she struggled to get her feet back on the ground.

Later, while Saskia slept – her skin dusted white with dried sea salt – Caro and he would sit in front of the fire and drink wine and talk about moving down to Cornwall and having more children. They were still young. They had all the time in the world.

Only nobody ever had all the time in the world, and that's where they'd gone wrong, and there never were any more children.

Saskia, upstairs asleep with the shells that had fallen out of her clenched fist and onto her pillow as she lost consciousness, didn't know that, and the young couple – Richard and Caro – sat in front of the fire downstairs, didn't know that either.

In the car, in the forest outside Burwood, Richard Greaves started to cry. He sat in the driver's seat of the post-divorce Skoda, shuddering, his mouth open.

Ruth, disconcerted, stared at him.

If they'd been parked on a headland, she'd have wrenched his hands off the steering wheel, convinced he was about to drive over the edge. But they weren't.

'What is it?' she said after a while, when he didn't stop crying.

He didn't respond, but did at least start wiping his face and breathing normally again.

Tomorrow morning he was going to get up early, sort out the kitchen and buy some food. He was going to eat breakfast with his daughter. He had a daughter still.

Right now he was going to reverse out of this forest and drive the seventeen-year-old girl in the passenger seat back home; return her to her family.

He switched the engine on, the headlamps unbearably bright as the edge of the forest in front of them was suddenly illuminated – the trees closer to the car than he remembered them being.

'I'm taking you home,' he said, putting the car into reverse and twisting to look through the back window.

'What – and that's that?'

'Yes,' he said, decisive. 'You're going to leave home, go to university and fall in love properly, Ruth.'

'I already did that.'

'I'm fifty-one years old,' he yelled.

'I don't care,' Ruth yelled back, 'and I don't want to go to university. Tonight, when you phoned, I thought it was to say we were leaving – that you were taking me away.'

'Where?'

'I don't know,' she cried out, helpless, then stared out the window, thinking. 'Away from here. We could keep goats – make cheese. There's this commune . . .'

He was watching her now, worried. 'Commune?'

'You always said you were nothing more than an old hippy – and you've got that book on your shelves.'

'What book?'

'Goat Husbandry.'

Caro had bought that when they were thinking about moving down to Cornwall.

'We can do this, Richard – right now. We can just go.'

For a split second, he considered it – and all it would entail – then he shook his head. 'You think you want to go, Ruth, but you don't.'

'You don't know what I want.' She hesitated. 'I could tell Saskia – about us.'

'If you did that I'd kill you,' Richard said quietly.

Ruth believed him.

Richard believed himself.

'You hate me.'

'I don't hate you, but this has to end, Ruth.'

'This isn't the end.'

'This *is* the end,' Richard concluded.

'No!' Ruth yelled, holding onto the door as though they were already travelling at high speed. 'I'm pregnant.'

His hand stayed on the gear stick and he remained twisted in his seat.

Then the engine cut out and they were sitting in darkness again. Cooked breakfast with Saskia, eaten al fresco on patio furniture from B&Q, followed by a cycle ride through the nature reserve, tumbled into the abyss.

'No.'

'Yes –'

'No.'

'Richard – I'm pregnant.'

'Shit. You're not just saying that?'

'Fuck you.'

'And it's definitely mine, yeah?'

'Fuck you.'

He rubbed his hand over his face.

'We'll get it sorted,' he said after a while, breathless again and no longer calm. 'Just don't worry about it.'

He squeezed her knee – something he'd never done before – and she felt suddenly revolted by him.

'Don't worry.'

She put her elbow up on the window and stared through it in silence as the engine went back on and they reversed out the car park.

He turned the wheels hard, gravel popping out from under the tyres.

'You haven't told anyone, have you?'

'No!' she said aggressively.

'Good girl,' he said automatically then wished he hadn't.

His hand went out for her knee again and, seeing it coming this time, she shouted, 'Get off me!' before he'd even had a chance to touch her. She pulled her legs and the rest of herself as far away from him as the limits of the Skoda would allow.

They drove back to Burwood in silence – Richard never so relieved to see the lights of the town.

26

The rain had started again when she was half way across Burwood, and by the time she got home Grace's hair was dark and heavy with it – the rain water running in rivulets down her neck, under her coat collar and across her back.

As she got off her bike a bus pulled up at the stop on the corner and a girl emerged backwards from it, pulling a buggy and a pitbull with her.

The buggy clattered onto the pavement and the bus pulled away, empty now apart from the driver.

It was Tina Branston, making her way towards Grace, the pitbull snorting and wheezing at her heels, the child – under its PVC rain cover – straining and screaming. Tina's head, in a hood, was sunk between her shoulders and light from the streetlamps bounced off the large gold hoops swinging from her ears as she thrust herself, the buggy and the dog through the rain.

Grace stood on the verge, waiting for her to pass. From where she was standing she could hear the TV on inside her house.

Tina and she stared wetly at each other. Living on

the same estate they often met, but never spoke. This time, Tina stopped.

It took a while for the pitbull to register that the buggy was no longer moving and he carried on walking until Tina pulled him forcibly back so that he stood to heel, panting placidly and rolling his eyes at Grace.

Through the rain-streaked cover, Grace made out an unhappy looking child.

Tina shook the buggy, hard, and yelled, 'Tyler!' Then stared aggressively at Grace, standing by her bike in a soaking wet Sainsbury's uniform.

Grace nodded – at first she thought it was the child Tina was speaking to, but then realised it was the dog.

Tina leant down between the buggy handles, peering through the rain cover at the child still crying inside. 'You gotta calm down, babes, or you'll cry yourself out.' She flashed an unexpected smile at Grace. 'He's teething. I've tried everything – gels, tablets, herbal stuff which was totally shit. My mum says rub whisky on his gums – can you lend me five quid?' she said without pausing, and waited. It wasn't a request.

She watched Grace take the rucksack off her back and open it, the rain pouring in.

Every now and then she gave the buggy a shake.

Grace dug around in the rucksack for her purse, found it then opened it.

'I've got two quid,' she said, shaking it under the street light.

Tina grabbed hold of the purse, shook out the two pound coins and pocketed them, handing the empty purse back to Grace. 'See ya,' she said, moving off through the rain again.

Grace could still hear the buggy wheels clattering

174

on the pavement as she locked her bike to the drain-pipe, looked up at the front of the house to check that the lights were off in Dixie's room, and went indoors.

There was the sound of laughter from the TV – loud – and, without bothering to put the hall light on, she pulled off her soaking Sainsbury's fleece, shoes and socks and went through to the kitchen to dry her hair and face on a tea towel.

After that she went into the lounge.

It looked as though Nicole was asleep on the sofa, but when Grace turned the TV off, she opened her eyes and took in her daughter.

'Is it raining?'

'Pouring.'

'Run yourself a hot bath.'

Nicole moved the empty cheese dunkers box and patted the sofa, rolling her head sideways as she continued to watch Grace.

'What is it?' she said after a while. 'There's something wrong.'

Grace shook her head. 'Mum – there's nothing wrong.'

'You don't look yourself. You shouldn't of gone to work tonight.'

'I'm fine.'

Grace collapsed on the sofa next to her and they both continued to stare at the TV even though it had been switched off.

'How was Dixie?'

'She spent about two hours practising the splits tonight.'

Grace smiled. 'And what about work?'

'I'm up early tomorrow morning – I've got to be at

175

that friend of your's house. Somebody Henderson –
they're having a party.'

'Yeah, that's Vicky,' Grace said, thoughtful.

'How was school?'

'Fine.' Grace tucked her chin down onto her collar-
bone.

'What's going on?' Nicole said, watching her
daughter.

'Nothing –'

'I know you,' she insisted.

Grace turned to her.

'I do know you,' she said again, tucking one of the
wet strands of hair behind her daughter's ears. 'There's
something wrong.'

Grace started to cry suddenly.

'Come on, love.'

'Mum –'

'What?'

She tugged on the ends of the Sainsbury's shirt and
suddenly Nicole knew. 'Oh, no, Gracie – not you. Not
that.' She paused. 'You are, aren't you?'

Grace nodded slowly, her face drained.

'Not that,' Nicole said again. Then, 'I saw one magpie
this morning – I should of known – it was a warning.
And Leila said a new life was coming. That's what she
said – literally – you've got a new life coming,' Nicole
carried on, talking to herself. Leila was the psychic she'd
been seeing since Dan the jazz musician, Dixie's father,
walked out on them the summer after Dixie was born.
He went out to take the dog for a walk and never came
back. It took Nicole until midday to realise the car had
gone from the road outside. They hadn't heard a word
from or about Dan since, and had no idea whether he
was dead or alive.

Leila, Nicole's psychic, had seen 9/11 coming. She'd had dreams of smoke and missing persons posters and skies that remained an unreasonable blue.

'I mean, when she said that – a new life was coming – I thought maybe I was going to meet someone –'

Nicole had been saying this ever since Dan left; so had Leila.

'But she was talking about this, wasn't she? This was what she meant when she said about a new life. This – She saw it coming.' This revelation about Leila's prophecy temporarily silenced her then, glancing at Grace's stomach. 'How far gone are you?'

Grace, embarrassed, put her hands over herself. 'Two months.'

Nicole nodded, aware that shock was giving way to anger in her. In fact, she hadn't been this angry since she watched that documentary on torture and the CIA; the one that had prompted her to join Amnesty International.

'And whose is it?'

Grace bit her lip.

'You do know, don't you?'

'Course,' she yelled suddenly. 'It's not like that.'

'Like what?'

'What you're saying – that's horrible,' Grace said, aware she sounded childish, but trying to distance herself from the image of Tina Branston shaking her buggy, asking for money in the rain.

'Well, I don't know, do I? So who is he?'

'He's at university – down in Brighton.'

'Another one with brains.'

'We miscalculated.'

'I'd say you miscalculated.'

'It's Tom Henderson.'

'Tom Henderson?' Nicole hauled her feet off the coffee table and sat up on the edge of the sofa.

'It started in the summer.'

'Tom Henderson?' Nicole said again. 'Bloody hell, Gracie, I've got to go and fill his mother's house with flowers tomorrow.'

'They don't know. He hasn't told them yet.'

Nicole leant forward and scratched at something stuck to the surface of the coffee table. 'Are you seriously thinking of going ahead with this?'

'I love him,' Grace exploded.

Nicole looked slowly at her. 'Gracie –'

'He's completely excited about it.'

'Gracie,' Nicole said again, shaking her head.

'We want this baby. We've got it all sorted –'

'You've got no idea.'

'Why are you being so negative?'

'Because I've been there – twice – and you've got no idea what's coming. What about university?'

'Tom graduates next year. Then he'll come with me – and the baby – to Cambridge.'

'If they still want you.'

Grace's face hardened, and Nicole looked away.

She sat staring at a clay candle holder on top of the gas fire; Grace had made it in primary school, and the dusty white candle wedged in it had never been lit. 'You were the last person this was meant to happen to. The last person. I wanted something different for you, Gracie.' Nicole looked around her bleary-eyed.

'It's going to be okay, mum,' Grace said, tearful again. 'This doesn't change anything.'

'It'll change everything!'

A mobile started ringing somewhere in the house.

'Yours,' Nicole said.

Grace didn't move.

'Your mobile's ringing – sounds like it's coming from the kitchen.'

'I can hear it.'

'So go and get it.' She broke off. 'It's him, isn't it? I want you to take that call because I think I'm about to cry and I want to do it on my own.'

'Mum – don't.'

'Just piss off,' Nicole said, her voice breaking.

Grace hesitated then went into the kitchen, shutting the door behind her.

Nicole could see the blue and orange uniform through the patterned glass panels in the kitchen door and didn't want to hear what her daughter was saying so put the TV back on and sat there with her mouth open and tears falling silently over her cheeks, chin and neck.

A few minutes later, Grace came back into the room, holding the phone out towards her. 'He wants to talk to you.'

Nicole shook her head. 'Not now.'

'Mum, please –'

'I don't want to speak to him.'

'Mum!'

Nicole hesitated then wiped at her face and took the phone, still sniffing. A clear-cut, sincere, inherently light voice – attempting weightiness for the occasion – came down the line.

'Mrs Cummings? I just want you to know –'

She cut him short, 'No, I want you to know that you're stupid – both of you – bloody stupid if you think you're going to get through this in one piece.'

'I didn't want Grace to tell you on her own, Mrs Cummings.'

'Stop saying that.'

'What?'

'Mrs Cummings.'

Tom hesitated. 'I wanted to be there. And I wanted her to wait until tomorrow night so that I could be there. She wasn't meant to do it tonight. And,' he carried on, rapidly now, 'I'm going to look after her. I want you to know that. We're going to work it out.'

'I hear you,' Nicole said at last, too angry to say anything else. She handed the phone back to Grace – who disappeared into the kitchen again – and lay along the sofa listening to the clipped excitement in her daughter's voice as she spoke to Tom Henderson, who really did believe things were going to work out. She'd heard the unhinged faith in his voice, but then everyone went through that first time round, before they realised that every beginning was only ever the precursor to a new ending – the law of nature.

She watched a documentary about a boy weighing half a ton being lifted by crane from his bed, and while she watched it, she lit a menthol – she quit cigarettes when she got the job at Fleurs because she wanted to be able to smell the flowers she was working with – and tried not to think about tomorrow.

the poker party

27

It was Saturday morning – the morning of Burwood's first ever poker party.

Bill had been sent out into the garden to move the fire pit because it had rained the night before and after rain the fire pit's feet left rust marks on the patio if it wasn't moved before the patio dried.

Only he hadn't yet moved the fire pit because he was too busy listening to a conversation Vicky was having on the phone. He was able to do this through the baby monitor he had in his hand.

'Well I need to see you. The whole weekend? Matt, come on –' Vicky broke off. 'I'm pregnant, Matt. Pregnant,' she said again. 'It's why I called you like about a million times, but you didn't pick up. Where are you? I can hear sirens and stuff.' Pause. 'I took a test, but I'm late anyway.' Pause. 'No – that's why I'm phoning. For fuck's sake, Matt.' Pause. 'What am I going to do?' Pause. 'What d'you want to do? Matt? My mum wants me to get an abortion.'

Bill instinctively spun round, looking for signs of Sylvia inside the house, but there weren't any.

'What – I shouldn't of? My mum kept going on and on about me not being able to fit into my jeans.' Pause. 'Six to eight weeks, but my waist has just like gone to pieces.' Pause. 'I had to say something –.' Pause. 'I don't know if I'm keeping it. Am I?'

Pause. 'So what, I make the appointment, check into a clinic and get this thing vacuumed out or whatever it is they do? A day out of my life? Completely straight forward. Is that what you want?' Pause. 'Why d'you think I'm asking you? 'Cause it's your fucking baby. You know – the Pentonville party.' Pause. 'A couple of months ago. Those Welsh guys – friends of yours, in Pentonville.' Pause. 'Yeah? Matt – don't do this. Please. You didn't leave early. It was you,' Vicky screamed. 'I know it was you.'

A sobbing that was difficult to bear. Bill's knuckles, clenching the monitor, were a mottled yellow and purple.

Vicky, crying and talking at the same time. 'What about the commune? You were thinking of giving up your course, moving down to Sussex.' Pause. 'But the commune – you said we were going to have loads of kids . . . keep a couple of goats, and make cheese . . . that's what fucking planet I'm on.'

Yelling rage followed by a clatter as, upstairs, Vicky threw her mobile across the room where it hit the wall and ripped her VIRGINS MAKE GOOD SUICIDE BOMBERS poster featuring a schoolgirl with bombs strapped to her.

Bill's thumb rolled automatically over the volume switch.

He was shaking – and somebody was calling his name.

Sylvia was making her way along the hallway plugging in the Ambi-pur air fresheners she'd bought last week

– Midnight Jasmine – at well-positioned olfactory points when Bill appeared on the other side of the patio doors, with his back to her holding what looked like a baby monitor.

She stood up and stared at him, trying to work out when exactly depression had become dementia.

It was difficult to believe – watching him now, standing on the patio in his old waxed jacket with the baby monitor clamped to the side of his head – just how much potential she'd once seen in him. In the beginning.

If she'd had the vocabulary at her disposal, she would have been able to articulate the fact that during the past twenty odd years of marriage Bill had not only failed to fulfil his potential, but instead succeeded in becoming the antithesis of his younger self. So saying, even if she had been able to grapple with this idea of antithesis, it wouldn't have helped her answer the fundamental question – why?

She pulled back the patio door. 'Bill! Bill!'

He spun round, wild-eyed, clutching the baby monitor. 'Vicky –'

This was beyond the male menopause. She held tightly onto the remaining three boxes of Ambi-pur Midnight Jasmine.

'Give me that, Bill, come on,' she said, gesturing at the monitor.

'I was worried about her last night, Syl. I thought she might –' he let out a wet sob '– do something stupid.'

'She already did something stupid,' Sylvia snapped, alarmed by Bill's tears.

'So I got the monitor out of the garage and put it in her room – under the bed.'

'You've got her wired up to a baby monitor? Jesus, Bill.'

'You never know,' he carried on, still shaking his head. 'There was that kid – he was only fourteen.'

'Was he pregnant as well?'

'Children are dying, Sylvia,' Bill gasped. 'Even here . . . in the green belt . . . where the schools are good and people have jobs . . . where the streets are tree-lined and . . .'

'Listen to yourself . . .'

'Yeah, I do that a lot.' He laughed – not a happy laugh. 'I've been thinking – about last night. What I said . . . sometimes I forget how much we've been through, and you're right.'

'About what?'

'Giving ourselves another chance,' he said, softly. 'Why don't we?'

'We already did.'

'When?'

'We're standing in it, Bill. We're standing right in the middle of our last chance.'

Bill swung round, disorientated. 'I'm not talking about this. I'm not talking about houses or places. I'm not even talking about countries,' he concluded, expansively – a covert allusion to the Gambia.

Sylvia was losing patience – time was running out – the fire pit still hadn't been moved and she was sure she could hear tyres on the gravel drive at the front of the house.

'You need help, Bill.'

'We need to start having sex again,' he implored her.

Sylvia was – momentarily – shocked. So shocked that she let her mind drift sideways, away from this insurmountable problem, and inadvertently lifted one

186

of the Midnight Jasmine air fresheners she was still holding, to her nose – sniffing at it. The patio and garden with its inhospitable vegetation fell out of sight. What if . . . she stared at Bill, who was staring intently back at her.

Could it really be as simple as all that? Was that all they needed to do – take off their clothes and peel back the sheets, and the mortgage, beloved son and estranged girlfriend, and pregnant teenage daughter would all just naturally fall into place around the nuptial bed? Sylvia felt herself start to lean towards him – and it was then that she heard the doorbell.

She straightened up immediately, her skin grey, breathing rapidly – like somebody in shock after an accident.

'We tried sex – it didn't work.' She paused. 'Remember?'

Bill wasn't to be deterred. 'Because you're menopausal. We need to try Viagra. Alan at work bought some on the internet – before he went to Tenerife, and he was hard for –'

The doorbell rang again and, relieved, Sylvia went to answer it.

She took in the person standing on her doorstep without recognising her.

'Hi – Mrs Henderson? I'm Nicole –.' Nicole's eyes flicked over the Midnight Jasmine air fresheners in Sylvia's arms still. 'From Fleurs? The flowers?'

'Flowers,' Sylvia said. Now she recognised her. She'd seen Nicole Cummings at Prize Giving when Grace Cummings wore out the soles of her shoes she'd collected so many prizes. Then there was the inauguration of the new Head Girl she'd had to sit through. At least she'd managed to squash Nicole's attempt to join the PTA. The point was – what was Nicole Cummings doing here?

For one awful moment she thought she'd found out about Vicky and come to say something condescending and commiserative.

'The flowers – for tonight?' Nicole prompted her again.

'Tonight?'

'The party –'

'The party,' Sylvia gasped. Then, 'You work at Fleurs?' Nicole nodded.

'Where's Angela?'

'She didn't tell you I'd be coming to do the flowers this morning?'

'I was expecting Angela.'

There was an awkward pause before Nicole said, 'I'll just start to unload the van. Is it okay if I park it there?'

Sylvia – disconcerted at the intensity with which Nicole Cummings was staring at her – said, 'I've got caterers coming as well.'

'Okay – I'll move the van.' Nicole smiled.

Five minutes later, after re-parking the Fleurs van next to a row of solar uplighters in the border, Nicole sat smoking a Menthol, her left hand gripping her upper right arm where the Nicorette patch was.

28

Nicole walked into number two Park Avenue with her arms full of potted Amaryllis.

Angela, who ran Fleurs, had tried to talk Sylvia out of the Amaryllis, but Sylvia was insistent because she'd seen them in a magazine – an interiors spread of a house in Gloucestershire where the linen-clad owner had achieved an incredibly sophisticated effect using Amaryllis against a backdrop of post-Gustavian neutrals.

Now, seeing the Amaryllis inside number two Park Avenue – which possessed the same post-Gustavian neutrals as the featured Gloucestershire home – Sylvia wasn't so sure.

Up close, in Nicole's arms – and still disorientated from the conversation she'd just had with Bill – they appeared self-confident and fleshy to the point of being obscene. Swaying heavily on their long stems they looked capable of randomly impregnating tonight's guests with alien spawn.

'Take them through to the sitting room – straight ahead.'

She watched as they were carried off down the hall,

turning their heads towards her over Nicole's shoulder and bowing mockingly. She saw them do it.

'Bill,' she called out with relief at the sound of footsteps on the stairs.

Only it wasn't Bill.

'Hey, Mrs Cummings,' Vicky said. 'Weird flowers.'

She'd only seen Grace's mum a couple of times, and Nicole had always made her uneasy.

'What are you doing down here?' Sylvia asked, worried.

'I came down for some water – is that okay? Or should I just stay up in my room and dehydrate?'

Sylvia followed Vicky closely round the kitchen as she opened and shut the fridge then checked the cupboards.

'What are you doing?'

'I don't know what's happened to my appetite, I'm like hungry the whole time.'

'Vicky!' Sylvia warned her, grabbing hold of one of her arms and digging her nails in hard at the wrist.

'What? Let go! You're hurting me.'

'I'm warning you.'

Nicole passed back through the kitchen and disappeared outside to the van.

'This is a big day for me, and while I can see that you're finding it hard to give a shit, you could at least try not to ruin it any further.'

'I came down for some water.'

'You know exactly what I'm talking about.'

Vicky rubbed sullenly at her wrist. 'There's blood – you made me bleed.'

Nicole passed down the hallway again with the next armful of Amaryllis.

Sylvia waited until she'd gone then grabbed hold of

Vicky's other wrist and hauled her out of the kitchen, dragging her upstairs and virtually throwing her into her room.

'Is that what this is about?'

'What?'

'You did it to spite me, didn't you?'

'It was an accident.'

'To think of the money we've spent on you.'

'That's all it comes down to with you, isn't it? Money. Well, sorry you got such poor returns on your stock.'

'Not half as sorry as me,' Sylvia concluded, panting with an anger she was trying hard to subdue.

'You really come out with them, don't you,' Vicky said loudly, unevenly – starting to cry in spite of herself.

Shaking now and less sure, Sylvia retreated to the bedroom doorway as Vicky lay on her bed and continued to sob.

'You're in shock.' She disappeared into the en-suite, and re-appeared with a pack of Sentinel. 'Take a couple of these – they'll help you calm down.'

'Trying to knock me out?' Vicky said, just about able to make out Sylvia and the pack of Sentinel through the glaze of tears.

'You're hysterical – you didn't sleep last night, I heard you – and you need to sleep.'

'I'm hysterical? You're scared I'll ruin the party.'

Sylvia hesitated in the doorway. 'No,' she said, slowly, 'you've never scared me, Vicky.'

Vicky sat up on the bed, crossing her legs, suddenly much calmer. 'I can't take those – I'm pregnant, remember?'

'Not for much longer,' Sylvia finished, coldly.

'You wish,' Vicky said.

'It's your life,' Sylvia responded evenly – the anger

191

had passed. 'But if you keep it you'll be the only one living with the consequences.'

'Are you saying you'll kick me out?' Vicky, shocked, started to cry again.

'I'm going to take a shower.' Sylvia started to shut the bedroom door.

'I hate you,' Vicky called out.

'You don't hate me,' Sylvia said. 'You hate yourself.'

She slammed the door shut before Vicky had time to respond, and went back downstairs into the sitting room to see how Nicole was doing.

Something was wrong.

And it wasn't the Amaryllis.

It wasn't the trees outside in the garden either, although she had heard faint laughter earlier, talking to Bill, and was fairly certain the eucalyptus used to be to the right and not to the left of the Oleander.

It was Nicole Cummings – standing over by the piano, holding the portrait of Tom they'd had done when he was the same age Vicky was now; the one in the silver frame.

Nicole started when she realised Sylvia had come into the room, dropped the portrait on the cream carpet, picked it up, and fumbled to stand it back on the piano.

'Sorry – I was looking at the picture of your son. That is your son, isn't it?'

Sylvia nodded.

'My daughter – Grace – she's friends with him.'

'With Tom?' Sylvia exploded.

'He looks a lot like you,' Nicole carried on, startled, and was about to say something else when there was a knock at the door, and Sylvia found herself running out of the sitting room to answer it, leaving Nicole by the piano, staring at the photograph of Tom.

* * *

Upstairs, Vicky – who'd taken 400mg of Sentinel – lay on her bed focussing fervently on the idea of Matt's commune in an attempt to counteract Sylvia's assault. After a while she started to draw strength from the pseudo-rural fantasy involving whitewashed stone walls, flagstones, open fires – and goats – until she realised that it wasn't Matt she was cavorting with on the rug in her dream, but Mr Sutton.

29

That evening, Sylvia walked slowly through the downstairs rooms lighting candles. The solid red Edwardian bricks of number two Park Avenue refused to echo the events of the past twenty-four hours and the house remained silent. Sylvia sensed a complicity in the silence that warmed her to the house for the first time since that desperate April day when she drove down from London on the campaign trail for the future of the Henderson Family and followed the estate agent – who wore pointed shoes and still smelt of his hangover – onto the crescent-shaped gravel drive.

So much had happened since then, but now she knew she could rely on the solid redbrick walls of number two Park Avenue to keep their façade unchanged. Despite having a pregnant teenage daughter in one of the upstairs rooms, the covering of Virginia Creeper on the front of the house would never think to do anything other than turn flaming red – because it was Autumn.

This complicity leant dignity to her suffering, which meant that despite having fallen to her knees in despair last night in the bedroom – while banging her head repetitively against carpet she wanted to replace – she was now able to move smoothly through the downstairs rooms of the house with a wipe-clean box of cook's matches.

Despite having a pregnant teenage daughter in one of the upstairs rooms, she was able to deftly switch on the Ambi-pur air fresheners and inhale deeply as fumes of Midnight Jasmine spread their olfactory benevolence around the perfectly laid out sitting room with sofas arranged ready to accommodate the poker tables arriving – along with staff to man them – from poker@home.

Even the Amaryllis had acquired a certain majesty now they were in situ and no longer tainted by the presence of Nicole Cummings.

Although she would never actually love number two Park Avenue in the way she had the London home – Bill would never understand what having to give it up had been like for her – the house could at least be relied on.

Life wasn't something you lived; it was something that happened to you, Sylvia thought. But at least she knew this about herself: that she still had the energy to stand in front of a mirror – despite what had happened in the past twenty-four hours; the past twenty-four years – and apply mascara with a steady hand.

The Hendersons might not be happy, but the Hendersons had survived.

There was the doorbell.

Here was the party.

195

30

Sylvia was pleased to see that people had taken the 'Dress Smart' clause in the invitation as seriously as she'd intended them to. Everybody, that is, apart from the elderly diplomat and his wife from number seventeen, who – while themselves immaculately dressed – had not only insisted on bringing their middle-aged Down's Syndrome daughter with them (excluded from the invitation by Sylvia) but allowed her to dress herself.

Lola had come to play poker; was addicted to poker online – according to the elderly diplomat and his wife.

Lola – why waste a name like Lola on somebody who was never going to have sex? – was wearing a purple tracksuit. Sylvia steered her out of the main arena and into a corner by the fireplace where Lladro shepherds and shepherdesses were displayed on a Regency-style side table, but Lola – it transpired – had no intention of being put in the Lladro corner.

Sylvia was furious, and did her best to ignore Lola's flat, unblinking stare, and excited squeals as the poker@home people started to get the tables ready

– guiding her instead towards Jill Fulton, the doctor's wife. Jill was also wearing purple – an undersize satin cocktail dress that toured school and charity events and whose acquired stains, Sylvia couldn't help noticing, had barely been dabbed at.

Jill didn't so much as flinch when Lola was foisted onto her, but then Jill was used to seeing people who didn't make regular mortgage payments and with far worse predicaments than Down's Syndrome – like her Yuletide needle exchange patients.

It took Sylvia a while to realise that Bill was tugging at her arm.

'Where's Vicky?'

'Upstairs – asleep.'

'She's not.'

'Bill – she's asleep,' Sylvia hissed, 'I gave her some Sentinel and she took 400mg.'

'You gave her sleeping pills?'

'She's exhausted – for obvious reasons –' Sylvia lowered her voice '– and having trouble sleeping.'

Bill jerked his head from side to side. There was a lot of room between neck and collar, Sylvia noted – far more than there used to be. She hadn't noticed Bill's weight loss until now – no doubt a side effect of depression – because tonight was the first time he'd had his dinner suit on since the move.

'It's my only claim to fame,' the elderly diplomat was saying, loudly, close to them. 'He was only with us a fortnight, but during that fortnight –'

The sounds of the party were closing round them, gaining momentum.

'Are you sure she's not upstairs?'

'Syl – she isn't there. She's nowhere in the house.'

'Have you tried her phone?' Sylvia asked.

'She's not picking up.'

'So, she'll be at Ruth's – or Saskia's, or somebody's.'

'I'll go and see.'

'What d'you mean *go and see*?'

'I mean, I'm going to see whether she's next door at Ruth's, or Saskia's or . . .'

'Bill!'

'What?'

'We're in the middle of a party here.'

'I taught him to ride,' the diplomat said, triumphant.

'Taught who to ride?' Sylvia said, spinning round with a wild, frantic smile on her face.

'Haile Selassie.'

'You did?' Sylvia gasped, holding surreptitiously but firmly onto Bill's very loose cuff in case he disappeared out into the night in search of their daughter.

'Incredible, isn't it?' Dr Fulton said.

'Extraordinary,' Sylvia echoed vaguely, making a mental note to check Haile Selassie on Wikipedia.

'Have you still got the bicycle?' she heard the doctor say as she moved away and Bill succeeded in pulling his arm free. Then she caught a whiff of derogatory laughter from Jill Fulton, standing shoulder to shoulder with one of the Amaryllis, and still talking to Lola who was getting fidgety for the poker to begin. Now she was worried again – about the Amaryllis.

'That's the door –' Bill said, terse.

'I'll go.'

It was Nathan Dent. He gave her two tight kisses then moved past to say hello to Bill, who managed to greet Nathan as though they didn't have a teenage daughter who had told them – less than twenty-four hours ago – that she was pregnant, and who was now missing.

'Where's Rachel?' Sylvia asked.

'Stomach cramps,' Nathan just about managed to say. His face was grey and loose – and he didn't look like he had any control over it.

Sylvia's hand went out for his arm, but he saw it coming and twisted instinctively away from the imminent contact. 'Is she okay?'

'No,' Nathan stated flatly.

Sylvia nodded, unsure what she was meant to do, and tried not to show excessive, visible relief when Bill interrupted – to ask Nathan whether Vicky was round at the Dents.

Nathan thought about this then shook his head and, distracted, allowed Sylvia to steer him straight into the diplomat and doctor's Liberia conversation, the periphery of which she glided through smiling and laughing knowingly while wondering how on earth a man who'd performed a vasectomy on himself managed to find the time to form an opinion on the past atrocities of someone called General Butt Naked and the Liberian Civil War.

She sustained her ambiguous nodding smile all through the cannibalism and human sacrifice jokes, then put a hand on the shoulder blade of each man and pushed them gently towards the poker tables now set up for play.

'Please don't feel you have to stay,' she whispered to Nathan, who just stared blankly at her, lost. 'Rachel,' she prompted him.

'There's nothing more I can do,' he responded, bleakly.

Sylvia, aware that he'd said far too much, turned away from him towards Dr Fulton – who had made a rapid turnaround in his estimation of Sylvia when he realised she'd made a point of inviting Lola to the party.

As she deposited him at table number three, he even squeezed her arm, and she felt suddenly, unexpectedly triumphant; radiant even. The newfound radiance enabled her to ignore Bill – cornered by the diplomat's wife – attempting to gesture irately at her (he didn't realise he was being irate, but then there were a lot of things depressed people didn't realise about themselves).

She was surrounded by the clicking of poker chips on baize; the deep slap of woven cards, voices and laughter – all taking place here in her sitting room, against all odds.

It occurred to her that they might actually get through this pregnancy debacle and out the other side without anyone finding out. If nobody knew about Vicky being pregnant then essentially Vicky wasn't pregnant at all. That was the point – only Bill didn't get it. But then he rarely did.

31

Rachel Dent stood next door at number four staring at herself in the mirror as another twinge passed through her abdomen.

Before Nathan Dent left to present himself at number two Park Avenue for Sylvia's poker party, he'd stood at the foot of the stairs, yelling at Rachel.

He had his right foot on the first tread and was smoothing his hair down with the palms of his hands, dropping them suddenly with frustration so that they hung large and loose by his hips. 'Rachel – COME ON! We were meant to be there TWENTY MINUTES AGO.'

A minute later – furious at the lack of response – he ran back upstairs.

Rachel saw him in the mirror as he appeared in the bedroom doorway, and another twinge passed through her abdomen. The colour had run out of her face and throat – something the make-up she'd just finished putting on accentuated rather than concealed.

'I'm not coming,' she said.

Nathan's reflection – in the mirror – stared at her.

'It's my period.'

'No,' he said, falling suddenly through the fabric of the evening into one of the deep dark places their marriage had become rhythmically pockmarked with since they started the IVF.

'I said – yesterday.' She turned away from the mirror and sank onto the bed feeling the too-familiar dull, aching internal pull.

Rachel was malfunctioning and full of need. She'd fallen backwards and pulled her knees up to her chest, hugging them tightly as she let out long, wet sobs.

Standing in the bedroom doorway, in his dinner suit, Nathan felt helpless then frightened then impotent then cold, and it was the coldness he stayed with because the coldness was familiar.

'You have to stop this.' It sounded like a command – he hadn't meant it to. 'We can't go on like this,' he added, feeling almost repulsed by the heap of agony on the bed – that was his wife – and yet unable to look away.

Rachel wrenched her head out of the duvet and twisted it until she could see him, blurred through tears. 'If it's the money –'

'It's not the money.'

'I can work.'

'Doing what?' He broke off. 'It's not that – it's got nothing to do with that. It's the constant rhythm of hope and despair, hope and despair. Most couples come crashing down once – some twice – but we come crashing down again and again. This isn't a life, Rachel – it's a life sentence.'

'But I want a baby, that's all.'

'I've got nothing more to give – and you don't even love me any more. What are we doing?'

'I do love you.'

'So show me.'

'I don't understand what you want.'

He strode across the bedroom and threw himself, kneeling, onto the bed – catching her hair under his legs. He saw her eyes – flat, wet and without depth – staring up at him, and could have killed her.

Why not, he thought – why not just kill her? Get it over and done with. He smelt freedom – a violent and beguiling means to an end – then pushed her roughly away and stood up.

'What are you going to do?' she asked, afraid.

'Nothing.'

'But –'

'What?'

'We can try again?'

'Yes, Rachel, we can try again – and again – and again. I'll tell Sylvia you're not coming.'

She nodded and buried her head back in the duvet as Nathan left the house. She heard his footsteps first on the gravel of their drive, and then – faintly – on the gravel drive of number two.

He was gone.

32

Ruth came home expecting the house to be empty. Dropping her towel and swimming costume into the laundry basket then turning round, she didn't anticipate seeing Rachel – across the hallway through the open bedroom door – lying on the bed, watching her.

The light in the bedroom wasn't on.

'Mum? I thought you were going out?'

She hung, awkward, in the doorway, aware that Rachel was dressed to go out – and fully made up.

'Where's Nathan?'

'He already went.'

'Aren't you going?'

Without answering this, Rachel said, 'You've been swimming – you went swimming last night as well.'

Ruth nodded, thinking that there was nothing stopping her telling Rachel now that she was pregnant. But there was something about the way she was lying – it reminded Ruth of the bedroom in the flat in Kilburn they'd lived in when they first arrived in London. In fact, that's all Ruth could remember about that time – Rachel lying on a bright pink bedspread that seemed to float, in her memory, unsuspended in a flat . . . other details, . . . furniture, the colour of the walls, etc . . . she either couldn't or didn't want to summon.

She used to come home from school and open the front door and know from the way the air hung in the flat – that she'd find Rachel lying on the pink bedspread and that she'd be crying, quietly. The pink bedspread filled her mind – day and night – the cheap, vivid nylon falling in ungracious folds, until she became convinced that the bedspread was holding her mother captive in some way. All she had to do was get rid of the bedspread, and Rachel would stop crying.

She knew now that it was depression and not the bedspread that had kept her mother pinned to her backdrop of crackling pink, but it left her with a deep hatred of the colour, and she never had got used to the sight of her mother lying on any bed fully clothed.

'I'm fine,' Rachel reassured her, instinctively reading her thoughts.

'So – why didn't you go to the party?'

Without turning the light on, Ruth went into the room and sat down on the edge of the bed. 'Did you have a row – you and Nathan?'

A dull rectangle of light fell onto the carpet through the gap in the curtains. She swung her foot in and out of it.

'A row?' Rachel, sniffing, pulled her head back to look at her daughter.

'You seem to row a lot – at the moment.'

'We do?' Rachel thought about this.

The room smelt of perfume, lipstick and shoes and above this the disorientating, intimate smell of a room slept in by more than one person: two people, in fact, who just about trusted each other enough to spend the night together lying side by side, unconscious.

'I'm sorry,' Rachel said at last. 'I don't want to upset you.'

'I know, but –' Ruth carried on lightly swinging her foot in and out of the patch of streetlight, thinking. 'It's the treatment, isn't it?' she said suddenly, realising that she'd known this as soon as she saw Rachel lying on the bed. 'It didn't work again, did it?'

'Not this time, no,' Rachel said, her voice far away.

'Are you going to try again?'

'I want to.'

'When will you stop?' Ruth said, aggression taking hold of her and making her tearful.

'Ruth –' Rachel's hands went out for her daughter's back.

'What? What if it never works?'

'I can't think like that. I have to keep trying.'

'Why?'

'It's not something I'm in control of. I'm forty-four!'

She'd raised her voice without meaning to, sounding almost angry with Ruth, who couldn't comprehend forty-four.

Ruth stopped swinging her leg and dropped her head on her chest. 'Why aren't we enough?'

Rachel sat up in bed and moved behind her daughter. 'You are – you really are – don't ever think that.'

'So why won't you just give up? It's like you're never here with us; it's like there's somebody else you're dreaming of the whole time who you want to be with, but can't.'

'I'm sorry.'

'Is it expensive – the treatment?'

Rachel nodded.

'Is that what the rows are about – with Nathan?'

'No, it's not that, it's – it's probably what you've been saying about me not being here.'

Ruth turned away. 'This is month after month, mum. You can't keep putting us through it. It's killing Nathan,' she said decisively, unaware that she'd even intended to say this.

'You love him very much, don't you,' Rachel said, running her hand over the ends of Ruth's pool-wet hair, and her spine.

Ruth nodded, the pink bedspread in Kilburn between them again. She thought about how Nathan arrived in their lives, and how she hadn't been scared of the bedspread after that. She loved him for that alone – and the way he made her feel those first few times they went out together when he would take hold of her hand to cross the road and keep hold of it. Nathan took her to places where other children went – where she could run and shout and forget the weight of Rachel.

'He's not going to leave us, is he?' she said, suddenly afraid.

'No – no,' Rachel replied, upset.

'Would you stop if . . .' Ruth started to cry.

'Ruth? What is it?' Rachel stared through the semi-darkness at her daughter, and knew – instinctively – exactly what she was going to say next.

'I'm pregnant, and I don't want to be, but –'

'It's okay,' Rachel interrupted, unaware of the words she was saying as she pushed her daughter's hair gently away from her face.

'It's not okay, mum,' Ruth said, choking, over-whelmed. 'None of this is okay, and I know I can't expect you to understand. You're not even angry are you? You're not even going to ask me whose it is.'

'Do I know him?'

Ruth shook her head. 'It doesn't matter, it's – it's horrible; the whole thing. I just want it out – as soon as possible. I want to forget it ever happened.'

'No!' Rachel shouted, hauling herself off the bed. 'I'm not letting you do that – I don't have it in me.'

They stared at each other, terrified, aware that they were thinking the same thing.

'You want me to keep it. I can't do that –'

'If you did . . . Ruth, listen to me.' Rachel caught hold of her hands. 'If you did, I'd stop the IVF treatment – I'd stop the treatment.'

Neither of them had heard Nathan returning from the party next door after only an hour. Neither of them heard him walk up the stairs and neither of them noticed as he slipped into the bedroom and saw Rachel sitting on the side of the bed, and Ruth standing in front of her.

She looked completely different.

He pulled slowly at his tie, staring at his wife, the chaos of passion at his elbows. 'I said some terrible things earlier – I'm sorry.'

She smiled at him. 'We're having a baby.'

He stared at her. 'So – the pains weren't what you thought? It's . . . it's actually worked? Rachel –'

'Ruth's having it for us.'

'Ruth –'

She nodded.

He stared down at her, afraid. 'So – you're not pregnant.'

'Ruth's pregnant.' She wasn't interested in Nathan or Nathan's reaction – the only person she was interested in was Ruth.

'But – how? How did it happen? She doesn't even

have a boyfriend.' He turned to Ruth in disbelief, his hand on his tie still.

'What does it matter?' Rachel cut in. 'We're having a –'

'Stop it – stop saying that.'

'Nathan, it's okay,' Ruth said, speaking for the first time.

'This can't happen, Rachel.' He turned to Ruth. 'You're only seventeen!'

'But don't you see – if I give her this,' she looked down quickly at herself, 'she'll stop the IVF, and then the rows will stop. There'll be no more rows, Nathan. You won't leave –'

'Leave? Ruth, I'm not leaving.'

'But the rows –'

'Are for us to work out.'

He went up to her and she collapsed into him immediately, pressing against his dinner jacket, which smelt of the dry cleaners still.

'It's okay,' he said, stroking her hair, no longer aware of Rachel. 'You just need to tell me about it – then we can work out what we're going to do.'

33

When Vicky eventually woke up – heavy from the 400mg of Sentinel – it was dark, and the shower in her parents' en-suite was on so she guessed the party hadn't started. She swung her legs out of bed then automatically got dressed – her hands shaking as she did up the buttons on her cardigan. After she'd put her make-up on, she picked up the small screwdriver she kept on her desk for changing batteries, and drove it through Girls World's forehead then left the house light-headed with hunger, and no real plan, walking fast – her stride awkward.

The night was dry, but full of the damp, earthy smell of gardens that had been rained on. There were stars to be seen, and a comet – passing through the sky in a bright descent – as she turned onto Hurst Road. But Vicky wasn't looking.

A group of boys from Danehill School passed in a laughing gaggle and called something out. One shouted her name – she recognised him from B-52s – but she didn't respond.

They had nothing to do with her.

She walked through the head high threads of dope they left behind them, unconsciously taking the route she took to school every day – the long route; the one that went past Mr Sutton's house on Dardanelle Drive. Traipsing wetly into a cul-de-sac of garages, she stood behind a cedar tree and took some Valium from the beaded purse she always carried with her, and waited for the shaking to stop.

Then she carried on walking, almost in a trance, and it took her a while to register that the girl approaching from the opposite direction was Saskia.

Vicky was almost at Mr Sutton's – she could see the curve of conifers shouldering his property. Unsure whether Saskia had seen her or not, she waited on the kerb by the conifers.

A car passed on the road, but Saskia didn't look up.

'Sas!' Vicky called out, aware that there were lights on in Mr Sutton's house.

Saskia stopped, staring at her.

'What are you doing here?'

In spite of the rain, somebody on Dardanelle Drive had, as planned, managed to finish creosoting their fence.

Standing on the pavement, her head throbbing, Vicky could smell Suburbia's definitive scent suddenly, strongly, taking its hold on the night and was over-whelmed by a foretaste of despair.

Saskia continued to stare until her face broke into a small, taut smile. 'More to the point, what are you doing here?'

'I don't know – having a walk – thought I might go to B-52s. D'you want to come?'

Saskia hesitated then nodded, turned round and started to walk with Vicky, in the direction she'd just come from.

Hours later, above the loud, hollow roar of a local band playing at B-52s, Vicky asked Saskia if she knew that Mr Sutton lived on Dardanelle Drive, but Saskia just smiled and Vicky guessed that she hadn't heard the question.

34

Bill came and found her just as Sylvia was about to start unwrapping the Mediterranean Buffet provided by Panino's.

'Vicky's not at Saskia's!' he said, loudly.

'Okay –' Sylvia said, in an attempt to pretend to Bill that she was processing this piece of information, while propelling him into the substantial cloakroom area beneath the stairs.

'I was speaking to her dad – just now. Richard? Is that his name?'

Sylvia shut the cloakroom door firmly behind them, taking the additional precaution of locking it. Bill's obsession with the idea that Vicky was going to commit suicide was clearly connected to his own depression – how did she tell him this? Without ruining the poker@home party?

'There's no point in starting a phone round, Bill – it's Saturday night. She could be anywhere.'

Bill wasn't listening – despite the confined space.

'I've checked all the phones – no messages – nothing,' he carried on, sounding genuinely helpless.

'Of course she hasn't left any messages,' Sylvia snapped,

losing patience. 'She wants us to be worried. She'll turn up.'

'Yeah, but turn up where – that's the point,' Bill said, suddenly conscious of the fact that they were in the downstairs cloakroom, and unsure how they'd got there. 'I mean, you were there at the table last night, weren't you? Or did I just hallucinate the whole thing? Please tell me if that's the case, and put me out of my misery.'

'Bill!' Sylvia warned him. 'Don't be absurd.'

'You *were* there, weren't you? Last night?' Bill said again, laying his hands suddenly on her shoulders and shaking her lightly.

'In case you hadn't noticed,' Sylvia said calmly, 'tonight we're having a party. Tonight we have over forty people on the other side of that door, playing poker and waiting to EAT.' She'd raised her voice – she hadn't meant to do that.

'Forty people? I don't even know half their names. This is our daughter we're talking about here. I mean – her world's just gone, Sylvia, fallen out from under her. How d'you think she's feeling right now?'

'How the fuck d'you think I'm feeling right now, Bill? I'm Chair of the PTA; on the Parish Council; Treasurer of the Residents' Association. I can't have a pregnant teenage daughter. This move to Burwood – this was our chance; our last chance. We don't have the option of it not working out, Bill. We both know that.'

There was a loud, frantic banging on the cloakroom door, followed by somebody calling out rapidly, 'Hello? Hello? Hello?'

Sylvia tore herself away from Bill and opened the door.

214

Lola, the diplomat's daughter, was standing there, her face screwed up.

When she saw Sylvia – and Bill jammed in the corner of the cloakroom – she stared down at the floor and said, 'I need to use the toilet.'

'Upstairs,' Sylvia said, 'first door on the left.' She slammed the door in Lola's face before she had time to blink.

A minute later they heard her climb the stairs above their heads.

'What if she's doing it for attention,' Sylvia said slowly, only momentarily distracted by Lola.

Bill's head was touching the underside of the staircase. 'This has got to stop,' he said quietly.

'She's been doing it since before she could even talk.'

'Sylvia –'

'The bulimia thing – and now this, the pregnancy thing.' Sylvia stopped. 'What if she isn't?'

'Isn't what?'

'What if she isn't even pregnant?'

'Stop it.'

'I mean – we just believed her. Like we did with the bulimia thing. What if she just made the whole thing up?'

'Why would she do that? Why would she put herself through that?'

'Attention.'

'That's fucked, Sylvia.' Bill shook his head, looking sadly at his wife.

'She needs help. She needs to see someone, Bill.'

There were footsteps coming down the stairs followed by more knocks at the door and then, 'Hello? Hello? Hello?'

Sylvia yanked open the door again, and there was

Lola, holding Vicky's old Girls World – a resplendent fusion of Goth and punk right down to the recently added screwdriver now vibrating in the plastic forehead.

'Can I mend it?' Lola asked, excited, eyes still downcast as she gave Girls World's synthetic blond hair some rapid strokes. 'She was in an accident,' she said, looking concerned for a moment before laughing suddenly.

'Fine,' Sylvia said, slamming the door for a second time. 'How did she know we were still in here?' she said, turning back to Bill who was now sitting on the loo seat.

'Because it's like an echo chamber in here – and we've been fucking yelling at each other.'

'An echo chamber?' Sylvia stared at Bill, mortified.

'Look at us,' he said, his hands dropping in his lap with frustration. 'This isn't a marriage. We're murdering each other – and we're doing it slowly.' As he said it, he sounded almost excited by the idea of murder.

'That's the depression talking,' Sylvia quickly responded.

Bill shook his head. 'We're just two lonely people living together. Out of habit.'

'So we're no different to everybody else we know,' Sylvia concluded, almost cheerful. This, she believed, was a positive point.

'But I want to be different –'

'That's always been your problem, Bill.'

'I wanted us to be different.' He looked at her suddenly with a sadness so acute it was verging on grief. 'And we did used to be different – remember? The way we went about loving each other – was different.'

'It's like that for everybody in the beginning.'

216

'No, it's not,' he said, vehement. 'We were special. We had something –'

'That's what everybody thinks.'

He nodded, thinking about this. 'Thing is, Syl, I still think it . . . how fucking sad is that?'

35

Saskia left B-52s early, but Vicky got talking to some-body called Frank Barlow, who kept buying her Tequila slammers, and who ended up inviting her back to his. Too drunk to think of a reason not to – and not drunk enough to want to go home – she ended up leaving B-52s with Frank at around ten.

The square outside was still full of young people, and Frank, casting his eyes over Vicky's head – with his arm locked firmly round her shoulders – couldn't help noting that he was in fact the oldest person there, and felt momentarily fretful.

A boy in an overcoat with a manic smile climbed onto the shoulders of the bronze drover – a sculpture commissioned by the Burwood Historical Society, and the unveiling of which had been covered by Frank. Two others, with traffic cones on their heads, ran across the square in front of Vicky and Frank and into the metal shutters covering the Waitrose windows. Another sat in a shopping trolley, his head in a bag of glue.

Vicky shook her head condescendingly at these antics,

then pressed herself tightly into Frank Barlow's confident embrace.

They drifted out of the square and round behind Waitrose towards the multi-storey.

'Where are we going?' Vicky asked, without caring.

'Mine –'

'Okay,' she agreed.

Frank noted the slurred words – Valium not alcohol, only he didn't know this – and hoped she wasn't too drunk. He led her up the concrete staircase, which smelt of paint, exhaust fumes and metal.

'Here we are – chez Barlow,' Frank said, turning the key in a door with the number '38' on it.

It was hot inside the flat, which smelt of Calvin Klein's Eternity for Men.

Frank turned on the lights and quickly cast his eyes round.

He nearly said, 'Here we are – chez Barlow,' again, but remembered just in time that he'd already said that only seconds before – Alzheimer's? – before opening the front door.

So he just sighed instead – an ambiguous sigh – and, smiling, crossed the open-plan living room to the red SMEG fridge he was busy paying for in instalments.

He'd taken the precaution – before going out – of stocking up on some bottles of Prosecco from Waitrose, as well as some jars and tins of what he referred to as arsey little nibbles that the girls he brought home watched him eat but rarely ate themselves because they'd been on diets since before they were born.

Since his split with Jenna, he'd got heavily into jazz, and the i-pod in its dock was barking out something low, jazzy and masculine.

He waited for Vicky to comment on the music, but she'd drifted over to the bookshelves and was standing, preoccupied, with her arms folded, her eyes roving over the spines. He watched now as she pulled *The Complete Guide to Fellatio* off the shelves and tried to relax into the stance she'd assumed because she knew he was watching her from behind his red fridge door.

He walked over with a bottle of Prosecco and two chilled glasses and stared, over her shoulder, impartial, at the illustrated page on deep throating.

'Here – take this,' he said, handing her one of the chilled glasses.

She put *The Complete Guide to Fellatio* back on the shelf, without comment, and took the glass.

'A drop of Prosecco?' he said, poised, holding his arms taut in his T-shirt as he started to peel off the foil.

'Yeah – anything other than Cava. Cava gives me migraine.'

He glanced at her, popped the cork and poured.

Vicky was a pony tail of a name, but there was some-thing – he felt – challengingly urban about her. Hard and sweet. After two months of masturbation following Jenna's soppy, tearful departure – culminating tonight in a doggy-style session against the Conran sofa – he was looking forward to some real live sex.

'Where d'you go to school, schoolgirl?' he said, bumping her gently.

'Burwood Girls'. In my last year,' she added, draining the glass and holding it out to be refilled.

He'd taken the bottle back to the breakfast bar, which – along with the SMEG fridge and microwave – was the kitchen.

'What is this music?'

'You like it?'

'It's okay –'

She went back over to the kitchen area, picked up an apple, took a couple of bites then put it down on top of the TV. She stopped in front of the palm – a palm he'd spend a lot of money on at the same nursery Sylvia Henderson had sourced most of her garden from. He had green fingers – something he'd inherited from his father's side of the family, only he didn't know this because he'd never met his father. The palm replaced an electric guitar he'd stopped playing when Jenna came along after he realised she knew more about guitars than he'd ever know. The only guitar he'd played since Jenna was the plastic Les Gibson that came with *Guitar Hero III*.

Frank had been brought up by his mother in a flat a mile from the one he and Vicky Henderson were now standing in. Frank's childhood hadn't necessarily lacked love, but it had lacked any sort of aesthetic – comprising as it had of bean bags, gas fires and the occasional man in a wool jumper. Men had only ever been visitors in Frank's life – colleagues of his mother's or the odd librarian – who came to the flat to have grunting sex with her, in front of the gas fire, their loose white bodies rolling and slapping together.

Frank fell heavily onto his Conran sofa, trying to affect a sprawl.

There was a patch on the carpet just to the right of his feet where he'd left a puddle of spunk after his early evening release on all fours. He'd managed to wash it out, but it was still damp, and he inadvertently toed the patch now, while keeping an eye on the ever restless Vicky, currently swaying slightly in front of the poster of Japanese schoolgirls committing seppuku that he'd put up last weekend to replace the

221

one of Che Guevara that used to hang there. His Asiatic schoolgirls were kneeling in their uniforms in various orgasmic states – their heads tipped back, their hands full of entrails – after having cut open their stomachs in the traditional Samurai manner.

'Where'd you get it?' she said, swinging unsteadily round to face him.

The thought that she might actually vomit struck him now for the first time, and while it was one thing, he thought, cleaning up your own spunk, it was quite another clearing up someone else's vomit.

'A shop,' he said, flatly.

'I like it.'

She sat down next to him on the sofa, curling her legs up under her. Her shoes were still on – he wanted to ask her to take them off, in case they left marks on the sofa, but didn't.

She sat picking at her nails, staring at the poster still only she wasn't really looking at it now – she'd become too self-aware.

'What is it you actually do?' she said after a while, her eyes scanning the flat again; making more of a point of it this time.

He was glad he'd got over his tie-dye wall hangings from Brighton phase.

'I'm a reporter.' He kept his eyes on hers over the raised glass of Prosecco.

She let out a short, loud laugh that came from the same cold place as the question. Girls didn't usually ask him questions.

'What?' He tried not to sound hurt; defensive.

'Here? In Burwood?'

Frank didn't say anything.

'Nothing ever happens here.'

'You'd be surprised,' he responded, aware that this time he did sound defensive, but it was a reflex action. 'We've got quite a cache of home-grown serial killers to our name. The acid bath murders?'

She shook her head.

'The wigmaker?'

She shook her head again then stopped. 'Wait – yeah. I heard about him.'

'A Burwood boy. Born and bred. Went to school with him.' He paused. 'Sure, I cover the school fêtes, carnivals, fight to stop the medieval town hall being taken over by Starbucks . . . I do all that shit. But when I'm not doing that shit, I open the bedroom door, and it's like . . .'

'What?'

'Hearing your parents fuck.'

'Totally, revoltingly, not possible.'

He nodded slowly. 'Burwood Studios – that photographer's on East Street? He's taken a lot of photos of children from local dance schools – not always in costume. Danehill School? Three suicides in the past year – all under the age of fourteen. Last Christmas a woman on Carlton Avenue beat her husband to death with a frozen turkey. Frozen meat's one of the most popular murder weapons there is.'

Vicky laughed.

'It's all happening right here in Burwood and *The County Times* won't even cover it.'

'So what d'you do?' she asked, genuinely interested.

'I sell the stories to the national press. I've got an agent and stuff who deals with it . . .'

After a while, Vicky said, 'So why don't you work for the nationals?'

Frank shrugged.

'I mean – what's the point in staying here?'

'I'm staying here for as long as it takes.'

'As long as it takes to do what?'

'Pull this place apart – bring it to its knees. Take yesterday . . .' he carried on quickly, before she had time to give him another one of her tight little smiles – ironic? Condescending? – that were making him nervous.

'I was sent to cover the closure of Burwood's oldest chemist – M.R. Cramplins. They've been chemists for five generations or something, but the latest Mrs Cramplin failed to have any children. Anyway –' Vicky was staring at him now. 'I was sitting there interviewing the Cramplins, chewing on my testicles to keep myself awake, when these schoolgirls walk into the shop. Why shouldn't they? No reason – only they were buying pregnancy testing kits.' Now he had her – *and* the tight little smiles had stopped appearing on her face. 'Again – why shouldn't they?' He paused. 'You want to know why they shouldn't?'

He was using a tone of voice he felt familiar with; the one that told virgins to undress.

'Because these girls – they live in a town with one of the country's lowest teenage pregnancy rates. Okay, it happens, but not to girls like these; these girls weren't even from Danehill School. They hadn't been giving blow jobs on stairwells from the age of eleven or having sex in the school toilets from the age of thirteen. These girls were nice girls. These girls were from Burwood Girls'.'

Silence.

'You were there,' Vicky said at last.

Frank nodded.

'I didn't see you.'

This had been obvious from the moment he bought her that first Tequila slammer at B-52s earlier. At the time the lack of recognition had hurt Frank – who thought of himself as deeply memorable; instantly recognisable.

'Well, I was right there – behind the counter. My photographer took the liberty –' He got up suddenly and pulled a photograph off the fridge door that she hadn't noticed before.

'This doesn't prove anything.' She pulled her leg up so that the knee was under her chin, and studied the shot of Ruth, Saskia and herself, taken only the night before – which already felt like a lifetime ago – as they were about to go into M.R. Cramplins.

'It's not meant to prove anything.'

'Is that why you came on to me tonight?'

'No. I came on to you tonight because I think you're beautiful.'

Frank wasn't lying.

'Why didn't you say something before? This is, like, raw embarrassing.' She pulled her cardigan round her so that it covered her legs as well and only her shoes stuck out the bottom.

'No reason. I'm opening some red wine.'

He got up and went over to the kitchen, watching Vicky tip her head back on the sofa.

'So – you took the test?'

'None of your fucking business,' she said. Then, a few minutes later, 'You said that "girls" – in the plural – bought pregnancy testing kits, but I was the only one.'

He eased himself carefully back onto the sofa so as not to spill the wine.

'According to the female Cramplin one of your friends was in earlier in the week buying the same thing. The tragic looking one.' He drank a mouthful of wine he'd paid a lot for. Paying a lot for things he knew nothing about was a trait of Frank's. 'You okay?'

He was talking about Saskia. He had to be. Vicky saw Saskia again – walking up Dardanelle Drive, past Mr Sutton's house. Saskia never did say what she'd been doing on Dardanelle Drive.

When she didn't respond, Frank said, 'You did know, didn't you – about your friend?'

Vicky shook her head. 'Clearly not.'

'You did take the test,' he said, watching her. 'And it came out positive, didn't it?'

She didn't reply at first. 'How d'you know?'

'So, who was it – boyfriend?'

'I don't have a boyfriend.'

'Immaculate conception?'

'No –'

'Aliens?'

'Not that I remember.'

'So if it isn't God and it isn't an alien – who is it?'

'I'm not saying –'

'Your dad?'

'Fuck off.'

'A one night stand?'

'No – nothing like that.'

Frank put his glass down on the coffee table and opened an old tea caddy. He rolled two joints – sourced from the same dealer Richard Greaves used – and passed one to Vicky.

'Wait. You're getting rid of it, right?'

'Yeah,' Vicky said, ambiguous, suddenly tearful but trying not to show it.

'I mean, I don't want to be responsible for turning your foetus into a disabled foetus or something.'

'This thing's coming out, so what the fuck,' she concluded, viciously.

'So – which teacher was it?' Frank joked, smiling

across the sofa at her – enjoying himself. He'd never seduced a pregnant teenager before.

She jabbed her foot into his thigh.

'Watch my wine.'

'That's fucked up.' She paused. Vicky had been thinking – all night. She'd been thinking while drinking with Frank at B-52s; thinking while talking to Frank here in his flat, and thinking while flirting with Frank. 'But true.'

Frank was shocked – and had to put a lot of effort into not showing it. 'I don't know,' he said, affecting a desperate loucheness, 'the things that go on under the auspices of education.'

She jabbed her foot into his thigh again.

'So – what does he teach?'

'Art,' she said quietly.

'Art,' he repeated, digesting this. 'Young?'

'For a teacher,' she said, realising as she said it that Mr Sutton was probably younger than Frank Barlow.

'Bit of a maverick?'

She nodded, not needing to warm to the idea she'd been fantasising about all afternoon under the influence of Sentinel.

'Doesn't plan on doing it forever – or so he thinks? Puts himself out there as un-con-ven-tion-al?'

'He takes lessons barefoot.'

Frank exploded. 'Wan-ker.' Feeling a sudden, conspicuous and inexplicable rage towards this Impregnator of teenage girls.

Vicky interpreted the rage as chivalric – a confusing notion given that the version of Mr Sutton she was serving up to Frank Barlow was in fact Frank Barlow. 'Yeah –' she agreed, aggressively, the image of Saskia walking towards her up Dardanelle Drive impossible to shake.

'Shit – so, you and him, you –'

'Once,' Vicky said, awkwardly, not looking at Frank any more. Frank was the first person she'd tried out this story on, and hadn't anticipated it going down so well.

'But that's all it takes, right?'

'Obviously,' Vicky counteracted, momentarily impatient with him. Then she started to improvise, pushing the night spent at the party in Pentonville to the back of her mind and giving in to fantasy. 'He was always watching me in class; finding excuses to get me back at break time, lunch . . . after school . . . showing me erotic stuff; going on about form and shadow.'

'Form and shadow,' Frank echoed, as Vicky's face fell suddenly to pieces and she started crying. 'He was grooming you.' He took the glass of wine carefully out of her hands – ever mindful of the Conran sofa – and once he'd done this was happy to make an attempt at comforting her.

'What a total, fucking cliché.' He slipped his hand across her back, unsure how far he could push it because – while without doubt an expert on seventeen-year-old girls – he'd never had one confess to statutory rape by her art teacher before (pretty much what it amounted to, surely), then break down.

She felt relatively suppliant beneath the palm of his practised hand, but that was down to confusion rather than desire. Plus, his diagnostic powers had been shaken during the two months of abstinence following Jenna's decision to leave him and become a Baptist.

'He was like totally predatory,' Vicky mumbled.

Frank, who'd been trying to move away from the

idea of the older, predatory male per se, was relieved
to hear that there was a serial aspect to the seductions.

'Have you told anybody – about being pregnant?'

'My parents.'

'Shit. That must have been heavy.'

'Like off-the-radar heavy.'

'But you're getting rid of it anyway, right?'

'Yeah,' Vicky said, ambiguous, tearful again.

'I'll get us some more wine.'

She stood up. 'I'd better be going.' Then, embarrassed. 'My parents have got no idea where I am.'

'Okay –'

She was going. Frank felt suddenly stranded, alone.
He wanted to know more – about this art teacher – the
likelihood of this other girl, Saskia, being pregnant. This
wasn't just a story; it was an exposé. This really would
bring Burwood to its knees.

'Listen, I can't drive you – I'm way over the limit –
but I can get you a cab.'

'Okay,' Vicky agreed, pleased. She'd never been in a
situation before where somebody had offered to get her
a cab, and felt suddenly grown up.

Not that Frank had actually offered to pay for the
cab, but then – in his experience – these girls always
had stashes of cash on them, doled out by guilt-ridden
middle-class parents.

'Are you doing anything Wednesday?' he said, after
phoning Fairway Cars.

'Wednesday?' She shook her head.

'Why don't you come round and I can cook us
something?'

'I'd like that.'

'Okay – Wednesday it is.' He paused.

She nodded, smiling properly for the first time.

36

'Big house,' the minicab driver said as they pulled up outside number two Park Avenue.

Vicky peered through the window at it, but didn't comment.

She had difficulty getting out from the back seat whose springs had long gone, and caught her legs on something sharp as she finally managed to pull herself out.

The street was full of cars parked for her mother's poker party. The rain had stopped, and it had got much colder.

She had a migraine from the number of pain relieving substances she'd indulged in that evening – combined with Tequila and Prosecco – and no idea what time it was.

There were people in dinner jackets on the drive, whispering, laughing and smoking, and she passed them without even trying to recognise them, aware of their eyes on her as she headed straight for the house.

The front door was open and she walked into the kitchen where she pulled a carton of milk from the fridge, ignoring the bleary comments made to her by a man dancing on his own with a tea cosy on his head – to the club mixes of A-Ha playing on the stereo.

Clutching the carton of milk, Vicky made for the stairs past unfamiliar shoulders, breasts, chests and faces, and the low strung laughter of people who didn't spend enough time with themselves.

A couple were sitting on the foot of the stairs, the man with his knees apart, mumbling to himself while staring at a spot on the wall. The woman leant in close, gripping tightly onto his arm.

Vicky couldn't get past, and the club re-mixes continued to boom emptily around her impregnated with the usual party screams nobody would remember screaming and laughter nobody would remember laughing.

Any minute now she was going to start crying; she was falling to pieces and there was nobody round to help put her back together again. There had to be a bona fide adult here somewhere, but all she could see were drunk strangers. Strangers on the stairs, in the kitchen, the hallway . . . who'd been invited to participate in the myth that was The Hendersons. There were no adults – only grown up children.

'Vick!'

She spun round.

It was Bill looking scared and sober, standing directly behind her.

He grabbed hold of her arms, pulled her hard against him then pushed her away. 'Where the fuck have you been?' He broke off, starting to wipe at her face. 'What's this?'

'Milk,' she said.

'Where the fuck have you been all night?' he said again, not listening. 'You don't go out like that without leaving a note. You don't go out without telling us. You-don't-just-go-out-like-that,' Bill finished, hanging his head, helpless with love, grief, fear and relief.

The couple on the stairs stared, too drunk to move away.

Sylvia, emerging from the sitting room with Dr Fulton in tow, saw Bill on the stairs talking to a young girl who she recognised with a start as their daughter.

'Vicky?'

She swung round to Dr Fulton, standing behind her, and affected a brave, nonplussed smile.

The music – which was loud – suddenly didn't seem loud enough, but this was only because the party sounds had died down. It took Sylvia a while to realise this – she was too busy wondering where she'd put the remote for the sound system – and how to get Bill and Vicky upstairs.

Nobody moved.

'Why didn't you say anything to us?' Bill was no longer shouting, but he could feel himself shaking still.

'Doesn't look like me going out exactly got in the way of the party.' Vicky scratched irritably at the side of her mouth where the rivulets of milk were drying. 'What are you all staring at?'

People started to stir. They unpeeled their backs from walls, emerged from low lit corners, drifted away from the window seat in the dining room, and stood up from where they'd been crouching confidentially on the stairs.

'I was worried,' Bill said, exhausted and unaware of the movement around him.

'This is Burwood, dad. People don't even lock their front doors.'

232

'Where did you go?'

'For a walk – okay?' Vicky was starting to raise her voice again.

Bill, looking lopsided in his dinner suit, said, 'It's gone midnight.'

'So it was a long fucking walk. What's your problem?'

'You don't disappear for over five hours without telling anyone. You're only seventeen, and –'

Sylvia cut in sharply with, 'Bill!'

'I didn't disappear.'

'We didn't know where you were –'

'Well, I wasn't getting drunk, I wasn't doing drugs and I wasn't having sex – okay? Not that that's really an issue any more.'

A couple of people laughed.

'Bill, please –' Sylvia hissed, trying to haul him away from the stairs, but he just shook her off and she ended up bruising her hand, which started swelling. 'Go to your room!' she yelled at Vicky.

But Vicky didn't go to her room.

'We were worried about you – we love you,' Bill said, his voice uneven.

'Yeah, I'm really feeling that love right now.'

Sylvia managed to catch hold of Vicky's arm with her bruised hand. 'You're drunk,' she said, breathless with the pain from her bad hand.

'I'm drunk?'

The sound system had stopped playing.

'Go upstairs,' Sylvia said again, pushing her daughter forcibly towards Bill while grappling with extreme exhaustion and the vague notion that she might still be able to bring the closing moments of the party together.

'I can't stay up there for the WHOLE NINE MONTHS.'

Vicky did then actually go upstairs, but these were the words that stuck as the party came down and the mass exodus took place, spilling furiously out the front door onto the drive. Nobody wanted to be the last man – or woman – out.

Couples exchanged terse, hissing enquiries as to the whereabouts of coats, bags, scarves, and as the rapid departures accelerated, some just gave up and left as they were, running.

Once outside people took to the streets either on foot or in their cars, with the overwhelming sense that they'd made a narrow escape. For a while, breathless from the speed of their departure, they didn't speak. Then they started to blame each other for whatever it was they'd had to leave behind, and argue about whose fault exactly it was. Then there was silence, then there was the gasping, 'Vicky Henderson's pregnant!' As if it was something viral they needed to protect themselves and loved ones from.

The Fultons were the last to leave – Dr Fulton shuffling, unsure, his perpetual optimism dented.

Jill Fulton finished shouldering on a navy wool coat, and turned to face her hostess. 'D'you want me to stay?'

Sylvia stared at her in disbelief, not understanding. 'Why?'

Jill pulled her hair out from under the coat's collar and smiled reassuringly at Sylvia, opening her arms to her.

The ripples started up in her left cheek again, violent and continuous. She felt something drop and started shaking her head to counteract it, while walking towards Jill. She was going to walk into Jill's clashing navy wool and purple satin warmth; a warmth that promised the sort of solutions to life Sylvia didn't have it in her to consider. If she walked into that embrace, life as she knew it would change forever.

She pulled herself up short – against the radiator on the wall opposite, and laughed lightly. 'We're fine, Jill. Hope you enjoyed the party.'

She kept the smile on her face – despite the constant ripples running up the left hand side of it.

'You're sure? I'll stay if you need me –'

Sylvia didn't.

37

Vicky had no idea what time it was when she woke up. There was sunlight moving across the duvet, and wood pigeons in the beeches circling the garden.

She was warm and felt safe, and that was enough.

Then, as the wood pigeons took flight, she became gradually aware of the fact that she was still wearing her clothes from the night before, and that there were people arguing somewhere close by.

It sounded like Tom's voice, but it couldn't be Tom – Tom was on the other side of the Downs.

She drank some water from the tap in the bathroom and went downstairs where an attempt to tidy up, post-party, had clearly been started then abandoned.

The abandoned debris gave the house a meaningless air – as if its purpose was being challenged – and it felt empty.

So empty that Vicky was surprised, when she walked into the sitting room, to see Sylvia standing motion-less by the piano, staring at the photo of Tom; Tom himself, sitting on the edge of the sofa, his eyes on her as she walked through the door, and Bill pressed up against the patio doors, his arm and forehead on the glass, staring out into the garden.

He turned around and smiled at Vicky as she walked into the room – a genuine smile, but weak – then turned back to the window again.

Tom waved.

'What?' Vicky said, looking at everyone.

'I heard –'

Vicky waited. 'About what?' Then remembered she was pregnant. Had they brought Tom home to help chloroform her and get her to the abortion clinic? 'Oh – that.'

'Yeah –'

'Tom's got some news as well,' Sylvia said. There was no life in her voice as she said it. Then, turning to Tom, 'I knew something was wrong – yesterday. I came in here and she was standing by the piano – just like this – holding your photograph. She asked me if it was you.'

Tom flicked Vicky a look. 'It's Grace – she's pregnant.'

'Grace?' Vicky exploded.

Sylvia, looking properly at her daughter for the first time since she'd walked into the room, said, 'You didn't know?'

'We've been keeping it close,' Tom said.

'Why?'

He shrugged.

'But – since when have you and Grace been you and Grace?' Vicky demanded.

Tom opened his hands expansively. 'Since the summer properly – I guess.'

'You guess?' Sylvia put in.

'It started before that – feels like it's always been there.'

237

'Why didn't you say, Tom? I can't believe Grace and you have been seeing each other since the summer and neither of you said anything about it.'

'And now she's saying she's pregnant – and that it's Tom's.'

'Mum,' Tom said, turning to Sylvia, 'she's saying she's pregnant because she is pregnant, and she's saying it's mine because it is mine.'

Bill continued to stare silently out the patio doors at the back garden, half wondering about the fox, and making no effort to follow the conversation going on behind him.

Sylvia appealed to Vicky. 'Has she been with anyone else that you know of?'

'Mum!' Tom yelled. 'When will you get it? We're in love.'

It was hopeless. The décor and soft furnishings in the sitting room at number two Park Avenue didn't do Tom's declaration any justice, and failed to give it any resonance.

Vicky – momentarily stunned, but believing her brother – said, 'I can't believe neither of you said, like, anything about this.'

'We didn't want people trampling over it.'

'Well they'll be trampling soon,' Sylvia said, almost triumphantly. 'And they won't stop until there's nothing left, Tom.' She pressed her hand tightly against her left cheek as the now familiar fluttering started up.

'She's not keeping it, is she?' Vicky asked.

'Apparently she is,' Sylvia said, before Tom had time to reply.

'She is?'

'We want this baby,' Tom said. 'It's *our* baby.'

'That's not fair!' Vicky rounded on Sylvia.

'Not fair?'

'If Grace gets to keep her's.'

'Well, hopefully her mother'll talk some sense into her. If not, I'm going round there later myself.'

'Mum –'

'This is about you, Tom – and the rest of your life.'

'I don't believe it,' Vicky said loudly. 'Every time –'

'Every time what?' Sylvia rounded on her, impatient.

'Every time I do something, Tom's already done it before me. I can't even get fucking pregnant –'

The front door bell rang.

Nobody moved.

It rang again.

'I'll get that, shall I?' Sylvia yelled suddenly at her immobile family.

It was Jill Fulton, the doctor's wife, in an old Flora London Marathon T-shirt – surely Jill hadn't run the marathon? – jeans and moccasins. She smiled brightly – bravely – at Sylvia.

'I just want you to know that if there's anything Vicky – or you – want to talk about, I'm here for you. Face to face – on the phone.' Jill trailed off.

Sylvia was outraged.

What right did Jill think she was exercising, talking to her like this – in an outfit Sylvia wouldn't have considered being the casualty of a hit and run in. And the tone – when *she* wasn't the one wallpapering her house in discontinued Laura Ashley.

There was something predatory about Jill's assaulting her with her charity like this, here in her own home. But then Sylvia had long suspected Jill of being the sort of person who compulsively gravitates towards disaster – towards the incapable, the incapacitated, and the incontinent. There was something gluttonous about it – and Jill did have weight issues. Well, she wasn't getting anything off them; she'd just have to go hungry – could starve to death for all Sylvia cared.

'Sylvia – are you okay?'

'What's that?'

'Are you okay?'

Sylvia gave her an alarmingly wide smile. 'I'm fine – fine. I was just wondering –'

'Yes?' Jill prompted her. Then, before Sylvia had time to pick up her thread, she said, 'Look – why don't you pop over.'

'Where?'

'Well – to mine. We could talk.'

'About what?'

'Vicky's pregnancy.'

'Vicky isn't pregnant.'

'Sylvia – I was there, last night, at the party. We all were.'

'Oh, that –' Sylvia let out a short, wild laugh. 'Vicky was drunk last night – I think we all were.' She felt the rippling start up in her left cheek, and saw Jill noticing it. 'She just made the whole thing up.'

'Made it up?'

'She's probably had some sort of undiagnosed attention deficit disorder since she was born.'

'You're saying Vicky was only pretending to be pregnant?'

'For attention – to piss me off – who knows? It's not the first time it's happened.'

'She's pretended to be pregnant before?'

'No – it was bulimia last time.'

'But –' Jill paused – momentarily at a loss, Sylvia noted with satisfaction. 'Why lie about something it would ultimately be almost impossible to physically fabricate?'

'I know,' Sylvia agreed. Then, cheerfully, 'Twisted, isn't it?'

'But – have you seen anybody about it?'

Sylvia made a show of considering this. 'I read a piece in a magazine about phantom pregnancies. There was this woman who was so desperate to have a baby that she convinced herself she was pregnant . . . right up to thinking she was going into labour.'

Jill wasn't listening. She was writing something down and Sylvia, staring at Jill's nails as she wrote, was disgusted to note that Jill clearly bit them. She had some stuff in the medical cabinet that she'd bought for Tom to try and get him to break his habit – maybe she should offer it to Jill.

Jill was handing her something. She glanced at the name and number on the piece of paper then up at Jill.

'She's very good –'

'At what?'

'Family therapy.'

After Sylvia left the room, Bill turned to face his children, observing them with an ambivalent warmth.

'So – what are you going to do?' he said to Tom.

'About what?'

'The rest of your life.'

Tom sighed. 'You really want to know?'

'Now seems like as good a time as any,' Bill said, sitting down on the sofa opposite and putting his hands comfortably behind his head.

'I graduate at the end of this year,' Tom stated, uncomfortable, using his hands a lot, which he only ever did when he got nervous. 'The baby's coming in the summer –'

Bill sat and listened, without interrupting.

'And over the next three years Grace will be doing her degree. At Cambridge.'

'She's still going?' Vicky asked.

Ignoring this, Tom said, 'And I was thinking of doing a part-time course at agricultural college.'

Bill sat up, surprised. 'Agricultural college?'

'It's a sort of follow-on to my degree – ecology, climate change . . . how it's affecting farming.'

'I never knew –'

'And there's this unit researching cultivation on Mars – I'd love to get in on that,' Tom finished, speaking quickly, shyly.

'Mars,' Bill echoed, preoccupied, as if it was a place he'd once been to as a much younger man. 'Mars,' he said again.

'Who knows – maybe one day Grace and me'll get to plant a field up on Mars.'

'Yeah,' Bill agreed, letting out an excited laugh. 'I can see you on Mars.' He paused, following his own train of thought. 'I used to think about becoming a farmer. Cattle – Australia. I spent a year there when I was about your age, castrating bulls.'

Just then Tom's phone went off.

'Hey – Ali. No, I'm good. I can't talk right now. What's that? Oh – oh, okay.'

He came off the phone as Sylvia walked slowly back into the room.

'That was Ali.'

She looked about her, distracted. 'Where?'

'On the phone – thanking me for a charm I never sent her. A pagoda or something – for her bracelet.'

'The Tiffany one?' Vicky said, suddenly irate.

'How would I know?'

'That was me,' Sylvia said, running her hand absently along the top of the piano.

'Why, mum?'

Sylvia gave a short, empty laugh.

'We looked at that one together – you knew I wanted it,' Vicky said. 'I thought you were getting it for me, but you weren't – it was for Tom.'

'Ali,' Sylvia corrected her.

'Same difference.'

Sylvia stared blankly at her.

Bill, who hadn't been following any of this, chuckled to himself and gave Tom a sudden sideways glance. 'Mars, eh?'

the burwood four

38

Sylvia Henderson was kneeling on the bench behind the kitchen unit that concealed the microwave, peering through a CNV150 night vision scope at the front garden and drive. The night vision scope was one of Bill's impulsive post-redundancy purchases that she'd been too depressed at the time – yes, she too had been depressed for a while when Bill first got his news, but unlike Bill she'd got over her depression – to question why he'd bought it. Something to do with bats – and later, foxes. It didn't matter. The CNV150's built-in infra-red illuminator was perfect for uncovering the stuff of suburban dreams – and nightmares. From the rarely seen crossbills spotted by keen amateur ornithologist, Mick Kedge over on Fletcher Way, to the panoply of British media on the trail of a suburban scandal involving four pregnant teenagers, now detected – with aching joints from kneeling – in the early hours by Sylvia Henderson.

There were two squatting by the small shed built to house all one hundred recycling bins, one actually nesting inside the Pampas grass on the drive, and another just by the drive of the evangelical, sci-fi-reading divorcee opposite. By 9:00 a.m. their number would have multiplied tenfold.

Sylvia chuckled to herself – calmly and without the aid of Diazepam.

Yesterday she'd fallen victim to this Paparazzi stakeout. She'd gone out with some aluminium cartons from the Mr Li's takeaway they'd had the night before – the first that year, typically – and five photographers had appeared from nowhere and started taking pictures. Of her. At first she thought they were council employees, sent to garner evidence of misuse of re-cycling bins, and in her panic she'd dropped the cartons, which fell about her feet only to be picked up by an icy north-easterly that blew them gratingly across the drive.

Then she realised.

'Sylvia – over here.' They knew her name? 'Where's Vicky, Sylvia?'

Too mortified by the debris from last night's take-away to think straight, she yelled inconsequentially, 'This is private property!' Then ran, stumbling in Vicky's UG slippers, back towards the house, hoping that they'd at least get some of the detached redbrick Edwardian façade in the picture – the Virginia creeper was at its best – because it was so much more indicative of who they, the Hendersons, really were than the wind-strewn cartons from Mr Li's now blowing around the advancing bank of Paparazzi. Please God let them get the house and – in the right hand corner of the frame – the new Lexus 4×4. The cameras snapped, clicked, chattered, juddered and whirred at Sylvia's stumbling retreat, the golden dragon on the back of her kimono rippling energetically. She never even thought – afterwards from the relative safety of her kitchen – to warn Rachel next door.

She was too busy booking emergency appointments with Barrie at Kutz, and Dr Forbes-Botox.

The arrival of the media had changed everything; checked the demise of The Hendersons in a way Sylvia herself, single-handed, simply no longer had the energy to do. She'd managed to fend off what was beginning to feel like an evolutionary culling once – at the time of Bill's redundancy – but this unexpected horror involving her children was beyond her.

She'd spent the days since the poker party in a Diazepam haze, refusing to speak to them and only managing one trip out – to the lingerie section of M&S where, in a vertiginous trance, she stocked up on ultra support briefs for Vicky. To stop *it* from showing – until she talked her round.

Other than this, she just about had the stamina to pursue low level, homespun attempts at abortion by compulsively giving Vicky food stuffs and herbal supplements harmful to pregnant women. Vicky succumbed unwittingly to this diet of Acai berry tablets, soft cheese (listeria), undercooked meat (toxoplasmosis), and raw shellfish.

For the first time in her life, Sylvia found herself seriously considering suicide, and often ran through in her head a list of the most pain-free options, the idea of an overdose gaining momentum to an almost companionable level.

Then yesterday morning she realised, with a frayed sense of enlightenment, just how lucrative the pregnancy she'd never considered as anything other than a total disaster – for herself, primarily, but also Vicky – could be. The chain of grimy and inconsequential events was broken and Sylvia decided not to die. The very thing that filled her with the worst fear – other people knowing – vanished with the realisation that while some people knowing might be 'shame', many people knowing was 'celebrity'.

Humming, she crawled towards the stairs and up the first few treads before evolving into a bi-ped once more. She went into the en-suite and – bypassing the medicine cabinet with its tri-coloured array of Valium – took a shower.

After this she went into the bedroom and, ignoring Bill's grunting protest, switched on the lights and laid out some Fahri she hadn't worn since her London days. She then chose Bill's suit, shirt and tie before crossing the hallway and going into Vicky's room.

The presence of Paparazzi outside the Henderson home thus led to an impromptu family breakfast.

'Okay,' Sylvia said, excited, pouring coffee for Bill and her, 'We've got two behind the wheelie bins, one in the Pampas grass – and one on the freak's drive.'

'The freak?'

'Opposite – the one who tried to get me to join her Sci-Fi Reading Group.'

Bill, interested, said, 'I didn't know there was a local Sci-Fi reading group – why didn't she ask me?'

Ignoring this – nothing more than a depressive's attempt at underplaying events – Sylvia said, 'And when you leave the house, you should put your sunglasses on.'

'I'd rather just go out there and tell them to piss off.'

'These people don't respond to threats, Bill – and we need them on our side.'

'For what?'

Sylvia treated this as a rhetorical question. 'According to Tom we're on the front page of every newspaper in the country.'

'We? When did you speak to Tom?'

'Earlier.'

'Earlier when? It's only half seven now.'

Bill carried on the laborious process of eating the new porridge Sylvia's nutritionist had recommended – with added spelt and cranberry.

'When we leave the house –' Sylvia turned to Vicky, taking her in '– just walk straight towards the car – I'll make sure it's open. You should wear sunglasses as well.'

'Surely she's not going in to school today?'

'She needs to go to school, Bill – she's got A Levels she's meant to be sitting.'

Vicky shrugged, thinking about Mr Sutton. Then pushed the porridge she hadn't touched to one side, looking at Bill. 'I'm not going through with it – I've been thinking, and thinking, and I just can't.'

'Can't go through with what?' Sylvia said, too pre-occupied with trying to decide which sunglasses Vicky ought to wear to confront the nation's media to really follow what Vicky was saying.

'I'm sorry, dad.'

'It's your decision, Vick. Come here –' Bill said, heavily as his daughter allowed herself to be held for the first time in weeks. 'Everything happens for a reason, right? We're here for you – whatever decision you make. I told you that.'

'You're not mad at me or anything?'

'No,' he said, truthfully. 'First thing I felt just then when you told me was relief.'

As they pulled apart, Sylvia – startled – noted two things. Firstly, that the left-hand lapel on Bill's Boss suit was smudged with foundation that came up peach on the black wool, and secondly, that Vicky had been crying.

'Your make-up!' she cried out instinctively then, latently picking up on the conversation. 'Decision about what?'

Bill and Vicky were both staring at her. 'The abortion,' they said together.

'You're getting an abortion?' Sylvia yelled, thinking about the exclusives she'd been talking about all day yesterday with various top-end people.

'No, Syl – she's keeping it.' Bill waited. 'We'll work it out,' he said, grabbing hold of her hands and pulling on them in an attempt to get her to focus on him.

'I was talking to Jill,' Vicky said.

'Jill?' Sylvia interrupted.

'Jill Fulton – she said I could talk to her any time, so I did. She went into all the details about procedure and stuff, and that's when I decided I just couldn't –'

'Jill?' Sylvia said again.

'Look at the space we've got here.' Bill rotated his head round the kitchen. 'I could take early retirement –'

Sylvia at last caught up with him and pulled her hands away. 'Early retirement?'

'To look after the baby.' It was the most animated Bill had been for years.

'But dad,' Vicky put in, worried, 'I don't want to keep it.'

'What d'you mean you don't want to keep it?'

'I mean – not after. I was thinking maybe adoption or something.'

'Adoption?' Bill stared at her. His chest felt tight. 'But, Vicky – I know you don't feel it now, but that's your child you're talking about. Our grandchild. Syl –' he said, trying to grab hold of her arm again.

Sylvia shook him off without even looking at him.

'Shut up, Bill. It's the first sensible thing she's said.

I'm not even fifty – I've got no intention of becoming a grandmother.'

'Don't worry – I wouldn't inflict that on any child.'

Sylvia turned to Bill, expectant, but Bill was almost in a trance now with the pain in his chest, and trying not to slip off the stool.

'I don't get it,' Vicky carried on, watching Sylvia. 'One minute I'm in ultra-support hell, and under house arrest until I agree to an abortion then the next – when I tell you I'm going to have this baby – you act like you couldn't give a shit. I thought you'd be, like, completely mad.'

'Mad?' Sylvia shook her head. She had to play Vicky carefully on this one. 'People can change.'

'Yeah –' Vicky conceded, unconvinced. 'Want to know what made me change my mind?'

'What?' Sylvia asked, uninterested.

Neither of them noticed Bill disappear down the hallway into the sitting room where he observed, through the patio doors – still in a daze – winter's first frost and a heavy orange sun. He shut his eyes and raised his head to the sun – which had risen over the lip of beech trees and was now shining directly through the doors – and felt another sudden dark tightening of his chest, much stronger this time. He held onto the curtains for a few seconds before collapsing onto the floor.

He came to a minute later, to find himself staring up at a tear-drop chandelier he had no recollection of.

Sylvia and Vicky didn't hear Bill thud to the sitting room floor after suffering a minor heart attack. The house was well upholstered enough to absorb small traumas such as this, which meant that his wife and daughter, arguing in the kitchen, remained oblivious to the fact that he was just down the hallway regaining consciousness and hauling himself back to his feet with the aid of the Sanderson curtains.

'I realised – after talking to Jill – that I don't have it in me to kill.'

Sylvia, disconcertingly, burst out laughing – with the bottom half of her face. 'To kill?'

'That's what abortion is, isn't it – murder?' Vicky insisted, adamant about the morality of her choice because she knew that murder had nothing to do with it.

'That's one way of looking at it – if you live on a tree-lined avenue with loving parents and a monthly fucking allowance.'

'Loving parents? Is that your definition of love – letting me live here rent free?'

'You've got no idea –'

'About what?'

'About anything, that's what. My point is – morality costs. It's a luxury item the majority of people can't afford – a Louis Vuitton handbag.'

'But you've got a Louis fucking Vuitton handbag – upstairs,' Vicky yelled.

'It's a FAKE!'

Sylvia and Vicky were staring at each other in silence as Bill appeared at the foot of the stairs then crossed the kitchen slowly and purposefully. His heart felt heavier than usual and it made him lurch rather than walk, but neither Sylvia nor Vicky commented on this.

As the front door opened, a crowd – with cameras – appeared on the drive only to drift away again when they realised he was alone.

Bill tried to think of something to say. 'Nice morning,' he mumbled and started to walk towards the park, beautiful under the frost and slowly rising sun. By the time he got to Pinnacle Insurance's offices on the other side of the park, the rising sun had been unexpectedly cut off by a bank of cloud.

Sylvia, resplendent in Fahri, made her way slowly, majestically towards the carefully parked Lexus. The crowd had multiplied. Photographers, journalists, TV crews – whoever, whatever they were – carpeted her immediate line of vision.

She opened the car with the remote, stretching her arms in a way that showed she worked out to opera. The Lexus responded to the remote with its usual barrage of high performance electronic sounds as Sylvia stood, with her legs slightly but provocatively parted, and her head tilted back in its wraparounds. Despite the morning's promising start, she felt the first few spots of rain, but ignored them – holding the pose.

Here was Vicky.

Running, lopsided, towards the Lexus, her cardigan pulled round her and up over her head – the sunglasses falling off, at an angle.

Sylvia quickly shut the car doors, once again using the remote – if she let Vicky into the car now, the only shot they'd have of her was stumbling across the drive looking like a recent convert to Islam – and made her way towards her daughter, who was spinning on the spot, terrified.

'Just open it mum!' she screamed, banging frantically on the car windows.

Even Sylvia was surprised at the ferocity with which Vicky clung to her as she re-opened the car.

The fraught mother/daughter embrace – the first in over a decade, and one that enabled Sylvia at close quarters to surreptitiously pull the cardigan down, and fluff up Vicky's hair – was caught on camera.

Sylvia was just making her way slowly round the front of the car – Vicky still clinging to her – when the front door to number four opened and Rachel and Ruth Dent appeared.

Sylvia, distraught at the distraction caused by the Dents, waited by the bonnet of the Lexus, keeping her abdomen pulled in and ignoring Vicky's scared face.

Then, before she had time to react, Vicky – with most of the crowd following – was gone, straight over the wall, using the branches of the pear tree that hung over both properties, headed for Rachel's car.

'I'll take them,' Rachel shouted over the wall to Sylvia, and above the noise – as Vicky flew into the back seat next to Ruth, tipping her head onto Ruth's shoulder while Ruth sat staring out the window, just as scared, and nervously stroked Vicky's hair and right ear.

Rachel, worried, glanced at them in the rear view mirror before opening the window as they pulled off the drive, yelling, 'Just leave us alone!'

It was shameful, Sylvia thought, watching Rachel from the bonnet of the Lexus as she screamed at the media. They weren't meant to be actually communicating with these people.

39

At number eighteen Willow Drive, over on the Meadowside Estate, Grace sat at the end of Nicole's unmade, optimistically king-size bed, unaware she was swinging her legs as she stared out the window at the rain then back at her mother, who was standing in her underwear, holding onto the open wardrobe doors in an attitude of nervous despair. The wardrobe was part of a legacy of G-Plan furniture from the previous elderly tenant of the house. On the matching dresser there was a figurine of a girl with an umbrella, and a miniature straw donkey – mementoes from a forgotten Spanish holiday – as well as a china pot with some locks of hair in.

'You don't have to come,' Grace said for the hundredth time.

Nicole ignored her and continued to stare into the wardrobe.

Grace, sighing, turned back to the rain, now heavy and relentless.

'Should I wear a suit?' Nicole said, after a while.

Grace shrugged. 'I don't know.'

Neither of them knew.

Nicole pulled out the only suit in the wardrobe. 'I bought this for Aunt Irene's funeral. I think.'

'Why didn't you buy a black suit?'

'Black wasn't in the sale.'

She started to get into the suit.

'Was Angela okay about giving you the time off work?'

'She was fine – why?'

'Nothing – just making conversation.'

'What time is it?'

'No idea.' Grace hauled herself off the bed and went downstairs to check the only clock in the house, which was the one on the cooker. 'Half eight,' she yelled up the stairs, then went back into the kitchen, her eyes scanning the debris on the benches. She had time to clear them before they left, but didn't. This feeling of inertia was new to her, and one of the few things that actually reminded her she was pregnant – something, disconcertingly, she often forgot. Probably because it was barely showing yet, and she just couldn't conceive that the outcome of the whole thing was going to be a child; her child.

Upstairs, Nicole – now in the suit – sat down on the end of the bed where it was still warm from Grace and lit one of the cigarettes she'd started smoking again.

She screwed up the left side of her face as she inhaled – a habit she'd acquired when she first started smoking, at fifteen, before she got addicted to nicotine.

She wasn't thinking about anything much and, when she got up to drop the stub in an empty cup by the side of the bed, was surprised to find herself dressed when she had no memory of getting into the suit.

'You ready?' she said to Grace a few minutes later as she walked into the kitchen.

Grace nodded, thinking that Nicole looked like she was going for an interview.

'I can do this on my own. Honestly.'

'Actually, Grace,' Nicole said, sounding tired. 'You can't. Did you take your iron pills?'

'I took them earlier.'

'You've got to take the pills – you were anaemic anyway – before this.'

'Mum – I took them.'

'I'm just saying, that's all.'

'I know you're just saying, and I'm just saying I took them.'

'Right.' Nicole paused. 'Car keys.' She started to rummage through the usual places and found them, eventually, in a basket full of elastic bands, pens that didn't work, and staples.

They left the house.

Nothing could have prepared them for the media barrage positioned behind the dying privet hedge at the end of the front garden.

40

Mrs Harris, Headmistress of Burwood Girls', was sitting behind her desk in an office she'd waited a long time to occupy.

Outside it was raining heavily, but the only light she had on was a desk lamp, which cast an intense halo of light over the pad she was writing in, and not much else.

She was a devout woman – a devotion fuelled from an early age by doubt, having seen Neil Armstrong's lunar landing as a child and surmised that on his way to the moon, Neil Armstrong passed through no place that could clearly be identified as Heaven.

This coming Sunday she was preaching at the low-rise Baptist Church she'd been a lay preacher at for the past twenty years, and was now going over some notes for a sermon she'd made the night before – primarily to take her mind off the fact that Grace Cummings and her mother had requested an appointment with her that morning. She had no idea what it was they wanted to see her about because Mrs Harris – unlike her PA, Lichelle, Burwood's only half-Somalian – hadn't yet laid eyes on a copy of the *Sun*.

She'd never properly met Mrs Cummings before, but knew she had two different children by two different partners and that both had walked out on her, leaving her a single mother. Mrs Harris felt no sympathy as this thought passed through her head, just a vague distaste – as though the situation came down to a lack of hygiene rather than a complex set of circumstances and personalities. Mrs Harris rejected, out of hand, life's complexities.

In her mind, Grace's story was simple: she'd risen above her inauspicious beginnings – single mother/ multiple fathers/council house – and been touched by talent. Grace had been given a gift; she'd been chosen, elected, and Mrs Harris felt an urge to see God's gifts fulfilled – and Grace succeed in life in a way she never had her own daughter. Which was why she had been unsettled to note – in September – what could only be described as an alien sensuality emitting from Grace. Not that this distracted her from her duties as Head Girl, which she took as seriously as Mrs Harris had anticipated she would. It was just that there was some-thing not quite right – barely discernable, but still, not quite right – about the way she held herself.

Mrs Harris wasn't an attractive woman, and had suffered very few physical temptations in life; some-thing that enabled her to preach propriety and abstinence to the girls with ease. She had no particu-lar feeling for men in general because they'd never had any particular feeling for her. She shared the planet with them, and was married to one. That was it. But since her appointment as Headmistress, she did enjoy having some of the younger male members of staff – such as Mr Sutton – in her office. At these moments, she felt a latent, burgeoning sexuality that sent her, late at night and in the privacy of her office at home, onto websites with adult content. She buried the shame of these late-night sessions by delivering favourite assembly maxims. Such as – *dress as you would expect to be addressed* – while stood up on stage behind her podium, in her Primark suit. She delivered the same banal maxims on the paths to success and roads to hell week after week.

Mrs Harris had been Deputy Head when the old Head left, and put in for the post when it was advertised, without hesitation. Ambition was a secret vanity – vice, even – of hers. She was passed over. An external applicant – Ms Russell – was appointed instead. An appointment backed up by a strong majority on the Board of Governors who decided that what Burwood Girls' needed was something new . . . a maverick . . . visionary.

Despite the humiliation, and in spite of the humiliations, Mrs Harris stayed on – her God was testing her – festered and prayed while Ms Russell brought in a flurry of gimmicky curriculum innovations: Transcendental Yoga . . . separate assemblies for the minority population of Muslims at the school . . . a weekly sexual health clinic. There was even talk of getting rid of the school uniform.

It was at around this time that all those good, honest, hard working-parents who'd put so much effort into getting their girls into the school got wind of the fact that a maverick visionary who'd turned round a chain of London sink schools was experimenting with their children. The Board of Governors, that enthusiastic body of electors, finally got cold feet.

This just wasn't Burwood.

And even though – for one year only – they got to number three on the League tables, a unanimous vote of no confidence was taken in Ms Russell and she was asked to leave.

Burwood had had its fill of 'something new'.

Mrs Harris was approached by the Board of Governors – the same Board who'd looked so wearily on her steadfast mediocrity only a year before – and invited to re-apply for the post of Headmistress. Because Mrs Harris knew Burwood; knew what Burwood was.

And this time – a year later than anticipated, but with just as much prayer – the Board of Governors . . . God Himself, elected Mrs Harris to be Headmistress of Burwood Girls', and she gave thanks for this by making God welcome once more in the halls, corridors and classrooms of the school.

So Mrs Harris's reign started, and although she would never inspire, she could at least control.

It seemed, if anything, even darker in the office now.

It was still raining.

There was nothing she could do about it, but she wished it would stop. She turned her attention sharply back to the sparsely annotated pad in front of her where she'd written an analogy about somebody who survives breast cancer (the Head of Art was the inspiration for this character) and who goes into their local post office to buy stamps. There's a long queue and she's told she can use the stamp machines to buy stamps, but replies, 'The stamp machines don't ask me how my chemotherapy went.'

It was no good – she couldn't keep her mind on stamps and chemotherapy. It kept drifting back to Grace – Grace as she had been when she appointed her Head Girl, and Grace when she returned to school in September, admitting to herself now for the first time that the disparity was marked.

263

Thinking about this disparity led her to the graffiti in school, and the fact that her mind had unwittingly made this connection, worried her even more.

Burwood Girls' had the same problem with graffiti as other schools, but Mrs Harris knew – although nobody else actually said – that the problem had become much worse since she became Head.

The graffiti gave her nightmares, growing in her unconscious mind . . . the words spiralling out in vicious, sylised felt tip . . . unstoppable.

No matter how many times she told herself that God Himself was the first graffiti artist – Daniel 5, *Mene mene tekel upharsin* – and Belshazzar's palace walls, the first blog site.

She woke up screaming.

According to Mr Harris.

He didn't ask why.

She now carried out spot checks on all the toilets – including staff ones – on a weekly basis, and no matter what had been painted over the week before there was always more writing on the wall. Here were the real chronicles of Burwood Girls' – the news that didn't make the newsletter or website or League tables or Ofsted reports.

There was always something about the younger male members of staff – predictably violent, smutty, erotic – and the art teacher, Mr Sutton, often made an appearance.

Last week, however, in the lower school toilets – the lower school, Mrs Harris had commented to the caretaker who accompanied her, and whose face remained unreadable – something much more disturbing had appeared. In conjunction with Grace and three other girls.

She realised that she knew exactly why Grace and her mother were coming to see her – had known as soon as the appointment was made.

A storm really was breaking over them and she inadvertently found herself poised; waiting – unsurprised when her PA, Lichelle, appeared in the doorway to the office holding a newspaper. It was a copy of the *Sun*, and was being proffered to her with apologies.

'I didn't know whether you'd seen – I didn't know what to do.'

The headline ran: THE BURWOOD FOUR, and underneath the headline there was a picture of three girls.

'There are only three of them,' Mrs Harris observed, then started to read, then stopped then started again.

On the floor above the Headmistress's office, a similar window with less in the way of height was crammed full of faces belonging to staff making the most of their pre-timetable freedom.

The Common Room had the same view of the world as Mrs Harris, only the occupants of the Common Room had already thumbed to tatters three copies of the *Sun*.

'I think,' Ms Hadley observed, balanced on her crutches close to the window, 'Burwood just lost its eighth-place ranking of towns in the UK with the lowest teenage pregnancy rate.'

On the floor below, the two women stared out the window, each as uncertain as the other what exactly – according to their job description – they were meant to do. They carried on staring as Grace Cummings and her mother – Mrs Harris presumed it was Grace's mother trying to hold onto a yellow umbrella that was collapsing over her head and shoulders – pressed through the crowd of photographers. Those *were* photographers at the gate, she realised with horror.

'You've taken the phone off the hook,' Mrs Harris stated, realising suddenly that she'd been aware of the silence all morning. Then, turning back to the window. 'They've got TV crews down there as well. Are they allowed to do that without prior notification?'

They weren't going to bring her down with this. She wasn't going to let that happen.

Lichelle didn't respond to the question.

'The other girls – are they in school today?'

'I'll check.'

'Wait – if they are, I want you to have them sent to me.'

This command was followed by the sound of the door to Lichelle's office opening and the next minute a soaking wet Grace and her mother, struggling with the now completely broken yellow umbrella, appeared – the water running off them and onto the carpet where it formed circles around their feet.

41

Lichelle was hyperventilating and forgot to take Nicole Cummings' umbrella off her, which meant she walked into Mrs Harris's office still carrying it.

The umbrella was dripping over Nicole's feet and the floor and she didn't know what to do with it.

'Please –' Mrs Harris said, indicating two chairs in front of the acre of desk and staring, pointedly, at the umbrella as if it was part of some initiative test.

The umbrella had left a trail of wet pockmarks across the office floor. At a loss, Nicole sat down, dropped it by the side of her chair, and undid her coat, which was sodden.

As she did so, Mrs Harris noted with horror that Nicole was wearing exactly the same suit as her. On over £80,000 a year, Mrs Harris didn't have to shop at Primark, but she'd made a conscious decision to out of a higher sense of purpose – and that was humility.

She nodded at Grace, who looked unwell and utterly devoid of the tearful gratitude she'd expressed the last time she sat in that very same chair – the day of her appointment to Head Girl.

Now the rain-battered, media-battered Cummingses were staring expectantly at her through the semi-darkness.

She didn't look at Grace. Her focus was on Nicole Cummings, the short woman sitting in front of her – and wearing the same suit as her – on the other side of the desk.

Mrs Harris had up until now, she realised, privately thought of Grace as an orphan – a foundling in need of salvation. These thoughts were hard to account for in the presence of Grace's natural mother. Out the corner of her eye, she saw Grace glance sideways at the photo montage of her recent trip to the Sudan.

When Nicole eventually stopped coughing, the office was too silent.

A silence interrupted by Grace saying, 'I'm pregnant.'

She made an effort, after saying it, to look directly at Mrs Harris.

Nobody said anything.

Nicole, making strange sniffing sounds, was looking proudly at her daughter.

Mrs Harris was again reminded that Nicole was Grace's mother and felt another wave of jealousy and resentment.

She'd often looked at Grace herself in that way.

Now mother and daughter were watching her, and all she could think to do was nod slowly.

'Right. I see.'

Nobody said anything.

'How pregnant?' she said to Grace.

'About two months. I think.'

'You think. And I presume you've considered all your options –'

Nicole cut in with, 'We've been through that –'

Ignoring this and keeping her eyes on Grace, Mrs Harris continued. 'You're only seventeen.'

'I've tried telling her,' Nicole put in.

Mrs Harris wished she'd stop.

'I've made up my mind – even though it's going to be difficult.'

'Difficult? You've got no idea,' Nicole said.

'But it doesn't change things –' her daughter insisted, stubborn, and suddenly sullen with defiance, the tears close to breaking.

'But, Grace,' Mrs Harris said, expansive, 'it changes everything.'

'In what way?'

'No obtuseness,' Mrs Harris warned her sharply. 'Not from you, Grace.'

Nicole sat back in her chair; aware that she was dropping out of the discussion, if that's what they were having; relieved to have a third person in on this.

'I'm not being obtuse – I just don't see how my being pregnant changes things.'

Nicole snorted and crossed her arms, giving an angry sideways look at a certificate framed on the wall.

'I still want to go to Cambridge; still want to work for NASA. Those things aren't going to change.'

'You're not taking into account the practical considerations of raising a child, Grace. The financial implications –'

'I can work.'

'And study for your degree and look after a baby? Grace –' Mrs Harris said, sadly.

'Why's everyone being so negative?' Grace exploded.

'Realistic,' Mrs Harris corrected her. 'You'll have to inform the university – I have no idea what they'll say.'

'I've got an unconditional offer.'

'There's no such thing as an unconditional offer in practice.'

'That's what it says – on the paper,' Nicole confirmed aggressively.

'On paper, yes, but in practice – When's the due date?'

Grace glanced at Nicole, inadvertently bringing her back into the conversation.

'End of June,' Nicole confirmed, defensive.

'June,' Mrs Harris repeated slowly, 'When all the exams are.'

'So I'll be finished by then.'

'If the baby comes when it's meant to. Which they rarely do. What if it comes a month early?'

'I am here,' Nicole said loudly, ambivalently. 'And nothing's going to stop her sitting those exams – I'll make sure of it.'

Mrs Harris rejected this relatively simple solution, insisting instead on hypothetically sensational scenarios. 'What if there are complications?'

'She's sitting those exams. Whatever,' Nicole stated – aggressively, Mrs Harris thought.

'And I am going to Cambridge.'

'You'll have to speak to your Admissions tutor.'

'What are they going to say? No – because I'm pregnant?'

'They could do.'

'On what grounds?'

'Grace – you have to understand the reality of all this.'

'I do. I do understand – why d'you keep going on about it when I don't have a choice?' The tears were threatening again.

Mrs Harris could see them, and she felt Grace was

suddenly much closer to her. They were at the turning point. 'Who's making you feel that you don't have a choice?' She paused, only half expecting an answer. The tears had broken and were moving slowly down Grace's cheeks. 'When you do,' she insisted quietly, 'when you absolutely do.'

The office had, if anything, become darker, and the rain outside, heavier. There was a stillness now in the room that Mrs Harris hadn't intentionally achieved.

They were poised – on the brink – and she wanted, more than anything in that moment, to save Grace.

Then Nicole Cummings did something terrible. She got out of her chair and went over to Grace, taking hold of her and mumbling something that sounded reassuring and that Mrs Harris couldn't hear.

The poise was broken.

'Mrs Cummings – would you mind just giving me a few moments with Grace,' Mrs Harris commanded.

Nicole held tightly onto her daughter before pulling awkwardly away, hesitating then standing up straight – suddenly taller than she'd seemed when she first walked in.

Mrs Harris was once more confronted with the suit they had in common, which looked different on Nicole. It disconcerted her all over again and made her feel suddenly less sure of herself; as though she might do something irrational or unpredictable.

She had to get Nicole out the room.

Nicole went into the outer office, sat down in a chair that made the suit skirt cling with static to her tights, and waited.

A few minutes later she stood up and went over to the window, stopping at Lichelle's abandoned desk where the phone was off the hook still and the *Sun* lying across her keyboard.

Momentarily distracted by the PA's screensaver – crashing meteors – Nicole looked over the front page without seeing it.

Then she saw. 'Fuck.'

42

Once the door to the outer office was shut, Mrs Harris went back to her desk, sitting on the edge of it with her hands in her lap.

'It's your choice, Grace,' she said.

'I've been through it all –'

'With your mother.'

'It's not her baby,' Grace pointed out. 'And Tom and me, we want this baby.'

'Tom?'

'My boyfriend.'

'And this . . . this . . . it's your boyfriend's?'

'I just said it was.'

'And you're sure – about wanting it, I mean?'

Grace nodded – then thought about it and sank in on herself, suddenly collapsing. 'I don't know any more. You think I should get an abortion, don't you?'

'I think you should consider your choices – fully.'

'Are you even supposed to say that?'

'I'm speaking to you as a friend. I think you've been hearing a lot of things from a lot of people, and I think now you need to spend some time listening to yourself. What do you want, Grace?'

'I thought you were pro-life?'

Mrs Harris picked up a pottery hippopotamus from the end of her desk and considered Grace's question as though it was a question she'd been told she wasn't obliged to answer – while trying hard to control her sudden rage at being challenged. Mrs Harris never responded well to being challenged, and had put up with it earlier on in her career by perfecting the art of submitting to challenge and criticism with the condescension of someone who holds their Self accountable to a Higher Authority. So while she was perfectly willing to have the pro-life discussion with God, she had no intention of having it with Grace Cummings.

Grace stared at the hippopotamus in Mrs Harris's hands. 'We haven't done anything wrong –' Mrs Harris remained silent. 'We just got caught out, that's all.' Grace paused. 'And we're happy to live with the consequences.'

'Happy?' Mrs Harris yelled suddenly, her face shot through with rage; an unappealing mix of red and yellow. 'Have you got any idea how selfish you're being?'

Grace had never seen the Headmistress look like this before. Other girls had – such as Theresa Robbins, who emptied out all the sanitary disposal units last term, leaving the school corridors full of their menstrual contents, and Louise Kessel who'd mugged someone at a cashpoint in town.

'I'm going to put it to you frankly,' Mrs Harris said, standing up and walking back behind her desk. 'The Head Girl of Burwood Girls' can't be pregnant.'

She saw – as she said it – that it was the first time this had actually occurred to Grace.

'In cases like this – and there rarely are cases like this, and never involving the Head Girl – a girl can come into school as normal, but once it starts . . . to show . . . work is sent down to the SEN suite and completed under the supervision of staff there. Public examinations are taken on site, but in isolation. These were the arrangements we put in place for Tina Branston – you remember Tina Branston?'

Grace was staring at her. 'Tina Branston?'

'We're a grant aided organisation so I'll have to talk to the Board, of course. Depending on what you decide –'

'I've decided.'

Ignoring this, Mrs Harris said again, 'Depending on what you decide,' before pretending to concentrate on the sermon she'd been writing on stamp machines and cancer prior to the interview with Grace and Nicole Cummings.

'I'm going to be able to sit my exams though, aren't I?'

'Ultimately that will depend on the Board.' Mrs Harris paused. 'And if not – the council run a unit, on your estate I think, for girls who've had to stop attending school. As I've already said – you've got to explore all your options fully.'

'You let Tina Branston stay on,' Grace said.

Mrs Harris's face turned red and yellow again. 'Tina Branston wasn't Head Girl.'

'You're punishing me.'

'That's your conscience speaking.' Mrs Harris rose, censorious, from behind her desk. The meeting was over.

Neither of them could think of anything to say after this and, in the silence that followed, became aware that the rain had eased up.

There was a brief brightness in the sky; the wrong sort – a queasy mix of orange and grey – then it became suddenly even darker than before as it began to hail.

The desk light flickered off, and uneasily back on.

'It's getting worse,' Mrs Harris shouted above the noise of the hail.

It took her a while to realise that the hail had driven the media away.

'You must save yourself, Grace,' she urged her suddenly with an overwhelming sense that time was running out. 'Will you save yourself? Will you?'

Grace, scared, started to back towards the office door, her hands searching frantically for the handle as Mrs Harris closed in on her.

'Grace!' Mrs Harris yelled, irate, as Grace finally managed to open the door, falling backwards into the outer office.

There was Nicole Cummings' umbrella still, on her office floor.

43

Julia Webster was making her way to the refectory when an irate looking Lichelle accosted her, asking her if she'd seen the papers.

'Who hasn't.' Julia disliked gossip.

'She wants me to get hold of the others. Grace is in there with her now.'

Julia felt suddenly depressed again at the mention of Grace's name.

'Only, the thing is, the rest of them are in art, aren't they?' Lichelle's point was that the art department was at the top of one of the old towers, and she'd had a major hip replacement operation only six weeks ago.

Other people's hip replacement operations were the kind of thing Julia remembered and kept track of only she was distracted at the moment so it took her longer than usual to pick up on Lichelle's point.

'You can't go up there,' she said at last. 'I'll get them – I've got a free period.'

'You will? I don't know what's happening – I can't cope with this,' Lichelle said, as the strain of the morning's events caught up with her, and she realised just how tired she was of people forgetting the major hip replacement operation she'd had done only six weeks ago, and the nervous breakdown she'd had only eighteen months before that. She was taken for granted that's what it was.

'It's fine – I'll go and get the girls.'

Julia made her way towards the staircase that led to the art department, which was housed in one of the two towers in the Old Building, and a long way from the new science block where Julia taught. It smelt different as well – disorientatingly different. The school, like the world, was too large to get to know intimately, so people tended to carve out a corner for themselves and stick to it. Julia was used to spending her days with her nostrils full of gas from the Bunsen burners, but here, even on the staircase – it smelt like the garage on Dardanelle Drive where Paul stored his canvases; where Paul stored almost everything, in fact. So little of him made its way into the rest of the house. Following the row they'd had – however long ago – over a Chinese takeaway and some IKEA bookshelves, she thought, smiling suddenly then feeling even sadder – life had become quietly civil, and unendurable.

After a childhood spent in institutions, normality – mortgages, babies, takeaway food; the butt of so much of Paul's artistic despair – felt like a sensational aspiration to Julia.

She wanted children of her own one day; children she would love in retribution because she knew what it was like to cry endlessly through nights that were in themselves endless – and for nobody to come. Not that she had been completely unloved as a child – she had a deep, abiding respect for the Barnados organisation and what they did – she just hadn't been loved especially.

She reached the top of the stairs where there was a forgotten stained glass window by Rossetti. The door facing her reminded her of similar doors in the Barnardos home – old, heavy and often shut. The school's entire Old Building reminded her of the Barnardos home, in fact – something which struck her now, forcibly, for the first time.

The realisation triggered old fears; irrational in a child, even more irrational in an adult. The stairwell no longer felt empty; something was heading towards her up the stone treads that shone in the storm's dull light.

Her panic gained momentum and she ran towards the door, but the handle wouldn't turn; the door wouldn't open. Something terrible was going to happen; she could feel it.

It was first period and, although silence doesn't exist in schools, prisons, hospitals or other places where fate and circumstance throw vast numbers of strangers together, no sounds reached her from elsewhere in the building.

She really felt she might be on the verge of screaming when the door opened suddenly from the inside.

There was Paul, surprised, distracted, his mouth open in mid-sentence.

'Shut the door – just shut the door,' she said, leaning against him, into him, letting her head drop onto his shoulder.

But his arms didn't hold her.

There was no embrace.

She felt his hand, briefly, on her right arm; felt him step away so that she had no choice but to stand up straight or fall forward onto the floor – her nostrils full of aftershave from where she'd put her head onto his shoulder. Aftershave she'd heard him spray on that morning as she'd sat on the loo in the en-suite listening with ecstatic fervour to the sounds of him moving about the bedroom oblivious, semi-dressed.

Paul coughed awkwardly and moved even further away from her.

There were girls sat on stools, and among them Vicky, Saskia, and Ruth.

The girls carried on staring, their self-portraits forgotten.

'Sorry,' Julia mumbled, pathetically, to no-one in particular, 'I've got a message for Vicky Henderson, and Ruth and . . .' she looked at Paul and tried to remember the name of the other girl, 'Saskia.'

At that moment one of the girls fell suddenly, without warning, off her stool.

The other stools were scraped across the floor as girls moved out the way.

Pencils and charcoal fell to the floor and Julia moved rapidly, instinctively towards the girl lying unconscious on the art room floor, taking up space in the untidy way people do when they're no longer doing it consciously, deliberately.

Part of Julia came alive in a way no other part did when the untoward happened. She would have made a good doctor; a good soldier – all careers she'd considered earlier on in her life, before deciding on teaching.

But Paul got there before her – his arms going out for the girl.

'Don't touch her,' Julia said, automatically. She meant to say 'move' not 'touch'. Something she thought about much later that evening when she went over the scene again.

Paul was kneeling over Saskia – his hands pulling the hair off her face.

The room had gone silent.

It was all wrong.

'Sas,' he said, desperate with a worry he didn't even think to conceal as Julia checked her pulse.

'This is Saskia?'

He nodded.

'She's breathing,' Julia announced.

Paul sat back on his heels, one hand clutching his head. 'Did anyone see what happened?'

He appealed to the other girls, who'd unwittingly formed a circle round Saskia, Julia and him.

'She just fell – like, fell,' Ruth said after a while.

Vicky, standing next to her, didn't say anything.

Saskia rolled slowly onto her back, her eyes remaining closed – obviously in pain.

Paul was there again.

Too close.

Julia had her hand round his arm, forcing him back. 'Just give her some space,' she warned.

Saskia's eyes slowly opened, but they were empty in the way people's eyes are when they've been lost in sleep.

Julia recognised her now – she'd taught her physics in year nine, and been fond of her in the way she was of girls who didn't quite fit in.

She stood up, now fully in control. 'Okay, girls, I think we could all do with a short break. Just leave your things and go downstairs. Vicky – Ruth, you need to see Mrs Harris.'

Nobody moved; they were all staring at Mr Sutton, crouching over Saskia, who was trying to roll in to the recovery position.

'Shouldn't we get her down to sick bay or something?' somebody said. 'I mean, she just like blacked out.'

'It's okay. It'll be okay. I want you all to go to the refectory now,' Julia said again. 'Girls! I said the refectory – now.'

The girls, shocked, drifted slowly towards the class-room door.

Saskia was sitting on the floor in an uncomfortably poised looking position, stunned.

She had one leg hooked up under her and was balancing most of her weight on two clenched fists skewered behind her, in an attempt to get up.

'Sit back down,' Julia said, sounding harsher than she'd meant to. 'Put your head between your knees.' She pushed Saskia's head lightly forward, but after a few seconds Saskia raised it again.

She looked at Julia, not really seeing her or under-standing why she was there. 'What happened?'

'You fell off the stool,' Paul said.

Saskia looked around her for the stool she'd been sitting on.

'You just fell – straight onto the floor.' Paul's hands went out for her – his arm went round her shoulder and she let it rest there. He inadvertently kissed the crown of her head, mumbling, 'It's okay.'

Julia, who'd been crouching near Saskia as well, stood up suddenly and nearly tripped over a table with an old projector on it – whose plug clattered to the floor, raising dust.

Paul became suddenly aware of her again.

Saskia pulled herself awkwardly away, the pain sharp in her left shoulder.

'Have you got a history?' Julia asked her.

'Of what?'

'Fainting – high blood pressure?'

Saskia shook her head as Paul pulled her slowly to

her feet and got her over to the chair he rarely used behind the desk he rarely used at the front of the class.

'It hurts,' she said, sitting down.

'Where?' Julia asked.

'I don't know.' A few stray sobs escaped. 'Sorry.'

'What is it?' The colour had gone from Paul's face.

'I don't know – it just hurts.'

Julia ran her eyes over the girl, trying to remember where her body had been in contact with the floor. 'Head? Shoulder?'

Saskia nodded, 'And here.' She put her hand on her hip.

Julia focussed fully on Saskia, ignoring Paul who didn't seem to know what to do with himself and was moving in relentless and pointless circles behind the chair Saskia was sitting in.

'What is it?' he said again. Then before either of them had time to respond, 'She needs to go to the hospital.'

'Paul, she had a fall – that's all.'

'She's pregnant. But – I guess you knew that. I guess everybody knows. The news –'

As soon as he said it, Julia realised that she already knew. 'How many weeks?' she asked, quietly.

She asked Paul, not Saskia.

'Two and a half months – how many weeks is that? I don't know.'

44

Julia stood in front of her Year Seven class, her hands pushed down heavily into the pockets of her white lab coat, and tried to impart the secret of those freeways of energy – conductors – to them.

The girls sensed immediately – pack instinct – that Ms Webster wasn't on top form. They detected a weariness; an unnatural dishevelment almost, despite the fact that her physical appearance was the same as usual. The notes she gave them sounded inconclusive, and at one point she sat down on her stool mid-sentence and stared out the window until Lucy Claverton had to prompt her.

They were put into pairs and huddled enthusiastically over the circuit boards on the benches in front of them, noisier than usual. Ms Webster always moved around the class when they did pair work, challenging them about their observations and pushing them steadily beyond the narrow confines of the curriculum. Although too closed and remote to love, the girls certainly respected Ms Webster.

Today, however, she remained on her stool, staring out the window, strangely sunken.

She barely looked up when Sam and Alice's circuit board clattered to the floor.

It was as if she had simply stopped.

A rumble of spontaneous laughter started to run round the class, which was unsettled. The girls had seen the papers and were suffering from a suspension of belief in the authority that ruled their lives – although they didn't know this. They couldn't understand how this authority had allowed something so disruptive to happen. It felt as though nobody was in control, and this made them afraid. The fear, in turn, made them irritable.

Ms Webster – now totally oblivious to the activities of her class – didn't notice the laughter.

The post-storm sunlight was warm through the glass, and heating the varnish on the bench in front of her until the smell of it started to rise.

Girls were playing hockey out on the field. Beyond the copse of oaks, a group of reserves (the girls who were left behind after the captains of the A and B team had made their choice; a practice Ms Webster had campaigned to have abolished) were moving slowly, aimlessly in a game of their own devising.

There was a copse of oaks like that at the Barnardos home, and just beyond it, a ditch with an old Anderson shelter in it still. The Anderson shelter was one of the few places she'd found privacy; one of the few places she'd found where she could look out at the world without the world looking back at her, in a childhood wrought with the damaging contradiction of being constantly alone and never having any privacy. It was the only safe place she'd ever found to cry. She'd gone back to the home a few years ago – to give a talk about a career in teaching – but hadn't gone up to the Anderson shelter. She'd worked so hard at leaving that child behind that she was terrified of going up to the old shelter and finding herself there still, her scabbed knees – and their perpetual odour of TCP – pulled up under her chin, sucking on a strand of hair while tears slid soundlessly down her face for no particular reason other than that this was the only place they could.

She instinctively wiped at her face, now running with tears – and sniffed, leaving her hand under her nose.

Then turned to face the class, who were no longer hunched over their circuit boards, but grouped over by the window staring at her – all twenty-five of them.

45

Saskia was in a blue and beige room in a hospital about six miles out of Burwood, rigged up to a foetal monitor and reading a graphic novel.

Richard Greaves was outside sitting, restless, in a bank of blue plastic seating – the new Queen Elizabeth wing of the hospital was decorated in blue and beige throughout – and flicking repetitively through a leaflet on coping with epilepsy during pregnancy.

He'd been in the car park at school, doing a line from the Skoda's dashboard – parked in its usual place beneath the pines – when Saskia phoned to tell him they were taking her into hospital.

When he got there they asked him if he was the father and he'd said 'yes' then realised they were talking about Saskia's child, and not Saskia – and had thrown up in the toilets over a *please wash your hands now* sign and Mr Soapy dispenser.

'That sounds okay,' he'd said when the midwife showed him into the monitor room where Saskia sat alone, reading, to the full, watery beep of the baby's heart on the monitor.

She'd looked up and he could tell from her face that she'd been expecting somebody else.

'It's the baby,' she said, as if expecting him to disagree – feeling a disbelief he recognised.

He'd felt it himself a long time ago when Caro was pregnant with Saskia, but disbelief was inextricably linked to hope. He no longer hoped and therefore no longer experienced disbelief. There was only this numbness. Things happened in life – your wife wrote love letters to, and slept with other men; you became addicted to cocaine; you woke up in the morning in a town whose name you couldn't remember; you had sex with your daughter's friends and they got pregnant then your daughter got pregnant. This was how his life was.

Saskia's face, as she listened to the incessant amplified pounding of the baby's heart, looked the same as Caro's – maybe that's how all women looked rigged up to a foetal heart monitor, he didn't know. Caro and he had referred to Saskia, in her foetal stage, as Fred – because they couldn't quite believe that they'd made this baby who was going to grow into a child they were going to love and nurture for the rest of their lives . . . together. Who were those people? Had Caro and he really laughed so hard at ante-natal water aerobics they'd been asked to leave the pool?

He stared unblinking at Saskia, not really knowing what to say. After a while he got to his feet. 'I'm going to get a coffee – want anything?' He was desperate for another line of cocaine.

'I don't think I'm supposed to – not while I'm rigged up to this. Dad?'

Richard turned, his hand on the door.

'Thanks for coming.'

'Hardly.' He smiled at her. 'I'll be back in a few minutes.'

She nodded, pleased he'd left the room. It was Paul she wanted in there with her.

Paul, who'd made up an excuse to leave school mid-morning, and cycled to the hospital. Paul, who was locking up his bike down in the bike park and running up the hospital's main steps while Richard got his coffee – getting directions from desk staff for the Queen Elizabeth wing and not really listening.

It was the clatter of the studs on Paul's cycling shoes – difficult to walk in – that Richard could hear down the corridor now as Paul walked towards the reception desk and Richard stood up in the toilet cubicle and cleared his debris efficiently off the top of the cistern. It was Paul's voice he could hear as he left the toilets – asking where Saskia Greaves was – and Richard took one look at the young man, holding his cycling helmet and breathing rapidly – and knew.

Just as Paul, turning and seeing Richard, with his bloodshot eyes, in the corridor – knew.

After a moment, he walked hesitantly towards him, worry for Saskia keeping fear of Richard at bay. It struck him as he walked towards the large, lopsided man filling up the corridor that he didn't even know his name so he just said the first thing that came to mind. 'How is she?'

'Okay –'

'Okay?'

'She's fine – the baby's fine.' Richard stared at him.

Paul, on edge, hesitated. He didn't know what to do – or expect. 'I'm Paul,' he exhaled heavily at last.

The two men shook hands – something that should have made Richard feel ridiculous – but that didn't.

'Paul,' he repeated.

'Saskia blacked out – in art. She just slipped off her stool onto the floor.'

'You teach my daughter art? At school?'

Paul nodded. 'For the past year and a bit,' he croaked, coughing to clear his throat.

'You're her teacher. I never did make Parents' Evening – otherwise I suppose we'd already know each other. Would that make it any better – or worse? I don't know. How old are you?' Richard asked suddenly – before Paul had time to respond to the moral question – following his own train of thought.

'Twenty-six.'

Richard let out a strange laugh. 'That all?' Then, sharply. 'I love my daughter.'

'So do I.'

The two men stood quietly contemplating each other then Paul said, 'Is she up there?'

Richard nodded. 'The monitor room.' He watched Paul start to walk up the corridor then called out, 'Wait,' and lumbered, wheezing, after him, grabbing hold hard on his arm.

Paul let him.

'I need more than that.'

'I'm going to be there for Saskia – you have to believe that.'

Richard didn't say anything.

'I mean it.'

'This baby doesn't fit in with any of Saskia's plans – she wants to be a painter.'

'She will – I'd never take that from her.'

Richard considered this. 'I need you to tell me that you're going to give her a life. Tell me that –'

'I already did. Saskia is my life.'

Paul held his gaze, his eyes wide, intense – until Richard broke away.

'I should tell you – I've been talking to my ex-wife, Caro – Saskia's mother. Actually,' he corrected himself, 'I wasn't talking, I was listening to her yell at me. She thinks Saskia should get an abortion, and for once I feel the same way.'

'No!' Paul said, staring helplessly up the corridor as if he couldn't believe what Richard had just said. 'No.'

'Maybe you're putting pressure on her to keep it – she's only seventeen.'

'How old were you when you had Saskia – you and your wife?'

Richard, surprised at the question, had to think about this. 'Mid-thirties.'

'And you were married at the time?'

Richard nodded.

'And you and your wife, you had good jobs, lived in a nice house, etc.? What I'm saying is – you did everything right. You were in your mid-thirties, married, good standard of living – that's the right way of doing things, and yet it's been a total fuck up.'

Richard let out a loud, solitary laugh.

'I'm sorry, Saskia's told me stuff.'

'It's okay,' Richard conceded, interested.

'I mean you and your wife and Sas – you were 2.1 prototypes, and look at what happened: the divorce . . . your habit . . . Saskia and you.'

'What a fuck up,' Richard agreed, wondering what the diagnosis became when you added Ruth to that list.

Standing in the hospital corridor, they had nothing more to say to each other.

Richard watched Paul walk up the corridor into the monitor room and felt no inclination to follow so drifted back to the bank of seating and sat down again, watching the TV screen the hospital had installed to anaesthetise patients before they even got to see any medical staff. It was a show where contestants were forced to consume a three-course dinner in the dark, which must have been filmed, he guessed, on infra-red camera. It was the sort of show Caro produced, he thought – watching the contestants make their way through spaghetti Bolognese – while idly working out what the budget on the show must have been because old habits die hard.

46

Vicky sat curled up in the corner of Frank Barlow's sofa while Frank attempted to give her an Indian head massage – something he'd learnt to do to almost professional level during one of his Alternative deluges when he'd seriously thought about pursuing a career in Holistic Therapy.

Every now and then she jerked irritably away from him before relaxing back into it.

The flat's proximity to the multi-storey built to service Waitrose shoppers became unavoidable during daylight hours when the air hung heavy with petrol fumes. The bird's eye view out over Level 6 was about as inspirational as the petrol fumes that rendered the balcony – home to a display of minimalist garden furniture (Saarinen) bought off e-bay – obsolete.

But Vicky was too depressed to notice and Frank, too scared. He'd anticipated interest in The Burwood Four – national interest – but now the shit storm was raining down on them, he no longer felt in control. Plus, his feelings for Vicky had seriously grown.

'We were standing there in Harris's office and she was looking at us with this like . . . like . . .'

'She doesn't know what to do about you.'

'Yeah, well she made that clear when she told us to fuck off home – until further notice.'

'Well, at least now you don't have to face *him* every day.'

Vicky, distracted, said, 'Face who?'

'Well – *him*. Mr Sutton.'

'Oh. Him.' She saw Saskia falling sideways off her stool again, and Mr Sutton falling to the ground beside her.

'And no wonder she was freaked, Vick,' Frank carried on, unaware of just how distracted she was, 'there are four you. Four. And on her watch. This is Burwood Girls' we're talking about. I don't use the word sensational very often, but this definitely comes under the category of sublime sensation. It's so fucking sensational, it's dislocating.'

Vicky shook him off and turned to stare coldly at him. 'Dislocating? For fuck's sake, Frank, this is my life.'

'I know, baby.'

'No you don't know, baby, and stop using that word it makes you sound like an ageing pornographer from Essex with a Vauxhall Astra.'

'I'm sorry,' he mumbled, 'I didn't mean anything by it, it's just –'

'Shut up, Frank.'

They fell silent. Then, 'Sutton's getting his come-uppance, Vicky – you don't need to worry about that. They're going to skin him alive.'

'Just shut up about it.'

His hands hovered over the back of her neck then he

dropped them and traipsed over to the kitchen where he cut a slice of lemon and dropped it into a Coca-Cola. He stared at it for a while.

When he turned round, Vicky was about to put two blue Valium pills in her mouth.

He ran over and instinctively knocked them out of her hand.

'What was that?' she yelled.

'You've got to stop taking those –'

She stared at him for a moment then burst out laughing. 'What the fuck, Frank?'

'If you're keeping it, you've got to stop taking those.'

'How d'you know I'm keeping it?'

'Because you haven't done anything about losing it.'

'What d'you think about me keeping it?'

Frank drifted over to the window and watched a small red car below execute a complicated parking manoeuvre. The sky had cleared and a harsh white winter sun was cutting across the car and everything else on Level 6.

'Hey – this is revenue for you,' she said, patting her stomach.

'What are you talking about?'

'The Burwood Four. Don't worry, mum feels the same way. If I was to go and get this sucked out now, they'd have to re-brand the others, The Burwood Three and it just doesn't have the same ring, does it?'

'I don't give a shit about any of that. Now.'

'But you did. What changed?'

'You.'

Vicky chose not to pick up on this. 'You won't be saying that when I start getting really fat.'

'It's not fat – it's baby,' Frank said, focussing still on Level 6 just beyond his balcony. 'And I don't have a problem with that. I find it kind of sexy, actually.'

Turning, it was the first time he'd ever seen Vicky look surprised.

'I don't know what I'm talking about,' he said, scared again.

'Yeah,' Vicky responded, 'Thought so.' She sat for a while, able to hear the bubbles exploding in the glass of Coca Cola on the kitchen bench behind her then uncurled herself and stood up.

'Where are you going? Stay –'

He came over to her and tried to take hold of her, but she shook her head.

'I can't.'

'Wait,' he said, suddenly remembering. 'I got you this.'

'What is it?' She took the Body Shop bag he handed her and, pleased, pulled a small white and blue Mother-to-be pack out of the bag. She didn't say anything, and the next minute started to cry.

'Hey – what is it?'

Vicky, tearful, said, 'I don't know. Everything.' She wiped at her face and picked up the mother-to-be pack again. 'Why did you do this?'

'I was in there getting some shaving stuff and I saw it, and . . . the woman said it was good for stretch marks.'

'Stretch marks?'

'Those elastic looking marks you get towards the end when the skin's got a lot of body to stretch over.'

'Could it get any fucking worse?'

'If we massage this in on a regular basis you're a lot less likely to get them – plus, given your age, you probably won't get any anyway.' He dug around in the bag and pulled out a bottle of bath oil. 'This relaxes you – helps you sleep better, and this . . .' he pulled out another bottle, 'is some sort of jelly you're meant to put on your feet and legs to help prevent swelling.'

'Lots to look forward to then. God – why would anyone actually go through this of their own free will.' She took the pack out his hand and looked at the various bottles. 'How d'you know about this stuff?'

'I bought a book.'

'You bought a book? Frank –'

'What?'

He got up and went over to the kitchen, opening a drawer.

'What is this?' Vicky took hold of the book he handed her. '*Now We Are Two*?'

'I don't know how good it is, but at least it gives us some idea of what to expect.' He paused. 'Week by week. Look, you're about ten weeks at the moment – that's what the baby looks like.'

'I don't want to look.'

'He's got –'

'He?'

'For argument's sake.'

'Frank – I don't want to know. Okay?'

'Okay.' Frank carried on leafing through the book, preoccupied. 'Thought about a birth plan?'

'Birth plan?'

'It's something you need to think about, Vicky. Whether you want the baby in hospital or not; whether you're happy to accept painkillers or not – an epidural . . . inducement.'

Vicky remained motionless by the oven, staring at a 3-D postcard of an Indian goddess stuck to the fridge door.

'You should stay here tonight.'

'Why?'

'Because you need a lot of looking after.'

'I've got to go, but Frank? I've got my first scan in a couple of weeks' time – will you come with me?'

47

At number forty-four Dardanelle Drive, Julia was starting to pack her clothes, removing them from the wardrobe and folding them methodically into the case she'd bought years ago when it was still possible to get onto an aeroplane with more than two kilograms of luggage. She was quite certain that this was what she was doing. She'd semi-filled the out-size suitcase before, but only in order to provoke protest; to be stopped by Paul. This time she wouldn't be stopped. When she looked at the bed, covered in the duvet Paul had no opinion on, she couldn't believe they'd ever slept in it – or done other things in it – together.

Later, at her friend Laura's, where she'd be by ten o'clock that night, she'd open the case, drunk on Chardonnay, and all she'd be able to smell would be the Paco Rabanne she bought for Paul in Duty Free on the way to South Africa that summer because that's what the wardrobe her clothes had been hanging in smelt of. But she wasn't thinking about Paco Rabanne right then; she was thinking about how Paul had looked crouched over Saskia Greaves on the art room floor.

Outside, she heard the brakes on Paul's bike as he stopped on the drive, followed by the squealing of the hinges on the garage door. He was home late tonight – she didn't know why; didn't really care. She heard him moving around downstairs in the kitchen as she continued to pack, full of an almost reverential sadness for herself.

A few minutes later, he was standing in the bedroom doorway, in his coat still, a bottle of beer in his hand – watching Julia empty her underwear drawer.

She didn't turn round.

She'd heard him come up the stairs and felt him now in the doorway, watching her.

'I love her,' he said after a while.

'I know. That's why I'm going.'

'Julia –'

She carried on packing, as methodical but not as focussed as before. 'When were you going to tell me?' She turned to look at him.

'I don't know. Soon –'

'How did it happen?'

'It just did. I'm sorry. I am sorry.'

'I know,' she agreed quietly. 'Have you got any idea what you've done?'

'I'm sorry,' he said again.

'I'm not talking about me, Paul. I'm talking about –' She broke off. 'What about the others?'

'What about them?'

'You didn't do them as well, did you?'

'No!' he said, upset. 'No. It's not like that.'

'Like what?'

'You know me, Julia.'

'I don't know anything about you.'

'It's got nothing to do with Saskia's age – that's incidental.' He stared, distracted, at the sports sock in Julia's hand, and didn't see her face blanch when he said Saskia's name.

'You won't be able to convince anybody of that, Paul. They won't let you get away with it.'

'Get away with it?'

'They'll come after you.'

'Why?'

'Because these things just don't happen.'

'Who'll even care?'

Julia laughed. '"Paedo teacher gets girls pregnant –"'

'Girl,' he interrupted her.

'Okay "paedo teacher gets girl pregnant in affluent commuter town". Everyone will care – and they'll ruin it for you. They'll ruin you, Paul, because you haven't paid for it; it hasn't cost you – and it has to cost you. That's how things are.' She dropped the sock in the case and went back to the drawer.

'Who'll even find out?'

'Give me a break, Paul – we weren't the only ones in the art room today. This is a school we're talking about – rumours don't even hit the walls they just run and run.'

He sat on the edge of the bed and finished his beer, staring into the half empty wardrobe. 'Are you disgusted with me?'

'Don't ask me to judge you – you can't do that.' She paused. 'I'm devastated – but that's about me, not you.'

'She's almost eighteen. I'm only eight years older than her.'

Julia didn't respond.

He was watching her. He'd never seen her like this before – resigned; elegiac. The tension between them that had been building up over the past month until even trying to decide who was responsible for letting the milk run out became a row – was gone.

'It's not who I am you don't love – I can see that now – it's who I'm not.' She paused. 'It makes it easier – a case of mistaken identity. Although I'd still like to be her for a day – longer . . . the rest of my life.' She looked sadly at him.

'I really wanted us to work. In the beginning.'

'But that's just the point, Paul. There never was a beginning, and Saskia's always been there, hasn't she?'

He nodded. 'Since September.'

'September?' She sounded angry, for the first time. 'Obviously. The baby.' Then, sobbing without wanting to, and barely able to say it. 'September? God – Paul. How could you?'

'People do.'

She stared desolately at a green flip-flop belonging to him; that he'd worn in South Africa that summer – where was the other one?

After a while, he held up the empty beer bottle. 'I'm getting another one of these – d'you want one?'

She nodded without looking at him, listening to him go downstairs, open the fridge, take the caps off the beer then walk back upstairs.

She took a sip, swilling it round her mouth before swallowing.

'I could cause you so much grief – you and her.'

Paul stayed silent.

They sat on the end of their bed, drinking beer.

After a while, calm, she said, 'I should have known,' – more to herself than him. 'The way you talked about her all last year – your protégé – and then the way you stopped talking about her. I should have known.' She looked at him. 'Do her parents know?'

'Now they do. I met her dad today – at the hospital. That's who she lives with.'

302

'And?'

'Julia – it doesn't change anything. He's a fucked-up divorcee. I think he takes a hell of a lot of cocaine, and I think he loves his daughter – a lot.'

'She's keeping it, isn't she?'

'It's up to her.'

'But you want her to keep it, don't you?'

He nodded.

'Isn't she shit scared?'

'We both are.'

Paul went downstairs for a third beer and Julia sat on the bed thinking, and resisting the urge – before she went, because she really was going this time – to tell him all the things about herself she'd planned to tell him later, years down the line. She thought about giving him the whole story of herself, now, sitting on the edge of the bed. But she didn't.

Instead, she stood up and started packing again.

Paul re-appeared and looked around the bedroom, aware for the first time of what was happening.

'Where are you going?'

'Laura's.'

'Did I ever meet Laura?'

'About a hundred times.'

They smiled briefly at each other, suddenly shy.

'Are you hungry?'

Julia shrugged.

'I'll get us a takeaway – before you go – Chinese?'

She heard him leave on his bicycle then put her elbows on top of the chest of drawers, resting her head in her hands – and started crying again. When she finally stopped, she sat down on the bed, holding Paul's pillow to her.

48

It was a Monday night – and unusually busy inside Mr Li's, which was also an eat-in restaurant. Julia and he had eaten in once. At the beginning. If death had been a place rather than a state, it would have looked a lot like the 'eat-in' at Mr Li's. Previously the offices of an insurance broker who sank during the last recession, Mr Li had made very few modifications since moving in – apart from whitewashing the walls in blood-draining magnolia. The false ceiling, stained office carpet and tilted blinds were all still there – as well as the lingering smell of failed venture, which not even Mr Li's flourishing kitchen could dispel completely.

Paul ordered all Julia's favourites – and himself another beer while he waited, and tried to ignore the fact that the man sitting next to him was reading a copy of the *Sun*.

'Unbelievable,' the man said after a while, appealing to Paul by flicking his knuckles over the photographs of the three girls outside M.R. Cramplins. 'My daughter goes there.' There was outrage – as if some sanctuary he'd been led to believe was inviolable had just been penetrated.

'And she's been predicted As till they're coming out her ears,' he added, subconsciously distancing his daughter from what was going on by wrapping her in the immunity of predicted achievement.

Paul didn't comment – he was too busy thanking God that this man's daughter obviously didn't take art or he would have been recognised – and hoped that the ambivalent comment on his daughter's grades would bring closure.

It didn't.

'You just can't believe it, can you,' the man insisted.

'Let me see,' Paul said suddenly, aware that if he didn't respond in some way soon the man was going to launch a full scale attack on him.

Gratified, the man handed him the paper and watched as Paul pretended to read.

'That's what I'm talking about,' he said, satisfied. 'Nothing's sacred, is it?'

Paul grunted – uncertain whether he was talking about the town, the school or his daughter.

'Somebody's behind this,' the man leant in, confidential, and did an impression of lowering his voice. 'It stinks of cult. I mean, stuff like that just doesn't happen, does it? Four of them? All at the same time? Nice girls? Nice families? Nice part of the world? Doesn't add up. Somebody's got to be responsible,' he carried on, automatically getting up as his number was called out. 'It's a disgrace.' He peered inside the bags and sniffed, rounding suddenly on Paul. 'You wait till you have kids of your own,' he concluded, ominously, departing Mr Li's with an aggressive jerk of his head in Paul's direction.

Left alone, Paul jumped as Mr Li's home delivery moped pulled up on the pavement outside. He scanned the empty road, video rental place on its last legs opposite, and new development of flats – as though something was out there, waiting for him – and finished his beer.

By the time the order was ready, he was aware of being vaguely drunk.

On the way back to Dardanelle Drive the head and tail lights of the traffic on the roads had an almost hypnotic effect on him and, disorientated, he cycled onto the drive without noting the absence of Julia's black Peugeot.

Wheeling the bicycle and Chinese into the garage, he went into the house, laid the table, put the cartons of food onto a tray and called out, 'Julia!'

There was no response.

The only sound in the house was the buzzing of the fridge and loud, sporadic ticks coming from the cooker clock as its batteries ran low.

He called out again, 'Julia!' but he already knew.

He went to the front door and opened it.

Her car was gone.

49

Tom Henderson had driven over the South Downs to Burwood in his piebald red Volkswagen earlier that day and was now standing in the garden of number eighteen Willow Drive in the rain, which had become torrential again – and finally driven off the photographers and reporters.

He could hear the TV on inside the house and, rising above the rain banging down on him and everything around him, the recognisably hysterical voice of a game show host.

The net curtains at the front window – another legacy from the previous, elderly owner – were lifted slightly, and Tom saw Nicole's face peering out through the rain, trying to see if he was still there. The bulb in the porch had blown however long ago and never been replaced so he moved up close to the window.

The net curtain was dropped.

He waited. This had been going on for hours. At first he'd stood there yelling until a neighbour threatened to call the police. Then he'd started banging on the door, but since given that up and stood waiting instead. They couldn't stay in the house forever.

Then the front door did open, and Nicole stood there shivering, smoking and watching him.

Tom had liked Nicole as soon as he met her that first time. She had a poise and elegance or rather, a sort of grace she remained unaware of and so had never learnt to use in life – which was a shame because it would have helped her in ways she could never have anticipated. Nicole pulled some stray tobacco off her lip.

'Go home, Tom. She won't talk to you – she doesn't want to – so just go home.'

Exhausted and completely saturated with rain water, he leant against the door frame. 'Where's this coming from?'

Nicole stared beyond him, over his shoulders at the night, without expectation.

'You did see the papers today, didn't you?'

'Obviously. That's why I need to speak to her.' He broke off. 'Wait – you don't think I'm behind that do you? Tell me you don't think that.'

'Course not, but somebody is.' Nicole exhaled and threw the cigarette butt into the garden. 'And on top of all this we went into school today – to tell them.'

'She never said you were going into school.'

'She had to sit there, Tom, and – She's Head Girl, Head Girl of that school,' Nicole carried on, talking herself into anger, 'and she worked so hard for that, and I've been so proud of her.' She broke off, starting to cry with loud intakes of breath.

'She never said you were going in.' He felt the rain rebounding off the porch roof onto him, soaking his shoulders, back and feet, vengeful.

'Why couldn't you of just left each other alone.'

In the house behind them, the TV started laughing, momentarily distracting Nicole.

She rubbed hard at her wet cheeks. 'I just wanted her to get out, Tom – and she was.'

'Out of what?'

'This, for fuck's sake,' she yelled, shooting her arm out at the night, the front garden, the house.

A fleet of scooters, phlegmatic sounding, passed on the road behind them.

They didn't register with Tom.

'And she was getting out, and now –'

'She is getting out,' Tom insisted.

Nicole shook her head sadly at him. 'You don't know.'

'She's been given an unconditional offer by Cambridge. They're fighting over her, Nicole.'

'But when they find out –'

'When they find out – what? What difference does it make?'

'That Mrs Harris said they'd take it away from her.'

'On what grounds?'

'On the grounds that she's fucking pregnant, Tom. How's she going to study with a baby to look after?'

'I'm going to look after the baby. We've been through that. I do the childcare – Grace does her degree.'

'You think that's it – that's all it'll take?'

'I'll do whatever it takes – you know that. Just let me see Grace, Nicole – I need to see her.'

'That Harris woman was saying she might not even be able to sit her A Levels at school, Tom. She was talking about her having to do it at that unit they've got for pregnant kids.' Nicole jerked her head in the direction of the Pole Star and top end of Willow Drive. 'And I've seen the kids coming out of there – and that's not Grace. It's not her.'

Tom had never heard of the unit before – but then neither had most of the rest of Burwood – and was quietly shocked that there were enough pregnant teenagers to warrant the existence of one, even if it was buried up here on the Meadowfield estate.

He took hold of Nicole's elbows and tugged gently on them. 'That's not going to happen.'

'I see that girl from school who had a baby last year, pushing her buggy past our door and I can't even bear to look at her.'

'Nicole –'

'That Harris woman said stuff to Grace – scared her.'

'Like what?'

'About her options.'

'Is that why she's not talking to me?'

'She was sent home from school today – because of all the stuff in the news. They sent her home. Just let her be –'

'You don't get it, do you?' Tom said, raising his voice, angry with Nicole for the first time. 'I love her – and I'm not going away.'

Nicole looked at him. 'Just give her some time, Tom.'

'Why can't people just leave us alone,' he shouted, kicking at the wall and knocking off a lump of pebble dash.

'Because they won't – that's people.'

'I just want to be with her – what's so wrong with that?'

He lunged forward, grasping the doorframe for balance and shouting, 'Grace – Grace!' into the house. But Grace didn't come.

Nicole pushed him away, back into the rain.

'I like you Tom. I do like you,' she said, unsure why she was saying this.

'I don't know what to do –'

'Go home – you're soaked.'

She shut the door on him.

It didn't re-open.

Tom stepped backwards into the middle of the front garden again until his legs hit the plastic ride-on car Dixie had abandoned years ago, but still let her dolls drive, and looked up at the front of the house, but no faces appeared at any of the windows.

A dog and its owner passed, wheezing, on the pavement behind him and when the wheezing fell out of earshot, he went to the covered passage that ran between number eighteen and number sixteen, pulled one of the wheelie bins up against the passage door, climbed onto it – with difficulty because it was impossible to get a grip on anything in the rain – and then onto the roof of the passage, which he walked along into the back garden.

Through the patio doors of the house number eighteen backed onto he could see a family on a sofa, motionless in the moving blue light from a TV screen of cinematic proportions. As he was about to jump, a child in Action Man pyjamas slipped off the tightly packed sofa with a bottle of something psychedelic looking in its mouth and ran to the window, knocking on it and pointing straight at Tom, excited.

He ran back to the sofa, flapping his arms like wings, was hit round the head by a woman taking up at least half the sofa, then hauled back onto it where he sat, peering mutely round her at Tom still, until she dug him back with her huge arm. He didn't look again.

Tom jumped down into the Cummings's back garden where Nicole had spent the summer trying to grow flowers – and the family on their sofa disappeared behind a fence held together by unchecked ivy and bindweed.

Tom had never climbed a drainpipe before but he climbed one now in order to get onto the roof of the kitchen – a flat-roofed extension completed in the sixties, and situated directly beneath Grace's bedroom window.

He saw, through the kitchen window, Nicole sitting on the edge of the sofa, talking to Dixie who was standing in front of her, in her pyjamas, rubbing at her eyes.

Tom realised that he'd probably woken her up, and felt bad about that.

It took him three attempts to scale the drainpipe and once on the flat roof, he took his car keys out his pocket and threw them up at Grace's window.

Nothing.

After a few seconds, he threw them at the window again and this time a light went on behind the unlined curtains – faint; a bedside light.

He threw the keys a third time – and there she was.

Face, shoulders, and everything she was to him, staring out of the barely illuminated window.

50

Grace was lying in the dark listening to Led Zeppelin.

She didn't hear Tom knocking at the door, her mother pleading for her future, or Tom pleading for his, so we'll never know if she would have gone downstairs to argue her case or not; whether she even felt that she had a case.

Tom did wake up Dixie, however – who wasn't listening to Led Zeppelin – and who went downstairs and asked where Tom was; she'd heard Tom's voice over the rain, she was sure. Why wasn't he allowed to come in? Was Grace still famous? Was she still going to be an aunt?

Nicole told her Tom was gone, and ended up letting her watch *Celebrities Under the Knife* in order to calm her down.

Upstairs, Grace was thinking about the fact that she hadn't had a period now for three months and that this was the only thing pregnancy had going for it when the hairs on her arms stood up and she instinctively slipped the headphones off her ears, listening.

Outside, on the flat roof, Tom was throwing his car keys up at her window for the third time.

She knelt on the bed, lifted the curtain damp with condensation, and saw Tom – who was letting out indistinct, watery bellows as he lurched around the flat roof in the rain; making her frightened he might slip over the edge.

So – despite the fact that she'd vowed not to speak to him until she'd made up her mind about the baby . . . the rest of her life – she opened the window and he took a running jump at it, a leap of faith that propelled him through the storm and up patchy pebble dash, towards uPVC window frames the council put in last summer as part of the Meadowfield Regeneration Project.

He bellowed, 'Grace!' as his hands shot through the open window and tried to grab hold of the windowsill.

A cry that prompted the woman in the house opposite to dig her elbow into her husband's bulging midriff and send him unsteadily towards the patio doors where he stared aimlessly into the night, seeing nothing until his scrunched-up eyes picked out Tom, hanging from the back of the house opposite.

He turned away and said something to the occupants of the sofa, who struggled with grunting animation out of the sofa's grip and towards the patio doors, assuming the positions bodies assume and the facial expressions faces assume when they watch spectator sports.

It didn't occur to any of them to open the patio doors.

At number eighteen, Grace started to laugh, suddenly, uncontrollably at the sight of Tom, saturated in rain, frantically trying to maintain his grip on wet uPVC.

She collapsed on her bed in hysterics as he fell with a thud back onto the kitchen roof.

Nicole and Dixie – downstairs watching a 3-D reconstruction of what a head belonging to Tom Jones would look like, minus the surgery – heard the thud as well.

On the second attempt, Tom managed to haul himself over the sill and through the open window, straight onto Grace's bed where he lay, panting, through the water streaming down his face.

'Hannah Montana?' he said, looking at her T-shirt – bought by a blind aunt for Dixie, in the wrong size.

She pushed her foot into his soaking wet abdomen. 'I knew you'd say that.'

And this was how Nicole found them when she appeared in the bedroom doorway with a frying pan, a bread knife – and Dixie, who'd been told to stay downstairs.

'It's Tom,' Dixie yelped, excited, running across the room and launching herself onto the bed between Tom and Grace.

Nicole slowly lowered the frying pan, but kept a tight grip on the bread knife as she gave up and went into the bathroom and started to run a bath for Tom, smiling at the laughter coming through the bathroom wall and hanging heavily in the steam, but feeling none the happier for it.

suburban satyr

51

The day dawned darkly wet with smudges of glow from streetlamps covering pavements, roads, and front gardens at regular intervals. It was about now that the birds started singing and a light, cold wind started to blow. It rattled the swings in the Danish-designed, Polish-built play park, brushed the bells in Burwood's many spires, and scraped a plastic carton – Burwood's sole piece of litter – up West Street past recently shut down M.R. Cramplins chemist, whose painted eye stared out steadily from the erratically creaking sign that hadn't been oiled for the first time in living memory.

In Burwood's pre-dawn world, Mrs Remington – a neighbour of Paul Sutton's on Dardanelle Drive – was digging up her garden in search of her three children, who'd long since left home, convinced that they were buried at the end, beneath the distinctive yew tree she was so proud of.

Three doors up from the Hendersons, on Park Avenue, a soon to be divorced equities trader was injecting heroin into his scrotum in the Czech & Speake en-suite, but by the time the birds started singing and the wind started blowing, all traces of these dark goings on had vanished. The alarms rang and the lights came on, unashamed, behind the curtains at upstairs windows. Burwood was once more the place the people who lived there knew and loved, even on a day like today that didn't promise much.

At number two Park Avenue, Sylvia Henderson woke before the alarm and stared at Bill's back and shoulders, rising untidily out of the duvet. His head and arms were flung to one side in the posture of a diver about to walk off the edge of the board.

The bed was kingsize, but Bill had always taken up a lot of space unconscious, between the sheets, so Sylvia aligned herself with the edge of the bed and continued to stare at the moles on his back, and narrow creases in his neck. The next minute she was staring at a woman's hand moving across the familiar expanse of skin that grew a little looser each year, and realised with shock that it was *her* hand.

She had inadvertently started stroking her husband's back in a gesture of, if not exactly sexual provocation, certainly tenderness. What did she want? Did she want Bill to turn round and hold her? Did she want more than that? No, she just wanted to be held because it had been so long since anybody held her and terrible things happened, Sylvia thought suddenly, when people stopped holding each other. This was the thing she remembered most about their early years together – the way Bill used to hold her. The way he would steal up behind her and slip his arm round her if she was busy, and how the sudden warmth from being held would pull her out of herself in a way nothing else ever could. Once she'd discovered this warmth – a warmth that had never featured in her childhood and that she soon became addicted to – she'd been terrified of losing it . . . to the point of morbidity. In the beginning she'd lived with the constant fear that Bill would be taken from her in a road accident or that he'd contract a terminal disease. She could still see her face – anxious and tear-ridden because he was fifteen minutes late – watching for him coming home through the window of their first flat. What had happened to that fear? She'd let it go – she'd let it all go.

Bill woke up then snorting and munching his lips together in imitation of speech. He opened his eyes and stared at her.

For a moment they were looking directly at each other then they turned sharply away until they were both lying on their backs, staring up at the ceiling.

Next door, at number four Park Avenue, Nathan Dent slipped silently out of bed and into the en-suite. He'd always been able to cover the distance between fast asleep and fully awake in seconds. He performed his morning ablutions then, staring briefly at himself in the mirror without emotion, went back through to the bedroom where he fully intended getting dressed in the clothes he'd laid out the night before when he stopped, suddenly at a loss.

He stared, helpless, at Rachel – lying in bed asleep still – and the next minute fell to his knees, stretching his arms out along the edge of the bed and pushing his face into it, moaning. There was nothing about Nathan Dent that would have led the casual observer, or even those familiar with him, to the conclusion that Nathan was a man capable of anguish, but here he was assuming the same position he had most mornings since being told that his adopted teenage daughter was pregnant, and that position could only be described as one of anguish.

Rachel, who was in fact awake, lay staring at the wall opposite where some strands of cobweb blew in the draught coming through the sash windows. She lay listening to Nathan's sobbing moans, she listened to him stop, and she listened to him get to his feet again, sniffing, and go downstairs. Then she shut her eyes.

On his way downstairs, a door across the landing opened – Ruth's – and she stared out at him, hanging onto the handle, in a T-shirt and dressing gown. It struck him, glancing at her, that she'd been awake for some time, and that she'd been crying. She looked like she had something to say; something she wanted to impart to him.

'Are you going to work?' she whispered.

He nodded, and watched her consider this. She understood. He went to work as soon as he was able because he couldn't bear to be at home.

'I need to tell you something,' Ruth continued to whisper.

Nathan remained poised on the landing, his shoes in his hands, until he realised that she meant him to go into her bedroom.

He couldn't remember the last time he'd been in her bedroom – years ago when her desk, which was self-assembly, was delivered. He glanced around the room with a latent curiosity, his eyes watering at the brightness of the spotlight above her bed. The room was more like a library than a bedroom. Ruth had always been an avid reader, possessing the shy child's ability to disappear into books. That's how she spent most of her time – either in other people's lives or underwater. Only she hadn't been swimming now for the past fortnight and Nathan guessed that was because 'it' was beginning to show, although he hadn't noticed this particularly because she chose her clothes carefully.

It struck him forcibly, looking round the room now, that Ruth really was the last person anyone would have thought this could happen to.

She stood, lost, in the middle of the room before sitting down tidily on the edge of the bed and staring at her hands.

Nathan remained just inside the door, holding his shoes still.

'I can't go through with this,' she said, quietly, without looking at him.

He remained silent and motionless, watching her. 'Ruth –' he said, unsure whether he was reassuring her or asking something of her.

'So I've decided – to have an abortion.' She looked up at him then, but he had nothing to say. They both knew that it was the only logical option.

'When?'

'Today.'

'Today?'

'Ssh,' she hissed, looking scared for the first time. 'You're not going to stop me?'

'No – no.'

'I know what it means – mum – I'm not asking you to choose between us – this is something I've got to do. You're okay?'

'I'm okay.'

'You're sure?'

'God, I'm relieved,' he said, meaning it absolutely and feeling suddenly tearful.

She gave him a half smile that made her look open,

relaxed and like herself for the first time in weeks and seeing her smile like that made him realise just how much he'd missed her.

'You want me to come with you?'

'No – no, I don't want that. I just want to go and then I want to come back. I don't even want to talk about it any more – but I couldn't have gone in there without you knowing. It's not your approval I want – I don't mean that – but your knowing.'

She got up slowly from the bed, pulling her T-shirt nervously around her and a second later they were hugging in the quiet, undemonstrative way that their respective natures permitted them to seek solace – Nathan holding his shoes still.

Upstairs at number twenty-four Carlton Avenue, Richard Greaves woke to the sound of his mobile ringing – the ring tone had been manufactured by people who grew up in the eighties to sound like an eighties landline. Caro and he used to have a beige phone that stood on top of a tiled side table they brought back from Portugal – that sounded identical.

He rolled over in a bed even he now found smelled off putting, tried to pick up his phone with his eyes still half shut and knocked it onto the floor. It stopped ringing. Then it started again. He retrieved it from under the bed and stared at it.

Ruth. What did Ruth want?

'I've decided.' She sounded like she'd been crying, but he was tired and half asleep still, and the thought of Ruth crying left him cold.

'What?' he said, not even trying to control his impatience.

'To have an abortion'

'Okay. Good.'

'Fuck you.'

'What d'you want me to say?'

Grunting to himself, he switched his phone off and threw it to the end of the bed then rubbed at his face before letting his arms drop to his sides in an attitude of depressed inertia. He confronted himself for as long as he could bear – with the fact that Ruth was having an abortion – but the only feeling he could honestly muster was one of exhaustion, as if he'd been awake all night.

Then his mind moved on to Saskia, who needed breakfast because breakfast was the most important meal of the day – especially for pregnant women. It was strange, he thought – how much more worried he was about Saskia, pregnant, than he'd ever been about Caro, his ex-wife, when she'd been pregnant with Saskia.

On the Meadowfield estate, Nicole Cummings woke with her alarm, sat up then immediately fell back onto the bed again, her arm flung over her forehead, trying not to think about anything, and definitely not the day ahead. On the other side of the wall behind her, she could hear Dixie, who was an early riser and who had probably already been up for an hour or more, talking to herself.

Across the hallway, she heard Grace's alarm go off. Dixie must have heard it as well because she broke off her chatter, opened her bedroom door and crept across the landing. Nicole couldn't keep her mind clear or the thoughts at bay any longer and they soon came falling down from the ceiling, knocking the breath out of her. She couldn't remember when exactly morning had stopped being a beginning and become nothing more than a continuation, but it had been a long time ago.

She thought of Grace and Tom waking up in each other's arms and felt a stab of envy she contemplated for a moment before carefully tidying it away and getting up.

Across the landing, Dixie hung giggling in Grace's bedroom door and watched Tom and Grace wake up in Grace's childhood bed, which had been bunkbeds originally until split apart when Dixie became old enough to sleep in a bed and bedroom of her own.

'Dixie!' Nicole called out from behind her, on the landing, trying not to look past her through the open bedroom door. 'C'mon, Dixie – breakfast.'

Dixie groaned, reluctantly shutting the bedroom door and following Nicole downstairs.

The town was divided on the Burwood Four. There were those who thought the girls themselves were to blame and who cast a verdict of immoral behaviour – citing the influence of drink, drugs, the internet, Britney Spears, GTA, non-organic food, Al-Qaida, and the Labour government. Then there those who thought they'd fallen victim to a suburban guru-led cult. There was even a splinter cell – led by the divorcee opposite the Hendersons on Park Avenue – who believed that the girls had been impregnated, Midwich Cuckoos-style, by alien spawn intent on colonising Burwood.

Whichever camp you belonged to – and you had to belong to one – the general consensus was one of disbelief. For a town that prided itself on being a place where nothing ever happened, for holding the view that news was something that happened to other people, the revelation that a dark fecundity was ebbing and flowing beneath the everyday came as a shock. Beyond the shock and disbelief lay outrage, and beyond the surface of this outrage – scratched and threadbare at best – lay excitement.

If, in public, people showed themselves to be excessively censorious – especially those with teenage daughters – in private, it was as if something had snapped. People literally abandoned themselves to each other. There were too many instances of abandonment and transgression to list individually, suffice to say that a large number of men who'd been attracted to other men's wives and women who'd been attracted to other women's husbands (not to mention husbands who'd been attracted to other women's husbands, and wives who'd been attracted to other men's wives) – silently, and often for over a decade's worth of tedious dinner parties – started meeting up in the countless out-of-town motels lining the M23 between London and Brighton. Their cars were on CCTV footage that nobody would ever watch, recorded arriving and departing.

Grace, Vicky, Ruth and Saskia became household names nationwide, and households nationwide were divided on their culpability and innocence. Young girls wanted to dress like them, be like them . . . get pregnant like them.

There were already rumours of chain pregnancies at Danehill School.

And it was about to get worse – much worse.

52

Paul Sutton woke to a parched mouth and lurching digestive system that had been over-exposed to the MSG in last night's Mr Li's – consumed alone along with excessive quantities of lager.

He had his head jammed in the fern-green sink, drinking water from the tap, when the phone rang. He heard it in the distance – and ignored it. Nobody ever used the landline. But it kept on ringing, insistent.

'Paul?'

Paul groaned. Julia was too vast and complex a place for him to re-visit right then. He collapsed back on the bed.

'You weren't picking up your mobile.'

'I had my head in the sink.'

'You're drunk.'

'Probably.'

'How was your night – last night?'

'Can't remember.'

'Me neither.'

'You left.'

'It was time. Listen, Paul – don't go outside.'

He sat up. 'What?'

'Don't go outside.'

Within seconds he was standing at the bedroom window.

Then he saw.

He'd heard the noise in his sleep – just before waking up – and put it down to the fact that they'd just re-routed the flight paths into Gatwick. But it wasn't aeroplanes he'd heard in his sleep, it was a swarming media hive.

'Fuck,' he hissed into the phone, instinctively dropping onto the carpet and crouching with his back against the radiator, which was on, and which it took him a while to realise was burning him badly. 'Fuck,' he said again, shuffling away from the hot radiator, but remaining on the floor below sill level. 'How did you know?'

'Laura just bought a newspaper.'

'Laura?'

'Paul – we did this conversation last night.'

'Which newspaper?'

'It doesn't matter – you're in them all.' She paused. 'They know about Saskia.'

'This isn't just about Saskia, Paul. They're saying you're the father of all the children – calling you the "Suburban satyr".'

'"Satyr"?' Paul took in the discarded Mr Li's containers and empty bottles littering the room; the chunks of pineapple caught in the carpet's pile just near his feet and the luminescent red streaks from the sweet and sour sauce on the duvet, and on his legs. He'd fallen asleep in last night's meal.

'"Suburban satyr heads up pregnancy cult at posh girls school." Verbatim. This is what I'm looking at, Paul.' She hesitated. 'Paul?'

'For fuck's sake, Julia – it's not true, and you didn't ring to hear me say that. You rang because you already knew. Where did they get this from? Who would do this?'

'Somebody who hates you a lot – even more than me.'

'I wasn't thinking that.'

'Yes you were.'

'If you hadn't phoned I'd have walked straight into it.'

'You already did. What are you going to do?'

'I don't know, I just don't know.'

Paul rang off and remained crouched on the floor staring at the debris before doing a crawling tour of the bedroom in search of his mobile. He had to phone Saskia.

With his hand under the valance – he'd never heard of valances before meeting Julia, never realised how essential they were to the notion of domestic bliss – the landline started ringing again.

Only it wasn't Julia this time.

He'd spotted his mobile – in a crevasse in the duvet – grabbed it, wiped off some black bean sauce and stray pillow feathers that had stuck to it and then willed Mrs Harris, Headmistress of Burwood Girls' and his current employer – to fuck off the line so he could call Saskia. He didn't even attempt to follow the protocol she was talking him through – 'suspended . . . pending immediate investigation . . . necessary disciplinary action' – the only thing that mattered was trying to get through to Saskia.

'Yeah, well, I'd look in your own back yard before pointing any fingers. I heard that your husband likes to download kiddie porn while you're out the house busy running your school according to Christian principles.'

He rang off, threw the phone onto the bed and called Saskia on the mobile. She didn't pick up. He tried every minute, on the minute, for the next thirty minutes, his finger pressed into his free ear, trying to block out the sounds rising from the outside world.

Mrs Harris came off the phone to Paul Sutton and slowly stroked her neck with her fingertips before letting her arms drop to her side. A posture that made her immediately look much taller. Still in dressing gown and slippers, she was shaking.

She stared through the patio doors at her husband in the garden, standing waiting for his falcon, Elgar, to fly out of the half light back onto his outstretched, gloved hand.

The end was coming.

Whether for her, her husband, both of them, the school or the entire town of Burwood, she didn't know, but the end was definitely coming.

Paul abandoned his bedroom refuge, and went downstairs into the garage.

He'd seen through the back bedroom window that the swarm outside stretched round the corner into Ypres Crescent where he was hoping to escape, on his bicycle, through the side garden gate – the one that had worried Julia so much because she was convinced it would attract burglars – and onto the bottom end of Hurst Road.

He wheeled his bicycle out of the garage and into the lounge, his hands already gripped tight around the handlebars.

Then his mobile rang.

Saskia.

'Paul,' Julia's voice said for the second time that morning. 'You're going to try and see her, aren't you?'

'How d'you know?'

'Gut feeling.'

'She's not picking up.'

'Where are you now?'

'Standing in the lounge – with my bike. I'm going to try the side gate.'

'Stay where you are – I'll come and get you. I'll text you when I'm there.'

Paul continued to stare at the back garden, his hands still gripping the bicycle as he rolled it nervously backwards and forwards over the carpet.

'Okay –'

'Give me ten minutes.'

53

Paul's phone let out the electronic jingle that signalled the arrival of a text, and seconds later he was standing behind the garden gate hauling some forgotten bags of compost out the way before slipping through it towards Julia's car, parked on Ypres Crescent. Out the corner of his eyes, he was sure he recognised a group of Year 2 students – particularly Amanda Burton, who'd sent him a photograph of herself topless at the end of the summer. He'd never told Julia about that.

Once he was in the car, Julia accelerated hard, barely stopping at the junction with Dardanelle Drive.

Paul kept his eyes on the road ahead, but through the side window of the car, as it swung around, he saw a lot of irate movement, and in the wing mirror there were people with some serious equipment running up the middle of the road after the car.

'Is this the right way?' Julia said, without looking at him.

'No.'

'So where do I need to go?'

'Carlton Avenue – behind the station.'

'They'll be there as well.'

'The house backs onto a Unigate Dairy depot – if you drop me there, I can get over the wall.'

She turned to glance at him. Her face was tight and tired.

'Harris phoned.'

'Well, that was inevitable.'

'About disciplinary procedures and investigations.'

'What did you say?'

'I told her she had other things to worry about given that her husband spends most of his time downloading kiddie porn.'

'Staff room rumours, Paul.'

'You've seen the guy, Julia.' He balanced his elbow on the door and stared out the window, clutching at handfuls of his hair. 'I fucking hate this place.'

'I know – you never let me forget – like it was somehow my fault.'

'None of this was your fault, Julia,' he said, turning to look at her, suddenly adamant. 'None of this.'

'Do I make a right here?'

'No, we'll get stuck in the one-way system – take the next turning after this.' He carried on watching her. 'Why are you helping me?'

'To show you I believe you. Plus, it takes my mind off wanting to kill you.'

He brushed her cheek with his knuckles.

'Don't,' she said sharply. 'Okay – right here?'

'This one – yeah.'

Julia drove down Chester Street, which ran parallel to Carlton Avenue, and pulled into the Unigate depot, looking around her, unconvinced.

'How's this going to work?'

'I'm going over that wall.'

'That's a high wall, Paul.'

'I've done it before.'

She looked at him then looked away. 'What are you going to do?'

'Ultimately?'

'Ultimately.'

'I've got no idea –' He paused for a moment, his hand on the door handle, then got out the car. 'I'll phone – sometime.'

She nodded. 'Sometime. Take care of yourself, Paul, and –'

'What?'

'Nothing.'

He patted the car roof, absently, then started walking towards the wall at the end of the depot.

Before he got there, he heard Julia's car leave.

Richard Greaves was standing at the bedroom window in his underwear when he heard the bloodhounds next door start baying from the confines of their bloodhound-size Swiss chalet.

A few minutes later the part-time fireman, Derek, who owned them and who had constructed their Swiss chalet with pathological precision – a pathology concealed by the quiet, seemingly exemplary life he led – opened his back door and called out to the hounds to quiet down.

He then went back indoors and so didn't see Paul climbing over the wall and into his garden, nor the hounds, agitated, sliding their wet noses across the glass he'd had cut to size for the chalet windows.

Richard Greaves, however, did see.

He saw Paul hauling himself awkwardly over the wall of his neighbour – Derek's – garden, but didn't wonder too much about it.

He didn't wonder about anything much any more; he just watched.

He watched as Paul ran, lopsided, across Derek's garden and broke the fence separating their two gardens as he attempted to vault it.

He continued to watch – with what was now a habitual, frantic stillness – as Paul picked his way across the debris in their back garden then disappeared out of sight. The next minute, when the banging started on the patio doors, Richard opened the window and leant out.

Paul looked up. 'Saskia! I need to speak to Saskia.'

Richard stood scratching his chest through his vest then left the bedroom window and went downstairs. He'd barely got the patio doors unlocked before Paul slid them heavily back.

'I need to speak to Saskia,' he said again, staring at Richard, who was standing there in a pair of boxers, and a vest.

'Come in.' Richard backed away from the patio doors into the lounge, collapsing heavily into the sofa and not taking his eyes off Paul.

Paul, on edge, hesitated before stepping indoors.

'Caro phoned – this morning – talking about lawyers.' Richard sighed. 'That's Caro.'

'Mr Greaves –'

'Richard –'

'I really need to speak to Saskia.'

'Um.' Richard considered this then pushed it to one side, aware that he was hungry and that there was little chance of that hunger being satisfied. '"Suburban satyr". That's good.'

Through the open patio doors the bloodhounds started to sporadically bay again.

'So what's this about the others?'

'There are no others.'

'Not according to all the bloody papers. I'll go up and see what's going on.' He got up from the sofa with difficulty.

'Let me see her.'

'There's something I need to tell her – then you can see as much of her as she wants.'

Richard walked slowly, heavily up the stairs acutely aware of the weight of his own body. He went into the bedroom and knelt with difficulty on the floor then lay down on it, peering into the dark, congested space under his bed. Smoothly – for a man his age, size, and in his condition – he pushed his arm through the old shoe boxes, folders, sleeping bag and ice cream maker – to where Ruth's locket lay, caught in the carpet's pile. He'd seen it down there weeks ago, shining, wanting to be found – and ignored it.

Snorting with the effort, he stood up, the locket grasped in his hand – and went into Saskia's room.

She was lying on top of her bed in a cardigan, smoking a joint and gazing at the ceiling.

She exhaled slowly when he walked into the room, her eyes flickering over him without interest then back to the ceiling.

'You shouldn't be smoking.'

'I heard talking downstairs.'

'Paul's here.'

She didn't say anything.

'You don't believe that shit, Sas.'

She sat up on her elbows. 'Has it occurred to you that it might actually be true?'

'It's not true.'

'You sound pretty sure.' She sat up cross legged, watching him.

337

She didn't look well.

'You know him.'

She pulled in her face so that her lips became even thinner – a hard, impenetrable look she'd inherited from Caro; the look that Caro wore in the early years of marriage when they rowed properly and with a great deal of energy, knowing that reconciliation would come later.

'Do I? I've been with him for – what – just on three months? What's that? Nothing. You and mum were together for, like, eighteen years – and you had no idea she was screwing around.'

'She wasn't screwing around, there was only –'

'Eighteen years,' Saskia cut in, upset, 'and you didn't have a fucking clue. But then, who knows, maybe that's not a good example – maybe that says more about you than her. Eighteen years, dad! How could you not know? How could it come as such a surprise – after eighteen years?'

'We were both busy people – very busy people. The strain that comes with the loss of intimacy makes it difficult to gauge things – even in people you're close to.' He paused. 'Even in people you love.'

He felt shaken – this wasn't a conversation he'd anticipated having. Without his knowing it, Saskia had been having this conversation over and over again – with herself – since the divorce, and now they were actually having it, she knew exactly what she wanted out of it.

Richard was just blindly following her lead.

'But afterwards – after you found out – you didn't even try.'

'You plural – or singular.'

'For fuck's sake, dad,' she said, pulling her hands up inside her cardigan sleeves and trying not to cry.

'No, Sas – we need to get this straight. So – you're not blaming her for having the affair, but you *are* blaming me for not – what? Fighting for her? Forgiving her? I have forgiven her. That happened a long time ago, but as for the fighting – she didn't do it for attention, Sas, she –' he had more trouble saying the next few words than he thought he would, 'fell in love. We didn't stand a chance against that.'

'Says you.'

He watched, helpless, as she sniffed and pushed her face into her knees, and remembered – suddenly, without wanting to – her bedroom at the old house with its white iron four poster and pictures of horses. The pile of the carpet had been thick, and the quality of the furniture good, and the air smelt heavy and sweet with dreams, but none of that had been enough to protect her from what happened.

Then he saw her on the trampoline she spent a whole summer on – from morning till dusk when dew made it too slippery to bounce on; the pictures she used to draw for them in the morning before they woke up, and the way she'd creep into their room while they slept and put the pictures at the bottom of the bed so they'd see them when they woke up; how – on birthdays and at Christmas – she'd choose toys from her room for them and wrap them up with toilet tissue and sellotape.

'Saskia!' Paul called up the stairs.

'I don't want to see him.'

'He can make you happy – I know he can.'

'Dad – all he's done is make me pregnant.'

'That's not true.'

'And the story in the news – it fits. Not about Grace, but Vicky and Ruth? Why won't they say who made them pregnant? It figures –' she concluded.

'It doesn't figure.' Richard hung Ruth's locket from his index finger and started to slowly swing it.

'What is that?'

'Ruth's locket – she broke it when she was here in August. I found it under my bed. It broke while she was in my bed.'

Saskia carried on staring at him until his arm ached so much he had to lower it, the locket hanging cold against his leg. Then she got up and started to move round the room, fast as if she'd woken up in a hurry and just remembered that she had to be somewhere.

She hauled up armfuls of clothes from the floor, pushing as many of them as she could into her school rucksack. Her hair kept slipping over her face and she had to keep pulling it back behind her ears before picking up the swollen rucksack with difficulty, and checking round the room with a flushed animation.

'Where are you going?'

As she pushed past him, he grabbed hold of her arm, but she yanked it away with such force he had to hold onto the doorframe to regain his balance.

'Once – it happened once – and she's not keeping it,' he yelled after her as she ran down the stairs, and into Paul.

'Take me away – just take me away.'

54

At number two Park Avenue, Sylvia was busy washing the leaves of her orchids – bought by Bill at Victoria Station last month while running for the 18:24, when he passed a kissing couple and remembered that it was their anniversary. Cleaning orchid leaves was the kind of thing she usually did to music – Highlights from Wagner, Best of Mozart, Ultimate Chopin, Romantic Bach – but this morning the phone hadn't stopped ringing.

She'd had a string of publicists offering to handle press for her. She'd had someone from Stella McCartney talking about a new maternity collection and asking whether Vicky had ever done any modelling before, as well as Warner Brothers, Columbia pictures, Fox TV, and a whole host of publishers. She'd had new Burwood friends and old London friends responding to the morning's 'Suburban Satyr' exposé, unable to imagine what it was like having a teenage daughter who'd been made pregnant by a rapist who taught her art – and eager to find out.

Now, giving the orchid leaves a final polish with the

duster, she was explaining to the mother of one of Vicky's old school friends that as a Friend of Burwood Girls' she'd had extensive – intensive – dealings with Paul Sutton and the proposal for a new art block, and that he'd even come on to her.

'But I thought it was schoolgirls he was into.'

'Maybe he wanted me to dress up. I've got to go,' Sylvia said, automatically lowering her voice to a whisper, 'there's somebody at the door.'

She scuttled to the front door, the duster still in her hand.

'Tom,' she said, stepping back as Tom stalked into the house, enraged.

'Where is she?'

Sylvia, nervous – in the last few weeks she'd become terrified of Tom – followed him into the sitting room where he stopped, suddenly at a loss.

He glanced round the room – he'd lost weight, she noted – then at her, standing twitching in the doorway.

'Have you just driven up from Brighton?'

'No – I was with Grace last night. Where is she?' he said again.

'Who?'

'Vicky –'

'Why?'

Tom shook his head in disbelief. 'This whole "Suburban Satyr" thing – don't tell me you actually believe it.'

'But, Tom – it's terrible.'

'It's Vicky.'

'Tom –'

'And you know it.'

Sylvia hesitated. 'Think about it, Tom –'

'You know it,' he said again, loudly. 'You know it

342

because it's just the sort of cruel, selfish fucked-up thing she would do. For attention.'

'Vicky won't tell us who the father is, Tom, she refuses to. Think about it – it makes sense. Four girls fall pregnant – not just one, but four.'

'You don't give up, do you?'

'All four fall pregnant at the same time. All four go to the same school.'

'Grace has never been taught by Paul Sutton.'

Sylvia stared at the duster in her hands and tried to remember what she'd been doing before Tom arrived.

'I made Grace pregnant in the back of the Volkswagen you and dad bought me for my twenty-first.'

Sylvia tried to digest this and reject it at the same time. 'But how can you know, Tom?'

'I was there. Grace was there. There are *some* sacred things in life.'

'But –'

'Don't.'

'I'm just saying.'

'Don't!'

'Tom –' Sylvia went up to him and tried to put her hands on his shoulders. 'I know this is hard for you to accept, but –'

'Get off me,' he yelled, sweeping his arm across the lid of the baby grand, which was always shut – he was the only Henderson who played – so that all the photographs fell onto the floor. Then he kicked over the piano stool and this landed on the floor near Sylvia – who was in a state of shock – knocking over a plant stand with a bowl of hyacinth bulbs in it that she'd planted only the day before. Nothing broke, but the hyacinth bulbs and black potting compost fell out onto the carpet and Sylvia found herself instinctively gauging the damage as she followed Tom out the room and up the stairs.

Upstairs in Vicky's room, Ruth leant against the window, staring out at the crowd on the drive.

'So you'll cover for me – if my mum comes round here looking for me?'

Vicky nodded, scared, from the bed. 'You're sure about this?'

Ruth twisted away. 'It's all booked.' She was about to say something else when Tom walked into the room, yelling, 'You total – total bitch,' at Vicky, who was trying to sit up and shuffle as far back into the corner of her bed as she could, through the piled-up soft toys she'd been amassing since birth, inadvertently triggering the mechanism of a Christmas penguin, which started to sing, muffled, *'You'd better watch out, you'd better sit tight . . .'*

'Have you got any idea what you've done?'

Vicky kept her eyes on Tom, terrified – she didn't look at Ruth.

'What are you talking about?' Ruth said, from the window.

'"Suburban Satyr" – it was her,' Tom exclaimed, flinging his arm towards his sister.

Ruth stared at Vicky. 'You said it was Ms Webster.'

Vicky was scrunched up still in the corner of her bed among the soft toys, clutching her pillow to her. 'I didn't think it would blow up like this.'

Tom laughed. 'Art teacher makes four students at top ranking girls school pregnant – are you fucking serious? Vicky – it's not even true.'

'Sutton and Saskia – that's true.'

'Have you thought about what Sutton's going through right now?'

'He should have thought about it before he started up with Saskia.'

'This is Saskia we're talking about here, Vick, our friend Saskia,' Ruth pointed out.

'Why Saskia,' Vicky moaned.

'They fell in love – you can't hold people to account for that.'

'It's not fair.'

'Not fair? Shit, Vicky.' Tom sat down on the end of the bed. 'We're in a different place now – all of us. You've got to get beyond this moment – there has to be some realisation, for your own sake, of what it is you've done to people.'

'D'you think you could sound any more fucking parsimonious if you tried, Tom? And stop looking at me like that.'

'Like what?'

'Like nothing good's ever going to come out of me.'

'Come here,' Tom said, trying to pull her towards him.

'No –'

'Come on,' he said gently, at last managing to pull her out of the pile of soft toys so that she was resting against his shoulder. 'You've got to get beyond this. You've got to start giving yourself a chance, Vicky. It's all in front of you still – you're only seventeen.'

'Yeah,' Vicky agreed tearfully, 'and I never asked to be.'

'Tom,' Sylvia said, appearing in the bedroom doorway at the same time as Bill – who'd taken the day off work. 'You leave her alone.'

She'd been attempting to right the piano stool, and scrape up the potting compost from the sitting room carpet and was still clutching hyacinth bulbs in her compost-blackened hands.

'What's all this?' Bill asked, staring at Sylvia, then into Vicky's bedroom. 'There's no point getting worked up – what they're saying in the papers, it's bullshit. Tell them, Vicky.'

Bill had a natural aggression that he never used gratuitously – apart from a couple of incidents during the late eighties – that some women found sexually attractive, and that put most men on their guard, unsure whether he was running alongside them to keep pace or trip them up.

'Tell them about Matt.'

'Dad! How d'you know about Matt?'

'I've never heard her talk about anybody called Matt. Did you know about Matt?' Sylvia turned to Tom.

'Matt?' Tom was looking at Vicky. 'I met him – once. At a party. Total wanker.'

'This isn't Matt's – okay?' Vicky yelled suddenly. 'Thing is, I don't know whose it is – haven't got a fucking clue, in fact. I got so drunk at the party that night.' She looked at Ruth. 'That one in Pentonville. I don't remember anything.'

'But that's rape,' Ruth said.

'I thought it was Matt because I kind of went with him – to the party – but he said he left early and never laid a finger on me.'

Tom, angry, said, 'Yeah, and he told you this – what – after you told him you were pregnant?'

Vicky nodded.

'It's him,' Ruth said.

'Think so?' Vicky looked up at her. 'I don't know, he's got an alibi – girl called Ingrid.'

'It's him,' Ruth said again.

'I don't even care any more.' Vicky leant her head

346

on Tom's shoulder as he wiped at the smudges under her eyes with his thumb.

'God – I think I'd rather it *was* the art teacher.'

'Syl! It's alright, love,' Bill said, turning to Vicky, 'you just sit there and have a good cry.'

He propelled Sylvia by the elbow downstairs.

'What happened?' he said, looking around him at the compost on the carpet, sheet music balanced in an uneven pile on top of the piano next to another uneven pile of framed photographs. The ceramic pot with the dragon on it, which he associated – he realised, suddenly – with Christmas, was upturned.

Without answering him, Sylvia dropped onto her knees again and continued to brush with unnatural focus at the last patch of compost that had worked its way into the carpet's pile, and once this was done, moved on to the Carpet Right treatment.

The piano stool was soon in its usual place, and the sheet music shut inside. The dragon pot was back on its stand and full once more of potting compost and hyacinth bulbs.

Sylvia looked about the room – the bottle of Carpet Right gripped firmly in her hand – so that the only apparent aftermath of the past hour's events was Sylvia herself, looking like a Hausfrau in rubble after the Fall of Berlin. But then the Henderson Family was Sylvia's Berlin; built with the same neurotic diligence. Despite the collapse she could be seen now operating as usual among the improbable and the inconceivable.

She stood up and Bill came and stood behind her, both of them staring out through the patio doors at the winter garden. Unexpectedly, she leant back against him.

'What a fucking mess,' he breathed into her hair,

Sylvia allowing him to hold her tight in a way she hadn't done for well over a decade.

What d'you think about Dubai?' he said after a while, softly.

'Dubai? I don't know.' She paused. 'Middle of the desert, isn't it?'

'Yeah.'

'We need more than a holiday, Bill.'

'I know we do. I saw a job advertised there.'

'What – Dubai?'

'Yeah.'

'I never sent that application, you know.'

'What application?'

'Malawi.'

'Oh. Malawi.'

'And I've been thinking – if I had sent it, and we'd ended up in Malawi, then none of this would have happened, would it?'

'Who knows? Shit happens,' Bill said, sighing.

'Yeah, but why does it have to happen to us?'

'It happens to everyone. This is life – not the set for the fucking *Sound of Music*.'

'There *were* Nazis in *The Sound of Music*.'

'Yeah, singing ones.'

'D'you remember that documentary we watched – *Whatever Happened to the Von Trapps*?'

'No, Syl, I don't.'

'It was so sad – all those kids when they grew up.'

'The Von Trapps weren't real, Syl.'

'No – I mean the children who played them. The actors. The little one – with the dimples and brown curls – ended up in a strip club, Bill.'

'C'mon, Syl.'

'Why does that happen?'

'I don't know. How does Dubai sound?'

'I don't know.'

'Beaches.'

'I don't know, Bill.'

'We're not leaving anything behind. The kids are leaving us.'

She turned round and looked sharply at him. 'The kids are pregnant, Bill! And Tom –'

'What about Tom?'

'He hates me.'

'Tom doesn't hate you.'

She pulled away, suddenly distracted, starting to sort through the photographs stacked on the piano, willing herself not to tell Bill that she'd told Tom – about Isabella. She focussed instead on one of the photographs.

There was Tom, aged seven, on a beach somewhere hot, wearing a necklace made of shells, and a smile. Everything that was inside him lay in that smile, and he didn't think to hide it. Photographs were unbearable. Why did people take them?

She leant back into the familiar smell of him. 'Where's this?' she said, pushing the photograph of Tom towards Bill.

'St Lucia,' he said, without hesitation.

'How did you know that?'

Before Bill could answer, he dropped suddenly to the floor.

Ten minutes later an ambulance attempted to pull onto the drive at number two Park Avenue.

349

55

Bill Henderson had suffered two minor heart attacks in the past twenty-four hours. Rachel Dent heard the ambulance that took him to hospital and her first thought was – Ruth. Something had happened to Ruth – the baby – they were taking them to hospital.

She got as far as the front door when the landline started ringing. Ignoring it, she went outside and saw the ambulance trying to break through the crowds on the drive, the blue light washing rhythmically over them.

Then the siren started up, momentarily disrupting the cluster, and it was then that they saw Rachel standing outside number two. They were coming for her, but she didn't care any more; it wasn't important.

'Who's in the ambulance?' she shouted above the sound of her own name being repeated again and again.

She stood processing the two necessary facts – Ruth wasn't in the ambulance, but Bill Henderson was. Bill Henderson wasn't important. She went back inside and caught the tail end of Saskia's message – she recognised Saskia's voice – something about Ruth.

Why was Saskia phoning here, and why was she using the landline? Landlines didn't exist for that generation.

Rachel started to panic. The ambulance had unsettled her; something was wrong.

She stood in the kitchen, which seemed strangely quiet, and listened to Saskia's message and – before the machine had let out its series of impartial and conclusive beeps – leant forward and started to vomit over the kitchen floor.

She was shaking, her teeth and hands clenched, trying not to swallow while staring down at the vomit, which had splashed over her feet and the sink unit.

By the time Nathan, whom she called, came home, the kitchen had been cleaned, and Rachel was sitting in the dining room – reflected in the dining table's mahogany surface.

Nathan, even more neatly dressed and more sallow looking than usual, kept his eyes on Rachel. His throat was covered in shaver's rash, which he kept unconsciously scratching at. The dining room always felt cold and unused even with the heating on. The acoustics were different in here as well – much emptier than anywhere else in the house.

'My baby,' she said bleakly. Then, staring intently at him, appealing to him, 'Why didn't I know?'

She felt conspired against – not just by him, but by the dining room itself . . . this home she'd created without faith – she could admit that now. To be fair she'd done it as whole-heartedly as she could, but she knew what mortar shells could do to wallpaper (whatever the make), furniture and carpets . . . so what, really, was the point?

'You knew,' she said suddenly to Nathan.

'Rachel –' He walked round the table towards her,

his reflection keeping pace until he got to where she was sitting on the other side.

'You knew!' she said again, standing up.

He tried to take hold of her, but she threw his hands off easily.

'You knew – you knew – you knew.'

'Rachel – stop it.'

'You couldn't stand her being pregnant, could you. What a messy, messy thing to happen to a man like you. When did she tell you?'

'This morning.'

'This morning,' Rachel repeated. 'And you didn't try to stop her?'

'No.'

'And you didn't think to tell me?'

'No.'

'She's MY daughter.'

'She's my daughter too,' Nathan exploded. 'I've treated her as one – loved her as one.'

'Loved her?' Rachel started to laugh, loudly, uncontrollably.

'How dare you,' Nathan shouted, slamming his hand, palm-down, onto the table. 'How dare you. I love her – and I was devastated when she got pregnant. For all the right reasons.'

'It makes sense,' Rachel said, ominously bright.

'What makes sense?'

'You – persuading Ruth to have an abortion.'

'Rachel – I didn't persuade her.'

'It's a culmination of all the small, grinding, humiliating cruelties you've inflicted over the years, isn't it? The final cruelty – it makes sense. A man can't live like you live without there being any let up. It's unnatural . . . twisted . . . It makes sense.'

'Shut up, Rachel!' He got hold of her and started to shake her.

'If you'd told me this morning when she told you – I could have stopped her,' Rachel yelled.

'Ruth's only seventeen – a baby's the last thing in the world she wants. You have to see that Rachel.'

'But it's *our* baby.'

'This isn't about us, it's about Ruth,' he yelled, pushing her so that she lost her balance and fell backwards into the dining room curtains, falling through discount Sanderson – purchased with Sylvia – onto the floor.

She sat up slowly, the static in her hair making it spread out across the curtain's heavy fabric folds, and looked at Nathan as if he was a long way away. 'Are you happy now?'

'What have I ever done to you?' he shouted down at her, 'apart from love you.'

Rachel remained motionless in the curtains as he crouched down beside her, trying not to touch her.

'Is this the point you wanted to get me to?' she said at last, looking down at herself.

'I'm down here with you,' he responded, choking.

'I've had enough.'

'Of what?'

'This – it's been going on for too long.'

'Rachel – please. Rachel – Where are you going?' he said as she got slowly to her feet and started to leave the room.

'There's somebody I need to see.'

56

Richard Greaves had just done another line of cocaine from his Natural History Museum tray, and was sitting on the side of the bed in a pair of boxer shorts, one of his pre-divorce polo shirts the colour of tuberculosis, and one sports sock. It was difficult – even for him – to tell whether he was half dressed or half undressed. He heard the doorbell, but presumed it was somebody else's that was ringing – it was always somebody else's – the wind bringing the sound closer. He swayed instinctively as though the wind was passing through the house.

The ringing carried on.

A pizza delivery? What time was it?

He called out, 'Sas!' but there was no response so he got up and went into her room, faintly puzzled by the mattress on the floor and the piles of clothes, which he swooped at unevenly, lifting them up at random as though expecting to find her shrunken and concealed beneath. Was this really his daughter's room – or had they just been burgled and he hadn't noticed?

He gave up, dropping the last handful of clothes back on the floor.

Then he remembered – Saskia had gone – and sank under a throbbing wave of grief.

The doorbell was still ringing.

He went downstairs, clicking on light switches as he went, blinking at the harshness of the trail of light he left behind him, and slipping on the last tread of the stairs. Something in his right ankle hurt and it was much colder down here than upstairs; he felt the hairs on his legs stand up.

The bell stopped ringing as, limping, he opened the door.

There was a woman standing outside, staring in at him.

He knew instinctively who it was.

'Where is she?'

Richard stared stupidly at her, slamming himself inadvertently into the fridge so that they kept their distance in the tiny, shabby, stinking kitchen.

'My daughter – Ruth.'

He shook his head, staring at her and making no effort to conceal his terror. 'She phoned me – this morning.'

'You knew she was going to have an abortion – and you didn't try to stop her?'

'No!' Richard yelped, trying to follow the logic as it occurred to him that it wasn't the pregnancy she was angry about, but the termination of it. Was she religious? Was she some hardline pro-lifer? 'But that's a good thing, isn't it?'

'A good thing?'

'What have I done?' He said, staring wildly at her.

Rachel was watching him. 'She didn't tell you where she was going, did she – to have it done? There was no stopping this from happening was there?' She appealed to him. Then, quickly, before he had time to respond. 'And you don't love her.'

'I never thought about it. I mean – I don't know what it was, but no . . .'

'So – why? Why Ruth?' For the first time she was starting to break up and sound tearful. 'You should have left her alone.'

'I'm sorry – I'm so sorry.' Richard sagged forward. 'God –'

'You've got a daughter of your own – how would you feel if –?'

'I know.'

'You don't know. How old are you?'

'I'm completely fucked.'

'I'm not interested.'

'It wasn't Ruth's age – nothing like that. I don't have a thing about – about girls. I mean, I teach. I'm a teacher. I don't even think about the girls I teach. It was Ruth . . . who she was,' he said, facing her. 'You have to believe that.'

'Who she *was*,' Rachel repeated, carefully. 'When did it start?'

'It didn't start – it happened once.'

'France?'

'No – no.' For some reason he was upset that she thought it had started in France while Ruth was in his care. 'Here. It happened here.' He broke off. 'I can't talk about this.'

'We spoke on the phone,' Rachel said vaguely, 'about flights to France – what airport I needed to book her flight to. The baby . . .' she said after a while.

'There wasn't meant to be one.'

'You never wanted the baby?'

'No –'

'And now there is no baby,' she finished, helpless, 'and there's nothing we can do about it.'

He stared back at her – just as helpless – and saw, faintly, Ruth's eyes and mouth in her face.

Then it happened.

For the first time since the whole mess started he felt suddenly overwhelmed by the fact that what he had done was wrong. He hadn't felt it while plundering her naked daughter on his bed in the afternoon, but he felt it now, standing opposite the fully dressed mother. He had done a very wrong thing.

He breathed in deeply and exhaled as steadily as he could, momentarily shutting his eyes. The only thought that preoccupied him after this was that he was going to vomit – through fear and relief. It *was* relief, he felt at the onset – at last – of remorse, and the effect of it on him after having lived without it for so long, was almost spiritual. He let himself go – having found the one thing in this whole mess he was entitled to without remorse, and that was remorse itself.

Had the mother come alone or was there a raging bull of a father waiting in a car parked outside? Would he soon find himself on all fours on his filthy kitchen floor, his bare legs slapping against the tiles, gurgling blood, pleading . . .

Unbelievable – he had an erection, and not knowing what else to do, stumbled past Rachel towards the sink where there was a bottle of whisky and some glasses . . . there were always glasses by the sink at number twenty-four Carlton Avenue.

He stood with his back to her, and poured whisky into two glasses without thinking. 'I'm evil,' he con-cluded to himself. This corpulent grey body and these tight grey curls on my head – a distorted reflection was visible in the taps in front of him – harbour nothing but evil.

'Here.'

After a moment's hesitation, Rachel took the glass, their finger tips briefly grazing.

They stood listening to each other drain their glasses then Rachel crossed over to the sink and poured herself another one. 'I've been trying to have a baby for six years. I've been trying and trying and . . . nothing. I've seen specialists . . . therapists . . . gurus . . . psychics . . . nothing apart from seven miscarriages. So we started on the IVF. Four –' she put her hand up to her mouth '– unsuccessful courses of it.'

As she brought her hand away from her mouth, he saw the teeth marks on the back where she'd bitten herself.

'The night Ruth told me she was pregnant, I'd been getting these clawing pains, all day, and I just knew. I mean, you know, and . . . I knew.' She stared sideways at him. 'It's the worst feeling in the world, wanting something so badly – and getting nothing; staying empty. Full of emptiness. Emptiness is heavier than you think.' She looked up suddenly, staring straight ahead. 'Then Ruth told me . . .' Rachel trailed off. 'And I suddenly knew that this was it . . . this was the baby I'd been waiting for.'

She finished the second whisky then put the glass down by the sink. 'Okay.'

'Okay?'

'We're done.'

He stared at her and the next minute she collapsed against the kitchen unit under the weight of one, sustained choking sob.

He continued to stare, helpless.

'For God's sake,' she screamed at him, 'hold me or something. Just hold me.'

He shuffled awkwardly across the floor as she turned to him.

As soon as Rachel felt the weight of his arms, she fell onto him. His arms relaxed, but his hold on her became tighter, and within seconds they were taking handfuls of each other's clothes, tearing at them and pulling them apart.

Eight hours later, Rachel walked into number two Park Avenue.

Nathan was cooking, standing at the oven with his back to her.

'Where's Ruth?' Rachel asked.

'Upstairs,' he said, his back still turned. The spoon he was holding – forgotten now – was dripping a dark sauce over the immaculate hob. 'I didn't know if you were coming back. I mean, I didn't know if you were coming back – ever,' he said, turning round at last.

Then he saw her.

She'd been with Richard Greaves for eight hours, and was still wearing those eight hours – on her face, smeared with make-up that had half sweated off, on her clothes now beyond repair that had been slowly, disbelievingly shrugged back on again, and on her bleeding calves cut by shards of glass from tumblers broken by a falling coffee table.

'Where were you?'

'I'm going to shower,' she said, and disappeared.

His wrist had fallen over a gas flame and he hadn't noticed. He let out a short sharp scream that elicited no response from anywhere in the house and then went to hold it under cold running water.

57

Ruth lay in bed. It had been a long day, but she couldn't sleep and didn't know what else to do so continued to lie there in the dark with her eyes shut. She heard Rachel come in, and come upstairs, and waited, but Rachel didn't come into the bedroom. Nobody came to see her, and after a while it dawned on her with relief and sadness that they weren't going to.

She'd never been as afraid as she had been that afternoon when she was wheeled to the operating theatre down a brown corridor that seemed to tilt and whose windows had all been open, making it cold.

She'd been introduced to everybody in the operating theatre, even though she didn't want to know their names, and then had to move herself from the bed they'd brought her in on, onto the steel operating table when she lay, not seeing anyone, aware only of sound and movement while affecting to listen when people spoke to her.

They put the mask on her and she panicked and said she couldn't breathe, but they told her it would be okay. She couldn't remember what number she managed to count to before losing consciousness, but she did remember being pushed gently back onto the operating table.

She came to in the recovery room – to find herself staring at a panel of seemingly random green and red lights on the wall in front of her. They'd taken it out of her – it had gone. Then came the relief. That's all she felt – relief – and a sense of being alive.

Rachel stood under the warm water falling from the shower head, set to tropical rain. The simulated Amazonian downpour made it impossible to think, so she didn't. She just stood with her eyes shut, swaying lightly from side to side.

Downstairs, Nathan had stopped screaming, applied Savlon to the burn on his wrist and finished making his curry to the sound of the shower going on upstairs.

After a while, it went off.

He served himself and took the plate through to the lounge – passing the dining room whose doors he'd shut after Rachel left. He started to eat – on the sofa – staring round the room as if he wasn't really there and was expecting this fact to be made physically apparent to him at any moment.

He heard someone on the stairs and a couple of minutes later, Ruth appeared in the doorway. He hadn't been expecting Ruth. She looked ill, and he had no idea what to say to her.

'What's that?' she said after a while, jerking her head in the direction of his plate.

'Curry.'

'Thought so. I smelt it – upstairs. I'm hungry.'

'D'you want some?'

She nodded and followed him into the kitchen,

watched him serve up, then followed him back into the lounge where they sat on the sofa together silently eating.

'This is good.'

'Um,' Nathan agreed.

'What time is it?'

'No idea. About nine?'

'Is that all?'

'What time did you think it was?'

'I don't know – I fell asleep; thought I'd been asleep for ages.'

Nathan didn't comment on this.

After a while Ruth said, 'You need a bandage on that.'

'What?'

'Your wrist. Looks like a burn or something. It'll get infected.'

Nathan stared at his throbbing wrist without expectation as Ruth disappeared then reappeared with a roll of microfibre dressing. He flinched, instinctively, when she pulled his hand towards her then watched her bandage the burn gently, efficiently, preoccupied by the moment.

She looked up at him, pleased.

His hands were resting awkwardly on his knees, but then every posture he assumed looked awkward. He looked down at himself, aware of this for the first time.

'I could have come – I don't want to think of you going through that alone.'

He fought to look at her – forcing his head up.

The tenuous sense of peace had been broken, replaced by a fractious restlessness.

'It was my decision,' she said at last, defensive but calm.

She didn't want to talk about it. The endless brown

· 362

corridor with its open windows, the lights and stainless steel belonged to her and her alone – even if she didn't want them. She had to house them somewhere inside herself, and although one day she might lessen the load by sharing them with somebody else, that somebody else wasn't Nathan, and she wasn't about to do it now.

'I could have come, Ruth,' he said again.

'Well, it's done now.'

Nathan rubbed at his face.

'You did the right thing.'

Ruth considered this, unconvinced. 'You think so?'

They sat in silence for a while after this, able to hear the trees in the garden outside, disrobed by winter, scratching at the walls and fences.

'And you told mum – I'm sorry I left that to you.'

Nathan stared at her, helpless.

Ruth looked away.

'I love you, Ruth. I've always loved you, you know that, don't you.'

Ruth stopped in the doorway to her bedroom.

Rachel was sitting on the side of the bed in a dressing gown with the words Datchwood Spa embroidered in blue across the back. Some of the letters were obscured by her mother's hair, which was wet, but Ruth knew that's what they said. They'd spent the day there – for Ruth's sixteenth birthday – and Rachel had been intent on stealing one of the robes. They'd had an argument about it in the changing rooms, and laughed about it in the car on the way home.

When she turned round, she looked unnervingly young – not much older than Ruth, in fact – and she was smiling. There were no more secrets between them.

'Come here,' she said, standing up, her arms open.

Ruth, unsure, walked round the bed towards her.

In that moment everything changed.

It was the first real physical contact she'd had that day since being helped onto the operating table. She could smell the cocoa butter Rachel had always used on her skin – a soft, caramel smell that Ruth would associate with her mother, even after her death. Standing in her bedroom at number four Park Avenue, being held tightly by her, she didn't know that in forty years time, when she herself was fifty-seven and there was no longer a generation between her and death, she'd smell that same cocoa butter in the changing rooms at a swimming pool and collapse onto the bench in her cubicle, crying uncontrollably.

'I'm so sorry, mum,' she said, pulling out of the embrace.

Rachel nodded, pulled her back and kissed the top of her head. 'No, I'm sorry – I should never have let you go through what you went through today alone. What sort of mother does that? I should have been there.'

'It's okay,' Ruth mumbled.

'No – it isn't.' Rachel paused. 'But I think it will be.'

58

What a fucking day, Richard Greaves thought to himself, laughing. Had he just thought that – or actually said it out loud? The Natural History Museum tray slid off the unmade bed and landed unevenly among the heaped debris on the floor. He stepped on it as he made his way over to the wardrobe, still in the same state of acute disorientation that he'd been in since Rachel Dent's departure.

Richard had been brought up by an unimaginative mother to believe that morality was something you necessarily assumed in order to take part in society. Morality was civilizing. According to this principle, the child Richard expected to be rewarded for good behaviour, and anticipated being punished for bad. But as he grew up and bore witness to the fact that life was complex and that the opposite was often true – you got rewarded for bad behaviour and punished for good – he was presented with a choice and hit crisis point.

He chose the nobler road, and decided not to let others govern him, but to continue to govern himself instead. He chose a wife he thought shared his belief in self-government, and together they went into the world of TV and produced award-winning document-aries on unpalatable issues at just the right moment in entertainment history. Caro was with him all the way. Until award-winning documentaries on unpalat-able issues became unfashionable – and stopped winning awards. Caro said some very clever things about reality TV, a new floor-wiping genre at the time, and tried to convince him that this was something they should be focussing on. The men – and few women there were – at the top, agreed with her. Richard wasn't convinced, but they got given the promotion anyway. Then Caro got pregnant – some-thing she always looked back on as Richard's wilful sabotaging of her career, and the minimum six months she spent on maternity leave was long enough for somebody else to jump into their place. Richard turned back to the documentaries on unpalatable issues people were showing less and less interest in and Caro got post-natal depression. The world *had* changed, but Richard had no intention of changing with it. He got demoted then made redundant, and Caro knew exactly what he had to do to make it all better, but he refused. She got frustrated to the point of divorce, and then everything collapsed.

At this point, Richard realised that he had failed. But who was it he had failed?

At the end of the day, it didn't matter. Failure took up residency inside him, and it showed.

Other people, he soon realised, looked on his failure as something he was guilty of – not victim to.

Caro left. Just about everybody left – apart from Saskia. Saskia's presence was his litmus test. As long as Saskia wanted to live with him – he could live with himself, and the cocaine helped; a habit acquired during his big salary producer days.

Ruth had been a horrifying breach of self-government.

Rachel – terrifying.

Where did it end?

This evening, after Rachel left, he realised that he knew the answer to this: wherever he wanted it to.

Well, he wanted it to end here, now, and because the funny side of life was something Richard had always enjoyed he felt that a little elaborate symmetry wouldn't go amiss. Which was why he was going to hang himself with his old school tie.

Saskia had gone, but Saskia was loved – by a better man than him. He could let go. Life had, at long last, become suddenly and incredibly simple, and the only thing he had to worry about was finding his school tie.

He found it curled up in a shoe. He'd worn both to an Alumni fundraising event he'd masochistically insisted on going to over a year ago.

Pleased, he unravelled it, draped it loosely round his neck, and started to search for a suitable spot inside number twenty-four Carlton Avenue, from which to hang himself. This proved to be more difficult than he'd anticipated. In fact, he was amazed at just how few places there were in the average home for somebody approximately six foot tall, weighing fourteen stone, to hang themselves from.

The rail in the fitted wardrobe was only four feet from the bedroom floor, and the curtain rails upstairs could barely support the decomposing, unlined curtains let alone fourteen stone worth of man eager to die. The staircase had a solid banister and there was nowhere downstairs.

He sat down on the sofa where he'd made love to

Rachel and pulled the tie slowly from around his neck. What sort of knot should he use? He'd got a badge once for tying knots – at summer scout camp on Brownsea Island. He could picture the badge clearly now – green with a gold reef knot on it. In fact, a reef knot was about the only sort of knot he could remember how to tie.

He practised now, and after the third attempt managed to make a noose and slip this over his head. There wasn't much tie left to attach to anything else – apart from a hook, he thought eyeing the watermarked artex ceiling. Unless the flex the light was hanging off would hold. He dragged the armchair over, but even stood on that he wasn't tall enough to get the length of tie knotted to the flex.

He got the steps out enthusiastically – from the cupboard under the stairs – and took them into the lounge-diner. They weren't particularly steady, but gave him the right height. He switched off the light, took out the bulb with an oven glove – a protracted business – then removed the shade, and was about to knot the end of the tie to the flex when he remembered that he hadn't shaved that day. Shaving wasn't a particularly regular habit of his, but it suddenly bothered him that he was about to hang himself unshaven.

So he climbed down and went upstairs into the bathroom where, humming, he ran himself a sink of hot water and shaved.

Downstairs, he climbed the ladder again, confident, grabbed hold of the flex, lost his balance and fell off, pulling the flex, the rest of the light fitting and some of the ceiling with him. He lay twisted on the carpet, laughing and coughing – because of the plaster dust he was covered in.

A few minutes later, he hauled himself up, still laughing, and walked unsteadily towards the patio doors, sliding them open to get some fresh air.

The air temperature had dropped rapidly during the course of the day and now there was a cold mist. He stepped barefoot outside. Through the mist he saw the old swing frame that belonged to somebody else's childhood, at the end of the garden. Its blue and red frame was eaten by rust, but it would hold.

The bloodhounds next door had started up a low baying that sounded distant, muffled by the mist, as he stood on an old cane chair and tried knotting the tie round the top of the frame.

Derek, the part-time fireman who lived next door to Richard Greaves, was cleaning his bathroom. He did this on average twice a day, using the strongest skin irritant products he could, because he had a never-to-be-diagnosed cleanliness OCD. Moving onto the sink plug chain, he took out the toothbrush he kept for this job, dipped it carefully into an egg cup full of bleach and started to scrub at the minuscule balls and links in the chain. It was then that he heard the sound – distant – of somebody's mobile ringing, and it was coming from the garden. He heard the bloodhounds as well, and opened the bathroom window to see what was going on.

Through the mist, he saw in the garden next door – that he was forever phoning up environmental services about – a barefoot man attempting to hang himself from the swing.

The mobile continued to ring and, despite yelling at the dogs to shut up, the dogs carried on whining.

He ran downstairs and out into the garden, still

369

wearing the rubber gloves he'd been cleaning the bathroom in.

It took Richard a long time to get the knot right, but finally he managed – despite the fact that his feet were now freezing, and his hands covered in rust.

He was about to kick away from the cane chair he'd been standing on, and test the tie's two knots – one round the swing frame and the other round his neck – when his mobile started to ring.

Then he changed his mind about dying.

He wanted to take the call – even if it was only to talk to his network provider about price plans and upgrades. That's how much he didn't want to die.

But it was too late.

He lost his balance, the cane chair toppled, and a second later he lost consciousness.

His phone continued to ring.

Derek, the part-time fireman, was the sort of man who not only built a Swiss chalet for his bloodhounds, but who carried a Leatherman clipped to his belt.

After picking his way carefully but rapidly across the debris in the Greaveses' garden, he used the knife on his Leatherman tool set to cut through Richard Greaves's old school tie.

Derek was a tall man.

As he cut through the tie, their faces were on a level.

Once Richard had fallen to the ground, Derek rolled him into the recovery position and cut the noose round his neck, waiting for him to regain a choking consciousness.

The mobile was still ringing.

'You're okay,' Derek said, his hand on the other man's stomach. It was a statement – not a question.

'My phone,' Richard said, with difficulty, pointing to his trouser pocket.

But before Derek could get there, the phone stopped ringing.

Five minutes later, he followed Derek into Derek's immaculate kitchen where he sat while Derek cleaned up a quite serious laceration on his right foot from where he'd trodden on an old paint can – Dulux magnolia – in his garden.

The two men remained silent as Derek finished dressing the wound on Richard's foot then made them both mushroom Cuppa Soup.

'Thanks,' Richard said, taking the cup that was pushed across the table towards him. Then again, 'Thank you.' He didn't know what else to say. The man who'd been sending them notes on a weekly basis about the external appearance of their house had just saved his life.

'Life's a bugger,' Derek observed sullenly. 'I didn't mean to interfere.'

'No – no, I'd just changed my mind.'

'That's good then,' Derek said. His only other reference to the whole business was an accusation that Richard had scared the dogs. 'They'll be unsettled tonight – but there's nothing I can do about it.'

59

Thirty minutes later, after vomiting up the mushroom Cuppa Soup in Derek's downstairs toilet – something which fazed Derek in a way cutting down a man from a garden swing hadn't – Richard was behind the wheel of the green Skoda, driving away from Burwood on the same road that Tom Henderson had driven to Martha's Farm all those months ago.

He was out of cocaine and driving towards Hewitt's Farm, which belonged to Craig Hewitt, who bred gun dogs, repaired computers, supplied cocaine to – among many others – Richard Greaves, and who was a good friend of Paul Sutton's.

He turned off the main road and was soon in forest. Visibility had dropped dramatically along with the last streetlight and he could barely see beyond the first line of trees.

He passed the car park where Ruth had told him she was pregnant that night, drove for another five minutes then started to turn into the drive for Hewitt's Farm, but there were four deer – a family of them barely visible in the mist, two with antlers – across the entrance.

He pulled the wheel hard to the right, swerving to avoid them, but his illegally bald tyres lost their grip in the gravel and the car slid sideways into the trunk of an elm that local school children were always shown on their nature trail because of the burn marks at the base of the trunk, said to be a legacy from a dragon that once lived in the forest.

The deer stood watching the green Skoda. When it hit the elm they started to run deftly between the cypresses lining the drive in spite of the dark and the mist – until they came to what had once been a farmyard where, inexplicably, they slowed down.

There were lights on in the old barn, which had recently been given an architectural makeover.

Inside the barn Craig, glad for once of something other than canine company, was talking to Paul. Saskia sat by the window, the curtain pulled back, staring out at the mist. Nobody knew they were here and the nearest place was an old keeper's cottage set even further back into the woods, inhabited by a potter Craig had been having an on and off affair with for at least a decade.

She didn't even try to follow what Craig and Paul were saying. The only thing her ears really picked out was the popping and cracking of the wood on the stove – cut from pear trees in the Autumn. She didn't know what she was doing here and even though the last thing she wanted to do was go back to number twenty-four Carlton Avenue, part of her was still waiting to go home so that she could get up tomorrow morning and go to school. But that wasn't going to happen – ever again.

She blew on the window and traced an S through the condensation. It was then that she saw the deer in the yard, or the shifting outline of them anyway, the two pairs of antlers rising thick and dark through the mist.

Without saying anything, she went to the front door, opened it and stepped out into the yard. Behind her she heard Paul call out, 'Sas?'

She stood watching the four animals nose quietly at the ground, the mist falling around them. Every now and then the smallest one would stop what it was doing to stare straight at her. It looked sad.

They turned and ran as Paul appeared beside her.

'You'll freeze.'

'You frightened them away,' she said, angry.

'They'll be back.'

peace, plenty
and . . . babies

60

Summer was at its height, and at Hewitts Farm – along with a lot of other places on the same longitude – it was midday. Thirty-two degrees centigrade with humidity had been forecast, and Saskia felt the full weight of it – even inside the barn with its exposed stone walls. Sitting awkwardly in an armchair Paul had moved over to the window for her, she was making notes on the Tet Offensive for her last history paper in two weeks' time. The pad was balanced on what was left of her legs, which didn't seem like much after she'd taken her stomach into account.

Through the window, she could see Paul out in the yard, sketching one of Matt's spaniels. She turned back to the Tet Offensive in order to take her mind off the sharp prickling pain at the top of her legs, and the dull ache in her lower back. She read the paragraph she'd just read again, aware that the two different pains were amalgamating and swelling, making her feel light-headed. Was this it?

Unsure whether it was fear or excitement she felt, she closed in on herself, leaving the US marines and the VC fighters stranded in mud, blood and jungle as the book slipped off her lap. Then the immense pain stopped suddenly, and it was as if it had never happened. Dazed, she pulled herself out the armchair and walked towards the kitchen where she stood drinking a glass of water while staring at a spider crawl into a crevasse in the stone wall above the splash back.

Then the pain came back – as suddenly as it had disappeared before – and she dropped instinctively to the floor, the glass slipping through her fingers and onto the flagstones below.

Paul, out in the yard, heard the splintering glass. The sound could have been many things, but for some reason he knew the resonance was personal, and that it had something to do with Saskia. Without thinking, he dropped the pad, which started to immediately pucker and curl in the midday sun, and ran. Towards the barn.

61

Grace was lost in the probability section of her Advanced Mathematics paper. She was no longer aware of the room in The Unit where the Surestart parenting classes usually took place – and where she was now sitting the exam – or the other three candidates.

Tina Branston, sat directly behind Grace, wasn't taking Advanced Mathematics. She was re-sitting her Biology GCSE under the tutelage of Julia Webster, who'd been running revision classes at The Unit on Tuesday, Wednesday and Thursday evenings for the past six months, and who was invigilating today's exams.

In fact, Julia was enjoying her work at The Unit so much that she was seriously thinking about applying for enough funding to set up a maths and science centre for adults and young people the system had failed first time round.

Julia looked up then to find Grace staring at her, unseeing.

The thing Grace loved most about probability was the way it set mathematics – not only the laws, but the very nature of mathematics – up against itself. Probability was as much an acceptance of the improbable as an explanation of the probable. She was just coming to the conclusion of the penultimate question when a dull, ebbing pain filled her entire body then disappeared. Scared, she held her pen and waited, staring at the candidate number on the desk in front of her – 112; knowing that 112 was a number she'd always remember. The examination paper went into High Definition and, despite the continuing pain, she started on the next question because time was running out.

It was Tina, sitting behind her, who noted Grace's change in posture and saw the skin on the back of her neck flush. Tina knew exactly what was happening. She put up her hand.

By the time she'd spoken to Julia, and Julia had spoken to Grace, everybody in the room knew what was happening because all of them – apart from Julia – had already been through it.

Grace sat in her avid stillness, focussed. 'I can finish,' she whispered to Julia.

'You're sure?'

Grace nodded, and Julia, worried, went back to the front of the room where she made a note on Grace's candidate sheet to explain that during the last thirty minutes of the examination, Grace had in fact gone into labour.

By the time she'd finished the paper, the contractions were about six minutes apart. The answer to the last question was imprinted clearly in the surface of the desk where she'd carried on writing during a contraction because time was nearly up.

Julia collected the papers then called for a taxi.

Grace called Tom, who was working in the basement

of a bike shop with a couple of Polish mechanics over the summer holidays, and Tom called Nicole.

'Does it get any worse?' Grace asked Tina, waiting with her outside the office at The Unit.

'So bad you'd be happy for someone to fucking shoot you to make it stop.'

Julia looked at them both, terrified. For the first time in her life, she didn't know what to do.

'What did you call?' Tina asked her.

'A minicab.'

'Fuck that – she needs an ambulance.'

'I'll drive her.'

Tina nodded, and between them they got Grace to the car.

62

Saskia passed their daughter, Freya, carefully to Paul – sitting on the edge of the bed with the same expression of ecstatic terror he'd worn for the past six hours.

'Sas?' he whispered, not daring to change the position he was in.

'What?' Distracted, she didn't feel like talking.

'I phoned your dad. I know – I'm sorry. I just felt – I couldn't not.'

Saskia carried on stroking Freya's thick, black newborn hair.

'Sas,' Paul said again.

'When did you phone?'

'About half an hour ago.'

'He's coming here?'

Paul nodded. 'He was crying – on the phone when I told him.' He watched her get up from the bed. 'Where are you going?'

'For a walk. If he's coming – I don't want to be here.'

She was making her way haltingly towards the midwife's desk out in the hallway when she thought she saw Sylvia Henderson by the coke machine.

'Mrs Henderson?'

Sylvia turned round slowly, still in the act of pressing a Diet Coke against her forehead. She looked terrible under the hospital lighting as her eyes skimmed over Saskia.

'Hello', she said, flatly. Then, 'Is it just me or is it unbearably hot in here?'

'I thought you were in Dubai.'

'We were.' Sylvia paused, wondering how Saskia knew this. 'I've been going backwards and forwards.' She paused again worried that she wasn't making sense.

This was an impression she often had these days when speaking to anyone other than Bill, and it was connected to the intimacy they'd fallen – unexpectedly – into the middle of shortly after going to Dubai; an intimacy they hadn't known since their pre and post-nuptial days. This intimacy had had the strange affect on Sylvia of eroding her long-standing social confidence – or maybe she just felt that performing well socially was no longer important because she'd rather spend time with Bill than anybody else.

'Between Dubai and here,' Sylvia added, concluding awkwardly, 'Because of Vicky.'

'How is she?' Saskia asked, unsure. Vicky and she hadn't spoken once over the past six months.

Sylvia hesitated. 'Doing okay.'

'She's here?'

'They gave her a room to herself – after having it.'

'I'd like to see her.'

'I don't know, they're keeping her in for observation.'

'Mrs Henderson, please –'

Sylvia's eyes skimmed over Saskia again.

'What did you have?'

'A little girl – Freya.'

383

'Go down a level and through the double doors on the left – just for a minute though.'

Sylvia didn't say anything else, and Saskia was on the verge of turning away when she stopped. 'What about Tom and Grace?'

'Grace is in here now – they had to do an emergency Caesarean. The baby was breech.'

'But she's okay?'

'She will be.'

After Saskia left, Sylvia saw a bed being wheeled down the corridor towards her, and walking behind it was Nicole Cummings, and Tom – pushing a small trolley.

Grace – lying on the bed with an IV drip in her arm – smiled weakly as they drew level.

'Is everything okay?' Sylvia whispered.

Tom nodded, staring down at the vivid red baby tightly swaddled in a white hospital blanket.

'He?' Sylvia asked.

'He – yeah.'

'Tom, he's gorgeous.'

They stood in silence, contemplating the baby. Light bounced off the chain round Sylvia's neck over the baby's hair and face as she leant towards him, her breath making his hair move.

'He's got your eyes,' she said after a while.

'Mum – his eyes are shut.'

'I mean the shape of them.' Sylvia paused. 'Have you thought about a name yet?'

'Hector.'

She spun round, unable to control herself. 'Hector?'

'Mum –' Tom warned her.

'Hector? Tom – you can't.'

'Mum!'

'Bloody awful, isn't it,' Nicole put in.

'Don't you start,' he said, rounding on Nicole.

Sylvia hesitated. 'He's so tiny.'

'I phoned dad – to let him know.'

'Sometimes you can't get through.'

Neither of them commented on the fact that Bill had flown purposefully out to Dubai so that he wouldn't be there when Vicky had the baby she was giving up for adoption.

Sylvia looked down at her grandson.

'Ready to be a grandparent?' Nicole said, beside herself with relief after Grace's surgery.

Sylvia stared down at her arms, which were a healthy brown from the spray tan she'd had done yesterday – before Vicky went into labour – ready to fly out to Dubai and meet Bill. 'Grandparents? I'm not even fifty yet.'

Nicole was about to say that she knew somebody up on Meadowfield who'd just become a grandmother at thirty-five, but in the end she said, 'You – fifty? You don't look anywhere close to fifty.'

Later, lying on the bed at number two Park Avenue, in the same clothes she'd been in for over twenty-four hours now – Sylvia phoned Bill in Dubai, and got through.

'What was the weather like – the day Tom was born?'

'Scorching. Brilliant blue sky.'

'I knew you'd remember. Bill – we're grandparents.'

63

Vicky was lying on her side with her earphones in when Saskia appeared in the doorway. She wasn't asleep.

She stared at her for a while before pulling one of the earphones out.

'What are you listening to?'

'Metallica.' Vicky rolled onto her back.

They could both hear the music, still playing, at a distance.

'You've had it,' Vicky said, without looking at her.

'On the kitchen floor.'

'The kitchen floor?'

'Up at the farm – the ambulance didn't get there in time it all happened so quickly.'

'Lucky you.' Vicky turned to look at her at last. 'So?'

'A little girl.'

'Why do people say that? A little girl or a little boy. I mean, they're going to be little, aren't they? They're babies.' She broke off. 'You'd think, wouldn't you, that maybe they'd be able to find me a room where I don't have to lie listening to a whole load of fucking babies screaming and crying, but clearly it's beyond their logistical capabi . . . capabi.' She gave up trying to get the word 'capability' out. 'What's her name?'

'Freya.'

'Who chose that?'

Saskia hesitated.

'He did,' Vicky guessed.

Saskia stood up to go, but Vicky grabbed hold of her wrist. 'It's okay – stay with me for a bit,' she said, loudly.

So Saskia stayed sitting on the bed until Frank Barlow walked into the room – stopping when he saw her.

'Is she asleep?' he whispered.

'I don't think so.' Saskia stood up.

'I'm Frank – I'm a friend of Vicky's.'

Saskia nodded. 'Okay –'

'I've been with her since they brought her in.'

Saskia recognised Frank, but was too disorientated still by the past twelve hours to place him. 'How did it all go – the birth and . . . stuff.'

'Badly – lasted for eighteen hours.' He sat down on the edge of the bed where Saskia had been sitting, and took hold of Vicky's hand. 'She's asleep,' he said, pleased. Then, turning to Saskia, 'What did you have?'

'A girl – Freya.'

'Nice,' Frank said, meaning it.

They were both staring at Vicky, asleep now.

'What about Vicky?'

'She hasn't asked me that yet,' Frank said. 'Maybe she won't. So I can't tell you. You will come and see her again, won't you?'

64

Somewhere between the ante and the post natal wards, Richard Greaves, who'd already asked at least four people for directions, got lost, and ended up in intensive care. The maternity wards had changed a lot in the past eighteen years, he thought, walking through the overheated corridors, disorientated. There were so many men. When Caro had Saskia he'd been begrudgingly tolerated during visiting hours and not a second beyond. Now, he supposed, he'd be expected to deliver his daughter himself, and any man worth his salt would be able to give a minute breakdown of their child's birth.

He looked around him.

Where was he?

Somewhere, close by, a can rattled into the dispenser of a drinks machine, but nobody appeared.

In front of him there was a long window and beyond it, a bank of miniature trolleys. It was then that he realised where he was. These were the premature babies; the ones who had come into the world before their time. He walked up to the glass, instinctively drawn by the overwhelming sense of potential and hope in the critical mass of newborns laid out before him.

Then he saw her.

It was Ruth Dent.

Standing on the other side of the glass, in the middle of the room. She looked up then, and saw him, and her face made it clear that he was the last person in the world she'd expected to see not just here, but anywhere. She hadn't anticipated seeing him ever again. Her emotional immune system, robust with youth, had easily and effectively fought him off.

Somebody was standing beside him.

'It's mine – don't worry,' Rachel Dent said.

They turned to look at each other, watched by Ruth on the other side of the glass.

'Two months premature – but they say she's out of danger.'

There was a crack as Rachel opened the can in her hand, offered him some – Richard shook his head – and started to drink.

'Sorry, for a moment, I thought – I mean, I saw Ruth, and –' He stopped himself. 'So – it worked out for you.' It sounded wrong, but he couldn't think what else to say.

Rachel smiled. 'It worked out for us – yes.'

'For you and –' He'd forgotten the husband's name.

'Nathan. We have a little girl – Marina.'

They didn't say anything after that; they both just carried on watching Ruth beyond the glass.

'I got lost,' Richard said suddenly. 'I was looking for Saskia.'

'She's had the baby?'

Richard nodded. 'A girl – just over seven pounds.'

'Well – congratulations – post natal's back down that corridor there.'

'Okay – congratulations to you too,' Richard said, hesitating, before receding then disappearing out of their lives.

Almost.

Once he'd gone, Rachel remained standing in the corridor as, on the other side of the glass, Ruth bent over the tiny baby weighing barely three and a half pounds, called Marina.

Now she knew what it was she recognised in the almost inhuman face. Now, as she looked, she saw Richard's nose and mouth.

She looked up – a look of disbelief – at Rachel, standing on the other side of the glass, staring back at her.

Richard finally found his way to the right ward.

He knew it was the right one because Caro was standing by the bed, cradling her granddaughter by the window, her body assuming the rocking motion parents never forget.

She turned round then, instinctively, and saw him – and smiled.

65

The media had its hook.

The Burwood babies had all been born within hours of each other. A phenomenon that remained precisely that, given that none of the experts sourced by researchers and willing to appear on camera, could find any explanation – despite filling hours of programming.

For a while, Burwood was to teenage pregnancy what Bridgend was to teenage suicide.

The jist of the reporting was that the developed world – as everyone knew it – was coming to an end.

The developed world couldn't get enough of its own demise.

Then the developed world forgot.

Frank Barlow got a job offer from a national he'd never dreamt of getting in his lifetime, finally left Burwood and moved up to London. Vicky joined him in September when her BA in photojournalism started.

Paul and Saskia stayed on at Hewitts Farm for another year, with Saskia commuting up to London every day until Paul got the job he'd been wanting as Art in

Education Projects Manager at Tate Britain – and then they moved away from Burwood. With baby Freya.

Ruth changed her mind about university, deciding to spend a year in Zagreb with her cousin instead. She never came back – and didn't keep in touch with any of her childhood friends.

In October, Tom and Grace packed their piebald red Volkswagen and headed out of Burwood towards Cambridge. Hector, three months old, slept all the way. Grace's answers on the probability section of her paper were published in pamphlet form, and became the basis for Government research into why the world had fallen into economic recession.

While all happy families are a profound achievement – each unhappy family is a work of art.